C0-AUT-466

A History of the Eragny Press 1894–1914

Lucien Pissarro at the press; undated. (Photograph courtesy John Bensusan-Butt)

A History of the Eragny Press

1894–1914

Marcella D. Genz

Oak Knoll Press
The British Library
2004

First Edition, 2004

Published by **Oak Knoll Press**
310 Delaware Street, New Castle, Delaware, USA
Web: http://www.oakknoll.com
and **The British Library**
96 Euston Road, St. Pancras, London NW1 2DB, UK

ISBN: 1-58456-107-6 (USA)
ISBN: 0-7123-4862-X (UK)

Title: A History of the Eragny Press, 1894–1914
Author: Marcella D. Genz
Editor/Designer: Gregory R. Suriano
Publishing Director: J. Lewis von Hoelle

Library of Congress Cataloging-in-Publication Data
Genz, Marcella.
A history of the Eragny Press, 1894–1914 / Marcella D. Genz
p. cm.
Includes bibliographical references and index.
ISBN 1-58456-107-6
1. Eragny Press—History. 2. Private presses—England—History—19th century. 3. Private presses—England—History—20th century. 4. London (England)—Imprints. 5. Pissarro, Lucien, 1863–1944. 6. Pissarro, Esther. I. Title

Z232.P65G45 2003
070.5′93′0942—dc21

2003050628

British Library Cataloging-in-Publication Data
A CIP Record is available from The British Library

This work was printed in the United States of America on 60# archival, acid-free paper meeting the requirements of the American Standard for Permanence of Paper for Printed Library Materials.

Contents

To Fanny

Acknowledgements

I would like to thank the Ashmolean Museum, Oxford, and its staff for making the Pissarro Collection openly available to me during my extended stay in Oxford. I would like to specifically cite Anne Thorold whose ceaseless work in calendering the Pissarro Collection and her intimate knowledge of the papers of Lucien and Esther Pissarro and the Eragny Press, which she gladly shared, facilitated this research.

I would also like to thank Robert Harlan who devoted a great deal of time to a careful, patient, and sensitive reading of numerous drafts. His perceptive comments and unflinching standards helped shape both the ideas and the text.

I am indebted to various libraries and their librarians for access to Eragny Press books, especially: The Bancroft Library, University of California at Berkeley; The British Library; Special Collections, Strozier Library, Florida State University, Tallahassee, Florida; The Huntington Library, San Marino, California; The New York Public Library; the San Francisco Public Library; and the William Andrews Clark Memorial Library, University of California at Los Angeles.

I would also like to thank Nicolas Barker and Roderick Cave, who provided advice concerning publication, and Sue Easun, who never wavered in urging the publication of this work. Julie and Jonathan Harwell also helped in countless ways, far too many to enumerate.

Part I

Introduction

Lucien Pissarro had the daunting task of being the first son of an immensely talented father, Camille Pissarro, the French Impressionist painter. As a painter, working under his father's direction, Lucien found it difficult to earn a living. Camille's position in the Parisian art world did not make it any easier for Lucien to achieve his own reputation. Rather than continue trying to develop a name as a painter, under Camille's guidance, Lucien turned to the decorative arts. His decision to move to England in 1890 brought Lucien into contact with a very different strain in art and gave him the impetus to continue to develop his art in another genre, namely printing and book illustration. Inspired by the example of William Morris who founded the Kelmscott Press in 1891, Lucien and his wife, Esther Bensusan Pissarro, established the Eragny Press in 1894, named after the Normandy village, Eragny-sur-Epte, where his family had lived since 1884.

Other private presses soon followed in this period of typographical ferment, sharing in common fine craftsmanship and the use of well-made materials. St. John Hornby issued the first book of the Ashendene Press in 1895.[1] Charles Ricketts, who had been experimenting with book design, published his first Vale Press book in 1896. The Essex House Press of C. R. Ashbee and the Doves Press of T. J. Cobden-Sanderson and Emery Walker followed in 1898 and 1900, respectively. These private presses comprise an extraordinary group, which greatly influenced book design and typography in Europe and the United States.[2]

A number of factors contributed to this sudden burst of creativity in the area of book design, illustration, and production. As a part of the larger Arts and Crafts movement, the private press movement was a reaction to the Industrial Revolution, where the individual worker had become debased, his traditional role as craftsman obliterated and replaced by machinery. The primacy of the machine paralleled a decline in craftsmanship and taste. Machine-made products were often, in the Victorian era, ornate, ugly, overdecorated, and nonutilitarian. William Morris' efforts to restore simplicity, utility, and beauty to textiles and furniture provided stimulus for the revival in the aesthetics of the decorative arts.

In founding the Kelmscott Press, William Morris furnished the catalyst to revitalize a craft, which had fallen, like many others, with the swift rise of technology, into a deplorable state. His greatest contribution to the private press movement as well as to commercial presses was his emphasis on the importance of excellent materials and well-designed typefaces as well as his concept of the architecture of the page.

> Whatever the subject matter of the book may be, and however bare it may be of decoration, it can still be a work of art, if the type be good, and attention be paid to its general arrangement. . . . A book quite un-ornamented can look actually and positively beautiful . . . if it be, so to say, architecturally good. . . . *First,* the pages must be clear and easy to read; which they can hardly be unless, *Secondly,* the type is well designed; and *Thirdly,* whether the margins be small or big, they must be in due proportion to the page of letters.[3]

His basic theories provided the revivalist presses with a design scheme from which they did not deviate.

Morris set out to combat the Gothicky contagion that was disfiguring bookmaking and so much else in Victorian England.[4] Kelmscott books are not direct imitations of medieval books, but restorations to earlier conditions of craftsmanship, "carrying on the development of the arts of the book as if the intervening centuries had never existed."[5] The other private presses continued this restoration, modeling their books after the incunables of the early printers. Charles Ricketts went one century further and based his Vale Press designs on Renaissance books. An Eragny Press book, however, can be regarded as an attempt to produce a book wholly of its time within the confines of the renewed typographical tradition. Lucien Pissarro aspired to create a modern vision of the book by employing contemporary sensibilities.

Modern critiques have tended to diminish Lucien's place within the revivalist private press movement, dismissing his books as inconsequential, partly because of their small format and the limited output of the Press, but also because they were outside the mould of the other private presses. Lucien Pissarro brought foreign and unfamiliar sensibilities to his books. The distinctive use of color wood engravings which explore the Impressionist sensation endow Eragny books with a vital character unlike any other revivalist private press.

Until recently, Lucien's work as a painter has been ignored in favor of that of his father and his contemporaries.[6] In fact, many critics and historians in writing of his role as a link between French and British Impressionism have been particularly condescending toward his work. Douglas Cooper, the English critic, wrote, "As a painter, Lucien's gifts were of a secondary order. . . ."[7] and John Rewald in his *History of Impressionism*[8] mentions Lucien's role in the Impressionist movement only in association with his father.

As a graphic artist, Lucien has gained some recognition. Lucien's wood engravings were first studied in the late 1950s by Alan Fern in his unpublished Ph.D. dissertation, which includes a catalogue of the wood engravings, prefaced by a short essay on Lucien's career as a wood engraver and by necessity, a brief history of the Eragny Press.[9] Fern also edited a little Christmas book, "Notes on the Eragny Press, and a Letter to J. B.

"Et de le foille autresi, une belle loge en fist," wood-engraving (frontispiece). *C'est d'Aucassin et de Nicolete,* 1903. (Special Collections, Florida State University, Tallahassee)

Manson,"[10] for the Cambridge University Press, which consists of notes written by Lucien for James Bolivar Manson for an article he was writing and a short essay by Fern on Lucien's work. Colin Franklin, the chronicler of the history of the private presses in England, described this work "as the last word about the Eragny Press."[11] The importance of this little book and Fern's dissertation is not that Fern wrote the "last word" but that he wrote some of the first words. He reintroduced Lucien Pissarro and his Eragny Press to a world that had forgotten him. Certainly, these two pioneering works by Fern should not be overlooked as a starting point for any history of the Eragny Press. However, because he had access to relatively few of the letters and documents, Fern's work on the Eragny Press is incomplete. Access to the archive at the Ashmolean Museum was not readily accessible at the time of his research. It was still in boxes in the basement of the museum.

In 1950, through the generosity of Esther Pissarro, the Ashmolean Museum in Oxford acquired the Pissarro Collection. Located off the Print Room of the Department of Western Art, the archive includes paintings, drawings, prints, woodblocks, letters, and other documents which had belonged to the Pissarro Family. It was Mrs. Pissarro's intent that the gift be representative of the Pissarro family as a whole. Subsequently, the original gift was augmented by additions made by Lucien and Esther's daughter, Orovida, until her death in 1968, and then by her executor, Mr. John Bensusan-Butt. In the early 1970s, Anne Thorold voluntarily undertook the calendering of these materials, which made them readily accessible to scholars for the first time. The resulting collection embraces a broad time span and touches upon different artistic phases in both France and England between the years 1883 and 1933. The Pissarro Collection provides one of the richest and most valuable sources for the study of revivalist printing in England and its impact and influences on the Continent and the United States. Moreover, the archive is an invaluable source for studies on Impressionism, Neo-Impressionism, and Post-Impressionism in England, movements which influenced and motivated the Eragny Press.[12]

Holdings important for this study are the letters between Lucien and Esther, the letter books which record almost every letter written by Lucien from 1896 to 1914 and beyond, and the many thousands of letters written to Lucien and Esther concerning the Press' activities, the trial designs for the books, the sketches for the engravings, the woodblocks, the account books and receipts, and the books themselves.

The correspondence between Lucien and his father forms the nucleus of material concerning the early Eragny Press and Lucien's artistic development. Camille's letters were originally edited by Dr. John Rewald, with Lucien's guidance.[13] The goal of the editor was to present as clear a picture of Camille's life and work as possible. But in doing so, cuts were made and almost all reference to the graphic arts deleted, creating an unbalanced portrait of Camille's involvement in the graphic arts and his interest in Lucien's work. Janine Bailly-Herzberg has restored these omissions in her careful editing of Camille Pissarro's letters.[14] Lucien's letters to his father were edited by Anne Thorold and published in 1993.[15] This phenomenal documentation, though mostly in French, affords a rare insight into the evolution of the Eragny Press and all phases of its operation.

Several themes are essential to any discussion of the Eragny Press. Camille Pissarro's influence on Lucien and his role as patron of the Eragny Press are unquestionably important. Lucien pursued a career in the decorative arts to avoid the influence of his father on his work. His importance as an artist rests in his book designs because there he was finally able to cast off the conventions of his father, finding his own emerging style. Yet, Camille's appraisal and criticism of Lucien's wood engravings and designs for the Eragny Press were important to Lucien, who continued to seek his father's approval.

One of Lucien's major reasons for embracing the English Art and Crafts movement was to find a balance between the ideal (art) and the practical (trade), which, if they could be merged, would result in a way for him to make a living. Art and trade did not merge effortlessly for Lucien. But his skill as a designer enabled him to integrate his art with his craft, thereby succeeding in restoring aesthetic values and integrity to craftsmanship.

Esther Pissarro's position at the Press has remained ambiguous in past writings about the Eragny Press. Her own aspirations to be an artist were subjugated by the period in which she lived, but she found her place with that of her husband and his art. The Eragny Press would not have been possible without her tireless labor. Esther's influence upon the Press is not as well documented as that of Camille's, but it did exist and needs to be recognized. In fact, both Lucien and Esther looked upon the work at the Press as a full and complete partnership. Their roles were different, but both were indispensable in supporting and sustaining the Eragny Press.

A further theme underlying the history of the Press is the wistful longing Lucien had to return to France. He often believed his decision, made under Esther's persuasion, to live in England rather than France was a mistake. Lucien's uneasiness in England, his difficulties with the language, and his sense of alienation made the promotion of his work more difficult. Moreover, as an Impressionist in a Pre-Raphaelite milieu, Lucien was obliged to modify his style in order to gain support for his art.

Finally, at the center of the history of the Eragny Press is the bittersweet irony of what might have been. Constrained by lack of capital and often lack of opportunity, Eragny Press books are less than they might have been, due to the compromises Lucien had to make in order to produce his books. While larger, more impressive volumes were planned, they were not completed because of the expense and time which would have been involved in their making.

The purpose of this work is to offer a complete account and reassessment of the Eragny Press based on the Pissarro Collection. It begins with a close scrutiny of Lucien Pissarro's early career in France in order to establish the influences and motivations for his later work, then proceeds to examine Lucien's association with Charles Ricketts, the establishment of the Eragny Press, and the Press' relationship with Hacon & Ricketts. Chapter Two addresses the physical plant, its operations, and the materials of the Press as well as costs and profits. Chapter Three considers the Eragny Press publishing program, the marketing and distribution of the books in England, America, and the Continent, and commissions from French book clubs. Chapter Four looks at the influences and theories which are the basis for Eragny Press books as well as their significance and place in the history of the English revivalist private presses.

The main text is followed by "A Descriptive Bibliography of Eragny Press Books," which includes a brief history of the design and production of each book.

Notes

1. Colin Franklin in his *The Ashendene Press* (Dallas, 1986) reports that the first book of the Ashendene Press was begun in December 1894 (p. 3) and appeared in 1895. Lucien Pissarro began his wood engravings for *The Queen of the Fishes*, his first book, in January 1894. The book was printed by the end of 1894 but was not bound until early 1895.

2. Colin Franklin, *The Private Presses* (London: Studio Vista, 1969) and Roderick Cave, *The Private Press*, 2nd edition (New York: R. R. Bowker Company, 1983) provide overviews of the English private presses. Interest in the private press movement has been primarily the domain of booksellers and bibliophiles. The publication of William Peterson's history of the Kelmscott Press by the University of California Press in January 1990 was the first major study of a private press and its cultural significance.

3. William Morris, "The Ideal Book, A Lecture Delivered in 1893," in *The Ideal Book: Essays and Lectures on the Arts of the Book* by William Morris, edited by William S. Peterson (Berkeley: University of California Press, 1982), 67–68.
4. Peterson, *The Ideal Book,* xiii.
5. Ibid., xxiv.
6. See Ann Thorold, *A Catalogue of the Oil Paintings of Lucien Pissarro* (London: Athelney Books, 1983). A full analysis and interpretation of his work as a painter and his influence on Impressionism in England has yet to be written.
7. Douglas Cooper, *The Courtauld Collection: A Catalogue and Introduction* (University of London: The Athlone Press, 1954), 33.
8. John Rewald, *The History of Impressionism,* 4th rev. ed. (New York: The Museum of Modern Art, 1973).
9. Alan Maxwell Fern, "The Wood-Engravings of Lucien Pissarro with a Catalogue Raisonnée," Ph.D. diss., University of Chicago, 1960.
10. Lucien Pissarro, *Notes on the Eragny Press, and A Letter to J. B. Manson,* edited with a Supplement by Alan Fern (Cambridge: Privately Printed, 1957).
11. Franklin, *The Private Presses,* 92.
12. For a detailed account of the Pissarro Family Archive, see Anne Thorold, "The Pissarro Collection in the Ashmolean Museum, Oxford," *Burlington Magazine* 120 (1978): 642–645.
13. Camille Pissarro, *Letters to His Son Lucien,* edited with the assistance of Lucien Pissarro by John Rewald (Santa Barbara and Salt Lake City: Peregrine Smith, Inc., 1981).
14. *Correspondance de Camille Pissarro,* edited by Janine Bailly-Herzberg: tome 1, 1865–1885 (Paris: Presses universitaires de France, 1980); tome 2, 1866–1890; tome 3, 1891–1894; tome 4, 1895–1898; tome 5, 1899–1903 (Paris: Editions du Valhermeil, 1986, 1988, 1989, 1991).
15. *The Letters of Lucien to Camille Pissarro, 1883–1903,* edited by Anne Thorold (Cambridge: Cambridge University Press, 1993).

Chapter I

Early Years and the Establishment of the Eragny Press

Lucien Pissarro was born in Paris on 20 February 1863 to Camille Pissarro, the Impressionist painter, and his then mistress, Julie Vellay.[1] The eldest of seven children, Lucien spent his childhood at Osny near Pontoise. From an early age, he displayed abilities for observation and draughtsmanship which pleased his father immensely, but his mother, too familiar with the poverty and struggle of an unsuccessful artist, was sharply opposed to Lucien following in his father's career. In 1878, at the age of fifteen, Lucien left school at Pontoise, mainly to alleviate his family's poverty, and went to work in Paris for a firm that sold English fabrics. There he learned to string and wrap parcels.[2] Lucien was eventually dismissed, the employer telling Camille that while he was an excellent boy, he lacked any trace of talent for business. Lucien returned home to Pontoise, where he continued to paint and draw under the observant eye of his father, who had recently been joined by Paul Cézanne and Paul Gauguin.

In January 1883, Lucien, not quite twenty, went to England to stay at the home of his uncle, Phineas Isaacson, whose wife was a half-sister of Camille, his two sons, Rudolph and Alfred, and his two daughters, Alice and Esther. The main objective of Lucien's stay was to learn English with the hope that with this accomplishment he would have less difficulty in obtaining a commercial post in Paris. One of Camille's underlying intentions was the hope that the new experiences would help mature the shy young man and contribute, at the same time, to the development of his artistic gifts outside the realm of his influence. His mother, on the other hand, hoped that his stay in England in a less artistic climate would prompt him to surrender his aspiration of being an artist and to take up a more lucrative career. Lucien tried to please both of his parents.

Shortly after Lucien's arrival in London, he applied for an office position with a manufacturer of oil cloth. Although Lucien was willing to work for nothing, the owner was not interested in him. He soon found an unpaid position with a music publisher, Stanley, Lucas, Weber and Co.[3] Instead of a salary, Lucien was given tickets to concerts and recitals, beginning a lifelong love of music. Both parents, however, were disappointed with his decision to work. His mother reminded him that his reason for living in England was to learn English. Camille, while understanding that a position in a firm would force Lucien to learn English, also questioned the necessity of taking a job. Camille reminded him of the necessity of devoting all of his time to drawing as a preparation for some profession that might be closely connected to art.[4]

In trying to please his father, whom he worshipped, Lucien met with many difficulties. He grew discouraged by his lack of time and with the lack of appropriate accommodations at his uncle's home. He foundered without direct guidance from Camille. Camille suggested that Lucien enroll in some free evening art classes where he could draw from nude models, for only after long hours of practice could Lucien expect to reach the point of rendering subjects in their true character. Camille also expressed his misgivings about the dangers of following the theories of other artists too closely and of being influenced by more skilled students. He urged Lucien to have the courage and will to develop his own style, to shun servile imitation: "The end is to learn to see forms, but with your own eyes, even with their faults, to look for perfection in the absurd (from the point of view of execution)."[5]

In mid-June, after he had asked his employer for a salary and was refused, Lucien quit his job with the music publishers. Without his position Lucien had more time for drawing and for learning English, as Camille had thought he would. Lucien began to go every day to the British Museum to draw Egyptian statues, which he praised for their simplicity. Continuing to encourage and advise Lucien, Camille also recommended the drawings of Charles Keene, the English caricaturist, popular in the pages of *Punch,* as examples of fine draughtsmanship. When Lucien had been in England for about a year, he began to attempt to learn to draw the figure. Lucien continued to draw daily and sent his work to Camille for criticism. Camille found Lucien's drawings too rigid, stilted, and mechanical—without any feeling for nature. Camille suggested that Lucien study carefully the drawings of Delacroix and Daumier as examples of what he meant. Drawing was essential to all artistic endeavors and a solid foundation could be acquired by drawing the nude.

Late in 1883, Gauguin visited Camille with a proposal to design Impressionist tapestries. Camille accepted Gauguin's offer because he thought this would be a viable and easily exploited branch of the industrial arts to which Lucien could make contributions. He reminded Lucien of the importance of drawing in this endeavor. Gauguin's idea was not new, for William Morris had set up his first tapestry loom in 1877[6] and was the leading exponent of industrial arts in Europe. Camille had been introduced to the decorative arts movement by his niece, Esther Isaacson, who was a disciple of both John Ruskin and Morris. For the Pissarros, the decorative arts were seen as a means for an artist to remain an artist, but with more tangible ware to sell than a canvas. Camille, realizing how difficult it was for an established artist to earn a living, naturally was interested in finding other ways for his sons to have an artistic life without all the financial hardships which he had endured. The industrial arts, providing an opportunity to blend the artistic with the commercial, also required a certain amount of capital which the Pissarro family lacked. But design was the crux of industrial art; if Lucien could not draw he would not be able to exploit his talent. While Gauguin's idea of designing tapestries did not come to fruition, the Pissarros continued to pursue those decorative arts which used drawing as a basis.

In early 1884, the Pissarro family made the decision to move from Pontoise-Osny to Eragny-sur-Epte, a small village not far from Gisors, three times farther from Paris than Pontoise. Camille, convinced of the importance of Lucien returning to France to work with him, began to entice him with the attractive things near Eragny and what the two of them could do together. Eragny had churches, markets, farms, a railroad station, and open fields; together they could paint, make lithographs, etchings, and drawings. Camille also suggested to Lucien a means by which he could capitalize on his drawing skills: by selling illustrations to the art and literary journals which were becoming popular in France. Camille's aversion to the new reproductive method of gillotage (a photo-relief process)[7] prevented him from contributing to these journals which were inclined to pay only those artists who had achieved some renown, but considered this to be a worthwhile venture for Lucien to attain some recognition, especially if he could develop original satiric qualities. Camille was interested in the revival of direct printmaking processes, but he realized that again it was a question of money, original prints being time-consuming and costly to make.[8]

After a series of bombings in various rail stations in London by Irish terrorists in February, Camille did not think it safe for anyone to be in London. He used this as another argument for Lucien to come home. With much imploring on Camille's part, Lucien finally made the decision to return home and begin the serious training and work which Camille had promised him. He arrived in late March in time to provide the family with the assistance they required for the move to Eragny, made in early April. His return also helped alleviate the family's unusually tight financial circumstances.

The camaraderie between Lucien and his father resumed. Lucien either spent his time in Paris or at Eragny helping Camille. In 1885, the Pissarros met and became enthusiastic followers of Paul Signac and Georges Seurat, who introduced them to the analytical technique of "pointillism," the division of color values in a conscious and scientific manner, intended to facilitate color synthesis. Lucien, as well as Camille, became an enthusiastic participant in this new technique, which would be given the name of Neo-Impressionism. Lucien, as a part of this group, became friendly or closely associated with a large circle of supporters of this new method. His personal relations with Seurat, Signac, and Félix Fénéon, the principle literary advocate of Neo-Impressionism and its chief interpreter, were particularly close.[9] This innovative group in which the Pissarros moved would provide Lucien with some of the connections he needed to establish himself as a printmaker and book illustrator.

Once home, Lucien took up Camille's suggestion of contributing illustrations to the Parisian journals, but while he was waiting for opportunities to come his way, he conceived the idea of attempting to earn his living by producing his own illustrated books, especially books for children. Inspired by the works of Randolph Caldecott, Walter Crane, and Kate Greenaway which he had seen in England, Lucien set out to produce a set of watercolor designs illustrating the ballad "Il était une bergère," which he began working on in late 1884.[10] Lucien continued working on his illustrations throughout 1885. When, late in the year his illustrations were ready, he made plans to lithograph and then color them with lithographic pencils.[11]

Camille, acting as Lucien's agent, took Lucien's finished illustrations to Hughes Leroux, a writer and critic. There he met an art critic who was excited by Lucien's work, but thought it would be difficult to reproduce the color tints. Leroux planned to show Lucien's work to Edmund de Goncourt who generally liked this "type of thing"[12] and who was influential with publishers; Leroux also promised to take Lucien's work to the publisher Calmann-Lévy, with whom he had a great deal of influence. Leroux believed that if Calmann-Lévy wished to publish the work, the firm would find a means of satisfactorily reproducing it, contrary to what his friend, the art critic, had suggested.[13] It was agreed that Lucien and Leroux would collaborate on the work, Leroux supplying the text, Lucien the illustrations. In spite of all of Leroux's enthusiastic promises and flatteries, he never placed, nor attempted to place, Lucien's story with a publisher.[14]

Disappointed with his first venture into the publishing world, Lucien

"Il était une bergère," watercolor drawing, 1885. (Ashmolean Museum, Oxford)

realized the need to have complete control over his projects, without dependence upon a publisher or printer to distribute his works. In order to have command over his projects, Lucien became motivated to learn wood engraving, which would allow him to engrave the line himself and thus reduce the cost of production. Woodcut engraving required only the simplest of tools. Sometime before the end of 1885, Lucien began to learn wood engraving. Camille took Lucien to see Auguste Lepère, a well-known and commercially successful wood engraver with a busy atelier.[15] Lepère explained to Lucien an uncomplicated system of making simple engravings, gave him a burin and a tool used to carve away large areas of white, and urged him not to fall into the ways of professional engravers in attempting to duplicate photographic effects. After this one important lesson, Lucien attempted his first wood engravings.

Fully aware of the difficulties and expenses of producing a book, Lucien sought commissions from literary and artistic journals. His first commission, obtained by Camille, was from the weekly newspaper *Le Chat,* named after the cabaret of the same name. The paper was well-known for its humorous drawings and caricatures. Lucien's first contribution was a series of "Types suburbains" which appeared in the 27 February 1886 issue. His drawings, highly praised by the painters Jean François Raffaelli and Federico Zandomeneghi,[16] were excellent publicity for the young artist. His second commission, again procured by Camille, came from *La Revue illustrée,* directed by M.F.G. Dumas. Lucien was to illustrate the ironic short story "Infortunes de mait'Liziard" by Octave Mirbeau, a friend of Camille's. Camille worried that Lucien might have trouble getting his drawing published, in spite of his commission, because the drawings were not refined.[17] They lacked adequate finish—not enough contrast within the tonal areas—and they were not decisive enough, but Dumas did not find Lucien's drawings too bad. Camille believed that Lucien could easily correct these faults when he made the actual wood engraving (which he prepared with the help of photography).[18] The four wood engravings Lucien completed for the "Infortunes de mait'Liziard" were published in the 15 June 1886 issue of *La Revue illustrée* along with a fifth engraving, "La Gare." Because of their roughness, the published engravings brought down a storm of protest on Dumas. But Dumas continued to ask Lucien to submit drawings regularly, thus enabling Lucien to supplement the family income.

Another opportunity to contribute illustrations to a journal arose for Lucien later that year. Gustave Kahn, symbolist writer and friend of the Pissarros, had recently taken over as editor of the journal *La Vogue.* He wished to transform *La Vogue* into a symbolist publication, illustrated solely by Neo-Impressionists. In addition to making format changes, Kahn also intended to take great care with the quality of printing and paper. While Kahn could not initially pay Lucien for his illustrations, this opportunity would provide Lucien with a vehicle for displaying his drawings, as well as introduce him to middlemen and agents who could contribute the financial backing for the book that Camille and he were planning to make.[19]

Apparently Lucien's contract with Dumas at *La Revue illustrée* prevented him from contributing illustrations to other publications.[20] Camille believed his agreement could be negotiated once Dumas understood Lucien's financial problems. Moreover, Dumas was not advancing Lucien's work; issue after issue went by without any of Lucien's illustrations included in the magazine. By contributing to *La Vogue,* Lucien would benefit, if not financially, at least from greater exposure. Risking his arrangement with Dumas, Lucien submitted his drawings to *La Vogue,* only to have Dumas retaliate by refusing all submissions. Without the income from *La Revue illustrée,* the Pissarros were in even more of a financial dilemma.[21]

Lucien renewed plans for an illustrated children's book while continuing to submit drawings to various publications. With Lucien in Eragny, Camille called on several publishers, but his contacts were few. Learning that the publisher, Quantin, had had much success with children's books, as well as drawings by Caran d'Ache and Théophile Steinlen,[22] Camille suggested that Lucien take his book to that house. Aware that Quantin was about to discontinue publishing children's books because illustrators were demanding compensation appropriate to their growing reputations, Camille advised Lucien to quickly and aggressively present Quantin with a sample from the children's story on which he was currently working. Camille coached Lucien on the appropriate style: simple drawings enhanced by several colors. By accepting a small fee, much less than an established artist would ask for, Lucien might be able to establish his reputation at the publishing houses.[23]

With Lucien's story "La Poupée qui éternue" in hand, Camille went to the Taverne anglaise, a meeting place of the Symbolist writers and the Neo-Impressionists, hoping to see Félix Fénéon, who happened to be at the café that evening. Fénéon liked the work and even agreed to edit the text before its submission. Fénéon was delighted to be of service to Lucien in his attempts to establish himself as a printmaker and illustrator. Gustave Kahn, who also was at the café, offered his help and his connections as well. Through Kahn's help, G. Lebre, editor of *La Vie moderne,* promised to publish Lucien's "La Poupée qui éternue" in several issues of *La Vie moderne.*[24]

Several other publishers, introduced to the Pissarros through friends, were contacted. Albert Dubois-Pillet, a follower of Seurat and fellow painter, suggested that the Pissarros approach the publisher Léon Vanier.[25] Dubois-Pillet had been successful in placing a few of his drawings at Vanier's. As publisher of the *Petite bibliothèque des jeunes,* albums by Caran d'Ache and Willette, and *Les Hommes d'aujourd'hui,* where each issue carried a caricature of the author, Dubois-Pillet thought that Lucien's style would be well-suited to Vanier's needs; but when approached by Camille, Vanier could not be bothered.

Octave Mirbeau had warmly recommended Lucien's work to Paul Ollendorf,[26] publisher of Mirbeau's recent novel, *Le Calvaire.* Ollendorf specialized in publishing foreign language study books, travel guides, novels, and other diverse publications, but he was not particularly interested in illustrated books.[27] In early May 1887, Camille called on Ollendorf with one of Lucien's proofs.[28] Zacharie Astruc, an editor at Ollendorf's, did not care for Lucien's work, finding it inappropriate for a deluxe edition he was planning. Astruc preferred the work of Jean Béraud, the painter of contemporary Parisian social life,[29] who currently was contributing drawings for the covers of Ollendorf novels. Astruc suggested that Lucien model his work after Béraud.

The contacts with well-established publishing firms were few. With so little success Lucien grew discouraged, though he had fully expected these rejections from commercial publishers who did not find his crude, naïve drawings to their liking. He believed he had been an idiot to think a commercial publisher would be interested in his work.[30]

Lucien, now twenty-four, knew that he should be supporting himself or at least bringing in enough money to supplement the family's income. With eight years separating Lucien from his next sibling, his role within the family was more as a second father to his younger brothers and sister than as an older brother. When Camille was in Paris, Lucien usually stayed in Eragny to help manage the large family. This responsibility surely weighed heavily on the young man, who was finding so much difficulty in establishing himself. While all of Camille's sons were brought up to be independent thinkers, to hold firm to their beliefs, both artistically and politically, Lucien had real difficulty in separating himself from his father. In addition to wanting to please Camille, Lucien was also Camille's assistant, whether it was in helping with the family, in setting up exhibitions and promoting his father, or serving as Camille's confidant. The burden of family responsibility combined with the difficulty of gaining an entrance into the publishing world made it very difficult for Lucien to establish himself as an artist.

Camille's brother, Alfred Pissarro, a respectable bourgeois businessman, was as conservative as Camille was radical. When he saw the family floundering financially, he stepped in with a job offer in early May for Lucien at a business firm.[31] Alfred insisted that Lucien make his decision uninfluenced by Camille who he believed would talk Lucien out of taking such a position. Outraged that his uncle should make such a suggestion, Lucien discussed the matter with Camille, who did not think that seeking a position in Paris while waiting for his current undertakings to come to fruition was such a bad idea. Lucien, rejecting his uncle's offer, began to look for a position at a bookseller or publishing firm in Paris, where he would be better positioned to place his illustrations. It was a difficult time to look for a position as the publishing season was coming to a close, but Edgar Degas, whom the Pissarros consulted, was able to provide Lucien with an introduction to his friend, François Marie Manzi, who was director of illustrated publications for Goupil.[32]

This contact proved worthwhile; in July Lucien began working for Manzi, learning chromolithography. While mastering the separation of the constituent colors of the subject to be reproduced, a technique which still required the discriminating and practiced eye of an artist, Lucien was left exhausted and with little free time to pursue his own artistic interests.[33] Because Lucien lacked the skills necessary for the position, he worked for a number of weeks without pay. His technique, not yet precise enough for

"Un Voyage au pays des pommes," drawing for children's story, c. 1889–90. (Ashmolean Museum, Oxford)

the tedious work, did not meet with the foreman's approval. The firm would soon be producing chromolithographs of subjects requiring more difficult techniques which demanded even more skill. In order to maintain his apprenticeship, Lucien agreed to work for half the wages of an ordinary worker who earned sixty centimes an hour. Lucien's thirty centimes an hour earned just enough to pay for his meals. Although he was finally learning a trade which would satisfy his mother's desire for stability, Lucien was apprehensive that this industry would soon disappear when a photographic technique was discovered for color. No matter how senseless and oppressive Lucien thought the work, he realized how indispensable drawing skills were to chromolithography.

While working for Manzi, a number of independent commissions came Lucien's way. These commissions were from men who were part of the Pissarro circle. Lucien submitted drawings for publication to various journals, including *La Vie moderne* and *La Revue indépendante*. By October, now more adapted to his work at the chromolithography firm, Lucien went in the evenings with his friend Louis Hayet to draw at the École municipale de dessin et de sculpture de la Ville de Paris.[34] Lucien left the firm probably sometime in the early part of 1888. He was anxious to return to Eragny where he could paint and draw in tranquility.[35]

In March, Lucien returned to Paris, having contributed drawings for *La Vie Franco-Russe,* a new periodical which had made its debut in February. Three of his drawings, accepted for the 31 March issue, illustrated stories by Edmund Pelletier, Gardine, and Ivan Turgenev. Lucien began to submit drawings to the journal and was bringing in about fifty francs a month; but, more importantly, Lucien believed that through this journal he would gain recognition as an artist. In early May, *La Vie Franco-Russe* ceased publication. Lucien again returned to Eragny to paint and draw with Camille, working through the fall season and into the next year. He continued the occasional contributions to *La Vie moderne* and *Le Chat noir* throughout 1889 and began making regular contributions to the anarchist journal, *Le Père Peinard,* in the summer of 1890.[36] He sold twenty-five proofs of one of his engravings to the Goupil Gallery for 125 francs (a hundred of which he sent to his family). During this period, Lucien also continued to write and design children's books—*Le Long nez, Un Voyage au pays des pommes,* and *L'Aventure en sabot*—although he was never able to interest a publisher in his work.

By 1890 the Pissarro family's financial position was greatly improved. In returning to his original and popular impressionist style, Camille's

"L'Aventure en sabot," drawing for children's story, c. 1888. (Ashmolean Museum, Oxford)

paintings began to sell. From this point the family experienced a modicum of financial security. With the improving financial situation, Camille began to seriously rethink a career in the applied arts for his sons. As an established painter with a considerable reputation, he had recently come through a lengthy phase with little financial success. How could his sons survive as painters?

With guidance and information from his niece, Esther Isaacson, Camille successfully enrolled Georges, his wayward second son, at Charles R. Ashbee's Guild and School of Handicraft at Toynbee Hall in London in June 1889. This school provided Georges with the needed discipline he was not receiving in France under Camille's guidance, as well as skilled advice and a serious working environment. Moreover, he was learning English while staying with his cousins, Alice and Esther Isaacson, who were now running a boarding house. Esther Isaacson, proponent of the Arts and Crafts movement, contributed toward financing Georges' training. He took up metal répousée work and showed considerable talent for woodcarving.[37] Camille's purpose in placing a son at an English school of applied arts was to enable him to bring knowledge and experience of this genre of art back to France. Camille believed that while the applied arts were commonplace in England, the concept of applying art to home furnishings was virtually unheard of in France. This exclusion within the decorative arts left the field wide open. The biggest challenge would come in marketing these objects to French collectors, who were, Camille believed, inclined to be faddish.[38]

Now that he had more money to finance this enterprise, Camille urged Georges to produce at school a variety of furnishings, frames, sconces, candelabra, andirons, etc., in an assortment of decorative styles for an exhibition where these objects could be displayed for sale. With his five sons, Camille intended to launch a distinguished and important decorative arts workshop. As Camille's plan evolved, each son would undertake an area of the decorative arts to which he was most suited. Lucien, Georges, Félix, Rodolphe, and eventually Paul-Emile, the youngest, would find their places within the Pissarro Brothers atelier. Each son would participate in the actual manufacture of the furnishings with the help of workmen, but would be involved in different aspects of design and decoration.[39]

Georges returned to Eragny in the summer of 1890 and plans were made for Lucien to go to London in the autumn. Lucien would support himself by giving art lessons, while at the same time gaining an entré into the world of the decorative arts movement. Lucien was sent because he was older and would be more respected by the English than the recalcitrant Georges. When Lucien had established himself with enough students to defray his expenses, Georges would then come back to London to continue learning his craft.

When Lucien returned to London in November 1890, his career was foundering. Working with and for Camille, Lucien's own creativity had been sapped and imposed upon, despite Camille's original intentions otherwise. His strong belief in his father tended to negate his sense of his own work and his reticence in networking with acquaintances limited his career substantially. In his work outside his father's medium, Lucien was not succeeding either. He had made no breakthrough in selling his book illustrations to French publishers. His involvement in anarchist politics, his Jewish background,[40] as well as the burden of his father's often troubled reputation, all worked against Lucien gaining entré into publishing firms, who were conservative in their outlook. Lucien was still single-handedly promoting the revival of original print media, especially wood engraving, but his shy temperament was not well-suited to the difficult task of advancing an idea before its time. Lucien, who had heard reports of a thriving wood engraving community, believed he had a greater chance of finding a sympathetic circle in London, as well as a publisher who would appreciate his work.

Establishment of the Eragny Press

A convenient, though arbitrary date for the start of the private press movement is November 1888, when Emery Walker gave his lecture on "Letterpress Printing and Illustration" accompanied by lantern slides during the first Arts and Crafts Exhibition. William Morris who had experimented with typography and illustration over several decades in the publication of his own writings, was astonished and excited to see the letter forms of the early Italian printers enlarged on the screen and went home determined to try his hand at type design. From this developed the Kelmscott Press, which between 1890 and 1898 produced fifty-two titles in a style quite unlike that of book production of the time. Morris' books were conceived as architecture, each detail contributing to the whole, so that paper, ink, typeface, word and line spacing, placing of margins, and the integration of illustration and decoration were considered in detail and in relation to the complete book.

In defining his aims for the Kelmscott Press, Morris laid the foundation for the twentieth-century renaissance in typography and book design.[41] But William Morris was neither the first nor the only man to experiment with a more vigorous and traditional typography. At the time when Morris was beginning to establish his Kelmscott Press, there was a brilliant flowering of commercial book design, promoted by a group of publishers of belles lettres, chiefly John Lane, Elkin Mathews, Grant Richards, Fisher Unwin, and Charles Kegan Paul.[42] A. H. Mackmurdo, founder of the Century Guild of Artists, launched, with the help of Herbert Horne, the quarterly magazine the *Hobby Horse* in April 1886, the first magazine to treat modern printing as a serious art and which, with its careful layout and typesetting and handmade paper, anticipated Morris' printing venture and the preoccupation of the private press movement.

Through a fortuitous letter of introduction from Félix Fénéon to the English poet John Gray,[43] Lucien, upon his arrival in London in November 1890, became acquainted with the circle of Charles Ricketts, instantly conferring upon him access to the world of English book illustration, typography, and binding. Ricketts had connections with a number of publishers and moved in an important circle of influential artists. He would become

Lucien's closest English friend, his second most influential mentor, and his publisher. Ricketts provided Lucien with a forum for discussion of artistic theory, while introducing him to his own theory of book design, especially to the harmonic unification of text and type and the essentials of book production.

Ricketts had a quick mind, was a fascinating and incessant talker, and spoke fluent French, which immediately put Lucien at ease. Ricketts, although acquainted with Impressionism, actually knew very little about the movement; yet Lucien had finally found someone who was knowledgeable about printmaking—wood engraving, lithography, and etching.[44] Lucien was introduced to and became friends with the members of the Vale group, which included Charles Shannon, Thomas Sturge Moore, and Reginald Savage.[45] In addition, he was also introduced to the broader circle of Madox Brown, William Rossetti, Walter Crane, Oscar Wilde, Herbert Horne, Selwyn Image, and Emery Walker.[46]

Ricketts, born on 2 October 1866, was the son of a naval officer and a Naples-born Frenchwoman, Helène de Sousy.[47] In 1882, after a childhood mainly spent on the continent, he began training as a wood engraver at the City and Guilds Technical Art School in Kensington Road, Lambeth, where he met Charles Shannon, who was to become his lifelong companion. Upon finishing their training, Ricketts and Shannon traveled to Paris to seek advice from Puvis de Chavannes about studying art in Paris. Puvis did not encourage them to study there, but thought it would be better if they returned to London where they could earn a living through their professional wood-engraving skills. After returning from Paris, the pair moved to the Vale in Chelsea, taking a Regency house formerly occupied by the painter James McNeill Whistler. The outside was unremarkable, but the inside, with walls colored distempered yellow and hung with prints by Hokusai, was remarkable and charming. Edith Cooper in her diary described the Vale "as a muddy retreat from the highway, edged by gardens in which snowball-trees grow from the soil like wands that are full of sighing."[48]

From the Vale, Ricketts, Shannon, and Reginald Savage issued their first number of an occasional magazine, called the *Dial*, in 1889. Four more issues appeared irregularly between 1892 and 1897. The design and layout were their own, as well as the risk of publishing a collection of writings and illustrations by unknown names. Typographically, the work owes much to the book designs of Whistler,[49] but its large quarto format, good paper, and fine printing resemble most closely the *Hobby Horse*. The text took a more avant-garde stance, inspired by symbolist ideas which were little known outside of France and Belgium at the time.

In addition to designing and publishing the *Dial*, Ricketts also produced work for the publisher Osgood, McIlvaine, and Co., whose authors included Oscar Wilde and Thomas Hardy. Wilde had introduced Ricketts to the firm, and Ricketts went on to design and illustrate Wilde's books from 1891 on, with the exception of *Salome*. In 1892, when Osgood, McIlvaine closed—after publishing Hardy's *Tess of the d'Urbervilles* with a binding and title-page by Ricketts—Ricketts received commissions from Elkin Mathews and John Lane, Wilde's new publishers. Ricketts was beginning to move independently towards the idea of the unity of the book, all elements complementing each other. In 1891, before the first Kelmscott Press book had appeared, Ricketts expressed his ambition to be the Morris of the book,[50] but at this early stage he was not able to take an entirely independent course. He lacked the financial resources to establish a press. From 1891 until 1894, continuing to design books for Mathews and Lane and others, Ricketts also undertook his own projects. *Daphnis and Chloe* is modeled after Aldus Manutius' *Hypnerotomachia Poliphili* (1499), a work which Ricketts admired considerably. For this ambitious work, the design and engraving of thirty-seven illustrations and over one hundred initials occupied Ricketts and Shannon for more than eleven months. The type, a commercial Caslon, was set at the Ballantyne Press and the printing supervised by Ricketts. Issued in a small edition by Mathews and Lane, the work was well enough received that Ricketts undertook another volume, Christopher Marlowe's *Hero and Leander*. The shorter text allowed Ricketts to devote more attention to detail, balancing the weight of the Caslon type with the illustrations. The book was printed on specially made paper with a watermark design of the letters VP (for Vale Press) interlaced with a sprig of wild thyme. In effect, Ricketts had begun operation of his own press.

With Ricketts, Lucien shared a mutual interest in wood engraving. He found Ricketts' engravings to be very well done in the tradition of the old masters. They had the same ideas on engravings, though Ricketts was the more technically skilled engraver. Under Ricketts' tutelage Lucien began to understand drawing as it applied to the medium of wood engraving. The two also possessed an interest in book design, especially the integration of text and illustration, which they articulated in a collaborative work, *De la typographie et de l'harmonie de la page imprimée* (1898).

It took little time for Lucien to come under Ricketts' influence, though he was troubled by Ricketts' derivative style. Shortly after Lucien's arrival, the Vale group planned another issue of the *Dial*, to which Lucien was asked to contribute one of his wood engravings.[51] Ricketts also had been solicited by the director of the American magazine *Harper's* to undertake the design of a new magazine which would be published in London. This commission by a major firm would provide Ricketts with firsthand experience of production processes, and with the income earned, enough capital to purchase his own press. He could then begin to produce his own illustrated books in limited numbers. If Ricketts succeeded, so would Lucien as long as he remained in collaboration with him.[52]

Although Lucien was surprised to find in Ricketts someone so sympathetic and supportive of his own artistic ambitions, he continued to pursue connections within William Morris' circle, believing it would ensure success in the industrial arts. In 1889, before Georges Pissarro, Lucien's brother, had been placed with C. R. Ashbee's Guild of Handicraft to learn metalworking and cabinet making, the Pissarros sought to place him in an apprenticeship with Morris without success. Lucien believed, now that he was in London and able to contact Morris directly, the Pissarros would

L'art est-il utile? Oui. Pourquoi? Parce qu'il est l'art.—Ch. Baudelaire.

4

DE LA TYPOGRAPHIE ET DE L'HARMONIE DE LA PAGE IMPRIMÉE.

à Georges Lecomte.

I.

DANS un renouveau des métiers le livre paraît, au premier abord, la chose la plus facile à régénérer. Sa technique restreinte, l'emploi d'une ligne noire sur blanc, la parenté de cette ligne avec le trait de plume, corrigé seulement par l'œuvre du graveur (dans la typographie et dans la gravure sur bois), n'offre pas les difficultés d'une matière plus complexe ou retorse: tels, la technique du brocart, du tapis ou l'agencement d'un vitrail.

Et, malgré cela, depuis trente ans qu'agit sur les métiers, en Angleterre, une préoccupation d'intimité curieuse dans les arts, le livre est le dernier venu.

Nous ne nous soucierons pas ici d'un renouveau purement artistique du trait,

5

Charles Ricketts and Lucien Pissarro, *De la typographie et de l'harmonie de la page imprimée: William Morris et son influence sur les arts et métiers,* 1898; pp. 4–5. (Ashmolean Museum, Oxford)

have a better chance of interesting him in their work.[53] His cousin, Esther Isaacson, introduced him to Emery Walker, to whom he showed his wood engravings. Walker admired the engravings, but was unable to publish them in the *English Illustrated Magazine*, of which he was artistic director, because the English public was not advanced enough to appreciate them.[54] Walker circulated proofs among the "Morris entourage," as Lucien referred to this group, who were astonished by his color engravings because they had seen nothing like them before.[55]

In order to facilitate his introduction to Morris' group, Lucien began to attend socialist meetings in Hammersmith.[56] Though he became acquainted with the men surrounding Morris, Lucien soon realized that a place could not be made with him. It quickly became obvious that his way would be through Ricketts, with whom he shared so much in common.

In early October 1891, Lucien reported to his father that he and his brother Georges, who had recently joined him in London, were casually discussing "a project for the future, which would be a kind of association uniting furnishings, the book, etc., etc."[57] The venture, to produce unique useable art, would require capital, but certainly would earn money.[58] Gustave Kahn, who was passing through London, suggested that they issue shares to interested people in order to obtain a small capital which would enable them to begin production.[59] But even more agreeable to Lucien was the idea Ricketts and Shannon were now proposing: to form a guild. Lucien was sure that Ricketts would accept their work, but as in any commercial affair it would be better if Georges and he were able to contribute capital to the venture, thereby insuring their own success. If one branch of the venture failed, their general interest in the guild would still give them a return on the work of the community.[60] Lucien's role in the guild had been discussed with Ricketts—he would design and execute bindings.[61]

If the collaboration between brothers came to fruition, Lucien believed that they would have a better chance of gaining a reputation in Paris, where they were known and had friends to defend and publicize their enterprise. They planned to begin the venture in London and then extend production to Paris, but the main thrust was to get production underway. The Pissarro brothers' plans were interrupted by a series of personal events, including Lucien's marriage to Esther Bensusan in August 1892. Moreover, neither one was financially astute nor confident enough to secure the needed investments.

Ricketts had been ambitiously establishing himself in the publishing field. In addition to the *Dial,* Ricketts and Shannon had published Lucien's first portfolio, *Twelve Woodcuts in Black and Colours.*[62] Moreover, Ricketts acted as an agent for the sale of Camille Pissarro's etchings and gouaches in England. It was only a matter of time and money before Ricketts established his own firm. In late October 1894, Ricketts signed an agreement with his financial backer, Llewellyn Hacon, a conveyancer by profession. Hacon, a man who preferred art to real estate, was introduced to Ricketts by the painter William Rothenstein. Hacon had offered to finance Rothenstein in his career as an artist by buying so many paintings and drawings each year, but Rothenstein, young and proud, and already with a steady income from his father, had declined Hacon's offer. However, he knew that Ricketts was "eager to design type and embark on book production,"[63] so he urged Hacon to finance Ricketts' venture. Hacon invested £1,000 into the business with a vague understanding of a half share of the profits. Ricketts contributed £500 from his grandfather's estate. In late 1894, Ricketts wrote to the poets Katherine Bradley and Edith Cooper (the aunt and niece who wrote under the name Michael Field), " . . . I am about to become a printer-publisher-bookbinder with a small shop of my own. You must imagine a little brown mouse with his two hazelnuts to realize the size and conditions of this future firm."[64] The firm was named Hacon & Ricketts, although Hacon remained very much a silent partner.

The year 1895 was devoted to preparing type, woodcut initials, and blocks as well as finding a suitable shop. Ricketts had conceived his shop as an artistic gathering place for all of London and as a place where the "new school" of art could be showcased. Looking for a shop that was small, well-located, and inexpensive, Ricketts found one at 52 Warwick Street at Regent Street. After a series of delays, Hacon & Ricketts opened in mid-March 1896, with an exhibition of Lucien's and Ricketts' wood engravings. The shop consisted of two rooms: the front room was painted apple green and white, and a smaller back room was painted white for exhibitions. As Ricketts wrote to the poets Michael Field:

> The shop positively drips with paint and white wash & we will invite you to tea when we are established there. We are so near to the New Gallery (on the condition that you do not allude to the outside which is ugly). The shop is painted green inside the colour of hope—. . . .[65]

Charles Holmes described the shop at Warwick Street as "a dismal hole"[66] which was occupied on the upper floors by "lodgers of another ancient profession."[67] But the shop was made palatable by the exciting melange of visitors.

The months following the opening of the boutique were difficult. Lucien noted in a letter to his father that Hacon & Ricketts was boycotted by the trade and in the month or so that the shop had been open, Ricketts had sold only twenty copies of the two books which he had prepared for the opening, *The Early Poems of John Milton* and Walter Savage Landor's *Epicurus, Leontion, and Ternissa,* under the Vale Press imprint.[68] In addition to these two works, Hacon & Ricketts also had for sale a portfolio of Lucien's prints, *Les Travaux des champs,* as well as the Eragny Press' first book, *The Queen of the Fishes.*

E. Le Breton Martin was hired as business manager, but left that same summer to take more remunerative work at a large daily paper. Charles Holmes, with seven years of publishing experience with the firms Rivington and Co., and the Ballantyne Press, came to work for Hacon & Ricketts for a salary of £80 a year in the summer of 1896.[69] By the time Holmes took over as business manager, the original £1,000 had been spent and Holmes had to borrow £50 more from Hacon to keep the shop solvent.[70] Holmes' considerable experience and natural business skills reversed the fate of the shop. He describes the situation:

> Ricketts had attempted to sell his books in person to friendly booksellers who, after exasperating him by their criticisms, had extracted such discounts from his helplessness as no professional publisher could afford. I was no trained traveller myself, but there was nothing for it but to make a round of the London shops, and reduce their allowance to a reasonable and uniform rate. Although a year or more passed before I could take a new book into a shop door without a preliminary stroll outside to summon up the courage to enter, the booksellers, for the most part, soon became friends, who actually appeared glad to see me, especially when the book I brought was sure to go "Out of Print" at once. I was greatly helped by the confidence of my chiefs, being allowed, for the first time, an absolutely free hand in finance and the details of negotiation;—so much so that once when Ricketts, in my absence, wished to draw some money from Barclays, the Bank hesitated about cashing his cheque. They had seen no signature but mine.[71]

When Hacon & Ricketts closed on 30 June 1903, the shop, according to Holmes, had become a financial success. After seven years of business, when the accounts were audited it was found that the "original capital had been returned to them more than eight times over, and that the goodwill of the business might fairly be valued at some £3,500 in addition."[72]

Parallel to, but seemingly independent of the founding of Hacon & Ricketts, Lucien established the Eragny Press. In early January 1894, Lucien was preparing engravings for a small book, *The Queen of the Fishes,* but did not know if it could be completed because of the problems involved with obtaining type and paper, printing, and binding.[73] The obstacles were overcome and the book was finished in early January 1895,[74] carrying the imprint of "Vale Publications." *The Queen of the Fishes* was ready for over a year before Hacon & Ricketts opened its doors and it was marketed independently. Lucien's work, at this point, was connected to Ricketts only through their artistic association, which had merged under the imprint of "Vale Publications."

little fish & the crayfish in the pools &
rock crevices. She did not mind cat-
ching the spiteful crayfish who nipped
her bare toes, but when she heard the
other poor little fish singing so sadly
in her basket her heart was touched
& she put them back in the river. Then
when she went home with almost
4

"Girl Reaching into Stream," wood engraving. *The Queen of the Fishes,* 1894; p. 4. (Ashmolean Museum, Oxford)

In spite of the earlier preliminary discussions concerning the guild and Lucien's role in it, when Hacon & Ricketts opened Lucien was only a peripheral associate. Although Ricketts was willing to sell Lucien's books and prints, he was unable to undertake financial responsibility for them. He urged Lucien to find his own financial backer. Lucien's ideal investor would be either French or Dutch and, for the sake of vanity or some other viable reason, would like to place a certain sum in his business. Lucien preferred that the backer provide him with a fixed sum, as Hacon had provided Ricketts, which would give him time to design his own type.[75] While this did not seem like a particularly lucrative venture for an investor, the books themselves would be the return and would continue to increase in value with time. Lucien, at least, believed an investor would not lose any money. However, the backer Lucien envisioned was so wealthy that if his investment should be lost, it would be little more than an annoyance.[76]

Lucien, via Camille, enlisted the help of Charles Destrée, a salesperson at Durand-Ruel Galleries, who was well connected in both Holland and in Paris. He was enthusiastic about Lucien's work and, because he was discreet, would not spoil Lucien's chances of finding a financial backer. Destrée, who had just returned from a trip to Holland when Camille approached him, knew of a possible backer—a Mr. Groesbeck, a wealthy collector and head of the art gallery Van Wisselingh and Co. of Amsterdam. Destrée suggested that Lucien go to Amsterdam and present his proposal in person to Groesbeck. With a letter of introduction from Destrée, Lucien could have presented himself quite suitably to Groesbeck, but his lack of confidence and his natural shyness prevented him from doing so. Lucien preferred to have an agent or an intermediary who would go to Groesbeck and outline the proposal before he arrived.

Lucien asked Camille to speak to friends who might be interested in making an investment in his business. Camille suggested Dr. Georges Viau, a dentist and collector of Camille's paintings; Dr. Paulin, Camille's dentist and a collector; and Paul Gallimard, a wealthy collector and publisher. Camille urged Lucien to come to Paris to speak personally with these men, especially Gallimard, who, as Camille described him, was enthusiastic about Lucien's work. Again, Lucien did not have the courage to make his proposal to these men.

By mid-October 1896, Camille had found a possible investor in Jérome Doucet. An active and enterprising man, already the sponsor of the painter Delâtre, Doucet was resourceful but not particularly wealthy. As manager of the Théatre des arts in Rouen and member of the Société de bibliophiles de Rouen, Doucet was engaged in publicity work. He knew the bibliophiles of Rouen as well as a large number of prominent people in the arts. Camille suggested that Lucien go to Rouen to discuss his business with Doucet, but again Lucien did not follow through.

In the meantime, a rift was developing between Lucien and Ricketts. Lucien believed that Ricketts was trying to ease him out of the Vale group. While he did not understand exactly why, Lucien offered several possible reasons for this. Perhaps it was their differing art philosophies, or perhaps it was for financial reasons. Ricketts, knowing that there was a limited market for his publications, might be trying to eliminate his competition. Lucien felt Ricketts had used him to form his group and now that they had been recognized he was dropping him.[77] This early misunderstanding between the two faded with the success of Hacon & Ricketts, and Lucien's place within the establishment became secure.

Esther Bensusan Pissarro

When Lucien started the Eragny Press in 1894, it had not yet been determined that he would devote the next twenty years of his life to producing books in England. It was assumed that he would bring his skills back to France and to his family's proposed atelier. The one event which Camille had not foreseen when he was carefully planning the business and careers of his sons was that Lucien would fall in love with and marry an English woman who refused to live in France.

Lucien first met Esther Bensusan[78] in 1883 when he was living in England. They were introduced by Esther Isaacson, Lucien's cousin and Esther's best friend. Lucien saw little of Esther that year, but when the Bensusan family visited Paris in August 1889 the two became reacquainted. Lucien found in Esther, who at eighteen was both attractive and intelligent, an attentive and sympathetic listener to his views on painting, music, current events, and anarchism. When she returned to London, the two began to correspond regularly and Esther sent her drawings for criticism to the Pissarros. She had become a follower of the School of Eragny.

Esther Levi Bensusan, born 12 November 1870, was the daughter of Jacob Levi Samuel Bensusan, a prosperous feather merchant, and his wife Minnie. Esther was brought up in a well-to-do Jewish family which adhered strictly to the observances and rituals of the Jewish faith. Her father was a knowledgeable musician, with a profound love of sacred music, and he frequently took Esther to concerts at the Crystal Palace. Her upbringing was rigid, but her independent and headstrong character would cause her to rebel against her father's orthodox religious practices as well as his conservative political views. She showed an early interest in art and could draw with skill and ease, taking lessons at the Crystal Palace Art School,[79] where she met a coterie of life-long friends, among them Diana White, who would become an adherent to the precepts of Impressionism and Lucien's confidant after the death of Camille. Esther had artistic inclinations and aspirations. Under the influence of Esther Isaacson, Esther became involved, against her father's wishes, in socialist politics, regularly attending the socialist meetings at Hammersmith with William Morris in attendance.

It is little wonder that Esther found herself attracted to this gentle, anarchist artist, for whose lifestyle of freedom she herself longed. When Lucien moved to London in 1890, Esther promised to be his student. Her father, however, upon hearing of her intentions, quickly intervened. He considered Esther's friendship with Lucien both undesirable and dangerous. He objected to Lucien because of his lack of religious training (Lucien would remain an atheist all of his life), his politics, and the fact that Lucien was an impecunious artist with no apparent future. He feared that by associating with Lucien, Esther's reputation would be ruined. By being seen in public with him, Esther might be mistaken for his model and would thus be considered a loose woman. Esther, forbidden to see Lucien, soon began to meet him secretly. Their favorite meeting place was the British Museum, where they met often to draw. Esther's father soon found out about these secret trysts and again forbade Esther to see Lucien.

This second intervention precipitated Lucien's declaration of love and a marriage proposal. When the declaration and proposal arrived in the mail, carefully packaged in a small box which Lucien had carved and colored himself, Esther's father was incensed. He feared Lucien was interested in Esther only because of her money and he refused to provide Esther with a dowry if she married Lucien. In marrying Lucien, Esther would give up the middle-class prosperity to which she was accustomed and begin a life of financial struggle. Esther did not need her father's consent to marry and the two went ahead with their plans. They were married on 11 August 1892 at the Richmond registry office with Ricketts, Shannon, and Camille Pissarro as their witnesses. In addition, Esther's father sent his confidential clerk as a witness to ensure that the marriage actually took place.

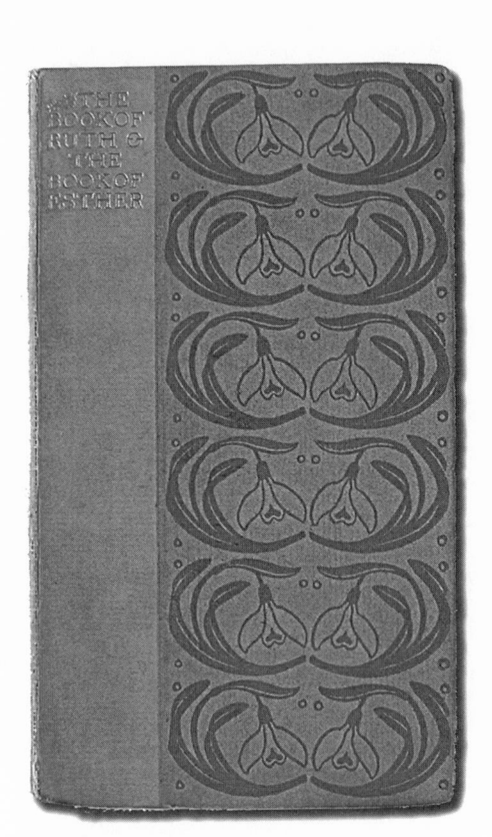

"Snowdrop" binding. *The Book of Ruth and the Book of Esther,* 1896. (Special Collections, Florida State University, Tallahassee)

Mr. Bensusan was not the only one to object to the marriage. Lucien's mother, Julie, also objected on the grounds that Esther, who had been brought up with all the comforts of life, would be unable to adapt to the poverty of an artist's existence. Lucien later assessed their marriage as an ideal union, except for the "difficulties of life, I mean money."[80] The Eragny Press would become, as Lucien suggested, the expression of their mutual love.

Lucien had discovered the perfect mate in the independent and outspoken Esther, a spouse who would run his house, mother him, and work with and for him. She was a companion he could depend upon, who believed in him and his life as an artist. Esther was a person of boundless energy and vitality, who knew no half-measures. She was a reservoir of goodwill, frank to a fault, outspoken in her opinions, and difficult to get along with. Her qualities of devotion and stubbornness saw her through her impoverished life with Lucien. Unfortunately, like Lucien, Esther did not have a sense of money. When they had a little extra money, she would spend it recklessly on her house, was generous with friends, but seldom spent any money on herself. Stern and severe, she was a woman of resolute integrity.[81]

Lucien and Esther honeymooned in Rouen, then spent eight months in Eragny before finally returning to England. They settled in the small village of Epping, Essex, which Lucien chose because of its similarity to Eragny. Orovida, their daughter, was born in October 1893. Esther, early on in her marriage, took a course of instruction in wood engraving and began to help Lucien in engraving the borders and initials for the books, which allowed the Pissarros to dispense with the services of a professional wood-engraver.

The Eragny Press was a joint venture between Lucien and Esther. What Esther's function was to be in the venture is difficult to establish. It is not unfair to assume that Esther's role was to be minor; that she would engrave some of the more simple blocks, provide a helping hand now and then, and serve as an artistic advisor to the Press. But her position at the Press altered considerably after 1897.

In the spring of 1897, Lucien and Esther moved from Epping to 62 Bath Road, Bedford Park, London, a choice of locality influenced by Ricketts, who considered Bedford Park synonymous with the elect of his art world. About this same time, Lucien began having attacks of vertigo, weakness in his legs, and stomach problems. In April, Lucien had a mild stroke, which paralyzed his left side. By day, Esther devoted herself to Lucien; in the evenings she worked at the Press. Her first independent printing project was the cover for *De la typographie*, which Lucien had begun before the stroke, printed in red and green.[82] Lucien's recovery took several years; by the end of 1899, his health had returned, but his left side remained slightly paralyzed and he still had trouble walking. Physically he was never the same; the stroke left him awkward and clumsy, and the fingers of his left hand remained paralyzed for life.

In late 1898, after a break of almost two years, the Pissarros began to print in earnest. They acquired a larger press, and Esther took on the major burden of running the shop, since Lucien was unable to do any hard work and they could not afford to hire a printer. Lucien started to engrave again, employing drawings which had been done before the stroke. Esther took over the presswork with the same zeal and enthusiasm that she put into every endeavor which she undertook. She became the technical skill behind the Press. It appears that Esther learned to print from Lucien and perhaps a hired workman. While Lucien would eventually rejoin Esther in the printing, for the years shortly after his illness he tended only to mix the printing inks to obtain the colors that he envisioned for his colored woodcuts.

After Lucien's recovery, Esther continued to work every bit as hard, if not harder, than Lucien, and was as involved in the actual production as much as he. While she was not responsible for the design of the books, she heavily influenced Lucien's decisions. Many of the decorations and the charming paper covers of Eragny Press books are modeled after the flowers which Esther, an ardent gardener, grew in her garden.

The Eragny Press

The Eragny Press, established as a commercial venture, was expected to provide an income to Lucien and his family. The Press followed the aesthetic of the Arts and Crafts movement, allowing Lucien to reunite the artist and the craftsman within himself. He hoped that through his labor as a craftsman his art would find financial compensation.

The Eragny Press, financed with Camille Pissarro's limited funds until 1903, was consistently undercapitalized. But this dearth of capital enhanced the Arts and Crafts aesthetic of the Press by forcing Lucien to be an authentic artist-craftsman. Neither William Morris, as the designer of Kelmscott books, nor Charles Ricketts, as the designer of Vale Press books, performed the actual work of printing; Lucien did. Because almost all the work was done by the Pissarros, from the design of the books and the engraving of the illustration and decorations to the actual production, the result is a genuine Arts and Crafts product. The output, however, was modest: thirty-two books over a twenty-year period.

The production of the Eragny Press can be divided into two series—the Vale and the Brook, named after the types that the Press employed. After the first book of the Press, *The Queen of the Fishes,* whose text was done in manuscript and then process-engraved, the next fifteen books of the Press used the Vale type, designed by Charles Ricketts. The loan of his type was a generous and friendly gesture on the part of Ricketts, since so many of the proprietary types of this period took on an aspect of self-identification. Fifteen more books printed in the Brook type, designed by Lucien, constitute the second series. Of the Brook series, two books were commissioned by French book clubs: *Histoire de la reine du matin et de Soliman prince des génies* (1909) by Les Cent bibliophiles and *La Charrue d'érable* (1912/13) by Le Livre contemporain. These commissions enabled the underfinanced Press to pursue designs which had previously been too expensive to undertake. During the twenty years of the Press, the Pissarros attempted color printing, printing with gold leaf and gold powder, printing on vellum, and music printing. The Press maintained its original integrity until the end.

Cul-de-lampe (NIF). Gerard de Nerval, *Histoire de la reine du matin et de Soliman prince des génies,* 1909.

The onset of World War I provided the Press with a convenient stopping point. Materials were difficult to procure, especially the paper which the Pissarros imported from France. The distressed war economy depleted their clientele. Lucien realized that no more commissions would be forthcoming. French book clubs were inclined to ask an artist to contribute only once. While there were many more active book clubs in France, Lucien had no connections with them. Producing books was a laborious task, not only was the actual printing time consuming, it was also hard work. The woodblocks were also becoming more difficult to cut as Lucien's eyesight was no longer as sharp as it had once been. The tedious work of printing, especially of five-color woodblocks, had taken its toll. Both Lucien and Esther were exhausted after completing *La Charrue d'érable* (1912/13). Esther went to Switzerland to recuperate while Lucien began assessing what they should do next. The Impressionists were now better understood in England and Lucien's paintings were more acceptable than when Lucien first moved to England in 1890. Lucien believed it possible that a return to painting full-time would prove to be more lucrative and less laborious. His paintings had been selling and he judged that this would be the easiest way to make money.

With Lucien's decision to return to painting full-time, he fully expected Esther to carry on the work of the Press without him. Lucien wrote: "I really want to try seriously to make you the printer of the firm."[83] He feared, however, that her generosity would cause her to take printing jobs that would not make a profit; she was never an astute businesswoman. She printed one book on her own, a work commissioned by Michael Field, *Whym Chow,* but the onset of World War I put an end to her venture.

In 1914, the Pissarros met Jean François van Royen, a Dutch postal official and an amateur printer who was intent on establishing his own private press which he called the Zilverdistel Press. He commissioned Lucien to design a proprietary typeface for him, based on the Carolingian minuscule. This brilliantly designed type, cut by Edward Prince and finished in late 1916, was named the Distel type.[84] Lucien also designed Van Royen's pressmark and watermark. While Lucien designed the type, Esther instructed Van Royen on the rudiments of printing. She also ordered an Albion press, as well as other printing materials for him. In this way, during the war years, the Pissarros, in helping Van Royen, were able to continue printing vicariously.

The war years were especially difficult for the Pissarros. It was difficult to sell paintings because few were buying and the price of food escalated. By the time the war had concluded, their financial situation had worsened. Their intention had not been to give up the Press—with the end of the war there had been a revival of interest in fine printing—but they did not have enough capital to undertake the work. The prices they would need to charge for the books would be so high that collectors would be reluctant to buy them. While the idea of printing a book seemed very far off to Lucien, Esther was still planning to do "a book of carols, then perhaps another bibliography—but we have no plans. . . . "[85]

In the years that followed the Press' closure, Lucien developed as a painter. His vision was steady and sensitive rather than original, but it was marked by a delicate perceptiveness and a gentle candor. With his increasing reputation, sales of his paintings increased and the Pissaros' financial burden eased. Lucien continued to paint until the end of his life. He died quietly on 12 July 1944 in Heywood, where Esther and he had gone to sit out World War II; his last words, "quoi bon!"

Esther survived another seven years, but never recovered fully from Lucien's death. In her usual fashion, she set about perpetuating his memory through the organization of memorial exhibitions. In order to have materials to show from the Eragny Press, she set about printing some of Lucien's engravings. Mr. Taylor, their printer, came out of retirement to assist her. When Esther died on 20 November 1951, her ashes, mixed with Lucien's, were scattered in the garden at the Brook.

Notes

1. Lucien's biography by W. S. Meadmore, *Lucien Pissarro: Un Coeur Simple,* introduced by John Rewald (London: Constable and Company Ltd., 1962), was written with extensive input from Orovida Pissarro, Lucien's and Esther's daughter. The information for the early years of Lucien's life has been taken primarily from Meadmore's work.
2. This early experience was not for nothing. The parcels shipped from the Eragny Press were always elegantly done up.
3. Stanley, Lucas, Weber and Co., Music Publishers, Foreign Music Importers and Dealers in Musical Instruments, 84 New Bond Street and 308 A Oxford Street, London.
4. Camille Pissarro, *Correspondance de Camille Pissarro,* ed. Bailly-Herzberg, tom. 1, letter 120.
5. *Correspondance,* tom. 1, letter 160. Translation mine.
6. Linda Parry, *William Morris Textiles* (London: Weidenfeld and Nicolson, 1983), 100.
7. *Correspondance,* tom. 1, letter 224: "Le gillotage est à la gravure ce que les faux tapis turc sont aux vrais, voilà se qu'il faudrait faire reprendre, la lithographie, eaux fortes, bois, tout ce qui est directe mais voilà c'est une questions d'argent! . . . "
8. Ibid.

9. For an erudite description of the relationship of Fénéon with the Post-Impressionst painters, see Joan Ungersma Halperin, *Félix Fénéon: Aesthete and Anarachist in Fin-de-Siècle Paris* (New Haven and London: Yale University Press, 1988).
10. *Correspondance,* tom. 1, letter 263, to Esther Isaacson (s.d. between 25 and 30 January 1885). "Lucien est bien portant, il travaille toujours pour sa publication, il a du mal, il faut qu'il trouve sa note c'est pas facile. . . ." Lucien's drawings for "Il était une bergère" were exhibited at the eighth and last Impressionist exhibition in 1886.
11. "I have near fifty drawings and sketches from nature and images. Compositions are ready. I shall engrave them on zinc, after they will be printed on stone and I shall color them with lithographic pencils." Lucien Pissarro to Esther Isaacson, about December 1885, quoted in *Correspondance,* tom. 1, letter 366.
12. *Correspondance,* tom. 1, letter 302.
13. Ibid., letter 302.
14. Ibid., tom. 2, letter 306.
15. For more information on Lepère and an account of his meeting with Lucien, see Jacquelyn Baas, "Auguste Lepère and the Artistic Revival of the Woodcut in France, 1875–1895" (Ph.D. diss., University of Michigan, 1982) and *The Artistic Revival of the Woodcut in France, 1850–1900,* ed. Jacquelyn Baas and Richard S. Field (Ann Arbor: The University of Michigan Museum of Art, 1984), 40–49.
16. *Correspondance,* tom. 2, letters 316 and 321.
17. Ibid., tom. 2, letter 310.
18. Lucien was helped in this by Signac. See *Correspondance,* tom. 2, letter 309.
19. *Correspondance,* tom. 2, letter 364. This is the first mention of a collaborative project Camille and Lucien were planning entitled "Travaux des champs." The first series was eventually published by the Vale Press in 1893; the work comprised six wood engravings and was the result of over a decade of planning and working. The original plan was a much more ambitious project: a book with a text and accompanying illustrations as opposed to the unbound portfolio it eventually became. The second series never came to fruition, but many of the drawings Camille did for the series were used in the Eragny Press' *La Charrue d'érable* (1912/13). For a description and analysis of this collaborative project, see Richard Brettell and Christopher Lloyd, *A Catalogue of the Drawings by Camille Pissarro in the Ashmolean Museum, Oxford* (Oxford: At the Clarendon Press, 1980), 66–85.
20. *Correspondance,* tom. 2, letter 364: "Dumas te laissera-t-il faire? Je crois qu'il ne pourra se refuser à cela; tu pourrais lui dire que ce qu'il te donne ne peut suffire à te faire vivre."
21. Ibid., tom. 2, letter 364. Financial backers for *La Vogue* were not particularly sympathetic with Kahn's idea of having only the Neo-Impressionists contribute illustrations to the magazine. When the cover of the first issue under Kahn's editorship was given to Albert Besnard to illustrate, an artist whom Camille considered his worst artistic enemy (because he used the Impressionists' ideas and then vulgarized them), Camille could not risk having his drawings included: "We must not expose ourselves to enemies disguised as innovators" (7 January 1887). However, Camille believed that Lucien could risk appearing anywhere because he needed the exposure. By 9 January, an agreement was reached with *La Vogue* for the Post-Impressionists to be the only illustrators, but by 12 January the financial backers had suspended publication of *La Vogue* for two or three months.
22. Maison Quantin specialized in children's books, both French and foreign, the "Encyclopédie enfantine" in chromolithography, humorous fantasies, picture books of the famous, as well as monographs on the great masters of art and the "Bibliothèque de l'enseignement des Beaux-Arts."
23. *Correspondance,* tom. 2, letter 378.
24. Lucien Pissarro, Paris, to Camille Pissarro, Eragny, 4 June 1887, Pissarro Collection, Ashmolean Museum. Lebre decided in the spring of 1888 that he could not publish "Poupée qui éternue" after all. *La Revue indépendante* then offered to publish it. This may have been a more appropriate place for it, since *La Revue indépendante* was producing a deluxe edition with original prints.
25. Léon Vanier (1847–1896) published modern editions, illustrated fantasies, literary curiosities, poetry, modern novels, and works by decadent and symbolist writers. His shop was located at 19 quai Saint-Michel, below the apartment where Dubois-Pillet lived. *Correspondance,* tom. 2, letter 394.
26. Paul Ollendorf's publishing house was located at 28 bis rue de Richelieu.
27. *Correspondance,* tom. 2, letter 412.
28. Ibid., tom. 2, letter 420.
29. Béraud did not himself engrave, but contributed his drawings to Ollendorf, who sent them to professional engravers.
30. Lucien never approached a publisher himself because of this expectation of rejection.
31. Lucien Pissarro, Eragny, to Camille Pissarro, Paris, 6 May 1887, Pissarro Collection, Ashmolean Museum.
32. *Correspondance,* tom. 2, letter 439. The Goupil ateliers and offices were situated at rue Forest and 55 rue du Cherche-Midi.
33. Lucien Pissarro, Paris, to Julie Pissarro, Eragny, 11 July 1887, Pissarro Collection, Ashmolean Museum. ". . . J'ai les yeux fatigués de faire ces maudits petits points, et malgre mes efforts je ne puis pas arriver à les faire nets, ma planche bleu a été imprimée elle est venue toute molle, pas assez de fermeté, la jaune que j'avais faite avante n'est pas trop mal venue, il est vrai que j'avais la permission de faire les points assez gros—Je fais en ce moment la planche bistre, toujours la même cathèdrale c'est une des dernières

après, on me mettre sur la figure, gare! Il faudra que les points soient perlés!" In a letter to Signac, dated 11 August 1887, he explains what his work entails: "I'll s'agit de faire sur pierre un dessin au point, à l'encre lithographique représentant le modèle d'une des couleurs comprises dans le modèle. Je travaille en ce moment d'après des aquarelles anglaises qui se convertiront en almanachs. Ce travail de chromiste est idiot, c'est le point perlé . . . et le beau coup de plume qui font ses seules connaissances. Je gagne zéro franc trente de l'heure ce qui fait deux francs soixante dix par journée de neuf heures et pendant mois je n'aurai que ce maigre salaire, après quoi je m'estimerai heureux si je fais mes mille huit cents francs par an. C'est maigre! Cependent les habiles ont un franc vingt cinq par heure. . . . Mon atelier (celui de Manzi) est a 55 de la rue du Cherche-Midi et j'habite près du Cirque d'hiver d'où une heure de chemin à faire matin et soir. . . ." Quoted in *Correspondance,* tom. 2, letter 443 (p. 191, n. 1).

34. Lucien Pissarro, Paris, to Camille Pissarro, Eragny, 9 October 1887, Pissarro Collection, Ashmolean Museum. "Je vais à une école de dessin, 6 rue Bréguet, près de la rue du Chemin Vert, le professeur est un petit vieux microscopique à lunettes, véritable type de professeur, qui a trouvé moyen de me dire le premier soir que j'y suis allé que l'on voyait bien que je n'avais pas l'habitude de dessiner. Je n'ai pas encore fait l'académie car c'est seulement demain que nous aurons en modèle vivant . . . une semaine de nature et une semaine d'antiques . . . telle est la règle. Nous [Lucien and his friend Hayet] avons dessiné de discobole ce qui est bien ennuyeux, je t'assure. Mais nous l'avons fait pour avoir l'air de suivre les cours, plus tard nous ferons des croquis les semaines d'antiques. . . . "

35. Lucien Pissarro, Paris, to Julie Pissarro, Eragny, 27 January 1888, Pissarro Collection, Ashmolean Museum.

36. For a short-title catalogue of Lucien's contributions to French periodicals, see Janine Bailly-Herzberg and Aline Dardel, "Les Illustrations françaises de Lucien Pissarro," *Nouvelles de l'estampe* 54 (November–December 1980): 8–16.

37. *Correspondance,* tom. 2, p. 280, n. 1.

38. Ibid., tom. 2, letter 578.

39. Ibid.

40. While the Pissarros were Jewish, neither Camille nor Lucien were religiously inclined. They realized, however, that as Jews they lived in a particularly hostile environment. The full fury of anti-Semitism in France arrived with the Dreyfus Affair in the 1890s.

41. See William Morris, *The Ideal Book: Essays and Lectures on the Arts of the Book,* ed. Peterson.

42. For a careful examination of one commercial press, see James G. Nelson's excellent study, *The Early Nineties: A View from the Bodley Head* (Cambridge, Mass.: Harvard University Press, 1971).

43. John Gray, born 2 March 1866 into a working-class family, was apprenticed as a metalturner at Woolwich Arsenal and in his spare time studied languages (French, Latin, and German). In 1882 he became a clerk and in 1888 he worked as a librarian at the Foreign Office in London. He began to find his way into the literary and artistic circles, and his first essays and stories appeared in the *Dial.* Charles Ricketts designed Gray's first book of poems, *Silverpoints* (1893), regarded by many as the quintessential nineties volume. One of the last pieces he wrote before setting off for Rome in 1898 to study for the priesthood was a prospectus for the Eragny Press edition of Laforgue's *Moralités légendaires.* He had met Fénéon in the summer of 1890 in Paris.

44. Lucien Pissarro, Bayswater, London, to Camille Pissarro, Eragny, before 26 November 1890, Pissarro Collection, Ashmolean Museum.

45. Ibid., [after 3 December 1890].

46. Ibid., [before 10 February 1891].

47. The definitive biography of Charles Ricketts is J.G.P. Delaney's *Charles Ricketts: A Biography* (Oxford: Clarendon Press, 1990). Two very good summaries of Charles Ricketts' life can be found in Joseph Darracott's biography, *The World of Charles Ricketts* (New York and Toronto: Methuen, 1980) and Stephen Calloway's *Charles Ricketts: Subtle and Fantastic Decorator* (London: Thames and Hudson, 1979). Ricketts' own diaries—of which excerpts have been published in *Self-Portrait Taken from the Letters and Journals of Charles Ricketts, R.A.,* collected and compiled by T. Sturge Moore; ed. Cecil Lewis (London: Peter Davies, 1939)—are helpful for determining Ricketts' personality.

48. Quoted in Calloway, *Charles Ricketts: Subtle and Fantastic Decorator,* 12.

49. For a discussion of Whistler's designs see A.J.A. Symons, "An Unacknowledged Movement in Fine Printing. The Typography of the Eighteen-Nineties," *Fleuron* VII (1930).

50. Lucien Pissarro, Bayswater, London, to Camille Pissarro, Paris, 19 April 1891, Pissarro Collection, Ashmolean Museum.

51. Lucien Pissarro, Bayswater, London, to Camille Pissarro, Eragny, [after 12 December 1890], Pissarro Collection, Ashmolean Museum.

52. Ibid.

53. Lucien Pissarro, Bayswater, London, to Camille Pissarro, Paris, [before 14 January 1891], Pissarro Collection, Ashmolean Museum.

54. Lucien Pissarro, Bayswater, London, to Camille Pissarro, Eragny, [before 11 December 1890], Pissarro Collection, Ashmolean Museum.

55. Lucien Pissarro, Bayswater, London, to Camille Pissarro, Paris, 6 January 1891, Pissarro Collection, Ashmolean Museum.

56. Lucien Pissarro, Bayswater, London, to Camille Pissarro, Eragny, 2 March 1891, Pissarro Collection, Ashmolean Museum.

57. Lucien Pissarro, Bayswater, London, to Camille Pissarro, Paris, 4 October 1891, Pissarro Collection, Ashmolean Museum. Translation mine.
58. Ibid.
59. Lucien Pissarro, Bayswater, London, to Camille Pissarro, Paris, [before 19 October 1891], Pissarro Collection, Ashmolean Museum.
60. Ibid.
61. Lucien Pissarro to Camille Pissarro, 22 October 1894, Pissarro Collection, Ashmolean Museum. Lucien planned to learn bookbinding with information given to him by Herbert Horne (Lucien Pissarro to Camille Pissarro, 25 May 1891). Lucien's influence on Vale Press bindings is perhaps a vestige of this early stage.
62. London: Published by Ch. Shannon and C. Ricketts in the Vale, Chelsea, 1891. Although dated 1891, Lucien's portfolio did not actually appear until January 1892. See Lucien Pissarro, Bayswater, London, to Camille Pissarro, Paris, 14 January 1892, Pissarro Collection, Ashmolean Museum.
63. William Rothenstein, *Men and Memories, 1872–1938,* ed. Mary Lago (Columbia: University of Missouri Press, 1978), 85.
64. C. S. Ricketts and C. H. Shannon, Chelsea, to [Michael Field], Reigate, London, [1894]. In *Some Letters from Charles Ricketts and Charles Shannon to "Michael Field" (1894–1902),* edited by J. G. Paul Delaney (Edinburgh: The Tragara Press, 1979), 9.
65. Charles Ricketts, Chelsea, London, to [Michael Field], [April 1896], Ms. ADD58097, Department of Manuscripts, British Library.
66. Charles Holmes, *Self and Partners (Mostly Self)* (New York: Macmillan Co., 1936), 173.
67. Ibid.
68. Lucien Pissarro to Camille Pissarro, 28 April 1896, Pissarro Collection, Ashmolean Museum.
69. Holmes, *Self and Partners,* 162, 171.
70. Ibid., 172.
71. Ibid.
72. Ibid., 174.
73. Lucien Pissarro, Epping, to Camille Pissarro, Paris, 24 January 1894, Pissarro Collection, Ashmolean Museum.
74. Lucien Pissarro, Epping, to Camille Pissarro, Paris, 8 January 1895, Pissarro Collection, Ashmolean Museum.
75. Lucien Pisarro to Camille Pissarro, 31 August 1896, Pissarro Collection, Ashmolean Museum.
76. Ibid., [before 10 October 1896].
77. Ibid., [before 28 September 1896].
78. The Pissarros distinguished between the two Esthers by identifying Esther Bensusan as either Esther B., Esther II, or Sterbee.
79. A careful combing of the Victoria and Albert Museum Library resulted in no information about this art school.
80. Lucien Pissarro, Finistère, to Esther Pissarro, London, 22 February 1910, Pissarro Collection, Ashmolean Museum.
81. This assessment of Esther Bensusan Pissarro is based on comments made by John Rewald in his introduction to *Lucien Pissarro: Un Coeur Simple* and from remarks made by her nephew, John Bensusan-Butt, in conversation with the author.
82. The Ballantyne Press completed the printing of the text.
83. Lucien Pissarro, Paris, to Esther Pissarro, The Brook, Hammersmith, 5 February 1914, Pissarro Collection, Ashmolean Museum.
84. Correspondence about this type is in the Meerman Museum in The Hague.
85. Esther Pissarro, London, to Jean François van Royen, The Hague, 20 March 1920, The Van Royan Papers, Rijksmuseum Meermanno-Westreenianum, Museum van het Boek, The Hague.

Chapter II

Production and Materials

The English private press movement of the 1890s was closely allied to the larger ideal of the Arts and Crafts movement. Deploring the aesthetic as well as the social effects of industrialization, William Morris and his followers sought to improve the quality of life, art, and craftsmanship. Their aesthetic was based on social and moral considerations, celebrating the virtues of individualism. In establishing the Eragny Press, Lucien Pissarro entered into this political and aesthetic atmosphere, intending to bridge the arts and crafts with life, to combine art and commerce.

One of the larger ironies of this "art made by the people, and for the people, as a happiness to the maker and the user,"[1] with its emphasis on fine quality materials and hand craftsmanship in a machine age, is that the products which resulted were only readily affordable to the upper-middle class and aristocracy, both as producer and consumer. Lucien Pissarro was not a member of the English upper-middle class. Although his socio-economic origins lie with the French upper-middle class, his immediate family lived the life of a poor, struggling artist. When Lucien was determined to establish his private press, not only did he wish to express himself artistically, he also wanted the Press to be commercially viable. His notion that the Arts and Crafts movement could become a way of life, both artistically and financially, was naïve.

Many who had come before him in the Arts and Crafts movement were wealthy enough to be more concerned with ideology than with practical reality. The Pissarros were not so fortunate. While Lucien and Esther wished to follow the ideals of the Arts and Crafts movement ". . . to do good work, for good ends, and . . . to be allowed unimpeded to pursue it. To be paid that he may work, not to work that he may be paid,"[2] some tedious realities stood in the way of achieving this goal.

The most important reality confronted by the Eragny Press was the lack of capital. The demonstrated financial success of William Morris and his design firm, Morris and Co., which had launched the Arts and Crafts movement on a commercial footing, led Lucien to believe that it was possible to earn a living by adopting the Arts and Crafts philosophy. What Lucien did not realize is that Morris and Co. was successful because it followed astute business practices without sacrificing aesthetics. Moreover, Morris and Co. had considerable capital to invest in the firm. The Eragny Press was consistently underfinanced. Lucien fully understood the aesthetics of the Arts and

Crafts movement, but he had difficulty in realizing that a successful business requires a certain scale of production and enough capital investment to achieve its goals.

The Arts and Crafts philosophy advocated the unity of labor—"the work should be conceived as one, and be wholly executed by one person, or at most by two"[3]—but the practical way of running a business concern was to divide the labor among the workers. The Kelmscott Press was William Morris' last major undertaking in a life that had been devoted to reviving the crafts. In this endeavor, while he contributed designs and supervised the printing, he employed engravers and a number of printers to actually execute his designs. His output of fifty-two titles (sixty-four volumes) in seven years would not have been possible if he had undertaken the work himself with the help of his wife alone. Conversely, Lucien and Esther did almost all the work themselves, from the design and the engraving of illustrations and decorations to the actual production and marketing. Their maximum output was never more than four books per year. Over the twenty years of their press, they produced thirty-two books, half the number which Kelmscott had produced in seven years. While this lack of capital enforced the Arts and Crafts movement's ideal of the unity of labor, it also prevented the Eragny Press' ability to maintain a profitable level of production.

The intention of the Eragny Press was to combine the arts and crafts with commerce while retaining artistic individualism. The resolute artistic integrity of both Lucien and Esther made it impossible for them to compromise—even when compromise may have meant commercial success. Their lack of business skills and financial means prevented them from establishing a thriving enterprise. In this chapter, the materials, methods and cost of production of the Eragny Press are examined, demonstrating that the Pissarros were, above all, artists and the aesthetics of their books came before any practical considerations. The Pissarros adapted convoluted printing methods to make a more perfect product and took great pains to make Eragny Press books works of art. Unfortunately, all the care which was lavished upon each book did not make the venture commercially viable.[4]

PLANT AND MATERIALS

THE PRINTING STUDIO

Eragny House (1894–1897)

Returning from their honeymoon in France in June 1893, Lucien and Esther settled in Epping, Essex, a district outside London. Lucien was particularly attracted to the area because of the proximity of Epping Forest and the many open areas. Lucien found the country setting of Epping to be a perfect place to pursue painting. He planned to use paintings as studies for his wood engravings. When a suitable place was found in Hemhall Street, Lucien wrote to Camille: "Epping resembles Eragny a lot, but the view is vaster."[5] Lucien named the cottage Eragny House, after the village in which his parents lived, and, here, in this small cottage, the Eragny Press was established. The cottage, rented for twenty-one guineas per year,[6] provided Lucien and Esther with a well-lighted studio in which to make their engravings.

62 Bath Road, Bedford Park (1897–1903)

Due to the difficulty and expense of travel, Epping was soon found to be too isolated from London. With the birth of the Pissarros' daughter, Orovida, and the acquisition of additional printing equipment, the house proved to be too small for a family of three with a maid and a growing business. By moving to London, Lucien could take care of his business more directly and make better contacts. In the spring of 1897, Lucien and Esther moved from Epping to 62 Bath Road, Bedford Park, a suburb of London—a choice of locality influenced by Ricketts, who considered Bedford Park suitable for the elect of his art world. The house, which had belonged to an artist, had a studio in the garden which Lucien could use for his print shop.[7] Although the Pissarros resided here for six years, producing several books, no description of the house and print shop exist.

The Brook (1903–1951)

In April 1903, the Pissarros moved to Brook House,[8] so named because of its location near the Stamford Brook, which forms the boundary line between Chiswick and Hammersmith districts. The abandoned house, which Esther discovered while on a walk, is a large structure converted from two seventeenth-century cottages. At the turn of the century, Brook House, remote and quiet, was surrounded by orchards. The house soon became Esther's obsession and continued to be for the greater part of her life. She spent any money she had to make the house and garden a showpiece. The Pissarros took a lease on the cottage in 1902, buying it in 1919.[9]

Two rooms of The Brook were set aside for the Eragny Press. One room in the front, formerly the coach house, was Lucien's studio; at the back, the pressroom was set up. When J. F. van Royen visited The Brook in 1914, he described it thus:

> The nice little house is well back from the street . . . you go through a white gate and find all sorts of strange and attractive leaves and flowers just like those that appear in his books; on your left is an extension, formerly a stable . . . low, small, with four deep windows in which there are all kinds of flowers.[10]

Lucien Pissarro at the press; undated. (Photograph courtesy John Bensusan-Butt)

PRINTING TYPES

Type, for the private presses of this period, was the most important element of the book. Proprietary types, designed specifically for each private press, provided a personality and distinction not possible with commercial types. The Eragny Press took great pride in the two typefaces which it employed, Vale and Brook. One, however, was borrowed from another private press.

The Vale Type (1896–1903)

The Vale type, designed by Charles Ricketts and based on Nicolas Jenson's and Johann Spira's roman letters, which Ricketts particularly admired for their logic, balance and control, was the first type used by both the Vale and Eragny presses. As a type designer, Ricketts believed that type should be translated from script or chiseled letters into forms that would be natural to metal. The Vale punches were engraved by Edward P. Prince and founded by the type founding firm Sir Charles Reed and Sons. While no details remain concerning the circumstances of the design, engraving, and founding of the type, we do know that Lucien began composing trial pages of the unfinished font in mid-October 1895 to see the effect of the type on the page.[11] Lucien, on seeing the composed page, declared the Vale type to be "one of the most beautiful which has ever existed."[12] The complete font in 13 point was finished in December 1895. Ricketts described this revivalist type as his "bold roman fount shaped on a broad base and resting on solid serifs."[13] The type creates a dark, heavy letter, and with generous spacing is particularly well suited to the weight of both Ricketts' and Lucien's wood engravings.

Ricketts furnished the type to Lucien on the condition that any book which Lucien printed in the Vale type would be published by Ricketts. The loan of the use of the proprietary Vale font appeared to be a friendly and generous gesture on Ricketts' part, and may have been a means to manage Lucien and the output of the Eragny Press. Because Lucien could not afford his own typeface at the time, the withdrawal of the Vale type would force Lucien out of business. Lucien was thus reluctant to do anything which might displease Ricketts. Lucien paid for the actual type with money he received from John Lane for the purchase of his first book, *The Queen of the Fishes*.[14]

Lucien printed fifteen books, which he referred to as the Vale Series, using the Vale font. The first book using the Vale type was *The Book of Ruth and the Book of Esther* (1896); the last, *C'est de Aucassin et de Nicolete* (1903).

In 1904, with the closing of the Vale Press, Ricketts, introducing a private press tradition, threw the punches and matrices of his types into the Thames river to prevent others from using his type. The type itself was melted down. He decided to destroy them because ". . . it is undesirable that these founts should drift into other hands than their designers' and become stale by unthinking use . . ."[15]

The Brook Type (1903–1944)

The possibility of doing work for a French publisher, and the unavailability of Vale type once the Vale Press closed, prompted Lucien to begin thinking about designing a type of his own. In February 1900, Lucien and

Design for Brook type. (Ashmolean Museum, Oxford)

Camille began discussing a typeface for the Eragny Press.[16] Camille had found Ricketts' Vale type to be a little heavy,[17] but Lucien defended the heaviness of the type. According to Lucien, it was necessary to have a "thick, heavy" type to match the weight of the wood engravings. If a "thin, pale" typeface were used then one had little range in the weight of the wood engraving. For a wood engraving to harmonize with a weak type, the lines of the engraving would have to be engraved with wiry strokes.[18] As a point of departure of Lucien's type design, he intended to return to early typography, freely using fifteenth- and sixteenth-century French types, as models.[19] He had nothing but disdain for the new and original type of Eugene Grasset, which he found too artistic, "that is to say picturesque and by consequences without style," failing because it abandoned the classical forms of letters.[20] Another option Lucien considered if a commission came from a publisher, in lieu of designing his own type, was to use the commercially available imitation of William Morris' Golden type.[21]

Georges Lecomte, a writer and friend of Lucien who had received several commissions from the publisher Editions Artistiques du Pavillon de Hanovre, sought a commission for Lucien at the firm. The director of the firm, Paul Gaultier, was interested in fine printing. His firm, with considerable capital, paid its writers and artists generously. Lecomte had shown to Gaultier several of Lucien's books—which he admired, especially for the type.[22] Because Ricketts forbade the use of the Vale type for any "commercial" purpose, Lucien, if he were to do any work for the firm, would need his own type. Lucien believed that if Gaultier really intended to produce

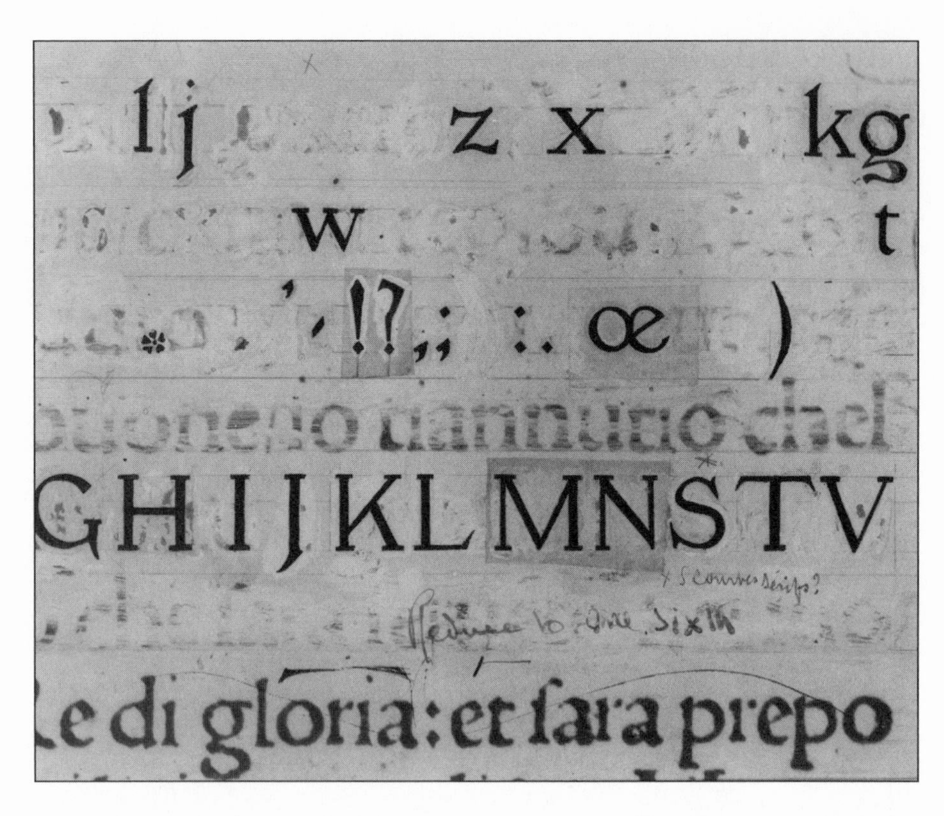

Design for Brook type. (Ashmolean Museum, Oxford)

beautiful books, he would seize the opportunity of having a type designed for his house. By having a publisher commission and pay for the type, Lucien would have the financing to design his type.[23] While this chance never came to fruition, it did provide Lucien with the impetus he needed to begin his design.

The greatest expense in commissioning one's own typeface during this period was the engraving of the punches and striking of matrices. Once the matrices were struck, the letters were usually sold by weight for about the same price as the cost of the metal. Because Lucien would design his own type, he would not have the expense of paying a designer. Lucien estimated the cost of engraving each character would be twenty-five francs (about £1) or about six hundred to one thousand francs (about £24–£40) for a complete font.[24]

With the decision to design a type, Camille advised Lucien to create a type quite different from Ricketts' Vale type. He urged Lucien to give his type a French character, to avoid the Italian school of Ricketts and to make the design lighter than the Vale type. Camille had no real knowledge of early French typography and Lucien's knowledge had been gained through the teaching of Ricketts. Lucien realized that he could not pretend to design original letters, nor could he make any major differences in a given form, based on a calligraphic tradition. Lucien did not actually begin to design his type until early 1901. In August, he was convinced he could pay for the type himself with the profit from his previous books, but when the time came for the punches to be cut and the matrices struck, Lucien asked Camille for the money.[25]

In spite of Camille's strictures concerning the Eragny Press type, Lucien modeled his closely on the Vale type. Lucien had to consider a number of other factors in addition to actual aesthetics. He was concerned about the public's reception of his type. A certain number of collectors bought Eragny Press books simply because they wanted to have a complete collection of books printed in the Vale type.[26] This surely had a major influence on Lucien's decision to design his type based on the Vale font.

When Camille first saw a specimen page of the Brook type, named after Lucien's home, he noted the similarity to the Vale type.[27] Lucien agreed with his assessment, but noted that while the Brook type resembled the Vale type in isolated words, the page itself would have a much different appearance. The major difference between Vale and Brook type is the density; the Brook type, when printed, is grayer, more condensed, and (at 12 point vs. the 13-point Vale type) smaller. The actual x-height of the letters is the same size as Vale, but the ascenders and descenders have been shortened. Lucien's primary goal in designing the Brook type was to ensure that the weight (or as Lucien referred to it, color) of the type harmonized with wood engravings.

In July 1902, Lucien contacted Edward Prince, who agreed to cut the Brook font. He suggested that Lucien find a foundry which would relinquish control over the punches and matrices.[28] Lucien wanted to retain the right to destroy his type if it should become in the best interest of the Press.[29] Lucien approached Sir Charles Reed and Sons, which had cast the Vale type. Sir Charles Reed and Sons, since the casting of the Vale type, were

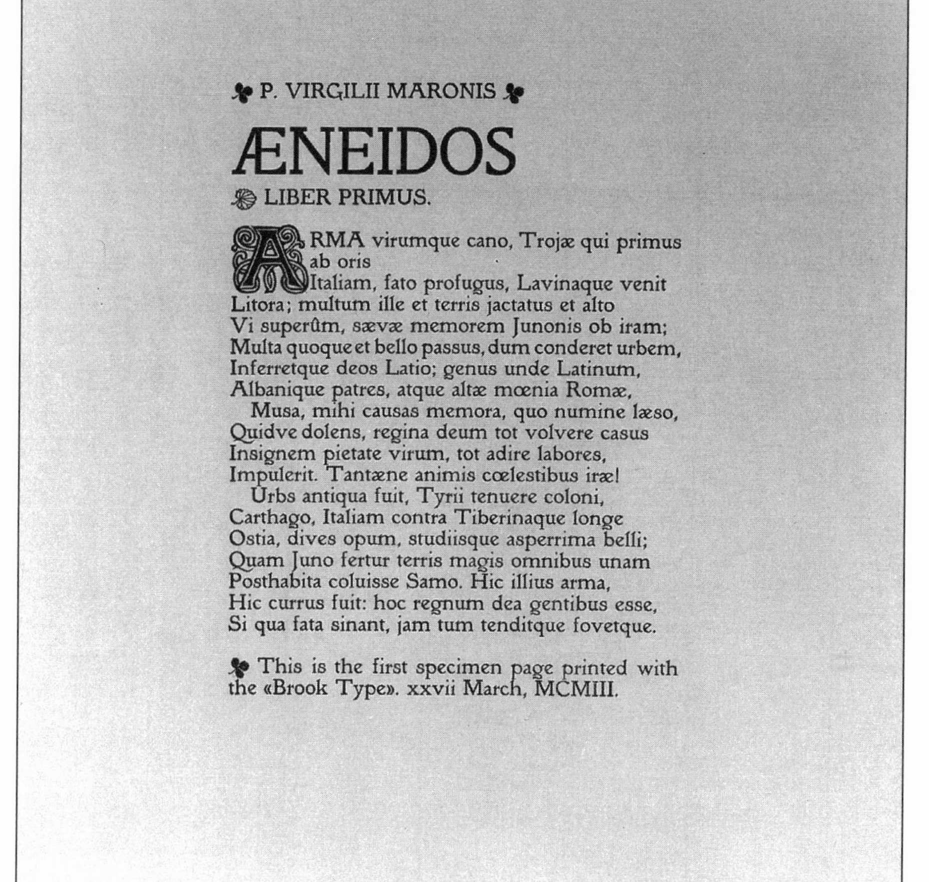

P. VIRGILII MARONIS

ÆNEIDOS

LIBER PRIMUS.

ARMA virumque cano, Trojæ qui primus ab oris
Italiam, fato profugus, Lavinaque venit
Litora; multum ille et terris jactatus et alto
Vi superûm, sævæ memorem Junonis ob iram;
Multa quoque et bello passus, dum conderet urbem,
Inferretque deos Latio; genus unde Latinum,
Albanique patres, atque altæ mœnia Romæ,
Musa, mihi causas memora, quo numine læso,
Quidve dolens, regina deum tot volvere casus
Insignem pietate virum, tot adire labores,
Impulerit. Tantæne animis cœlestibus iræ!
Urbs antiqua fuit, Tyrii tenuere coloni,
Carthago, Italiam contra Tiberinaque longe
Ostia, dives opum, studiisque asperrima belli;
Quam Juno fertur terris magis omnibus unam
Posthabita coluisse Samo. Hic illius arma,
Hic currus fuit: hoc regnum dea gentibus esse,
Si qua fata sinant, jam tum tenditque fovetque.

This is the first specimen page printed with the «Brook Type». xxvii March, MCMIII.

First trial page of Brook type, 1903. (Ashmolean Museum, Oxford) now declining to undertake the casting of proprietary types unless they were allowed to retain control over the matrices. Lucien then wrote to P. M. Shanks and Sons asking them to cast his type.[30] Finally, after certain legal wrangling, Shanks and Sons agreed to cast the type and to allow Lucien control over the matrices.[31]

In mid-August, Lucien sent Prince a photo of his type design. Prince began by cutting the punches for the lowercase "h" and "p," as was his practice, "to determine the size as to room on the body"[32] of the type. Cut within three days of receiving Lucien's design, these punches were then sent to Shanks for striking "to see what room we have on the body . . ."[33] The "p" did not fit well, so Prince suggested that either the "p" stem could be shortened or a small piece could be taken off both the "h" and "p" stems, with the "h" pushed higher up on the shoulder.[34] He was ready to send Lucien smoke proofs of the lower case letters on 1 October 1902.[35] The letters pleased Lucien except for the dot on the "i," which he found too small, a consequence of his lead-pencil drawing not photographing well. Before altering the "i," Prince cut the "j" to "see how this will do for size of dot."[36] By November, Prince began working on the punctuation, capital letters, and single- and double-leaf type ornaments. Each steel punch cost Lucien ten shillings or £13 for the complete lower case.

One repercussion of Lucien's inexperience in designing type was the difficulty Prince had in cutting the punches to Lucien's satisfaction. Lucien had definite ideas about what he wanted, but had difficulty in drawing the letters clearly in his design. When the original punches were finished, Prince was instructed to alter those for the lowercase "n," "h," "v," "p," and upper case "N," and to cut a new punch for the lowercase "m."[37] Lucien had difficulty in discerning the letterforms from the smokes. Only when the type was cast could he see any problems. Prince, though irritated, did not charge extra for the alterations, but he did charge for the recutting of punches. Lucien was also dissatisfied by the quality of Shanks' typecasting, finding some sorts straight and others crooked.[38] The standard of perfection which the Pissarros sought was difficult for others to match.

Some seven months passed from the beginning of the punch cutting, until Lucien was first able to make up trial pages. The Brook type consists of the following characters: twenty-six upper- and lower-case letters, accents, ligatures, an ampersand, punctuation marks, and two leaf ornaments.[39] No numbers were designed for the font; rather Lucien used numbers which he purchased from Shanks and Sons.[40] The total bill for the Brook type punches was £41.19.0.[41]

Not knowing how the public would accept his type, Lucien thought it prudent to begin with a well-conceived design and a popular text. He considered printing Baudelaire's *Fleurs du mal*, unillustrated, but with a border.[42] Perhaps knowing that Ricketts was about to publish a bibliography of his Vale Press books, Lucien decided to produce instead, as a companion volume, a bibliography of Eragny Press books printed in the Vale type. Thus, the first book in the Brook type was *A Brief Account of the Origin of the Eragny Press*, dedicated to Ricketts, which included a selection of wood engravings used in the Vale Series, as well as a text by T. S. Moore. Fifteen more books would be printed in the Brook type, which for the Eragny Press format was a much more successful type than the Vale. Its slightly smaller point size better conforms to the proportions of the page of an Eragny book and to the dimensions of the wood engravings. The weight of the Brook type also corresponds better to Lucien's wood engravings. Lucien had succeeded in designing a type which harmonized beautifully with his engravings.

The Brook punches and matrices met the same fate as the Vale Press typefaces. During Esther's first channel crossing to France after the end of World War II in September 1947 on the boat *Aramanche,*[43] she, with the help of her nephew, John Bensusan-Butt, cast the punches and matrices in the English Channel somewhere between Newhaven and Dieppe. Though Esther regretted it, it had been Lucien's wish. Throwing the punches into the Channel, rather than the Thames River, was symbolic of the blending of both the French and English artistic traditions which are so apparent in an Eragny Press book. The surviving type is now at the Cambridge University Press.[44]

Music Type

The Eragny Press was the only private press of the period to use music type. Based on sixteenth-century models, the type was specially cut (at one shilling six pence per note) in brass and cast by Shanks and Sons in 1904.[45] Because of the way the type was cast, the Pissarros found it troublesome to obtain perfect register. The minims of the notes had little lumps of metal in their centers, so each note had to be touched up by hand.[46] The music type was first used in *Some Old French and English Ballads,* edited by Robert Steele (1905) and again in *Songs by Ben Jonson* (1906).

Music type. *Songs by Ben Jonson,* 1906. (Ashmolean Museum, Oxford)

Greek Type

A Greek type, borrowed from Macmillan, was used by the Eragny Press in John Milton's *Areopagitica* (1903). This Greek type was designed in 1892 by Selwyn Image, with the technical assistance of Emery Walker. It is based on a Greek type from "a certain tenth century MS in the B. Museum, and on a Spanish printed book there of the fifteenth or early sixteenth century, which was itself founded on a MS of the 10th century."[47] William Morris used this Greek type in his edition of Swinburne's *Atalanta in Calydon* (1894).

PAPER AND VELLUM

With the exception of *The Queen of the Fishes* (1894/5), and *Les Petits vieux* (1901), which were printed on Japanese vellum, the Vale Series books were printed on Vale paper until 1902. The paper was an Arnold's paper, handmade from an unbleached mixture of linen and cotton rag. The Vale paper was manufactured in two sizes, a demy (20 x 15 ins.) bearing the watermark V[ale] P[ress] and a double crown (20 x 30 ins.) carrying the watermark of an engraving tool and two wreaths. C. J. Holmes referred to the Vale Press as "the dearest paper made with the exception of that made for Morris,"[48] the demy size costing about £2 per ream, the double crown size, £3.9 per ream. Lucien was not pleased by the Vale paper. He found the finish rough and the texture unpliable.

Late in 1898, Lucien began to think about commissioning his own paper. Paul Signac had recommended the firm of Perrigot-Masure, located in Paris at 30 rue Mazarine, beneath the École des arts décoratifs. Perrigot-Masure were distributors of the high-grade paper made by hand at the mill at Arches, Vosges, France. For his part, Lucien believed that he would be able to purchase superior paper in France at a better price than he could in England.[49] But he did not contact the firm until July 1901, inquiring whether they could provide him with handmade paper with a special watermark. Perrigot-Masure did accept orders for specially made paper but noted that prices were higher for small quantities.[50] Lucien placed his order and Perrigot-Masure began to make up samples for him. Three trials were necessary to make a paper which was satisfactory to Lucien. The first sample was too thin; the second, too thick and gray with irregular watermarks and unseen laid lines. To remedy these faults, Lucien suggested that the manufacturer dilute the pulp more. Finally satisfied, Lucien placed a trial order on 16 October 1901 for ten reams of no. 852, but made with a more diluted pulp to create a pure linen, laid paper, measuring 400 x 520 mm. One half of the order was to be sized, the other half unsized. The result of the more diluted pulp was a paper with a smoother deckle edge and more visible chain lines and watermarks. The bill was forty francs, including fifteen francs for the watermark, for a total of sixty francs per ream.

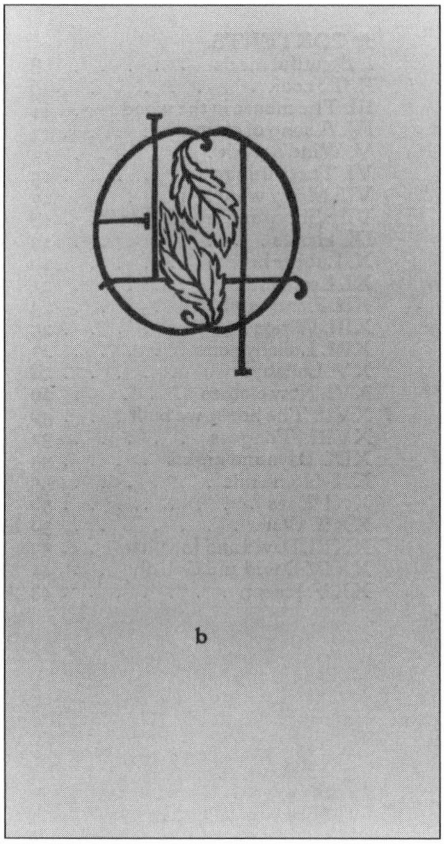

Each sheet has four marks: the watermark is the Eragny Press monogram, the countermark that of Arches. The watermark and countermark were placed on opposing corners, two centimeters from the edge of the leaf in such a way that the paper could be gathered in eight to show the marks to their best advantage when the paper was cut in half. Placed in the corners, the watermarks do not compete with the wood engravings.

Watermark and monogram.
(Ashmolean Museum, Oxford)

Lucien finally decided on two dimensions of paper, an ecu (crown) vergé (laid) no. 852 at fifty francs per ream, and a demy vergé no. 852 at fifty-five francs per ream. The total cost of the paper, delivered in April 1902, was 492.50 francs. In August, Lucien placed another order for the demy vergé, but was unhappy with the quality, which he found to be inconsistent. Perrigot-Masure reminded Lucien that handmade paper has irregularities and that identical paper could not be guaranteed with each new order.[51] Lucien soon accepted these imperfections as standard, and continued to use paper manufactured by Perrigot-Masure throughout the existence of the Press. He would later place orders through their London agents, P. Prioux and Co., until the Press' closing.

Lucien first began printing on vellum in 1897, although he much preferred books printed on paper. He believed that rarity, which vellum copies imply, had nothing to do with beauty. Vellum also reminded him of the smooth, glossy papers which were in fashion in France.[52] It is likely that Lucien began printing ten copies on vellum to satisfy the clientele of Hacon

& Ricketts.[53] The vellum copies were later given as gifts to close friends and were also sold to regular collectors of Eragny Press books. The supplier of the vellum was Henry Band of Brentford, Middlesex. It was not always easy to get vellum of the size and quality desired. Often the dimensions of the vellum sent by Band would be slightly off, or the sheets themselves would be greasy and one side would not take the ink. Or the sheets would vary, some being too thin, others too thick. The Pissarros preferred their vellum to be made from lambskin and usually ordered 40–150 sheets of vellum at a time.[54]

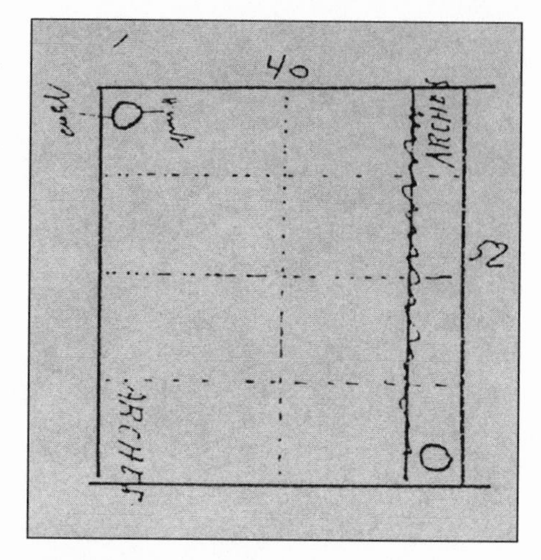

Drawing of watermark and countermark placement. (Ashmolean Museum, Oxford)

INK

The supplier of black ink for printing texts was Gebrüder Jänecke of Hannover, Germany. Although a difficult ink to handle because it was stiff and had to be worked up very thoroughly for even distribution, it produced a deep, dark color. For several of the later books of the Press, Lucien used a delicate gray ink, also manufactured by Jänecke. Suppliers of other inks, mostly for woodblock printing, were Winsor and Newton of London and Ch. Lorilleux and Co. of Paris. Lucien often mixed the inks to create his own subtle shades of color for the woodcuts or used paints, rather than ink, to realize colors not available in printing ink.[55]

The Eragny Press also attempted printing with gold leaf and gold powder. Lucien found printing in gold "a rather tiresome process," but he used it to good effect in his woodcuts, especially in *Reine du matin* and *Livre de jade*. While he considered himself to be an amateur when it came to printing with gold, he did provide Jean François van Royen with a few hints, the result of numerous failures:

> The gold block must be the first printed else the gold will stick to your black type—you ink your block with a colourless ink [varnish] and apply your gold leaf on the print and it will adhere to the impression so printed, but it requires a great deal of quick dexterity to prevent the metal to stick [from sticking] to the wet paper as well. I found the work much easier on dry paper like the "Livre de Jade" than on wet like the Soliman Ben David.[56]

ILLUSTRATIONS, INITIAL LETTERS, BORDERS, AND ORNAMENTS

Lucien was the designer and principal wood engraver for the Eragny Press for almost all the major color woodblocks. Esther, who did not design any of the engravings, usually engraved the simpler one-color blocks, the woodblock initials, and the ornaments. Three Eragny Press books contain major engravings which were created by other artists. T. S. Moore contributed engravings for *Peau d'ane* (1903) and *The Little School* (1905), Diana White for *Ishtar* (1904), and Laurence Binyon for *Dream-Come-True* (1905).[57]

The major illustrations were designed for each individual book, but

"Balkis au Lavis," wood engraving (Fern 156 [SB 227]). *Gerard de Nerval, Histoire de la reine du matin et de Soliman prince des génies,* 1909.

borders and initial letters and ornaments were reused. The arrangement of the text and initial letters would often be decided by how many of the same initials could be repeated. *The Little School* (1904) and *Songs by Ben Jonson* (1905), for example, both utilize the same style of initial letters. These initials were originally designed for *The Little School* and were used in *Songs by Ben Jonson,* for which Lucien and Esther created additional initials in the same style. In this way the Pissarros added to their stock of initials without having to duplicate the same initial letters which had been used in a previous book. Borders were used again as well, especially if the book was considered to be a companion volume. For example, in François Villon's *Les Ballades de Maistre François Villon* (1901) and the companion volume, *Autres poésies* (1901), the same border is used but printed in different colors, with *Ballades* using red and black and *Autres poésies* green and black. The repetition of these decorative elements, in addition to saving on the time needed to create new ones, also provided the books with a continuity. New initials, borders, and ornaments were designed when they were needed to harmonize with the style and tone of the book and its major illustrations.

Unlike the proprietors of other fine presses of the period, with the exception of Charles Ricketts, Lucien personally engraved his woodcuts because he was convinced that nobody else could meet the standard of quality he demanded, and also because he could not afford to pay an engraver. Because of this, the major illustrations of an Eragny Press book are autographic engravings rather than reproductive art, as are the engravings in a Kelmscott or Ashendene book.

Lucien was not reticent about using newer technologies in his work.

His designs were usually transferred photographically to the surface of the woodblock and then engraved. He also used photography to increase or decrease the size of his drawings, especially for initial letters, before they were photographed onto the block. The woodcuts were then sent out for electrotyping to preserve the original woodblocks. Woodblocks were usually supplied by T. N. Laurence and Co.; the electrotype and zincographs were made by Richardson, Koolman, and Isger.[58]

PRINTER'S MARKS

The Eragny Press had three pressmarks. The first mark, used only in *The Queen of the Fishes,* portrays a young woman holding an open book, with blocks of text on both pages, facing the viewer, with Eragny Press as a headline. The young woman is seated on grass, surrounded by flowers, underneath a fruit tree. The shape of the mark is rectangular and measures 71 x 51 mm. Lucien's monogram is at the bottom left corner, and Esther's initials, EP, are at the bottom right corner, indicating that it was Esther who actually cut the woodblock. It is highly likely that Esther served as the model for the young woman.

Pressmark I. (Ashmolean Museum, Oxford)

The second pressmark first appeared in Laforgue's *Moralités légendaires,* volume two (1898). Lucien designed and engraved the block in 1896. In a rondel shape, 76 mm. in diameter, it portrays a young woman, seated, holding a closed book, the back binding face-up with the words "ERAGNY PRESS." The woman is surrounded by foliage, and also sits on grass, surrounded by flowers. A ribbon flows across the top half of the roundel with the Eragny Press motto, *Fructus inter folia* (fruit among the leaves) inscribed on it. The motto had been chosen some years before during a discussion with friends. In September 1899, Elkin Mathews notified Hacon & Ricketts of an infringement on his trademark by the Eragny Press pressmark's motto. The motto, *Fructus inter folia,* was the very same motto that Mathews had used for over fifteen years in some 20,000 copies of the various books which he had published. The motto also appeared in every reissue of his trade catalogs and he used it in his bookplate.[59] As a matter of courtesy, C. J. Holmes thought it best that they adopt some other motto, but did not think it wise that they use a literal translation of *Fructus inter folia.* Holmes suggested using *Folia non sine frutus* or *Feuilles non sans fruits,* the latter he thought best because it has "no suggestion of the original motto in appearance or language, but means exactly the same."[60] It was finally decided that "E ET L PISSARRO LONDON." (the E and L representing Esther and Lucien) should be substituted for the motto, and the pressmark remained the same except for this change. This third pressmark was used first in Flaubert's *St. Julien* (1900) and continued to be used until the Press closed in 1914.

BINDINGS

From the beginning, Eragny Press books, like many of the other private presses (Kelmscott, Vale, and Ashedene, for example) and Bodley Head

Pressmark III. (Special Collections, Florida State University, Tallahassee)

books, were sent to the bindery of J. J. Leighton, Son, and Hodge of London. The first book, *The Queen of the Fishes*, was bound in full green calf as well as a variant binding of full white vellum. Looking for a less expensive but still attractive binding, the Eragny Press adopted a style of quarter bound paper over boards, with the paper usually printed in a botanical theme.[61] This was an ingenious solution, also employed by the Vale Press, to the high cost of leather binding. Two books, printed for French bibliophile societies, were bound in calf, as well as *Album de poëmes tirés du livre de jade*, which was produced between these two commissions. *Riquet à la houppe* (1908) employed a vellum binding. The last book of the Press, *Whym Chow*, was covered in red suede. Vellum copies were sewn, but not bound. As a testament to the charm of an Eragny Press binding, John Quinn, one of the Eragny Press' major American collectors, insisted that his vellum copies be bound in the corresponding Eragny Press printed paper covers.

It generally took Leighton, Son, and Hodge about a week to deliver an edition of 225 bound copies, either to the Vale Press or to the Pissarros directly.[62] The relationship between the Eragny Press and Leighton, Son, and Hodge was not always an easy one. The Press expected the bindery to work much more quickly (and much more perfectly) than they actually did because the Press itself was always behind in its work schedule. Often, too, the binders would be sloppy, not always cutting the papers straight, or using too much glue, for example.[63] While the printed texts remain crisp and bright, the bindings show the lack of care in their production. The glue has discolored the paper covers and the acidic boards have caused foxing of the end-leaves.

PRESSES

The Eragny Press had four presses, the first of which was acquired in early 1894. Probably a proof press, it was intended to "facilitate [Lucien] in making impressions"[64] of his woodblocks. On 12 April 1897, Lucien wrote to his father of his intentions of purchasing a larger press "to be able to make my books at home which would be better than printing at Epping where the material is in bad condition and the workers atrocious.[65] The press was not purchased until late September 1898; Lucien announced to his father that he had finally bought "a large press."[66] The press was a demy size Albion which Lucien purchased from Frederick Ullmer's for £24.19.00.[67]

In March 1902, the Pissarros ordered a royal size Albion Press from Hopkinson and Cope. The price of the press was £45 delivered and erected, but in paying cash (with money set aside from book sales)[68] they received a 10 percent discount, which brought the cost of the press to £40.10.00. In October 1911, a small, second-hand press was purchased for £1.2.0, to help with completing the printing of *La Charrue d'érable*.[69]

METHODS OF PRODUCTION

The Pissarros' lack of capital, which prevented them from undertaking large-scale productions, required that they do most of the work themselves.

This contributed to their having greater control over the quality of the composition and presswork. Since they were self-taught printers, for the most part, many of their production methods were unconventional. The methods they devised were mainly intended to obtain perfect register, important for the successful printing of color woodblocks. These rather convoluted and untraditional methods were costly—in both time and effort. Had the Pissarros been more experienced or less discerning, they might not have perceived the need to adopt these techniques. However, the Eragny Press was the only private press of the period to attempt multiple color woodblock printing. In this endeavor alone, which only a master colorist could attempt, it may not have been feasible, even if financial circumstances had permitted, to hire printers who were untrained in this aspect of printing. Moreover, the superb results they achieved with their printing methods seem to indicate the appropriateness of adopting these procedures.

The small format of Eragny Press books are not so much the result of the Pissarros' preference for the diminutive size, but because the smaller format allowed them to create books with far less capital than a larger format would have required. Moreover, the wood engravings, by necessity, needed to remain small. The small format for Eragny Press books is a reflection of technique as well as capital investment. Twenty Eragny Press books are octavos. The Pissarros produced one quarto, one tricesimo-secundo, five duodecimo, four sextodecimo, and one "fancy" format—for example, many of the books, especially those with a number of multiple color woodblocks (*Riquet à la houpe* [1908], *Reine du matin* [1910], and *La Charrue d'érable* [1912/13]) and books containing music (*Some Old French and English Ballads* [1905] and *Songs by Ben Jonson* [1905]), were imposed in 2's. Rather than half-sheet imposition, the Pissarros adopted a method of quarter-sheet imposition.

By choosing relatively short texts, the Pissarros cut down on the cost of composition as well as presswork, and could devote the majority of their time to working on design and decoration for each book. An average book generally took the Pissarros about four months to complete. A spoilage rate of almost half the production when undertaking the printing of a multi-colored woodblock contributed substantially to the amount of time needed to produce a book. Considering that most of the books usually required less than eight formes to be printed, the composition, and presswork, using their technique took a considerable period of time.

The first three books of the Press were produced in Epping. Records do not survive for the Press' first book, *The Queen of the Fishes.* With the second work, *The Book of Ruth and the Book of Esther* (1896), Lucien's methods had become more standardized. The Vale type, which he was using on loan from Ricketts, had become available in late 1895, and he had established contact with the local printing shop of Alfred B. Davis in Epping to rent a press and hire a workman.[70] As Lucien explained to Camille:

> I can, while providing my own paper and ink use his machine and his best workman for about 1/- an hour with the right to install myself there to oversee and if necessary lend a hand and I hope for

Initial A (Fern 307 [SB129]). Used in: *The Book of Ruth and the Book of Esther,* 1896; Villon's *Ballades,* 1900; *Ishtar,* 1903; *La Belle dame sans merci,* 1905. (Special Collections, Florida State University, Tallahassee)

> the same price to have a man come to the house to compose under my direction.[71]

The arrangement allowed Lucien flexibility; he did not have to invest time and money to keep a workman constantly busy. Hacon & Ricketts, as publisher, furnished Lucien with ink and paper and paid his printing bill.[72]

For his third book, Laforgue's *Les Moralities légendaires,* Lucien again worked with the Epping printing house:

> I am right in the middle of printing my Laforgue, you cannot imagine what confusion! I assure you that it is not a small matter—my days are filled from morning until evening— . . . , correcting proofs, supervising the compositors and the printers all at the same time . . . having the need to make rapid decisions and with discernment. . . ."[73]

The fourth book, *De la typographie,* which he co-authored with Ricketts, was begun under Lucien's supervision at Davis' shop, but when Lucien fell ill in the spring of 1897, the work was transferred to the Ballantyne Press and completed there under Ricketts' supervision. In 1898, after the move to Bedford Park, Lucien set up his own printing studio; the first book issued was Laforgue's *Moralités légendaires,* volume two.

Commencing with *Moralités légendaires,* volume two, the Eragny Press books were printed at Lucien and Esther's studio. Because Lucien's illness left him in a weakened state, Esther assumed more and more responsibility for the presswork and in time would take charge of all printing except for the multicolored wood engravings. The work was too strenuous for either Lucien or Esther to do alone. A printer was hired from a local printing shop for the duration of the job. When the work was finished, the printer would return to the shop until the Pissarros needed help. Often, however, the shop would be too busy to send a printer on short notice to help the Pissarros, so they had to plan their time schedules carefully. While they were compelled to hire a printer, it was difficult to find one who could perform to their standards. When a printer the Pissarros had hired from Phillip John and Co. left Lucien "in a lurch," Lucien noted that he was

> glad to be rid of our printer as he worked so badly lately in fact we are very disgusted with parts of the book [Flaubert's *Hérodias*] & are looking forward to our little books which we mean to do ourselves.[74]

But Lucien had other problems with his workman than his standards of quality. His anarchist beliefs were called into question when his employee joined a union:

> And for the crowning glory the worker that I have employed just joined the Trade Union of the kind that he no longer has the right to touch a press being a compositor of his trade. Damn the social vindictiveness!! and the worker organizations—it is still despotism—I understand completely that I am an exception and that the end is to struggle against the industrial giants, but from another

side, the division of labor is established in principle and man is no more than a machine, it's the fault of industrialization of production and the man-machine endorses this fault by its own attitude. It will be necessary that I find someone else and that I teach him his trade without counting the troubles in consequence of the contempt of the working class of this country for us—because we work with them instead of acting as an employer who must be respected—I also fear coming across a rough drunkard as they are numerous in this trade—and I have no strength to show an insolent worker to the door—Finally let's hope that all will turn out for the best. All these troubles come when I am not organized to keep my worker all year and when I have finished a work I am obligated to let him go.[75]

As an anarchist, Lucien believed in individual liberty. It must have been difficult coping with the British class system, especially when it interfered with work. Because both Lucien and Esther worked like "slaves" in their printing shop, they did not earn the workman's respect. The Pissarros required their worker to perform all the jobs related to printing, from composition to presswork, and to assist in any task when necessary. A full day was the rule of the trade,[76] but the Pissarros' day ended when the work was finished.

About 1901, the Pissarros developed a particularly strong working relationship with a printer, Thomas Taylor, who was an employee of Bissley and Co.[77] Taylor became their loyal worker until the closing of the Press in 1914. With this alliance established, the Pissarros had no further problems with hired printers.

Because so much of their printing involved color, registration was perhaps the most important aspect of their work. The Pissarros' output was quite modest due to their extreme concern with perfect registration as well as flawless production. Even with both Esther and Lucien combining efforts to work the press, they were able to print at most thirty or so three-color frontispieces per day.[78] The entire day, however, was not devoted to the actual presswork. They spent a half-day reimposing the forme:[79]

The pieces of wood [furniture] which fix the blocks on the press continually move and destroy the guide marks [repérage] in such a way that each day it is necessary to spend 1/2 day to fix them over again. Voila 2 1/2 weeks we work at this frontispiece and we still have half to do.[80]

Printing text pages did not go much faster. With a printer and Lucien and Esther both working, they were able to print on average one octavo forme of 220 sheets per week.[81] In order to achieve the good register and equal color they desired, the Pissarros found they got better results by printing in half-sheets, even for a "black forme." Esther explained their work and turn method for an octavo and a sextodecimo format:

In working a black forme [printing in black ink only] if we have 8 pages we impose so that 4 pages of one side of a half sheet are on one half of the press & the 4 pages of the back are on the other half. We divide our paper before wetting & work from one half to the other—printing 8 pages at a time but 2 half sheets instead of a whole sheet printed only one side. If we have 16 pages we print 8 backed in the same way. If we have 8 pages on the forme in a book that has red & black we again divide our paper & have 4 pages of black and 4 pages of red. We turn our sheet on the centre points & other points in the centre of the inside margin to back the black & then pass to the red & do the same, but we have fresh points for each printing. By fresh points I mean this . . . we have holes made in each section of our forme so that the sheet can be only and always in the same order & if the points do tear it does not upset the register of the next printing. Handmade paper is too irregular to lay our paper to paper marks only we generally fold the paper, prick the paper on centre points, and lay to only one mark. The centre points control both the centre of the paper and the next set of centre points. We have a good many points but as we use fine needle

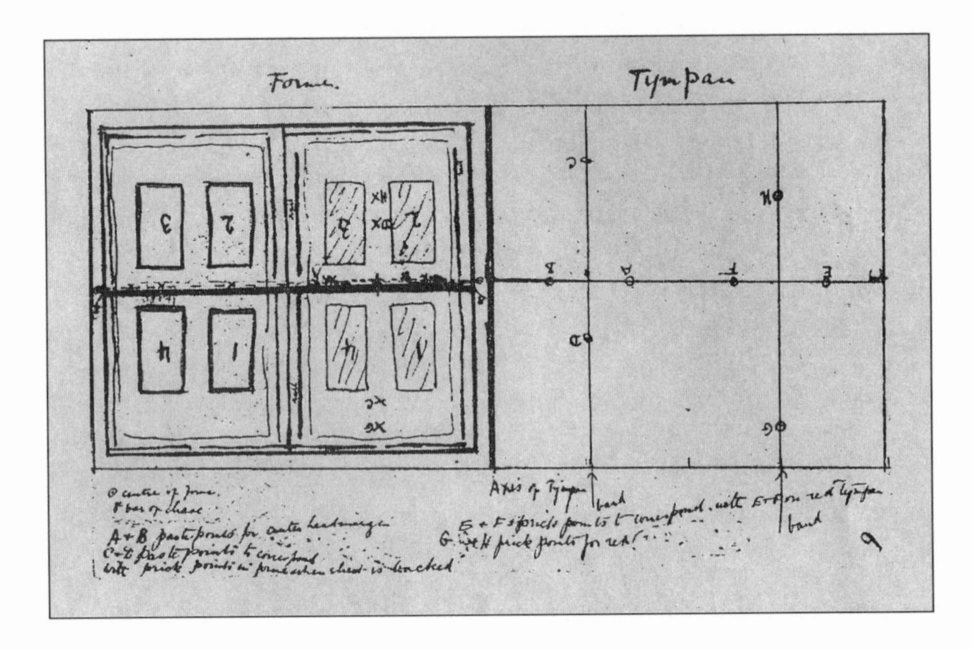

Layout of format. (Ashmolean Museum, Oxford)

points they do not spoil the paper. . . . We find we get better results by printing in half-sheets even for the black. We impose so. We have two paste points in the head margins of tympan and also two prick points in the forme head margins. Then to stretch the paper we have two paste points at the extreme edges of inner margin and two prick points in the forme. This is in order that no holes should be used twice. The paste points on the backing half correspond of course to the prick points in the forme of the 1st half.[82]

In addition to problems with imposition, they also encountered obstacles with dampened paper and two-color printing. Unlike other hand-press printers who use one press to print two colors, the Pissarros often set up two different formes on two different presses, printing the "black forme" one day and the "red forme" the next. Their difficulty came in trying to prevent the damp paper from drying overnight. The two centimeters' difference they found in their paper size between a dry sheet and a moist one could throw off the register substantially.[83]

They always used parchment on the tympan of their presses, which they acquired from Band of Brentford. Usually, a sheet of cardboard and brown paper was placed between the parchments and was changed for each forme. Finding that the parchment on the tympan frames changed with the weather, and moved the points, they had another frame made within the frisket frame, held to the frisket frame by steel hooks. On the two inner frames the parchments were mounted. The points were fixed to the outside frame's steel bands and secured with screws and bolts. If the parchment changed with the weather, the points did not change places. This modification facilitated the process of printing damp paper more easily and thus of obtaining perfect register.[84]

When the printed sheets were finished, they were then dried by placing them between clean sheets of paper and weighted with a light board set on top. The papers were sometimes changed two or three times and heavier weights were put on. Then the sheets, hung on wooden rails with rounded tops, were left to hang in the warm temperature of the printing room for two or sometimes three days. They were then placed in a wooden press between flat boards, removed, counted, packed, and readied for the bindery.

These glimpses into the Pissarros' printing procedures indicate that the methods they used were not often orthodox. They were quite inventive in their techniques, but their lack of knowledge of professional printing skills made their production expensive and their output rather low. Perhaps their ignorance of actual production methods held them in good stead for their creative endeavors, especially in color printing.

COST OF PRODUCTION

The account book for the Eragny Press survives from 1901, beginning with a record of *Un Coeur simple*, making it possible to reconstruct the cost and profit for many of the books printed from 1901 to 1914. A general summation of the Pissarros' financial situation[85] and an account of equipment expenses in 1898 when Lucien and Esther furnished their printing studio also exist. Because the account book is full of incongruities, it is not always easy to determine exact costs. Entries into the account book were made by both Esther and Lucien, though the main responsibility of record keeping was Lucien's, as indicated by the number of entries in his hand. For most books a new page was begun in the ledger; at the head of each page, reference was made to the book at hand, format of the book and production dates. At the end of each book's account, cost and sometimes profit (Table I) are noted (usually in Esther's hand). Entries appear to have been written as expenses were incurred.

Inconsistencies occur for two major categories of expenses, overhead

(Table II), and printing costs (Table III). Overhead was figured into the cost of the books if they were profitable. Even then only the studio (30 s/month) and heat (4 d/day) were considered as overhead. There is no indication of the purchase of new type to replace any that may have been worn, although if a particular implement, such as a rubber roller, were purchased during production, it would be included. Though new sorts were purchased when the Pissarros switched from French to predominantly English books, no record of this purchase exists in the account book.[86] When it appeared that a book would make a sizeable profit, wages for Lucien and Esther were figured into the cost. Sometimes the pair of them were paid the same as their hired printer; other times, they each received the same wage as the printer.

Another problem in figuring the cost of any one book is that if they did not actually purchase the material during the production, the cost of the material would not be recorded for a particular book. Even if a cost was incurred, no record of the expense exists. For example, ink (Table IV) is only incurred as an expense when it is purchased, not when it is actually used. This is also true for their handmade paper (Table V). Engraving-materials costs (Table VI) and binding costs (Table VII) are entered more consistently.

When the affiliation with the Vale Press ended in 1903, the account book entries records for the first and only time depreciation on equipment. This is noted in another hand, probably that of Albert Morelli, who was the business manager for about a year after the Pissarros began printing on their own.

In any case, there appears to be no particular logic to the account book. If anything it is a reflection of the Pissarros and their business practices. Neither one had a sense of business, nor any training in accounting practices. This account book is a rough record of expenditures and was neither used for any sound financial planning nor for making business judgments. In a period of especially tight finances, for example, the Pissarros undertook one of their most expensive books. It merely reiterates that the Pissarros printed what they wanted to without much thought to financial consequences.

The Pissarros were not wealthy, "gentlemen" printers, like William Morris, T. J. Cobden-Sanderson, or St. John Hornby, but were artist-printers. However, when the Press experienced financial difficulties, they had several means of avoiding insolvency. For the early period, the Press relied on the patronage of Camille Pissarro. Camille sent Lucien a monthly allowance of about three hundred francs until his death in 1903. This allowance was enough to cover minimal living expenses, but was not necessarily enough to provide the Press with materials. However, all the major investments—presses and type, for example—Camille covered. After Camille's death, the Pissarros supplemented their income from the Press with the sale of his paintings and with money from Esther's family. Once, when Lucien was in particularly difficult financial straits, he obtained a loan from Claude Monet. With the publication of *Songs by Ben Jonson* (1905), an expensive book to produce and one with poor sales, Lucien borrowed 3,500 francs to pay his

Table I.
ERAGNY PRESS BOOKS COST AND PROFIT

TITLE AND FORMAT	COST	PROFIT
Queen of the Fishes, 8°		
Book of Ruth, 12°		
Moralités I, 8°	34.06.11	
Moralités II, 8°		
Deux contes, 8°		
St. Julien, 16°		
Ballades, 8°		
Coeur simple, 16°	40.16.04	34.03.08
Hérodias, 16°	38.01.02.1/2	45.19.01.1/2
Autre poésies, 8°	46.03.10.1/2	54.07.00
Petits vieux, fancy	32.19.05	64.10.07
Of Gardens, 12°	22.07.06	
Choix de sonnets, 8°	76.12.08.1/2	
Peau d'ane, 8°	41.17.07	63.10.05
Abrégé de l'art, 8°	41.06.01.1/2	41.10.08
Aucassin, 8°	58.13.08.1/2	
Brief account, 8°	62.09.08	
Descent, 12°	38.15.09.1/2	20.10.09
Areopagitica, 4°	64.15.00.1/2	61.04.09
Areopagitica (reprint)	57.10.01	
Browning, 8°	67.00.07	74.16.05
Christabel, 8°	47.12.03	28.01.11
Some Old French, 8°	102.00.09	
Dream-Come-True, 12°	60.01.03	
Little School, 12°	54.10.00	36.19.07
La Belle Dame, 32°	26.15.11	
Songs by Ben Jonson, 8°	114.01.02	
Verses, 8°	69.03.11	
Riquet, 8°	39.19.10	
Histoire de la reine, 8°	179.14.07	
Livre de jade, 8°	103.02.09	
Charrue d'érable, 8°	122.18.07	
Whym Chow, 8°	13.04.05	

Note. British money before 1970 was expressed in pounds-£, shillings-s, and pennies-d. Thus, 5.07.03 would be read as five pounds, seven shillings, and three pennies.

Table II.
OVERHEAD

TITLE AND FORMAT	RENT	HEAT	INSURANCE
Queen of the Fishes, 8°			
Book of Ruth, 12°			
Moralités I, 8°			
Moralités II, 8°			
Deux contes, 8°			
St. Julien, 16°			
Ballades, 8°			
Coeur simple, 16°			
Hérodias, 16°			
Autre poésies, 8°			
Petits vieux, fancy			
Of Gardens, 12°			
Choix de sonnets, 8°	03.15.00	01.03.00	
Peau d'ane, 8°	02.10.00	00.11.00	
Abrégé de l'art, 8°	02.10.00	00.18.03	
Aucassin, 8°			
Brief account, 8°	03.06.08		
Descent, 12°	02.10.00	00.11.09	
Areopagitica, 4°	05.00.00	04.10.00	
Areopagitica (reprint)	03.15.00	00.15.09	
Browning, 8°	05.00.00		
Christabel, 8°	05.00.00		
Some Old French, 8°	10.00.00		02.02.00
Dream-Come-True, 12°	01.06.08		00.07.06
Little School, 12°	03.15.00		00.10.06
La Belle Dame, 32°	01.13.04		00.05.00
Songs by Ben Jonson, 8°	10.00.00		01.12.06
Verses, 8°			
Riquet, 8°		03.15.00	
Histoire de la reine, 8°	26.14.01		
Livre de jade, 8°	13.00.00		
Charrue d'érable. 8°	23.17.06		
Whym Chow, 8°			

Table III.

PRINTING COSTS

TITLE AND FORMAT	PRINTER'S WAGES	E. & L. WAGES
Queen of the Fishes, 8°		
Book of Ruth, 12°		
Moralités I, 8°	23.12.00	
Moralités II, 8°		
Deux contes, 8°		
St. Julien, 16°		
Ballades, 8°		
Coeur simple, 16°	14.16.00	14.16.00
Hérodias, 16°	13.04.00	13.04.00
Autre poésies, 8°	10.10.00	20.10.00
Petits vieux, fancy	01.13.00	
Of Gardens, 12°	10.02.00	
Choix de sonnets, 8°	52.10.00	
Peau d'ane, 8°	24.07.06	
Abrégé de l'art, 8°	25.09.06	
Aucassin, 8°	38.10.00	
Brief account, 8°	24.07.03	20.00.00
Descent, 12°	16.09.00	
Areopagitica, 4°	30.06.00	
Areopagitica (reprint)	25.18.03	
Browning, 8°	25.00.09	
Christabel, 8°	20.08.09	
Some Old French, 8°	53.04.06	
Dream-Come-True, 12°	12.07.06	12.07.06
Little School, 12°	17.01.09	
La Belle Dame, 32°	09.06.03	
Songs by Ben Jonson, 8°	65.16.06	
Verses, 8°	21.02.07	
Riquet, 8°	21.04.00	
Histoire de la reine, 8°	121.18.06	
Livre de jade, 8°	34.14.09	
Charrue d'érable, 8°	63.16.09	
Whym Chow, 8°	—.—.—	

Table IV.

INK COSTS

TITLE AND FORMAT	INK COSTS	GOLD COSTS
Queen of the Fishes, 8°		
Book of Ruth, 12°		
Moralités I, 8°	01.02.06	
Moralités II, 8°		
Deux contes, 8°		
St. Julien, 16°		
Ballades, 8°		
Coeur simple, 16°	00.07.06	
Hérodias, 16°	00.07.06	
Autre poésies, 8°	00.07.06	
Petits vieux, fancy	00.10.00	
Of Gardens, 12°	00.13.00	
Choix de sonnets, 8°	01.00.00	
Peau d'ane, 8°	00.00.00	
Abrégé de l'art, 8°	00.00.00	
Aucassin, 8°	00.08.06	
Brief account, 8°	00.00.00	
Descent, 12°	00.05.06	
Areopagitica, 4°	00.02.06	
Areopagitica (reprint)	00.07.06	
Browning, 8°	00.08.00	
Christabel, 8°	00.01.03	
Some Old French, 8°	00.08.06	
Dream-Come-True, 12°	00.02.06	12.07.06
Little School, 12°	00.02.06	
La Belle Dame, 32°	00.00.00	
Songs by Ben Jonson, 8°	01.14.00	
Verses, 8°	00.05.06	
Riquet, 8°	00.14.10	
Histoire de la reine, 8°	02.18.11	02.15.10
Livre de jade, 8°	02.02.06	01.13.00
Charrue d'érable, 8°	01.02.06	
Whym Chow, 8°	00.07.06	

Table V.

HANDMADE PAPER AND VELLUM COSTS

TITLE AND FORMAT	H.M. PAPER COSTS	VELLUM COSTS
Queen of the Fishes, 8°		
Book of Ruth, 12°		
Moralités I, 8°	05.00.00	
Moralités II, 8°		
Deux contes, 8°		
St. Julien, 16°		
Ballades, 8°		
Coeur simple, 16°	02.19.06	
Hérodias, 16°	04.03.01.1/2	
Autre poésies, 8°	05.08.10.1/2	
Petits vieux, fancy	10.16.00 (Jap. vellum)	
Of Gardens, 12°	00.06.03	
Choix de sonnets, 8°	08.02.00	
Peau d'ane, 8°	06.06.03	
Abrégé de l'art, 8°	00.09.00	
Aucassin, 8°	00.10.09	
Brief account, 8°	00.06.03	04.04.09
Descent, 12°	02.00.00	03.10.00
Areopagitica, 4°	00.00.00	11.04.06
Areopagitica (reprint)	07.00.00	—.—.—
Browning, 8°	06.10.00	09.03.06
Christabel, 8°	06.00.00	04.10.00
Some Old French, 8°	06.00.00	05.14.06
Dream-Come-True, 12°	02.00.00	02.03.02
Little School, 12°	04.10.00	03.19.04
La Belle Dame, 32°	03.00.00	00.17.06
Songs by Ben Jonson, 8°	06.00.00	07.15.00
Verses, 8°	06.00.00	07.10.00
Riquet, 8°	02.10.00	02.01.00
Histoire de la reine, 8°	Paper furnished	
Livre de jade, 8°	03.11.01 (Jap. vellum)	06.12.06
Charrue d'érable, 8°	Paper furnished	
Whym Chow, 8°	00.00.00	

Table VI.

ENGRAVING MATERIALS COSTS

TITLE AND FORMAT	ENGRAVING MATERIALS COSTS
Queen of the Fishes, 8°	
Book of Ruth, 12°	
Moralités I, 8°	
Moralités II, 8°	
Deux contes, 8°	
St. Julien, 16°	
Ballades, 8°	
Coeur simple, 16°	00.14.04
Hérodias, 16°	00.14.01
Autre poésies, 8°	00.06.11
Petits vieux, fancy	03.11.08
Of Gardens, 12°	01.13.00
Choix de sonnets, 8°	07.15.04
Peau d'ane, 8°	00.06.01
Abrégé de l'art, 8°	01.15.02
Aucassin, 8°	03.18.04
Brief account, 8°	01.01.09
Descent , 12°	01.01.09
Areopagitica, 4°	04.00.04
Areopagitica (reprint)	00.01.00
Browning, 8°	03.14.02
Christabel, 8°	02.09.03
Some Old French, 8°	02.02.07
Dream-Come-True, 12°	00.15.11
Little School, 12°	01.00.03
La Belle Dame, 32°	00.00.00
Songs by Ben Jonson, 8°	02.05.09
Verses, 8°	00.13.09
Riquet, 8°	01.06.06
Histoire de la reine, 8°	13.14.00
Livre de jade, 8°	04.13.10
Charrue d'érable, 8°	14.09.01
Whym Chow, 8°	00.11.03

Table VII.
BINDING COSTS

TITLE AND FORMAT	BINDING COSTS	PAPER COSTS
Queen of the Fishes, 8°		
Book of Ruth, 12°		
Moralités I, 8°		
Moralités II, 8°		
Deux contes, 8°		
St. Julien, 16°		
Ballades, 8°		
Coeur simple, 16°	05.14.09	
Hérodias, 16°	05.13.00	
Autre poésies, 8°	07.18.03	
Petits vieux, fancy	08.02.00	00.13.03
Of Gardens, 12°	07.07.11	00.04.10
Choix de sonnets, 8°	08.12.09	00.07.06
Peau d'ane, 8°	06.12.02	00.13.07.1/2
Abrégé de l'art, 8°	08.17.05	—.—.—
Aucassin, 8°	09.10.00	00.14.08
Brief account, 8°	07.11.09	00.06.09
Descent, 12°	06.00.10	—.—.—
Areopagitica, 4°	05.10.06	00.09.06
Areopagitica (reprint)	12.16.00	00.09.06
Browning, 8°	07.15.05	—.—.—
Christabel, 8°	07.16.06	00.08.04
Some Old French, 8°	09.05.11	00.03.00
Dream-Come-True, 12°	05.17.00	—.—.—
Little School, 12°	06.14.03	00.04.10
La Belle Dame, 32°	06.12.00	00.03.00
Songs by Ben Jonson, 8°	07.08.06	00.05.09
Verses, 8°	06.18.00	—.—.—
Riquet, 8°	04.06.09	—.—.—
Histoire de la reine, 8°	—.—.—	leather
Livre de jade, 8°	35.05.00	leather
Charrue d'érable, 8°	—.—.—	leather
Whym Chow, 8°	—.—.—	leather

printing expenses, which had already been assumed. As collateral he put up two of his father's paintings which he did not wish to sell.[87] Lucien repaid the loan over time, but it was difficult for him to manage the repayment. When the Press began to flounder financially in 1905, Lucien also returned to painting, thinking that it might be more profitable.

In order for the Eragny Press to make a profit, it was necessary to sell the entire edition. When Eragny Press books were sold to Hacon & Ricketts after mid-1899, outright at half the retail price, a profit was made. Profits per book during the Vale period ranged from £34.3.8 to £63.10.5, depending on the format, number of woodcuts, two-color printing, etc., of the book. Lucien noted that the books were:

> Very profitable, the worse thing is that it is necessary to have a sum of money for producing them and when they are produced one is not paid right away—I am obligated to pay my worker each week and me, it is necessary that I have unending credit.—Voila it is necessary to have capital.[88]

Lucien was never able to overcome this lack of capital. With Hacon & Ricketts paying Lucien on a regular basis, he had enough money coming in to continue to print his books. For the period before 1903, the Eragny Press output is greatest for this very reason. But when the Pissarros became their own publishers in 1903, they had difficulties selling their books and their profits and output dropped considerably. Profits ranged from £20.10.9 to £74.16.5, depending on how many books were sold, but more often than not little return was made on their considerable investment of both time and money.

With commissions from Les Cent bibliophiles and Le Livre contemporain, the Pissarros were no longer limited by their restricted resources. Both *Reine du matin* and *La Charrue d'érable* were books Lucien had planned earlier, *Reine du matin* dating from 1903 and *La Charrue d'érable* from the establishment of the Press, but was unable to carry to fruition due to the lack of capital. These two works in octavo format are the tours de force of the Eragny Press, displaying masterful color work in the woodblocks, a variety of decorative ornaments, and considerable texts. The cost of these books is at least triple the cost of earlier Eragny Press books, with the additional costs going to labor and materials. Engraving materials for these books were about three times the cost of materials for previous books. These works demonstrate the capabilities of the Eragny Press when money was not a factor and Lucien was able to create designs in tranquility without the burden of being unable to pay his creditors.

It is not unreasonable to think that in all actuality the Pissarros never earned a profit from the books. In figuring their profit, the Pissarros only accounted for the expenses and work done at the Press. They never considered either the time they spent on the design of a book and design and engraving of the pieces, or other miscellaneous work involved outside of the printing. They only looked at the cost of the actual materials and the hired labor. It is difficult to estimate their initial expenses in setting up their printing studio. In 1898 when the Pissarros established their own shop, the account indicates the purchase of a press (£24.19) and other equipment: an inking table (£1.10), paper racks (4s6d), a footrest (2s6d), pressing boards (12s8d), and type stands, strikes, etc. (£1.8.3). Opening capital expenditures, not including type or paper, would have been approximately £28. In 1902, with the cutting of punches and casting of the type (about £67) and the purchase of an additional press (£40.10), their plant expenditure rose to about £136. This figure again does not include paper and parchment stocks.

It appears that in both financial and production terms, the Eragny Press worked on a small scale in comparison with other contemporary private presses. By comparing the expenses of the Ashendene with those of the Eragny Press it is possible to determine somewhat the scale on which the Pissarros worked. St. John Hornby, the proprietor of the Ashendene Press, made an initial plant expenditure in 1901 of £171 and by the end of 1902 his expenses had risen to £634. Franklin, in his history of the Ashendene Press, does not itemize specific expenses for the Ashendene Press, nor differentiate between material stock and actual plant expenditures. Both the Ashendene Press and the Eragny Press employed an Albion Royal press (for the Ashendene Press, after 1901, it was the only press used); these presses were bought at approximately the same time. It must be assumed that the press costs were within the same range—about £40. Hornby maintained considerable paper and parchment stocks, as well as a full-time pressman, and a compositor was engaged as needed. Some of the discrepancy in initial plant expenditure between Ashendene and Eragny perhaps comes from a larger stock of material. Because Hornby was printing folios with a considerable amount of text (e.g., the Dante) he would have needed to have a substantial supply of paper and type. Perhaps then the Ashendene's initial plant expenditure of £171 is more in keeping with the Eragny's initial plant expenditure of £136.

By examining the printing costs for one of the smaller books of the Ashendene Press, *Un mazzetto scelto di certi fioretti . . . di . . . San Francisco . . .* (1904), a quarto printed in red and black in an edition of 125 paper copies (retail £2.12.6) and 20 vellum copies (retail 6 guineas), and an equivalent book from the Eragny Press, John Milton's *Areopagitica* (1903), the only quarto produced by the Eragny Press (paper copies retail 31s6d), it becomes obvious that the Pissarros were able to exist as printers only because they were able to do the labor themselves, without paying outside craftsmen.

According to the Ashendene Press ledgers, *Fioretti* cost £201.4.7 to produce; Hornby made a profit of £190. A portion of the production cost of *Fioretti* included £56.10 which Hornby paid to Charles Gere for his woodcut designs and £21 to William Hooper for cutting the designs on wood. *Fioretti* is not an elaborate book. Its woodcuts, while there are a number of them, are small, simple line engravings. *Areopagitica,* printed in red and black, does not include any illustrations, but has a border and about a dozen different initial letters. The production cost for this edition of 226 paper copies and 10 vellum copies, almost twice the size of Hornby's edition, was, according to the Pissarros' accounting, approximately £65. While any additional figures are somewhat arbitrary, if we add to the cost of *Areopagitica*, £77.10, the same amount Hornby paid for his woodcut designs and their engraving, and the Pissarros' labor, £31.6 (the figure based on what they paid their printer, £15.13), and paper costs of about £10, their costs amount to £183.16. These overlooked expenditures add considerably to the cost of production, bringing the Eragny Press expenses (£183.16) to somewhat of the equivalent of the Ashendene Press (£201.4.7). If they had sold the entire edition of 226 copies (not including the vellum copies) at 31 shillings 6 pence, a £45 profit would have still been possible. As we noted above, Hornby made a profit of £190 on *Fioretti*, but he also sold his book for about £1 more per copy. If *Areopagitica* had sold for £1 more as the Ashendene book, an additional £226 would have given the Pissarros a considerable profit of £271.

Many factors in this estimate have not been taken into consideration. It does appear that the Eragny Press undervalued their products (at least in comparison to the Ashendene Press) as well as their labor, but it may not have been possible for the book to have sold at a higher price. While most books from the private press period are monuments to great literature, Eragny Press books are, generally speaking, vehicles for wood engraving supported by minor texts. C. J. Holmes, when he was marketing Eragny Press books for Hacon & Ricketts, referred to them as "charming toys" which could not be sold at an "extravagant price."[89] The original prints of the Eragny Press are more valuable than an actual printed page of text, but the English book-buying public believed that a book was for reading and undoubtedly would not have bought an Eragny book if it had been priced higher to reflect the high production costs and the care and artistry which went into it.

Although Lucien and Esther established the Eragny Press as a commercial Arts and Crafts business, the care and workmanship and the quality of materials are reflections of personal and private tastes. No matter how much they may have yearned for commercial prosperity, artistic autonomy was placed above all else. Not having the capital resources at their disposal hindered Lucien and Esther in producing many of the books they had envisioned. If more assets had been available to them, the rate of production and the kind of books produced might have been more impressive.

Notes

1. *The Collected Works of William Morris,* with introductions by his daughter May Morris, vol. 22, "The Art of the People" (London, New York: Longmans, Green, and Company, 1910–1915), 47.
2. T. J. Cobden-Sanderson, *Four Lectures by Cobden-Sanderson,* edited by John Dreyfus (San Francisco: Book Club of California, 1974), 62–65.
3. *Arts and Crafts Exhibition Catalogue* (1988), 88–89.
4. Definitions for printing terminology used in this chapter may be found in Philip Gaskell, *A New Introduction to Bibliography* (1972) or in Geoffrey Ashall Glaister, *Glaister's Glossary of the Book* (Berkeley and Los Angeles: University of California Press, 1979).
5. Barbara Pratt, *Lucien Pissarro in Epping* (Loughton, Essex: Barbara Pratt Publications, 1982).
6. Ibid., 7.
7. Lucien Pissarro, Epping, to Camille Pissarro, Eragny, [after 2 December 1896], Pissarro Collection, Ashmolean Museum.

8. A brief history of Brook House is given in Brian Gould, " 'The Brook,' Chiswick: The Home of the Eragny Press," *Private Library* (1971): 140–148.
9. Meadmore, *Lucien Pissarro,* 166.
10. Quoted in Meadmore, *Lucien Pissarro,* 145.
11. Lucien Pissarro, Epping, to Camille Pissarro, Paris, [after 16 October 1895], Pissarro Collection, Ashmolean Museum. Edward P. Prince (1846–1923) was the primary type punchcutter for private presses. A biography of Prince is found in F. C. Avis, *Edward Philip Prince: Type Punchcutter* (London: n.p., 1967).
12. Ibid. Translation mine.
13. Charles Ricketts, *A Bibliography of the Books Issued by Hacon and Ricketts* (London: Charles Ricketts; New York: John Lane, 1904), xvii.
14. Lucien Pissarro, Epping, to Camille Pissarro, Paris, [after 16 October 1895], Pissarro Collection, Ashmolean Museum. John Lane joined the London book trade in the mid-1880s and quickly formed a partnership with Elkin Matthews, culminating in the creation of the Bodley Head in 1887. The Bodley Head published limited editions appealing to a sophisticated market and published such authors and illustrators as Oscar Wilde, Richard Gallienne, and Aubrey Beardsley. Lane's partnership with Mathews ended in 1894. Lane kept the Bodley Head imprint. In 1896, Lane opened a New York branch of his firm.
15. Ricketts, *Hacon and Ricketts,* [iii].
16. Lucien Pissarro, Bedford Park, London, to Camille Pissarro, Paris, 11 Februrary 1900, Pissarro Collection, Ashmolean Museum.
17. Ibid. In this letter, Lucien replies to Camille's opinion of Ricketts' typeface, " . . . que tu trouves un peu lourde. . . ."
18. Ibid.
19. Ibid. "Je n'ai pas du tout l'intention de faire une typographie gothique, ce serait trop archaïque— L'écriture romane a été le point de départ de notre typographie moderne et on est obligé, si on retourne aux source, d'avoir recours à eux—Naturellement si je faisais quelquechose dans ce sens je me servirait librement de l'écriture roman française d'avant le XVII et XVIII siècles époque où elle a commencé a dégénérer avec les Elzevier etc."
20. Lucien Pissarro, Bedford Park, to Camille Pissarro, Paris, 22 February 1900, Pissarro Collection, Ashmolean Museum. Translation mine.
21. Ibid.
22. Georges Lecomte, Paris, to Lucien Pissarro, Bedford Park, [January 1900], Pissarro Collection, Ashmolean Museum.
23. Lucien Pissarro, Bedford Park, London, to Camille Pissarro, Paris, [after 31 January 1900], Pissarro Collection, Ashmolean Museum.
24. Ibid., 22 February 1900.
25. Lucien Pissarro, The Brook, Hammersmith, to Camille Pissarro, Dieppe and Eragny, [August, 1902] and 1 November 1902, Pissarro Collection, Ashmolean Museum. The money came from the sale of a painting to the Berlin art critic Julius Elias. See Camille Pissarro, Eragny, to Lucien Pissarro, The Brook, Hammersmith, 4 November 1902, Pissarro Collection, Ashmolean Museum.
26. Lucien Pissarro, The Brook, Hammersmith, to Camille Pissarro, Eragny, [after 3 October 1902], Pissarro Collection, Ashmolean Museum.
27. Camille Pissarro, Paris, to Lucien Pissarro, The Brook, Hammersmith, 30 March 1903, Pissarro Collection, Ashmolean Museum. "J'ai reçu l'exemple de ton nouveau type, cela fait très bien, il faudrait voir tout un livre exécuté pour bien en juger, il me semble qu'il n'y a pas une très grande différence avec le type Ricketts, je serai curieux de savoir comment les Anglais le jugeront."
28. E. P. Prince to Lucien Pissarro, 22 July 1902, Pissarro Collection, Ashmolean Museum. "Messrs. Reed's have done Mr. Ricketts, but lately they and Messrs. Miller and Richards [of the firm Miller and Richard], decline to undertake this type of work unless they retain the matrices from which the type is cast."
29. Lucien Pissarro, Hammersmith, to Sir Charles Reed and Son, London, 25 March 1903, Pissarro Collection, Ashmolean Museum.
30. Lucien Pissarro, Hammersmith, to P. M. Shanks and Co., London, 6 August 1902, Pissarro Collection, Ashmolean Museum.
31. What exactly these legal concerns were, I have not been able to determine. In a letter written in 1914, at the time Lucien was designing a type for François van Royen, a similar legal process is alluded to.
32. E. P. Prince to Lucien Pissarro, 19 August 1902, Pissarro Collection, Ashmolean Museum.
33. Ibid., 22 August 1902.
34. Ibid., 29 August 1902.
35. Ibid., 1 October 1902.
36. Ibid., 10 October 1902.
37. Ibid., 1 April 1903.
38. Lucien Pissarro to P. M. Shanks and Sons, 25 May 1903, Pissarro Collection, Ashmolean Museum.
39. A brief discussion of the Brook typeface is in Robert Balston, *Private Press Types* ([Cambridge]: Printed by the University Printer for His Friends, Christmas 1951), 29–32.
40. Lucien Pissarro to P. M. Shanks and Co., 25 March 1903, Pissarro Collection, Ashmolean Museum.
41. Invoice from E. P. Prince to Lucien Pissarro, 15 April 1903, Pissarro Collection, Ashmolean Museum.
42. Lucien Pissarro, The Brook, Hammersmith, to Camille Pissarro, Dieppe, 12 August 1902, Pissarro Collection, Ashmolean Museum.

43. John Bensusan-Butt, personal interview, autumn 1984.
44. Esther Pissaro had consulted Oliver Simon concerning the disposal of the Brook type. Simon suggested she give the type to Cambridge University Press. The press now holds the Brook pica type, both lower and upper case; the lower-case capitals, ligatures, and punctuations; various ornaments and intitial letters (some on wood); and one pair of type cases. See Balston, *Private Press Types,* v.
45. P. M. Shanks and Sons, London, to Lucien Pissarro, The Brook, Hammersmith, [1904], Pissarro Collection, Ashmolean Museum.
46. Esther L. Pissarro to P. M. Shanks and Sons, 10 November 1904, Pissarro Collection, Ashmolean Museum.
47. *Selwyn Image Letters,* edited by A. H. Mackmurdo ([London]: G. Richards, 1932), 75.
48. Charles Holmes, London, to Lucien Pissarro, Bedford Park, 24 February 1899, Pissarro Collection, Ashmolean Museum.
49. Lucien Pissarro, Bedford Park, to Camille Pissarro, Eragny, 1 December [1898], Pissarro Collection, Ashmolean Museum.
50. Perrigot-Masure, Paris, to Lucien Pissarro, Bedford Park, 19 July 1901, Pissarro Collection, Ashmolean Museum.
51. Ibid., 7 October 1902.
52. Lucien Pissarro, Bedford Park, to Camille Pissarro, Varengeville sur Mer, [before 27 September 1899], Pissarro Collection, Ashmolean Museum.
53. Charles Holmes, London, to Lucien Pissarro, Bedford Park, 2 June 1899, Pissarro Collection, Ashmolean Museum.
54. Lucien Pissarro to H. Band, [1904], Pissarro Collection, Ashmolean Museum.
55. I am unable to place this reference.
56. Lucien Pissarro, The Brook, Hammersmith, to Jean François van Royen, The Hague, 7 February 1919, Pissarro Collection, Ashmolean Museum.
57. Thomas Sturge Moore, poet, playwright, essayist, and art critic, was introduced to Lucien shortly after his arrival in London in 1891. A member of Charles Ricketts' circle, Moore became a supporter of and collaborator with Lucien in several of the Eragny Press' publishing activities. Laurence Binyon, poet, art historian, and critic, was a Keeper at the British Museum, beginning in 1895, in the Department of Prints and Drawings; there he met Lucien, who was a frequent visitor to the department. Diana White, schoolgirl and then lifelong friend of Esther and a serious painter, became a confident of Lucien as well as a supporter of his art. She also served as an advisor to the Eragny Press, often suggesting ideas for what should be published.
58. The Eragny Press Account Book, Pissarro Collection, Ashmolean Museum.
59. Letter from Elkin Mathews to Lucien Pissarro, 29 September 1899:

> Re: Perrault Deux Contes
>
> I am a regular subscriber for the publications of the Vale Press and I may also claim to be an admirer of your work. At the same time when I saw the new Rebus you have designed as colophon for the above little book I must confess I was considerably astonished to find you had annexed my trademark motto ("Fructus inter folia") which I have been using for over 15 years, some 20,000 copies of various books I have published have borne it and it always appears on [the] front page of every re-issue of my trade catalogue (see specimens enclosed). You will also see it in my ex libris I enclose an example of the one etched for me ten years ago (1889) by Mr. Arthur Robertson APE.
>
> Mr. Holmes of the Vale Press is going to send me a written guarantee that the offending block shall not be used again for any Vale Press books, and I write to ask you if you will kindly either delete the motto from the block, or hand it over to me for my use, in which case "Eragny Press" should be deleted.
>
> In conclusion may I ask for a gratis copy of the book, and so amicably end a regrettable matter, a mistake I have no doubt you fell into through inadvertence.

Lucien's draft reply:

> As you are a regular subscriber of the Vale books, I am surprised to learn that you think my little block a new one. I used it in the second vol. of the Moralités Légendaires of Laforgue published in December last. I may mention that I designed and engraved the block before my illness in 1896.
>
> With regard to the matter I cannot understand how it can be regarded as private property. If I had in any way copied the design of your marks or taken the motto from your books I should owe you an apology but this is not the case. I chose the motto after discussion with friends some years ago.
>
> However, as a matter of courtesy to you & Mr. Holmes I will not use the motto again.
>
> At the same time you must pardon me if I decline to hand you my block & I regret I am unable to send you a free copy of my book as requested.

Charles Holmes thought Lucien's reply rather stern:

> Your answer makes me shiver. Being myself emphatically a man of peace, I wrote a simple note saying we were obliged to him for pointing out the coincidence in the motto, & would see it wasn't used again.

> He has, of course, at present, no grievance whatever, as there can be no question of damage owing to mistaking your books for his minor poets. Nonetheless I think you were quite right in saying you would not employ the motto again, as its continued use in defiance of his objection might aggravate the matter [Letter to Lucien, September 30, 1899].

60. C. J. Holmes, London, to Lucien Pissarro, Bedford Park, 21 November 1899, Pissarro Collection, Ashmolean Museum.
61. Lucien also thought about using cloth for his binding. He planned to produce his own printed cloth. See Lucien Pissarro, Bedford Park, to Camille Pissarro, Paris, [after 14 April 1899], Pissarro Collection, Ashmolean Museum.
62. Thomas Leighton, London, to Esther L. Pissarro, Bedford Park, 25 August 1902, Pissarro Collection, Ashmolean Museum.
63. The exact problems with each book are related in the Descriptive Bibliography.
64. Lucien Pissarro, Epping, to Camille Pissarro, Paris, 22 February 1894, Pissarro Collection, Ashmolean Museum. Translation mine.
65. Ibid., 12 April 1897. Translation mine.
66. Lucien Pissarro, Bedford Park, to Camille Pissarro, Rouen, 27 September 1898, Pissarro Collection, Ashmolean Museum. Translation mine.
67. General Book Working Account, 1898, John Bensusan-Butt Collection.
68. Lucien Pissarro, The Brook, Hammersmith, to Camille Pissarro, Paris, 30 April 1902. Pissarro Collection, Ashmolean Museum.
69. The Eragny Press Account Book, 1911 [3 October]: entry under *La Charrue d'érable,* Pissarro Collection, Ashmolean Museum.
70. As a small country printer, the employees of Mr. Davis would have been versed in all aspects of composition and printing. In 1897 the shop had two hand presses, a platen machine, a double demy cylinder machine, and eight men employed—six men and two apprentices. Alfred B. Davis also took up the slack after Lucien's illnesss. He printed the prospectus for *De la typographie* and would continue to print the prospectuses through at least 1899.
71. Lucien Pissarro, Epping, to Camille Pissarro, Rouen, 23 January 1896, Pissarro Collection, Ashmolean Museum. Translation mine.
72. Ibid.
73. Lucien Pissarro, Epping, to Camille Pissarro, Eragny, 26 November 1896, Pissarro Collection, Ashmolean Museum.
74. Lucien Pissarro, Bedford Park, to Charles Holmes, London, draft letter [probably written by Esther], 16 August 1901, Pissarro Collection, Ashmolean Museum.
75. Lucien Pissarro, Bedford Park, to Camille Pissarro, Paris, [early January 1899], Pissarro Collection, Ashmolean Museum. Translation mine.
76. Bisseley and Co., London, to Lucien Pissarro, Bedford Park, 16 October 1901, Pissarro Collection, Ashmolean Museum.
77. Thomas Taylor would later open his own print shop (by 1908) at 39, Berrymead Gardens, Acton W. He came out of retirement in 1945 to help Esther print some Eragny Press woodcuts for Lucien's memorial exhibition at the Leicester Galleries, which opened in January 1946. Looking forward to the exhibition, and expected at the gallery the morning before the opening, he died on his way there.
78. Lucien Pissarro, Bedford Park, to Camille Pissarro, Eragny, 26 July 1899, Pissarro Collection, Ashmolean Museum.
79. I have not been able to find a term appropriate for this problem. An experienced printer would not have had this much trouble in imposing the forme.
80. Lucien Pissarro, Bedford Park, to Camille Pissarro, Eragny, 30 July 1899, Pissarro Collection, Ashmolean Museum. The Pissarros were printing the frontispiece for Perrault's *Deux contes de ma mère l'oye.* This is the only book they produced in 1899.
81. Two hundred fifty sheets printed on one side was conventionally called an hour's work during the handpress period. See Gaskell, *A New Introduction to Bibliography* (1972), 139.
82. Esther Pissarro, The Brook, Hammersmith, to Jean François van Royen, The Hague, 10 October 1914, Van Royen Papers, Meermanno-Westreenianum/Museum van het Boek, The Hague.
83. Lucien Pissarro, Bedford Park, to Camille Pissarro, Paris, 11 February 1900, Pissarro Collection, Ashmolean Museum.
84. Esther Pissarro, The Brook, Hammersmith, to Jean François van Royen, The Hague, 12 October 1914, Van Royen Papers, Meermann-Westreenianum/Museum van het Boek, The Hague.
85. John Bensusan-Butt Collection.
86. Lucien Pissarro placed an order for more type with P. M. Shanks and Sons on 25 May 1903, Letterbook, Pissarro Collection, Ashmolean Museum.
87. Lucien Pissarro, The Brook, to Claude Monet, 27 September 1906, Pissarro Collection, Ashmolean Museum.
88. Lucien Pissarro, Bedford Park, to Camille Pissarro, Paris, 22 February 1900, Pissarro Collection, Ashmolean Museum. Translation mine.
89. C. J. Holmes, London, to Lucien Pissarro, Bedford Park, 9 June 1899, Pissarro Collection, Ashmolean Museum.

Chapter III

Marketing

Little has been written directly about the marketing of English revivalist private press books. William Morris, when he established the Kelmscott Press, intended to give away copies of his books to friends and colleagues. When the public expressed a desire to buy the books of his press, Morris, who was heavily involved in the commercial aspects of design, did not hesitate to make them available. First Reeves and Turner and then Quaritch published his books. When he grew disenchanted by Quaritch's business practices, Morris began to publish his own books. The Kelmscott Press was a commercial success from its inception.[1] St. John Hornby began the Ashendene Press as a hobby. He presented copies of his works to family and friends. As the reputation of Ashendene books grew, inquiries were made concerning the sales of the books. Hornby began to sell his Ashendene Press books, not with the intention of profit, but to cover some of his expenses. Often the books were sold for far less than their cost.[2] The Doves Press books were sold through subscription, but T. J. Cobden-Sanderson only anticipated breaking even in the venture.[3] For other private presses of the period, less information is available. Essex House Press books were published by Edward Arnold, who "held the stocks . . . and supplied to booksellers. At the same time Ashbee would advertise the books by means of a prospectus, inviting customers to order directly from the Guild [of Handicraft] or from his architectural offices, and presumably passing the orders on to Arnold."[4] No record of the Press' policy or success in marketing its books has surfaced.

Lucien Pissarro's major intention when he established the Eragny Press was to make a profit from his books and thus earn a living from his press. Artists who worked with his father struggled to sell their paintings and had difficulties with dealers. Lucien believed that the answer to this predicament was to embrace the industrial or decorative arts, those arts which are made to serve a practical purpose but are valued for the quality of workmanship and the beauty of their appearance. Wood engraving and printing, now part of the decorative arts movement, were, for Lucien, a natural answer to the financial problems of painters. Both Lucien and Camille were convinced that an easier living could be made by producing a more practical commodity than paintings. In establishing the Eragny Press, Lucien and Esther wanted to create books which both reflected their artistic sensibilities and would also be commercially viable.

In the 1890s, with the Arts and Crafts movement at the height of its popularity, these books produced in private studios, often for personal reasons, soon found a market. Kelmscott Press books sold briskly because of Morris' reputation and popularity. But by the end of the decade, the Boer War (1899–1902) brought a declining economy to England and with it a restrictive attitude toward money for luxuries. This decline made the sale of private press books more difficult, especially for those presses which were not surrounded by a coterie of friends and supporters.

This chapter examines the publishing program and the marketing of Eragny Press books for the two major periods of the Press, the Vale Period (1894–1903) and the Brook Period (1903–1914). While economic considerations were paramount to the Eragny Press, the Pissarros were not able to conceive a marketing strategy which would allow for financial success, although the books they designed and printed were created with an understanding of materials and the tools needed to create them as well as a genuine pride in the process of production. This understanding did not enter into their knowledge of marketing.

The Eragny Press Publishing Program

Many of the private presses printed books with substantial texts, and most of the works tended to be reprints of popular and literary classics. William Morris turned to his own writings or to literature which had inspired him—mainly early English texts—in deciding what to print. He also printed two books as favors to his friends who desired to see their work beautifully packaged. The Ashendene Press began by printing family ephemera and later Hornby would concentrate on printing the literature he enjoyed, especially that of Dante and his circle. The Doves Press tended to print classic works in the original language which were personally important to T. J. Cobden-Sanderson. The major concern of the private presses was with the form of statement rather than with new or original information. As Charles Ricketts wrote: "The aim of the revival of printing is . . . to give a permanent and beautiful form to that portion of our literature which is secure of permanence."[5] The texts did not include critical apparatus; the intention was for the reader to enjoy and savor the work, rather than grapple with it.

The Eragny Press was inclined, especially in its early period, to choose texts which were either more contemporary or which served as appropriate vehicles for illustration. Lucien preferred creating illustrations for symbolist literature and fairy tales more than for literary classics. He envisioned a program of printing contemporary French literature and fairy tales. His first book, *The Queen of the Fishes,* is an English translation of an old Valois fairy tale, undoubtedly a tale known to Lucien in his childhood. The second book, *The Book of Ruth and the Book of Esther,* was perhaps selected in honor of Esther's sister, Ruth, and for Esther, as well as being a popular text of the period. In 1896 Lucien outlined the works which he had in preparation—a series of French texts meant for the continental market. He planned to print Jules Laforgue's symbolist tales,

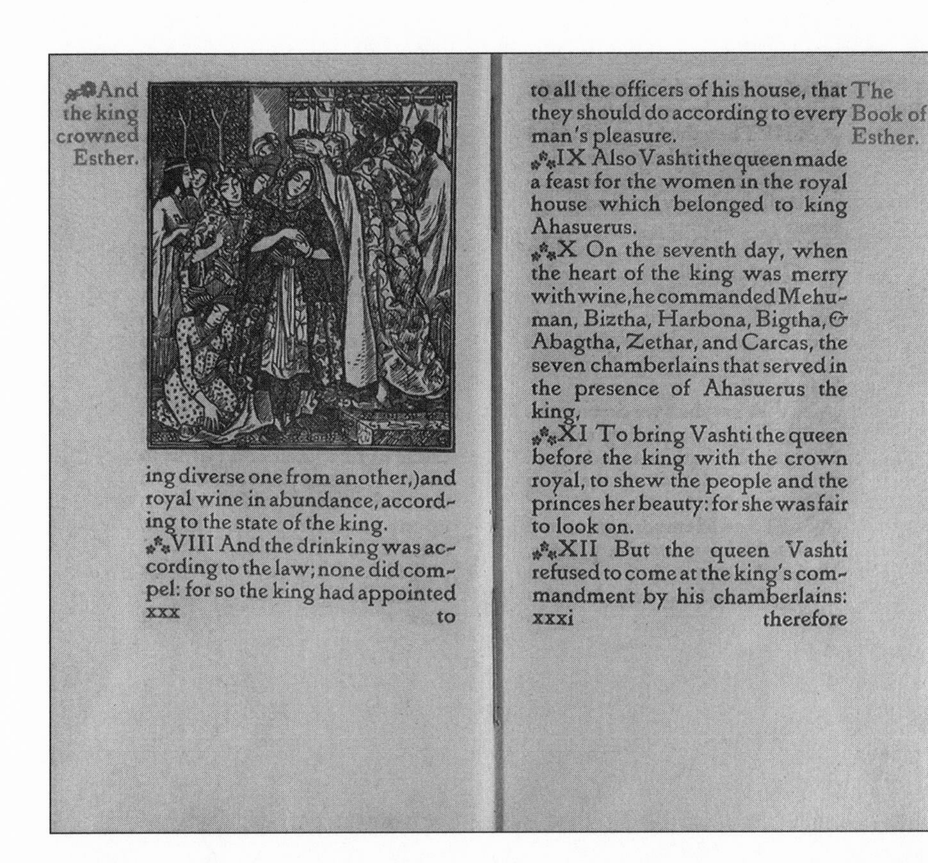
And the king crowned Esther.

ing diverse one from another,)and
royal wine in abundance, according
to the state of the king.
VIII And the drinking was according
to the law; none did compel:
for so the king had appointed
xxx to

to all the officers of his house, that
they should do according to every
man's pleasure.

The Book of Esther.

IX Also Vashti the queen made
a feast for the women in the royal
house which belonged to king
Ahasuerus.
X On the seventh day, when
the heart of the king was merry
with wine, he commanded Mehuman,
Biztha, Harbona, Bigtha, &
Abagtha, Zethar, and Carcas, the
seven chamberlains that served in
the presence of Ahasuerus the
king,
XI To bring Vashti the queen
before the king with the crown
royal, to shew the people and the
princes her beauty: for she was fair
to look on.
XII But the queen Vashti
refused to come at the king's commandment
by his chamberlains:
xxxi therefore

The Book of Ruth and the Book of Esther, 1896; pp. xxx–xxxi. (Special Collections, Florida State University, Tallahassee)

Moralités légendaires, in two volumes. This work was intended to be the first in a series of French Symbolist writers. Lucien did not realize when he began designing and engraving the woodcuts for the work that he would have to pay for the right to publish Laforgue's work which was still under copyright. Because he could not afford to pay an author or the expense of a copyright fee, Lucien abandoned his ambition to print contemporary works and sought out uncopyrighted works.

His own work on typography, written in collaboration with Charles Ricketts, met his ambition to print original materials without incurring additional costs. This work, *De la typographie et de l'harmonie de la page imprimée,* was intended to prepare the French terrain and to introduce Ricketts' and Lucien's theory of the aesthetic of the book to the Continent. Intending to make his books distinctive from other Arts and Crafts books, Lucien returned to using color woodblocks in his fifth volume, *Deux contes de ma mère l'oye* by Charles Perrault. To avoid paying for publishing rights, Camille suggested that Lucien print the *Trois contes* of Gustave Flaubert.[6] This work became Lucien's sixth, eighth, and ninth books.

During this early period, Lucien also planned two major projects, *Les Travaux des champs* and *Daphnis et Chloe,* in collaboration with Camille. Lucien's wood engravings were to be based on Camille's drawings. Two major factors thwarted the printing of these works: the lack of type prevented Lucien from composing an extended text, and stylistic difficulties with the translation of Camille's drawings to the woodblock remained unresolved.[7]

From 1900, when his publishing plan becomes less clear, Lucien continued to avoid texts which would require a copyright or author fee and sought many of his texts from medieval French literature, including two works each by François Villon (*Ballades* and *Autre poésies*) and Pierre de Ronsard (*Abrégé de l'art poétique françois* and *Choix de sonnets*); the tale *C'est d'Aucassin et de Nicolete*; and another fairy tale by Charles Perrault, *Peau d'ane*, a companion volume to the earlier Perrault. An English text was produced in 1902, *Of Gardens* by Sir Francis Bacon. Only one other work by a contemporary author in addition to Laforgue was published: a book of poems, *Les Petits vieux* by Emile Verhaeren. The production during this period of but three works in English demonstrates Lucien's commitment to the French market and, more obviously, his familiarity with French literature.

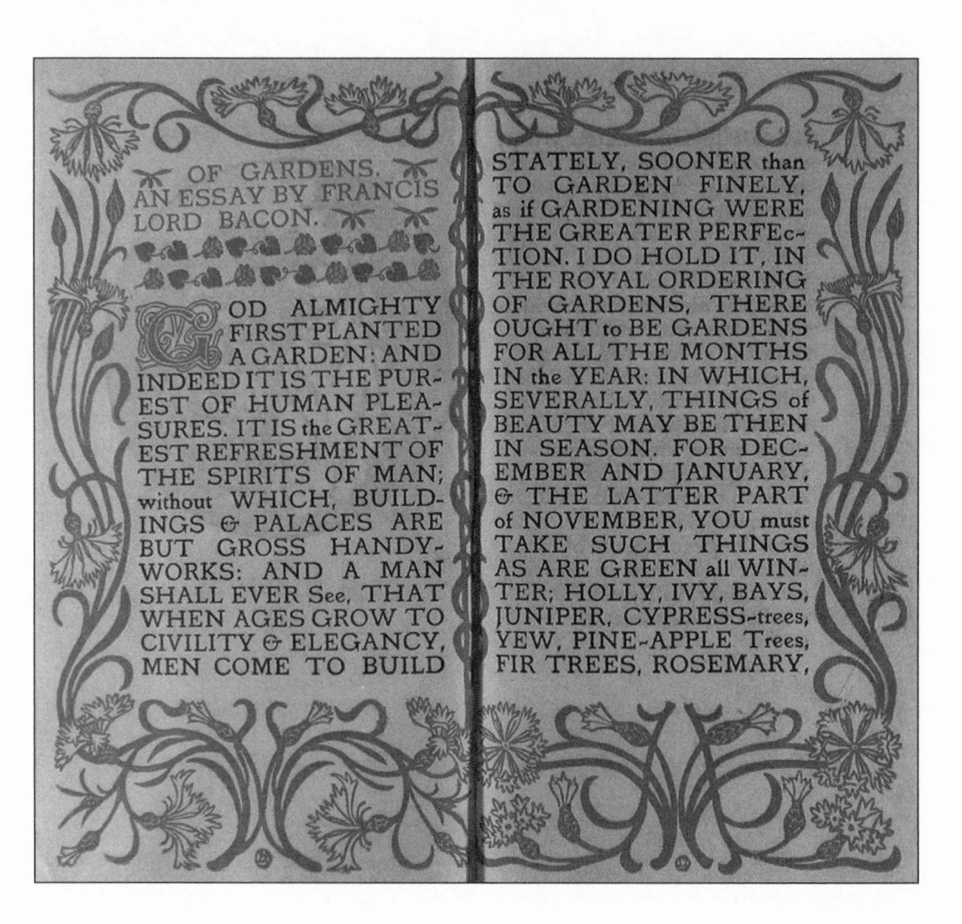

OF GARDENS.
AN ESSAY BY FRANCIS
LORD BACON.

GOD ALMIGHTY
FIRST PLANTED
A GARDEN: AND
INDEED IT IS THE PUR-
EST OF HUMAN PLEA-
SURES. IT IS the GREAT-
EST REFRESHMENT OF
THE SPIRITS OF MAN;
without WHICH, BUILD-
INGS & PALACES ARE
BUT GROSS HANDY-
WORKS: AND A MAN
SHALL EVER See, THAT
WHEN AGES GROW TO
CIVILITY & ELEGANCY,
MEN COME TO BUILD

STATELY, SOONER than
TO GARDEN FINELY,
as if GARDENING WERE
THE GREATER PERFEC-
TION. I DO HOLD IT, IN
THE ROYAL ORDERING
OF GARDENS, THERE
OUGHT to BE GARDENS
FOR ALL THE MONTHS
IN the YEAR: IN WHICH,
SEVERALLY, THINGS of
BEAUTY MAY BE THEN
IN SEASON. FOR DEC-
EMBER AND JANUARY,
& THE LATTER PART
of NOVEMBER, YOU must
TAKE SUCH THINGS
AS ARE GREEN all WIN-
TER; HOLLY, IVY, BAYS,
JUNIPER, CYPRESS-trees,
YEW, PINE-APPLE Trees,
FIR TREES, ROSEMARY,

Opening pages. Francis Bacon, *Of Gardens*, 1902. (Special Collections, Florida State University, Tallahassee)

With the closing of Hacon & Ricketts in 1903 and Lucien's and Esther's decision to self-publish, subsequent texts were chosen to appeal to a primarily English and American market. Lucien, unfamiliar with English literature, sought advice in his selections from Esther and her brother, Sam Bensusan—a writer—as well as from Diana White, T. S. Moore, and Laurence Binyon—trusted friends who as writers had some sense of the contemporary literary scene.

Works which were considered but rejected during this period, some in the planning stages, include Geoffrey Chaucer's *The Floure and the Leaf*, planned in a demy 16mo with a double frontispiece in color; selections from Robert Browning's *The Ring and the Book* and *Pippa Passes*, John Keats' "Isabella or the Pot of Basil," "Eve of St. Agnes," and "Eve of St. Mark";

sonnets of Elizabeth Barrett Browning; Percy Shelley's "Clouds," "Adonais," and his translation of Plato's *Symposium*; John Milton's "On the Morning of Christ's Nativity" (as a Christmas booklet), "Lycidas," and "Comus"; letters of Heloise and Abelard; William Wordsworth's *Prefaces*, the *Song of Songs*, and unidentified works by Richard Crashaw, George Herbert, Andrew Marvell, and Thomas Campion.

The Pissarros also embarked on a series of music books. *Some Old French and English Ballads* and *Songs by Ben Jonson* were completed in 1904 and 1905. A volume of the music and poetry of Robert Herrick was also planned but not produced.

The Série Camille Pissarro reached the planning stages in 1903–04 but was never printed because Lucien could not find an interested French publisher. The first volume was to be a biography of Camille Pissarro by Georges Lecomte. Six more volumes with French texts by prominent French writers accompanying Camille's drawings and engraved by Lucien and printed in chiaroscuro were to follow.

With the publication of Laurence Binyon's book of poems, *Dream-Come-True* (1904), Lucien and Esther—with the help of T. S. Moore, whose *The Little School* (1905) became the second work in the series—conceived of what they called the "Modern Series." Considered for inclusion in the series were works by Anatole France, Maeterlinck, Verhaeren, Michael Field, Bernard Shaw, W. B. Yeats, and Sam Bensusan.[8] The Pissarros were able to undertake these two works by Binyon and Moore because the books were mainly done as favors for the two men. The profits were split between the authors and the Pissarros; however, if no profit had been made, the Pissarros would not have paid the author. How they intended to pay the other authors whom they considered is not known.

The later books in the Brook series were, in many ways, the finishing of old business. Perrault's *Riquet à la houppe* may very well have been conceived as early as 1899. Nerval's *Histoire de la reine* was in the planning by 1902. *La Charrue d'érable,* which used the engravings based on drawings by Camille, had been in preparation in the early 1890s as a collaboration between Lucien and Camille. These works had not come to fruition earlier because of lack of capital.

The Eragny Press publishing program was initially very ambitious and innovative. Frustrated by copyright restrictions, the Pissarros turned to works without these confining limitations. Contemporary literature required compensating authors, something the Press could ill afford. If this had not been the case, Lucien undoubtedly would have persisted with his plan to print contemporary French Symbolist writers. When opportunities developed to print contemporary writers, the Pissarros welcomed and embraced them. These collaborative efforts with their author friends were financially successful, but as there was not a large coterie of authors with whom the Pissarros were well acquainted, this approach had its limitations. The French texts are a direct reflection of Lucien's inner self and are perhaps the most successful of the Eragny Press books. The reprints of brief selections from English literary classics are the weakest element in the publishing program, an expression of Esther's literary taste and her sense of the inclinations in the English market. Although constrained by financial considerations in the selection of texts, the Pissarros managed to create a publishing program that was a reflection of their tastes and unique vision, their most pleasing books outside of the private press "canon," including fairy tales and children's books, medieval French literature, and French and English songs.

Marketing of the Vale Series

Unlike Morris or Hornby, Lucien did not have the resources with which to begin a press. His only support came from his sole patron, his father. Without a large working capital, Lucien could not afford to be ambitious, yet he needed to produce distinctive works in order to succeed. Using for his models the color-printed works of the British illustrators Kate Greenaway, Randolph Caldecott, and Walter Crane, and inspired by Japanese color woodblock printing, *The Queen of the Fishes,* Lucien's first book, was a blend of his natural naïveté and his Impressionist background. When it came time for Lucien to market his book he knew little about what to do. He had had some experience with selling paintings and he had some idea about how art dealers worked. He also knew something of the importance of art exhibitions. But for the selling of books he had to rely completely on Ricketts' knowledge and his own uninformed assumptions about book marketing. While Ricketts had some contacts with London publishers due to his earlier work in commercial design, Lucien had few connections in England. In France, Belgium, and the Netherlands, Lucien had connections with painters, printmakers, and the literati, but his lack of familiarity with the book trade led only to frustration.

Each book of this early period was marketed somewhat differently. For many of them, it is essential to examine specific marketing methods. Early Eragny Press books carry the imprint of "Vale Publications" or "Hacon & Ricketts," but Lucien still played a major role in selling his works. This was partly because Hacon & Ricketts was still on shaky grounds financially at the time and was not completely established in the art and literary world. Lucien was, in fact, acting as an agent for the Vale Press and was in charge of expanding the market to the Continent. Other agents of Vale Publications and the early Hacon & Ricketts were Ricketts and Shannon (who acted as a traveling agent to the English provinces), both of whom dealt with the trade in Great Britain and America (via an arrangement made with John Lane).

The Queen of the Fishes, a Vale Publication, in an edition of 150, of which 120 were for sale, was marketed by a variety of methods. Seventy copies were sold to John Lane, the English publisher. These copies were intended for the English market and were sold at his shop at the Sign of the Bodley Head. An advertisement placed in the Dutch avant-garde periodical *Van nu en straks* resulted in thirty prepublication orders from Belgium and Holland. (Several wood engravings from *The Queen of the Fishes* were published in *Van nu en straks* as well.) Twenty copies then remained to be sold. It was Lucien's hope that these twenty copies could be sold in France, but Lucien's marketing efforts met with resistance.

Lucien's friends in France did what they could to help publicize the book. His friend, Félix Fénéon, in his capacity as editor of *La Revue blanche,*

THE QUEEN OF THE FISHES.

A STORY OF THE VALOIS ADAPTED BY MARGARET RUST BEING A PRINTED MANUSCRIPT DECORATED WITH PICTURES AND OTHER ORNAMENTS CUT ON THE WOOD BY LUCIEN PISSARRO, & PRINTED BY HIM IN DIVERS COLOURS & IN GOLD AT HIS PRESS IN EPPING. PUBLISHED BY C.H. SHANNON. (VALE PUBLICATIONS) 31 BEAUFORT STREET CHELSEA LONDON.

Ready very shortly 150 copies (120 for sale) crown 8vo. Price 1£ net each copy will be numbered & signed.

Printed on hand-made japanese paper & bound in apple green calf.

Subscribers are requested to use order form on the other side.

Prospectus. *Margaret Rust, The Queen of the Fishes,* 1894. (Ashmolean Museum, Oxford)

placed an advertisement on the back cover of that magazine[9] as a favor to Lucien. But Lucien's main promoter was his father, who took over the major marketing responsibility for France. Although prospectuses were sent, Camille's primary marketing technique was to talk about Lucien's book with his friends and colleagues, to booksellers that he personally knew, and to art gallery owners. Camille was most successful in selling *The Queen of the Fishes* to his friends. His American and Scandinavian friends living in Paris were the most enthusiastic about the book. Lilla Cabot Perry, the American Impressionist painter and student of Monet, had obtained a copy through subscription and had already shown it to her circle, whose members highly praised the book. By the time Camille arrived for tea at Perry's to promote the book, the group was well acquainted with *The Queen of the Fishes.* Perry had originally bought the book to give to her daughter, but she was so delighted by it that she kept the book herself and ordered another copy for her child, who, she reported to Camille, was captivated by it as well. Madame Perry also began to promote Lucien's book and convinced at least one friend to buy a copy; she also provided Camille with a list of possible buyers.[10]

Camille's success was limited in Paris. He left prospectuses with the trade book dealer, Achilles Heymann, who managed to sell a copy or two, but believed that he was hampered from selling additional copies because of the English text. Heymann also complained that the book's prospectus did not provide a clear indication of the design and suggested that the use of a color woodblock would make for a more striking prospectus. Camille sold two copies to a print dealer, Salvator Meyer, and he tried to place copies with André Marty, also a print dealer. Marty's clientele tended not to be interested in illustrated books. They preferred to buy individual prints. Camille also found that Marty did not like to deal with artists directly, preferring to work with a middleman.

A useful promoter of Lucien's work was the book dealer and publisher Martinus Nijhoff, at The Hague. He sold copies to the French as well as to the Dutch, and was more successful with the French market than the French dealers were. Nijhoff took a personal interest in Lucien, visiting him in Epping in March 1895. Lucien's work was highly regarded in Holland,[11] and Nijhoff had several Dutch collectors who were interested in Lucien's work, but the majority of Nijhoff's clients came from Paris. Knowing of Nijhoff's sales to the Parisian collectors, Lucien wondered how a Dutch bookseller could have so much success when Camille had had so little. Lucien was unable to fathom that Camille was not directing the book to the appropriate market. They were unable to tap into the traditional bibliophilic market, which apparently Nijhoff had done, because it was a market of which they were unaware. The booksellers, like Heyman, whom they did know, were not in fine books but were dealers of ordinary trade publications.

The Queen of the Fishes was not without detractors. As a convert to the Arts and Crafts style, Lucien was introducing a new style of book design to the French market. Elzeverian type, a thin, modern-style type, was still at the height of its popularity in France. Many French bibliophiles believed that books done in this lighter style, with much white space, were more elegant and refined. This new English style was thought to be crude and without taste. Moreover, the idea of integrating wood engravings with type was a rather startling notion to the more traditional French bibliophiles.

By the time his second book, *The Book of Ruth and the Book of Esther,* appeared in 1896, Lucien was convinced that with his previous marketing experience and "greater understanding" of the book trade, his next attempt would be more successful. He forged ahead. *The Book of Ruth and the Book of Esther,* illustrated with black and white wood engravings, was a less costly production than *The Queen of the Fishes.* Ready for the spring publishing season, *The Book of Ruth and the Book of Esther* was the first Eragny Press book sold by Hacon & Ricketts. Recently opened for business, Hacon & Ricketts were not in a position to buy the edition outright. The books, placed at the shop only on consignment, compelled Lucien to find other dealers to sell his books and other means of promotion. But it was difficult to find intermediaries. An advertisement and a wood engraving was placed once again in *Van Nu en Straks* but with disappointing results.[12]

By early November 1896, Hacon & Ricketts had sold sixty copies of *The Book of Ruth and the Book of Esther,* enough to cover the cost of production. Discouraged by the sales, Lucien blamed the English for having so little regard for art: ". . . in a country where everyone lives in bathrobes and slippers and drinks watered down wine what could be expected of them?"[13] French and continental friends were not particularly enthusiastic about *The Book of Ruth and the Book of Esther* either. The book was not to the taste of the Pissarro circle, mainly because it lacked the Impressionist colors so prominent in *The Queen of the Fishes.* Because the prospectuses were printed in English, it was difficult to interest the French.[14] Thus, the sales were for the most part limited to England.[15] The book was done very much in the English tradition and, moreover, had an English text.

By the time the Eragny Press made its formal debut in the French market in 1896 at the Exposition internationale du livre moderne, the French book arts had fallen into a state of decadence. This became even more apparent when French books were compared to English books. Edouard Pelletan, the major French publisher, wrote:

> The recent exhibition of the modern book, which was held in the original house of Art Nouveau (chez Bing), has shown with evident clarity into what decadence the French edition has fallen. This decadence was even more perceptible when one compared our books to those which came from England, reserved and elegant, rarer by the choice of type, the agreement of illustration, the quality of paper, the determination of the format, such that our volumes, decorated sonorous epithets, constitute a veritable offense to good taste.[16]

The Exposition internationale du livre moderne held at Siegfried Bing's gallery, Maison de l'art nouveau, played an important role in reviving the French book arts, as well as in advancing the decorative arts in France. Heavily influenced by the Japanese, Bing was convinced that decorative art was in no way inferior to fine art. He believed that the decorative arts were the "most appropriate vehicle for unifying all the Western arts into a cohesive aesthetic force."[17] Bing's gallery quickly became the center of design reform in France. Using the Tiffany studios in New York as a model, his ultimate goal was to have craftsmen working "to give shape to the carefully planned concepts of a group of directing artists, themselves united by a common current of ideas."[18] His exhibition rooms were modeled after those at the Maison d'art in Brussels, founded by Edmond Picard in 1894. The rooms at Maison de l'art nouveau were integrated rooms devoted to all the decorative arts: sculpture, prints, carpets, metalwork, furniture, stained glass, jewelry, etc., as well as paintings.

Camille, acquainted with Bing, urged Lucien to exhibit his works at Bing's gallery shortly after its opening in 1895. Believing that Bing had made a number of anti-artistic decisions concerning the decoration of certain rooms in his gallery, Lucien was reluctant to be associated with Bing. However, in early 1896, when Bing began planning an exhibition dedicated to modern book design, Lucien changed his mind. Bing's exhibition had the potential to be one of the most important exhibitions of Lucien's career. The organizing committee was international in scope and included Samuel P. Avery, president of the Grolier Club in New York, Gustave Geffroy, August Lepère, Roger Marx, Julius Meier-Graefe, all either friends or acquaintances of the Pissarros; Gabriel Moury, Bing's representative in London; Octave Uzanne, an active book promoter and president of a major bibliophile club; and Paul Gallimard, the publisher. Over 1,100 entries were selected for the exhibition, representing all aspects of manuscripts and the printed book, ranging from trade to deluxe editions. The exhibition catalogue was designed by Félix Vallotton.[19]

Both Morris and Ricketts were invited to exhibit. Ricketts' own work was not appreciated in France, but he believed that Lucien's work would be highly regarded there. Initially, Lucien had not been invited, but with Camille's intervention, an invitation was forthcoming. Unfortunately, Lucien did not have any new books ready to exhibit, but the frontispiece to Laforgue's *Moralités légendaires*, Lucien's first French book, was ready, and could be framed for display.

The exhibition opened on 9 June 1896. The installation was described as elegant.[20] Author manuscripts were prominently displayed on the ground floor of the gallery. On the first floor, printed books, bindings, and illustrations were displayed. A reviewer writing in the newspaper *Figaro* made special mention of an edition of Baudelaire's *Fleurs du mal*, published by Poulet-Malassis and illustrated by the sculptor Rodin; Oscar Wilde's *Salome*, illustrated by Aubrey Beardsley; and *Germinie Lacertaux*, illustrated by the painter Raffaëlli for the publisher Paul Gallimard—and quintessentially French by its limited edition of three copies. The reviewer, obviously biased towards French book art, dismissed the German, English, and American designers with ". . . they have sent their illustrations obtained by mechanical processes . . ."[21]

The more progressive reviewers spoke highly of the English. *L'Art moderne* noted that Bing's exhibit confirmed the superiority of the English book trade over the others, but thought that William Morris had indicated the wrong direction by turning to the medieval book as a model. Lucien was singled out for special mention:

> From the presses of Ricketts and Shannon come the pages of the *Book of Ruth* and of the *Moralités légendaires* illustrated by Lucien Pissarro. Their unusual character, the clear readable design, constitute a real progress on the results achieved by Morris.[22]

La Revue blanche also highly praised Lucien's books, referring to Lucien as a master engraver who was evolving into both a designer and a typographer. The reviewer, Edmond Cousturier, anticipated the publication of Lucien's *Moralités légendaires.* Of the English books represented, Lucien's received the most praise, but more than likely this was because Lucien was known in this particular artistic circle. This exhibition provided Lucien with a forum for presenting his work. While a certain degree of

"Salomé," wood engraving (frontispiece). *Moralités légendaires,* vol. 1, 1896. (Ashmolean Museum, Oxford)

publicity and recognition was received, it did very little to increase the sales of *Moralités légendaires* once it became ready for sale. Lucien had looked to Bing's gallery to buy part of his edition of *Moralités légendaires.* Whether Bing would have agreed to sell part of the edition is not known, but because of a copyright issue, Lucien could not have sold it to Bing in any case.

The spring of 1896 also brought forth an invitation from Ambroise Vollard, the art dealer who had opened his gallery on the rue Laffitte in 1893. His exhibitions of Cezanne's paintings had launched his career; it was, however, as a publisher and entrepreneur that Vollard would gain eminence.[23] In fact, Vollard attributed his career as a publisher to Lucien:

> The first work that came from his press, *La Reine des Poissons* [The Queen of the Fishes], disheartened me by its perfection; but in the end it helped to spur me on to attempt publishing myself.[24]

Vollard invited Lucien to exhibit his color wood engravings which had not been exhibited previously. Lucien had no new engravings ready to exhibit; moreover, he worried about a conflict if he should exhibit both at Bing's and Vollard's. In spite of this concern, Lucien exhibited at Vollard's gallery. His engravings were highly praised, though Vollard had placed them at the back of his gallery. Vollard must have been attracted to Lucien's work because he inquired of Camille whether Lucien would do a book by Verlaine for him.[25] But Vollard did not mention the book again for some time. Camille attributed this to Vollard's waywardness; he was so caught up in the flurry of his activities that he tended to forget his proposals.[26] When the matter came up again, difficulties with the rights to certain of Verlaine's work were encountered; the person who held the rights was asking five hundred francs for them. This made the project too expensive for Vollard to undertake at the time.[27] When Vollard was more established, he commissioned Pierre Bonnard to illustrate Verlaine's *Parallelement* (1900). By then Lucien was established in London and was no longer seeking work in France. But Camille had not completely trusted Vollard. He was concerned that Vollard would take advantage of Lucien. This mistrust of dealers and publishers did not help to further Lucien's career in France. Growing up with the notion of the independence of artists made it difficult for Lucien to advance his career in a medium which required so large an investment in equipment and materials. Artistic control was so important to the Pissarros that any financial intervention was seen with suspicion.

Hacon & Ricketts, still financially weak, were not yet in a position to cover Lucien's production expenses; and unable to obtain financial backing from the French, Lucien borrowed 1,500 francs from a family friend, which allowed him to begin printing the Laforgue.[28] Rather than passively waiting for his book to sell by subscription or through Camille's promotion, Lucien began to solicit continental dealers to buy his edition outright before the work was printed.

In August 1896, Lucien wrote to two booksellers with whom he was acquainted. If he could sell at least fifty copies outright in Holland, it would provide him with some capital and would have no effect on his negotiations elsewhere on the continent. To the Dutch book dealer, C. J. van Gogh, a cousin of the painter Vincent van Gogh, Lucien proposed a sale of fifty copies of *Moralités légendaires* at a 30 percent discount, granting van Gogh a monopoly in Holland. The entire edition could be bought with a 45 percent discount.

Lucien also wrote to Edmond Deman, a publisher and bookseller in Brussels, making the same offer and promising him a monopoly for Belgium. Lucien suggested to Deman that he was well situated in Belgium to place the entire edition of two hundred copies.[29] He heard from neither of these dealers[30] and grew anxious at the lack of response. If he went ahead

HAMLET ou les suites de la piété filiale.
C'est plus fort que moi.

DESAFENEtre préférée, si chevrotante à s'ouvrir avec ses grêles vitres jaunes losangées de mailles de plomb, Hamlet, personnage étrange, pouvait, quand ça le prenait, faire des ronds dans l'eau, dans l'eau, autant dire dans le ciel. Voilà quel fut le point de départ de ses médiations et de ses aberrations.

La tour où, depuis l'irrégulier décès de son père, le jeune prince s'est décidément arrangé pour vivre, se dresse en lépreuse sentinelle oubliée, au bout du parc royal, au bord de la mer qui est à tous. Ce coin de parc est le cloaque où l'on

"Ophelia," wood engraving (frontispiece). Jules Laforgue, *Moralités légendaires,* vol. 2, 1898. (Ashmolean Museum, Oxford)

and printed two hundred copies of *Moralités légendaires* and could not sell them, he would be risking a considerable investment. Lucien proceeded, however, taking the chance. The first volume of *Moralités légendaires*, finished in early December 1896, remained without a dealer.

With the book finished, Lucien was eager to find a publisher. He had earlier approached Félix Fénéon with the idea that *La Revue blanche*,[31] the literary journal with which Fénéon was associated, might undertake the publication of *Moralités légendaires. La Revue blanche* was not yet in a position to undertake a publishing venture, although earlier the review had published several portfolios of prints. Fénéon, however, had been checking into other publishers for Lucien's *Moralités légendaires.* But first there was the matter of publishing rights. Emile Laforgue, Jules Laforgue's brother, had inherited the rights to the writings of his brother upon his death in 1887. Without permission to publish *Moralités légendaires,* Lucien could do nothing and his investment would be lost. Fénéon, who had many literary connections in Paris, went to see Alfred Vallette of the *Mercure de France,* one of the leading symbolist journals and publishing houses in France. Vallette, who had an agreement with Emile Laforgue to be the sole publisher of the works of Jules Laforgue, was anxious to acquire Lucien's book. Lucien wrote to Emile Laforgue, who quickly agreed to the publication of Lucien's edition.[32] Mercure de France was unable to buy the book outright, but could undertake its sale. Lucien was in no position to negotiate. Mercure de France required a commission of forty percent of the selling price. Vallette also wanted Lucien, as part of the deal, to include the pressmark of the Mercure de France in the book. Lucien explained to him that because all of his works were printed with the Vale type, they made up a series called Vale Publications. While Lucien would not use their mark in his book, he offered to place the name Mercure de France in the colophon. Lucien assured Vallette that the sale in England would be minimal because of the French text and because Laforgue was so little known in England. Lucien also prepared prospectuses for Vallette, printed in the Vale type and carrying Vallette's address, with a list of works already printed by the Eragny Press and a list of proposed books.

Lucien did not have much choice but to accept the sale conditions which Mercure de France offered him. An identical agreement would hold for the second volume of *Moralités légendaires.* With a sale price of twenty francs, Lucien would make twelve francs on every copy. While this was not a particularly lucrative deal for Lucien at least he had found a publisher for his book. One hundred copies of *Moralités légendaires* were sent to Mercure de France and arrived in late March 1897. It took until August 1902 for *Moralités légendaires* to go out-of-print in France.[33] If Lucien had not been forced to sell his *Moralités légendaires* to Mercure de France, he may have done better at Bing's Maison de l'art nouveau. Perhaps in a shop more attuned to this style of art, the book would more readily have found a clientele.

Lucien still had one hundred copies remaining. He proposed to place a number of copies at Hacon & Ricketts (a number which would be agreeable to Ricketts) at a discount of 40 percent—the same arrangement that Mercure de France had. *Moralités légendaires* sold for sixteen shillings in England. By January 1898, a year after the book had gone on sale, Hacon & Ricketts had sold 58 copies.[34] Charles Holmes, Hacon & Ricketts' business manager, had only expected to market fifty copies and was surprised that the book had sold beyond his expectations. He ordered fifty copies of the second volume.[35]

After the two-volume *Moralités légendaires,* Lucien planned to print some tales of Perrault. This volume was envisioned to include a double-page spread in color surrounded by a black and white border. Lucien wanted to have at least five or six volumes completed, so that in the event his business did not succeed, at least his reputation in printing would have been made. In the meantime, in early 1897, Lucien was preparing *De la typographie.* Lucien believed that the idea of a harmonious book, the blending of type with engravings, would be met with much resistance in France for two reasons. First, the idea was from a foreigner; and secondly, the guild of photoengravers, finding themselves criticized for their small photographic vignettes, would oppose this revival of wood engraving.[36] Lucien had intended to print *De la typographie* in the spring of 1897. The book was already in production that spring when Lucien suffered a stroke which left him partially paralyzed and unable to work. The printing of the book was taken over by the Ballantyne Press, and was finally finished in December 1897, delayed by a printers' strike at the press.[37]

Lucien spent the summer of 1897 in France, recuperating from his stroke and working with Camille. He also used his time in Paris to make contacts with book dealers and to promote his work. He must have discussed *De la typographie* with the dealer H. Floury that summer.[38] In his letter to Floury on his return to London he described the book to him in full detail. Lucien explained that no ornaments would be used in the book, because he wanted to prove to his French clientele that a book could be beautiful simply with the arrangement of the type. He proposed to Floury to take half of the edition; fifty copies that would be bought outright and fifty more on deposit with a 40 percent discount.[39] The remaining one hundred would be sold by Hacon & Ricketts. In Paris the book would sell for six francs; in London, for six shillings.

In Floury, Lucien found a sympathetic ear.[40] In late November 1897, Floury agreed to buy fifty copies outright and take fifty more copies on deposit. Prospectuses were sent to Floury in February 1898. When the book reached him in early April, Floury, satisfied with the book, had already sold a number of copies through subscription.[41] Moreover, Hacon & Ricketts had had sufficient subscriptions to put the English edition out-of-print before it had appeared.[42] With the obvious success of *De la typographie,* Lucien's morale was considerably bolstered. At chez Floury, clients inquired about Lucien's next work.

With success so close at hand for Lucien, his illness, which left him unable to engrave and print, handicapped any immediate progress . The drive and momentum were gone. He would not resume working again until late 1898. The second volume of Laforgue's *Moralités légendaires* would be ready in the spring of 1899, and half the edition would automatically go to Mercure de France. While convalescing, Lucien began to plan his next book. In addition to the tales of Perrault, which had been planned for sometime,[43] Lucien, unable to draw, began translating into French William Morris' lecture on Gothic architecture which had been published by the Kelmscott Press in 1893. Lucien intended to use this work to further his way into the French and continental markets.[44] Floury had agreed to the sale of Lucien's translation, which Floury believed would be easily sold,[45] but the William Morris estate would not allow Lucien to print his translation.[46] Because *The Queen of the Fishes* was extremely popular in France, Lucien also considered doing a French version of it. Part of Lucien's reasoning was that *The Queen of the Fishes* would incur few expenses because no wood engravings would have to be made. He planned to substitute the Vale type for the handwritten text. It is not clear why Lucien did not print the French edition.

Floury, satisfied with the sale of *De la typographie,* looked forward to selling more of Lucien's work. With this sort of support in Paris, having someone to count on in placing his work, Lucien was given the encouragement he needed to continue. In 1899, Lucien planned to finish the second volume of *Moralités* and the tales of Perrault, for which he had begun working on the drawings for his engravings in mid-to-late 1898. The Perrault was finished in the summer of 1899. Charles Holmes, Hacon & Ricketts' business manager, suggested—contingent on Ricketts' approval—buying outright one hundred copies of the new book at half the published price, rather than continuing on a commission basis. Holmes put two conditions on his terms—that Floury buy half of the edition and that Floury not price the book any lower than Hacon & Ricketts. In addition, if Lucien were to print any vellum copies, that he either print ten copies or none at all. Three of the vellum copies would go to Ricketts, Hacon, and Lucien; the other seven to Hacon & Ricketts to be sold to their English collectors. He proposed to buy the vellum copies outright for £12.[47] Holmes, by buying half the edition, was securing from Lucien a monopoly for England and America.[48] Two hundred copies of the Perrault were designated for sale; one hundred copies to go to Hacon & Ricketts, and one hundred to Floury. With the advent of the autumn season, Holmes realized that Hacon & Ricketts was going to have a very successful season, and offered to buy one hundred thirty copies of Perrault, for which Holmes was certain he could find subscribers. Because only seventy copies would be sold on the continent, the success of the French edition was almost assured. When the Perrault arrived from the binders at Hacon & Ricketts in late September 1899, Holmes had sold almost all of the 130 copies.[49]

Binding. Gustave Flaubert, *La Légende de St. Julien l'hospitalier,* 1900. (Special Collections, Florida State University, Tallahassee)

By 1899, four years into the Vale Press venture, Hacon & Ricketts were doing well enough that they no longer took Lucien's books on a commission basis, but rather bought the complete edition. Hacon & Ricketts became Lucien's publisher. For Lucien's next book, Flaubert's *La Legende de St. Julien l'hospitalier,* Holmes requested samples of the illustrations, decorations, covers, etc., so that Hacon & Ricketts could decide whether they wished to publish it.[50] From thenceforth, until the closing of Hacon & Ricketts in 1903, the Eragny Press books were bought outright by Hacon & Ricketts at half the selling price, which was determined through discussions and negotiations between Lucien and Charles Holmes. By selling an entire edition to Hacon & Ricketts, Lucien recovered his investment quickly, enabling him to continue producing book after book without much financial worry. Hacon & Ricketts were conscientious publishers who paid their clientele regularly on a quarterly basis. With a steady income Lucien was able to continue to work without borrowing from Camille. Floury, however, had not been nearly as conscientious in making regular payments of sales. With seventy copies of the Perrault placed on deposit, Lucien was still owed 1,050 francs in mid-April 1900.[51] By late November 1900, Floury still had not paid Lucien for the books.[52]

It is unfortunate that no record exists of Hacon & Ricketts' clientele. Boycotted by the trade and the critics when they first opened,[53] once established, Hacon & Ricketts appears to have done rather well. Most of their editions sold out almost immediately upon publication. In addition to the fifty copies of an edition that went to John Lane for sale to America, Hacon & Ricketts undoubtedly had a lively business with the British trade, as well as with private clientele. While Hacon & Ricketts' success enabled Lucien to work with some degree of security and tranquility, it also thwarted him from continuing to establish a strong foundation in France and the Continent. Lucien was never really comfortable in his associations with the British. He spoke English quite well, but he was more comfortable speaking and thinking in French. Before moving to London, Lucien had an established circle of friends and colleagues in France, Belgium, and Holland. By isolating himself in England during those years of Hacon & Ricketts' success, he lost many of his continental connections. Reestablishing ties to the Continent would not be an easy task.

With Lucien living in England, even with Camille acting as his "agent," it was difficult for him to remain in contact with those who would have been able to promote his work. By choosing to live and work in England, Lucien gave up his "right" to be a French artist, and was soon considered by the French to be an English artist. Lucien was so seldom in Paris that many opportunities were undoubtedly lost to him. But there may have also been other reasons which hindered Lucien's success in France. Lucien was determined to be in complete control of his creations, from the choice of texts to the materials and formats of his designs. In France, the publishers and the newly flourishing bibliophile clubs were the arbitrators of taste. They decided upon the text, the format, and the design of the book, as well as the illustrator. The idea of complete control over a book, which Lucien believed necessary for artistic success, was foreign to the French publishers and book dealers who wished to set their own stamp upon a work.

Marketing of the Brook Series

With the closing of Hacon & Ricketts in the summer of 1903 and the death of Camille Pissarro in November of that same year, Lucien's two major sources of support were gone. Yet Lucien and Esther decided to undertake the publishing of their books themselves. Hacon & Ricketts provided the Pissarros with a list of their trade and private clients to get them started, but also, trying to finish up their publishing program, Hacon & Ricketts had saturated the market with many new Vale Press books in a depressed economy. In this difficult economic climate the Pissarros began as publishers, with little knowledge of bookselling and without a solid network to the trade.

Lucien and Esther considered several options, including selling their books by subscription to private buyers, as Cobden-Sanderson of the Doves

Press was doing. Holmes suggested that Lucien borrow Cobden-Sanderson's list of private buyers to begin,[54] but unfortunately neither Lucien nor Esther knew Cobden-Sanderson well enough to make such a request. The Pissarros hired a young man, Albert Morelli, who had worked for Hacon & Ricketts, to be the Press' secretary and business manager on a part-time basis. As compensation Morelli agreed to a 5 percent commission on the books that he sold.

The Eragny Press negotiated with John Lane for the American sales of their future publications. Lane, who had regularly bought the editions which Hacon & Ricketts published, sold them through his New York branch. Lane was not happy with the terms the Eragny Press proposed—30 percent of the retail price with three months' credit. To the trade in general, Lucien extended terms of 20 percent of the retail price for cash with order. Lucien explained to Lane the reasons he could neither submit better terms nor equal those which Hacon & Ricketts had offered. The cost of his production was high, and the Press produced fewer books than the Vale Press, as well as a smaller number of copies.[55] However, if Lane would promise to take a certain number, say fifty copies, the Eragny Press could offer a 35 percent discount off the retail price, two free copies (50/52), and three months' credit. Lane and the Pissarros finally reached an agreement. For 80 percent of the Eragny Press publications, Lane would purchase fifty copies, receiving two free (50/52), at a 35 percent discount. For the remaining 20 percent of Eragny publications, Lane would buy twenty-five copies at a 20 percent discount. If, however, Lane were to take an additional twenty-five copies, he would receive the full discount as if he had bought fifty copies all at once. This agreement would give Lane a monopoly on the American market for Eragny Press books. Lane began by buying twenty-five (and receiving one free) copies (25/26) of *A Brief Account of the Origin of the Eragny Press,* which were dispatched to him in late September 1903.[56]

Prospectus. *Some Poems by Robert Browning,* 1904. (Ashmolean Museum, Oxford)

Albert Morelli should have been a great asset to the Press. He knew how Hacon & Ricketts had negotiated the London and country trade as well as how they handled their accounts. While he did manage to sell a number of copies of *A Brief Account of the Origin of the Eragny Press* to private clients, his sales record was not particularly successful. Without a steady income from book sales, the Pissarros could not afford to continue printing. In 1904, four books appeared: *The Descent of Ishtar, Areopagitica, Some Poems of Robert Browning,* and Coleridge's *Christabel, Kubla Khan.* The sales continued to be discouraging. Lucien believed that Morelli had lost their London clientele.[57] Undoubtedly the reasons for the poor sales were more complicated. The Eragny Press bibliography, produced in *A Brief Account of the Origin of the Eragny Press,* was a very cautious debut for the Eragny Press. Rather than forward-looking, it was retrospective and nostalgic. The Pissarros must have believed that the clients who had bought the Vale series would like to have a bibliography and perhaps saw it as a marketing tool, providing potential buyers with enticing examples of Eragny Press publications. They were also influenced by the bibliography Ricketts planned to do of the Vale Press as its closing book; a far more appropriate choice than for a press that was beginning again. The second book of the Brook series, *The Descent of Ishtar*, used a slight text of limited interest and a frontispiece by an unknown artist. The first two books in the Brook series did not sell as well as they had anticipated. To survive between books and to enable them to continue printing, they borrowed money from a bank on the good name of Esther's brother, Sam Bensusan.[58]

The arrangement with Morelli lasted until December 1904. In addition to thinking Morelli had lost them the London trade, the Pissarros felt that he was not giving enough time to work their business "in a manner to make it satisfactory"[59] to both of them. The relationship which the Pissarros had with Morelli gives some insight into their business dealings. First, there is nothing that would indicate that either Lucien or Esther had much of a business sense. Because they were so personally involved in the production of the Press, any slight to the books was also a personal slight to them. This was more true for Esther than for Lucien. The Pissarros found Morelli "cheeky," but Morelli undoubtedly found Esther too fussy, too exacting. Since Morelli was receiving a commission as their business manager, it did not make much sense that they neither asked him for his advice nor, when he gave it, at least considered it. The real crisis came when, after three books and few sales, the Pissarros grew suspicious of Morelli.

Morelli had recommended printing *Some Poems by Robert Browning* and also advised them on the price they should charge. The Pissarros did not heed his advice. They priced the Browning at thirty shillings and made very few sales. Morelli had advised them to sell the book at a lower price. He believed they would make up in volume of sales what they lost in the selling price of each book. Perhaps what Morelli could not understand was how labor intensive their books were, as well as the need for the Pissarros to feel adequately compensated for all the work that they had put into each book. In any case, the Pissarros in late November 1904 decided to terminate their association with Morelli. In lieu of the obligatory three months' notification, the Pissarros promised to continue to give Morelli the commission on John Lane's order as long as the agreement continued. But Morelli was unsatisfied by their offer, and since he insisted upon a firm three-month termination notice, he felt that he had a right to more. His contract with the Pissarros entitled him to that notice or one quarter of the year's commission, which the Pissarros had estimated at £5 (Morelli estimated it at £8).[60] In order to settle with Morelli, Lucien offered him £10; Morelli wanted to seek out Ricketts' advice, but Ricketts did not wish to involve himself. Morelli believed that he should be compensated for all standing orders in addition to Lane's. But Esther, at least, considered standing orders no more the result of Morelli's efforts than the result of anyone else who had addressed prospectuses to persons whose names were given to them.[61] She disputed that Morelli had added 200 names to the Vale Press list and noted that there were only 248 names in Morelli's address book—77 trade customers and 141 private customers. The Pissarros finally gave into Morelli's demands, paying him £14.07.00.

In November, with the dismissal of Albert Morelli, Esther contacted Keith Johnston, to whom she was referred by the book dealer, Wilfrid Voynich,[62] hoping he would undertake the sale of Eragny Press books.

Johnston knew that the sale of private press books had fallen off in the last several years, and the book trade as a whole was depressed.[63] He proposed undertaking the sale of their books if he could receive a 15 percent commission on the paper copies and 10 percent on the more expensive vellum copies. The commission would be payable upon receipt of the orders by the Eragny Press. Johnston would be responsible for neither the delivery of the books, nor the collections of the accounts. Johnston also proposed that it would be best to fix no period for the arrangement between them, since the Eragny Press might find a better plan for selling their books, or because Johnston might not find the work sufficiently remunerative.[64]

The Pissarros and Johnston agreed to a 10 percent commission on the published price for paper copies and 10 percent for the vellum on the published price less the 20 percent discount to the booksellers.[65] They would pay his commission on the first of every month. In undertaking to sell Eragny Press books, Johnston faced a challenge. Since the closing of the Vale Press, the Eragny Press had published five books, of which two hundred copies of each title were for sale. The sales had not been of any great consequence and continued to dwindle.

Bibliography	150 copies sold
Ishtar	116 copies sold
Areopagitica	70 copies sold
(reprint ed., 134 copies for sale)	
Browning	110 copies sold
Christabel	58 copies sold[66]

Because Johnston was unable to earn enough commission from the poor sales, he gave up working actively for the Pissarros in April 1905. He would continue, however, to sell a few books occasionally for them for the next several years. They believed that Johnston had been fair and honest with them. The conclusion of the agreement was amiable, and the Pissarros often turned to him for advice.

Since Floury's purchase of the Perrault in 1899, Lucien had sold very few books to the continental market. With Hacon & Ricketts buying his editions outright, he no longer concentrated on the continental markets. In the fall of 1903 and the spring of 1904, Lucien spent a number of weeks in France, mostly for the purpose of settling Camille's will. He also used this time to resume his French contacts, seeing what might be available to him in France. Now, anything he could make would be valuable to him and essential if he were to continue to derive an income from the Press. It became a question then of making his books known to the French public, who were unaccustomed to his genre of publication. Lucien's complete control over the production of his books gave them a unity, he believed, impossible to obtain with production influenced by several people.

In November 1903, at the time of Camille's death, Lucien made contacts with some of his old friends—Gabriel Mourey and Georges Lecomte, who promised to announce Lucien's books in their new art magazine; and Roger Milès, who was going to introduce him to the book dealer at *Figaro,* who he believed would take a subscription for several copies;[67] however, this dealer did not think he could interest his clients.[68] He contacted Ambroise Vollard, who asked him to send prospectuses of Eragny Press publications. Vollard offered to give Lucien a list of Parisian bibliophiles and wanted to introduce Lucien to a dealer specializing in rare and antiquarian books.[69] Lucien later discovered the dealer was not interested.[70]

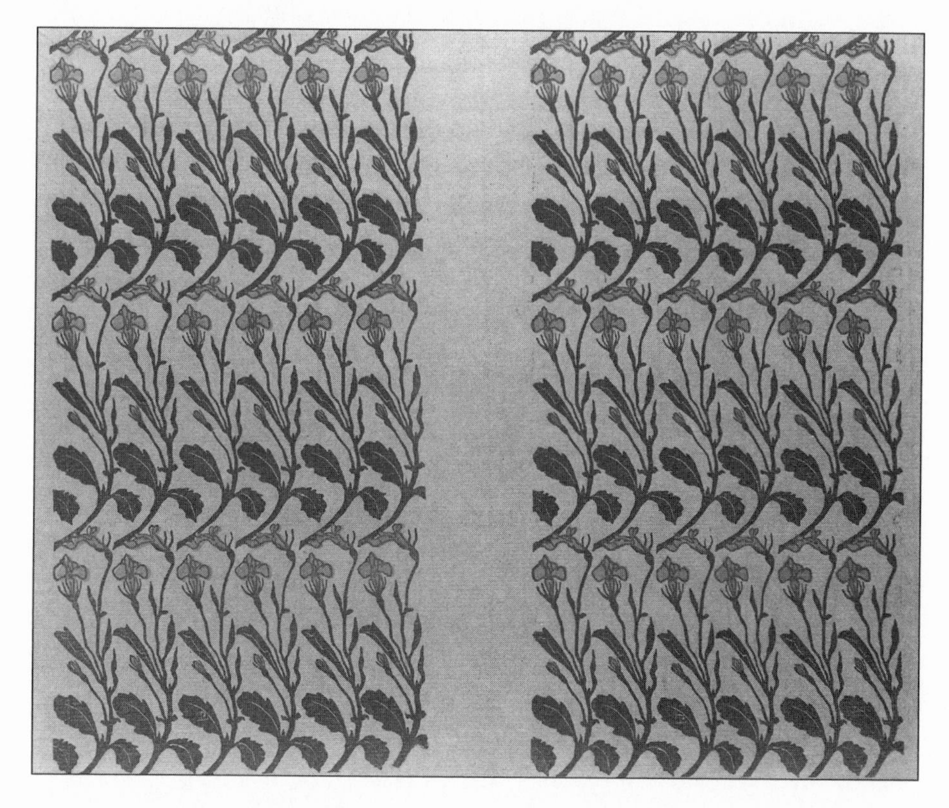

"Verbena" binding paper. *C'est d'Aucassin et de Nicolete,* 1903. (Ashmolean Museum, Oxford)

When Hacon & Ricketts closed in the summer of 1903, fifty copies of *C'est d'Aucassin and de Nicolete,* the last Eragny Press book done in the Vale type, remained unsold.[71] The Pissarros bought back these copies, and Lucien left copies of the book on deposit at Bing's Maison de l'art nouveau. The dealer was enthusiastic about Lucien's book. Lucien also began to promote the "Série Camille Pissarro." The dealer at Bing's thought he could place easily fifty copies.[72] The sale of books would be directed towards collectors.

Lucien began to seek a financial backer for his "Série Camille Pissarro" from the now powerful bibliophile societies. A commission would provide the Pissarros with a certain amount of financial security because the society would cover the expenses of the book as well as provide a ready market. In the best possible arrangement, a profit would be made. Félix Fénéon once again offered his services, introducing Lucien to Pierre Dauze, the founder of the Société des XX, established in 1897. The society regularly commissioned twenty copies of an original edition, the choice of which was dictated either by its literary, historic, or artistic interest. Often the club would choose unknown but promising young authors. Working in collaboration with a publisher, the society furnished the publisher with deluxe paper for these twenty copies. Once the twenty copies were printed, the publisher would have the work printed in a different format for the trade edition. The only expenses incurred by the society were the paper and the cost of printing the twenty copies.[73] Because the paper would be furnished, their expense would be minimal, but there were complications. The Eragny Press' agreement with John Lane prevented them from pursuing this commission or any commission. Because all books printed in the Brook type were promised to Lane, unless Lucien could get the society to have a special type made, he could not print them without risking his business with Lane. Because Le Société des XX was founded on the basis of few expenses, incurring the cost of a new type would not have been feasible for them. Fénéon was certain that Dauze could give Lucien useful information on which booksellers would take his books. Dauze highly recommended Floury with whom Lucien had had so much trouble previously. After visiting several bookdealers in Paris, Lucien came to the conclusion that Floury was the only man who was capable of promoting Eragny Press books in Paris; books illustrated with woodblocks had become his specialty. Lucien also understood that Floury was now in a better financial position than he had been in 1899. The other dealers recommended by Dauze (who are not identified) were willing to take two copies of each book with prospectuses on deposit. With too small a profit margin, the dealers were not willing to put much effort into selling the books. Preferring books with illustrations spilling into the margins and white spaces on the page, these dealers were still the tastemakers in Paris, their clientele buying what they declared to be in good taste. With visits to these dealers, Lucien was no longer convinced that his Camille Pissarro series would do well in Paris. It was necessary to wait before proceeding with it.[74] Lucien spent much time and effort in Paris to promote his work, but with very little result.

The books of the Brook series all had English texts, and Lucien had doubted they would be of much interest to the French market. However, in late 1904 with *Old French and English Ballads* in production, Lucien believed that he had a book in which the French bibliophiles would be interested. He began to reestablish his contacts in Paris which he had abandoned earlier that year. He approached Mazandier, a dealer at Bing's Maison de l'art nouveau, to see whether he would be able to find a clientele for his books. Lucien explained to Mazandier how special his books were, and particularly emphasized the care that was taken in making them. But Lucien was convinced that the purely typographic book was still not understood in Paris. He offered Mazandier a 20 percent commission. If he sold more than twenty-five copies, the commission would rise to 30 percent. But nothing came from their discussion.

Resigned, Lucien contacted Floury. He tried to mend the difference which had arisen over the settlement of the account of Perrault's *Deux contes de ma mère l'oye*. Floury had delayed paying Lucien, forcing him to borrow money to pay his expenses at the time. Lucien did not particularly trust Floury, but his financial situation, now precarious, forced him into renewing contact with him concerning the sales of his books in France. Lucien also approached the art critic Theodore Duret, who had offered to introduce him to Anatole France. Lucien thought that if he could print an unpublished work by a major French author he could attract the attention of the French bibliophiles. He was particularly attracted to Anatole France because he admired his work and because he believed that France might be sympathetic to his books. He was prepared to pay France for the rights to publish his work, but he would not be able to pay until the book was published and returning his investment. Contact with Anatole France was finally made through Félix Fénéon, but unfortunately, France had nothing prepared that would be appropriate to Lucien's format. Lucien also contacted the publisher Carteret,[75] a major dealer of classic editions in deluxe formats. He explained to agents at Carteret that while his clientele was presently made up of English-language bibliophiles, he would be pleased to prepare a book that would attract the attention of French collectors. But nothing came of this discussion with Carteret or from this trip to Paris.

In the spring of 1904, Esther's father, Jacob Bensusan, who had mellowed over the years in his attitude toward Lucien, also took an interest in the marketing of the Eragny Press books. He made arrangements with the Literary Agency of London, run by G. H. Perris and C. F. Cazenove,[76] to find and make arrangements with a publisher to sell Eragny Press books. Perris and Cazenove solicited the booksellers Brown, Langham and Co.[77] The Pissarros wanted Brown, Langham, in a general agreement, to buy one hundred copies outright at a discount of 33 1/3 percent and to act as their agents for the sale of fifty more copies at 20 percent of the published price. Of the eight vellum copies which the Eragny Press had for sale, seven of them were reserved for standing orders which the Pissarros would sell directly to their clientele.[78] As publishers, Brown, Langham wanted some control over the choice of books. Lucien was pleased to have advice and suggestions as to the choice of texts, but he would only undertake those works that distinctly appealed to him. It was necessary to preserve the freedom to choose the decoration, the arrangement, and the manner of production.[79] Thus this proposal was rejected; Brown, Langham countered with an offer to sell one hundred copies on sale or return, for which they would get a discount of 16 2/3, less 10 percent of the published price. In addition, the Pissarros would give them the names of their London trade customers and hand over any orders they might receive from the London trade. With this agreement, Brown, Langham became the sole dealer for the London trade and local customers. The Pissarros reserved the right to sell to private customers and directly to country dealers. Difficulties were encountered with London trade customers. The Pissarros worried that if their trade customers were not given the standard 20 percent for cash, the bookdealers would only buy the number of copies needed to satisfy the orders placed with them and would do nothing more to promote the sale of the book. The vellum copies could not be sold on deposit, but were to be sold outright to Brown, Langham, because these were especially delicate and susceptible to damp weather. The contract was finally signed in mid-June 1904, and fifty copies of Milton's *Areopagitica* with prospectuses were sent to Brown, Langham. The Browning edition, with three hundred prospectuses, was promised at the end of the month.[80]

The Pissarros provided Brown, Langham with a list of the dealers who were customers of the Eragny Press.

J. Zachendorf, 146 Shaftsbury Avenue
F. Denny, 147 Strand
Jones & Evans, 77 Queen Street, E. C.
Dobell, 77 Charing Cross Rd.
Williams & Norgate, 14 Henrietta Street, W. C.
Harrison & Sons, Pall Mall
Quaritch, 15 Picadilly W.
Grant Richards, 48 Leicester Square
W. H. Smith & Sons, Book Department, Arundel Street
Henry Bumpus, 335 Holborn
Bookshops Ltd., 9 Arundel Street, Strand[81]

With the commencement of their agreement Brown, Langham wanted the Pissarros to print their names in the books as they had done for Hacon & Ricketts. The Pissarros were reluctant to do this since Brown, Langham were taking the books on sale or return; they were happy to place the name on the prospectuses which Brown, Langham would send out.[82] As a precedent, Brown, Langham cited the arrangement the Essex House Press had with Edward Arnold. The Pissarros did not believe that any arrangement the Essex House Press had could be used as a standard. Considering the careful negotiations made through Cazenove, the association with Brown, Langham was not a smooth one. Typically, Brown, Langham were not particularly punctilious dealers; they did not keep the Pissarros informed of their sales; and, perhaps more importantly, they did not keep regular accounts. By early September 1904, no money from the sale of the books was forthcoming, although the date for the settlements of accounts was the fifteenth of each month. The Pissarros were also disappointed by their first-month sale after publication, which was far less than what Esther and Lucien Pissarro had sold to the London trade in the same amount of time. In three months' time Brown, Langham were not successful in marketing *Areopagitica* nor the Browning, selling fourteen *Areopagitica*s and seven Brownings. By early October 1904, the Pissarros terminated their contract with Brown, Langham and returned to self-publishing.

With the termination of their agreement with Brown, Langham, the Pissarros contacted various booksellers. To Frank Hollings, who sold both rare and miscellaneous books,[83] they proposed their ordinary trade terms of a 20 percent discount for cash. But Hollings could not agree to those terms and proposed a discount of 33 1/3 percent. The only way the Pissarros could agree to so high a discount would be if he could guarantee the sale of fifty copies. The Pissarros would also require quarterly payments. But no deal with Hollings was made.

They also wrote to Bernard Quaritch, seeking an arrangement with him to sell fifty to one hundred copies at a substantial discount. They wrote to Francis Edwards, asking him to publish Eragny Press books.[84] He replied that he could not possibly take over the agency for their books—"They are nice books but I have few customers who would care for them."[85]

In February and again in March 1905, the bookdealer Simpkin, Marshall and Co. offered to become London agents for Eragny Press books. The Pissarros sent a friend, E. L. Levetus, to act as intermediary to see what arrangements might be made with them. H. E. Barton, one of the sales people at Simpkin, Marshall, was not inclined to take any risk on the books by buying them outright, unless after experience they were to find a steady demand for the books.[86] Simpkin, Marshall were willing to distribute prospectuses and have their travelers push the sales of Eragny Press books, both in London and the provinces, in return for a 30 percent discount. The Pissarros agreed to this proposal, the 30 percent being a 10 percent commission over the trade price. In addition, Simpkin, Marshall were to avoid approaching the Press' steady trade customers. These were the trade customers whom the Pissarros reserved for themselves:

London:	*Country:*
Ellis & Elvey	Howell, Cardiff
Jones & Evans	Sherratt & Hughes, Manchester
J. J. Leighton	Cornish Bros., Birmingham
Maggs Bros.	W. Downing, Birmingham
Robson	Commin, Exeter
Elliot Stock	Otto Schultze, Edinburgh
Tregaskis	Blackwell's, Oxford
B. Quaritch	
Zaehnsdorf	*Foreign:*
Williams & Norgate	Schelteme & Holkems, Amsterdam
John Lane	Hiersemann, Leipzig
(American agent)	E. Meyer, Berlin[87]

Prospectuses were provided as well as a sample copy for their traveler. This agreement with Simpkin, Marshall lasted until 1907, but Esther believed, poor sales confirming, that their salesmen really did little to promote Eragny Press books.

Laurence Binyon, Keeper of the Department of Prints and Drawings at the British Museum, had been acquainted with Lucien since the early nineties. In September 1904, he wrote to Lucien concerning the printing of a book of his short love poems.[88] Binyon noted that it would be a great honor and pleasure for his poems to appear in the Brook type.[89] The book, *Dream-Come-True,* is illustrated with a woodblock frontispiece designed by Binyon. Lucien estimated the approximate cost of the book at £44.14.00, which included a 20 percent charge for Lucien's labor. With Lane taking fifty copies and with twenty-three regular clients, Lucien believed that seventy-three books would be sold in advance. This would cover the cost of production. If the edition of 150 copies were to sell out, Lucien calculated an additional profit of £50 to divide between them.[90] In fact, even with the split profit, the Pissarros did rather well with this book. Binyon, a young poet, had a wide circle of friends and many connections. *Dream-Come-True* sold well not because of its physical trappings, but due to the author's popularity.

Inspired by rapid sales of the book, Lucien conceived of a series of books by contemporary English poets. He was now convinced that original texts would sell better than the reprinted texts which they had been doing—texts which were available in cheap reprinted editions. His second and last attempt in this "series" was a book of children's poems written by T. S. Moore, entitled *The Little School.* Again, this book attracted more sales than usual, not on the merits of the Eragny Press, but on the reputation of Moore. With a combination of the steady clientele of the Press and the substantial circle of friends and colleagues of the author, they were able to make enough sales to earn a profit.

Even with these two successes, the Pissarros remained in financial straits. John Lane, in the summer of 1905, having sold his American business, wished to terminate his agreement with the Eragny Press. The Pissarros had relied on Lane's purchase of fifty copies to keep the Press solvent. Without that sure income, their thoughts turned to retiring the Press and relying on Lucien's engravings and paintings as a source of income. They considered augmenting their income by renting their printing studio to a sculptor who would lodge and take meals with them.[91] But somehow the Pissarros forged ahead. They began to seek other arrangements for distribution of their books in America. With one of their American collectors acting as an intermediary, they approached Scribner's in New York. The reply was discouraging:

I. BEAUTIFUL MEALS.

HOW nice it is to eat!
All creatures love it so;
That they who first did spread,
Ere breaking bread,
A cloth like level snow
Were right I know:

And they were wise and sweet
Who, glad that meats taste good,
Used speech in an arch style
And oft would smile
To raise the cheerful mood
While at their food:

And those who first, so neat,
8

"Mother and Child," wood engraving by T. S. Moore. T. S. Moore, *The Little School*, 1905. (Ashmolean Museum, Oxford)

> There are many reasons why the books issued by the Press should meet with good market, and should be readily sold in this country as well as in England, for the work of that Press is very beautiful, and is sure to have a future, if there is to be a future for any of the Privately Printed Presses. We regret, however, a re-action on Privately Printed Books, and this is so decided that it has become extremely difficult to place more than a very few copies of any book. . . .[92]

With word out that John Lane was no longer their American publisher, several offers, however, came to them. Gardner C. Teall, a dealer for the firm of Robert Grier Cook, was highly interested in acting as their representative, but found their terms quite impossible. These terms were for the sole agency for the United States and Canada:

> 1. That the agent shall buy outright 50 paper copies of all books issued by our press. The edition being never more, and sometimes less, than 226 copies of which 200 are for sale (of the last two books only 175 have been printed of which 150 for sale) also 10 copies on vellum of which 8 are for sale
> 2. That he should buy them at 35% less than the English published price
> 3. That we should have absolute liberty as to choice, arrangement and price of books issued, also date of publication
> 4. That the agent shall receive informal notice of the next book as soon as the work is started, but particulars as to price, date of publication will be communicated later
> 5. That the book shall be dispatched carriage forward by first mail after publication

6. That the agent shall send a cheque in payment three weeks after dispatch of books
7. That the name of the agent shall be printed in the books
8. That any orders for paper copies of our books sent to us direct from the United States and Canada shall be handed to the agent
9. That to end the agreement six months notice shall be given on either side.[93]

Teall, evidently an astute businessman, found that while it would be a great pleasure to handle Eragny Press books, "at the same time it would appear to be a luxury that could not be sanctioned immediately by conservatism."[94] Teall complained that with custom duties, carriage fees, etc., nothing would be left for the dealer "but the glory of handling the products"[95] of the Eragny Press. The contract that Lucien had proposed struck Teall as "thoroughly impracticable and unproductive of solid results, artistically or financially."[96]

In November 1905, not finding an American agent willing to agree to their terms, the Pissarros resolved to publish their books in America themselves with no real notion of how to do so. How would they advertise, send prospectuses, set prices—the English published price plus duty?—and would buyers have to go to the custom house each time to pick up the book? Fortunately, Lucien's cousin Alfred Isaacson, who resided in America, was willing to help. One of their major American collectors, J. M. Andreini of New York City, an attorney, to whom they dedicated *Songs by Ben Jonson,* also acted as an American intermediary.[97] He sent them lists of potential collectors.

The first book which the Pissarros tried to publish in America was *La Belle dame sans merci,* a New Year's gift book, which sold for five shillings. Prospectuses were sent to possible clients and dealers, but because the book appeared too late for the season, the Pissarros decided to reserve their major effort for *Songs by Ben Jonson.* The book, published in April 1906, had sold only three copies in America by late July. (In England, thirty-five paper and six vellum copies had been sold.)[98] Obviously, their self-publishing program was not satisfactory.

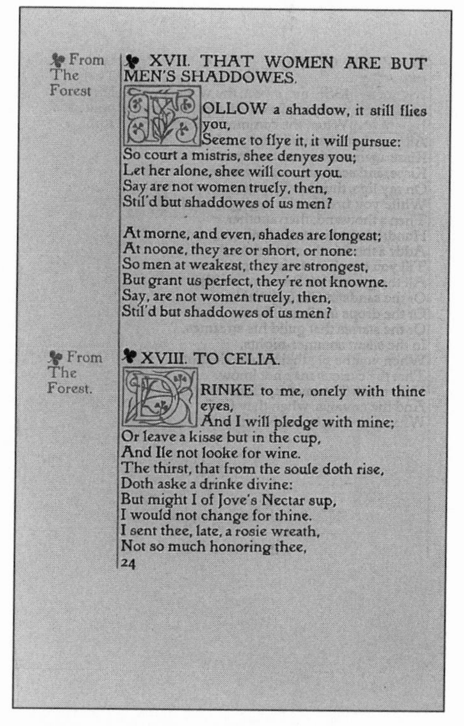
From The Forest

XVII. THAT WOMEN ARE BUT MEN'S SHADDOWES.

FOLLOW a shaddow, it still flies you,
Seeme to flye it, it will pursue:
So court a mistris, shee denyes you;
Let her alone, shee will court you.
Say are not women truely, then,
Stil'd but shaddowes of us men?

At morne, and even, shades are longest;
At noone, they are or short, or none:
So men at weakest, they are strongest,
But grant us perfect, they're not knowne.
Say, are not women truely, then,
Stil'd but shaddowes of us men?

From The Forest.

XVIII. TO CELIA.

DRINKE to me, onely with thine eyes,
And I will pledge with mine;
Or leave a kisse but in the cup,
And Ile not looke for wine.
The thirst, that from the soule doth rise,
Doth aske a drinke divine:
But might I of Jove's Nectar sup,
I would not change for thine.
I sent thee, late, a rosie wreath,
Not so much honoring thee,
24

Songs by Ben Jonson, 1906; p. 25. (Ashmolean Museum, Oxford)

In late April G. P. Putnam's Sons' London office contacted the Pissarros. Putnam's had seen in the *Athenaeum* magazine an announcement of *Songs by Ben Jonson,* and expressed an interest in arranging for the American market, but were informed that an arrangement had already been made for its American sale. By late May, the Pissarros were writing to Putnam's, letting them know that the sale of *Songs by Ben Jonson* had proved unsatisfactory and they would be willing to reconsider an arrangement for selling their books in America.[99] For the sole agency in America, the Pissarros offered these terms to Putnam's: a 35 percent discount with the purchase of fifty copies; 40 percent discount with the purchase of one hundred copies. The books would be delivered to Putnam's London office, with payment required seven days after delivery.[100] But Putnam declined the Pissarros' offer without giving any definite reason.[101]

Alfred Issacson put F.E.L. Watson in contact with the Pissarros.

Watson, a bookdealer from Lenox, Massachusetts, was willing to undertake the sales of their books on a commission basis. Under their agreement he would receive a 20 percent discount off the English prices. Watson suggested that if the Pissarros could allow for a larger commission it would be better, ". . . not that it would put any more money into my pocket but because it would make the selling price a little lower. You see as it is now I have to pay for the books 5% more than you charge for them in England, and have to add my profit to that."[102] Lucien and Esther thought the matter over and decided to allow Watson a 25 percent rather than the originally proposed 20 percent discount.[103] By the end of 1907, Watson had "a lot of people interested"[104] and planned to devote a great deal of his time to promoting the books. Watson appeared to be enthusiastic about the books, but with time he grew lax in his accounting, probably because the sales were not large. He did not keep the Pissarros informed on a regular basis. They grew frustrated by this because they were desperate for every pound they could bring in from sales of the books, but undoubtedly they were unreasonably expectant.

The disappointing sales of *Songs by Ben Jonson*, a book which cost £112 to produce, not allowing for their labor, yielded £89. Lucien returned to painting in the morning, and he and Esther printed in the afternoon by themselves. They were working on Christina Rossetti's *Verses*, a work which had been privately printed in 1847. In late July 1906, all but three formes of the book had been printed when they received notice from Macmillan and Co. of their copyright infringement. William Rossetti, who was trustee of his sister Christina Rossettti's estate, called Macmillan's attention to a notice of the Eragny Press edition in the *Athenaeum*. The Pissarros had thought the work public property. Because some of the poems had not actually been published until 1896, after the author's death, the copyright dated from 1896 rather than 1847. To abandon the edition at this point would have meant a serious loss for the Pissarros. They argued with Macmillan and Co. that they could hardly be regarded as competitors to such a great publishing firm since their edition of 150 copies would appeal to a very small class of collectors. They asked Macmillan to permit them to publish the edition with due acknowledgement to Macmillan and W. M. Rossetti, who actually owned the copyright.[105] Because they were also printing poems which did not appear in the 1896 volume entitled *New Poems* but were in the 1847 privately printed edition, these pieces were still considered to be private property of William Rossetti. He preferred those particular poems to be omitted from the Eragny Press edition, but he agreed to their publication in consideration of a payment of £25. This demand was yet another blow the Press could ill afford.

Lucien, convinced that no matter what type of text they printed, whether a popular English classic, a contemporary one, or one in the French language, made no difference in their sales, concluded that their only option was to reduce the size of the edition.[106] When they printed *Riquet à la houpe* in the spring of 1907, they decreased their output and printed eighty paper copies and eight vellum copies. With so limited an edition they were printing for their regular clientele, a clientele they could depend on to buy whatever they would print. By limiting the size of the edition, the expenses of paper and presswork were greatly reduced. The choice of a French text was another attempt to attract French bibliophiles. The next book the Pissarros planned was an edition of some songs of Robert Herrick to be sold on a subscription basis. The Herrick was seen as a companion volume to the two previous songbooks the Pissarros had done, *Some Old French and English Ballads* and *Songs by Ben Jonson*. Surely they must have thought that their clientele would want to complete their series of music books by the Eragny Press. They planned to close the subscription period in September 1907. The Pissarros turned more and more to America to sell their books. Through Andrieni, contact was made with the Grolier Club, which the Pissarros hoped would commission them to do a book. For the Herrick, the Pissarros suggested that if the Grolier Club cared to subscribe, they would be willing to make some difference in the printing of part of the edition.[107] Neither subscriptions nor commissions for the Herrick were forthcoming, and during the summer of 1907, the Pissarros abandoned the Press and Lucien returned to painting. When notice of the "failure" of the Eragny Press appeared in the *Academy*, the publisher Grant Richards wrote to the Pissarros "in order that I could see whether this house could not make some arrangement by which the continuation of your work should be assured."[108] However, after careful consideration of the question of the publication of the Eragny Press books, Richards came to this conclusion:

> . . . for the present at least it is unlikely that it will be possible to revive the Englishman's interest in the private press. That interest will come back, but it will not be, as far as I can judge, until the public has absorbed the various productions of other presses not so worthy that the bookselling trade is at present saddled with. It would have given me great pleasure to have been associated with you, even in the secondary capacity of distributor, in the production of a series of books which I admire so much as those for which you have been responsible.[109]

Grant Richards summarized the Pissarros' dilemma perfectly. They were creating beautiful books which were much admired, but were working, and had been working, for four years in a depressed market. Their prices were too high to attract a large number of customers in a competitive market. Perhaps if they had found someone who could have aggressively marketed their books, they may have found a larger market. It certainly was not for a lack of hard work, integrity or artistic ability. *Riquet à la houpe,* aimed at the French market and steadfast Eragny Press collectors, was the Pissarros' last attempt at marketing. Printed in an edition of only eighty copies, this small book sold rather well.

The Pissarros produced one more book in 1911, *Album de poëmes tirés du livre de jade,* printed between commissions, for which they sought subscriptions from their regular British and American clientele and from members of the French bibliophile clubs. Written by Judith Gautier, *Livre de jade,* based on Chinese tales, was conceived as a "pot boiler,"[110] an album of stunning engravings with very little text. Lucien entered into negotia-

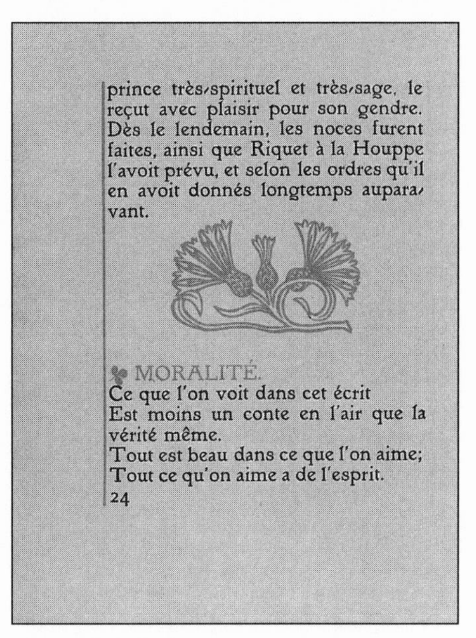
prince très-spirituel et très-sage, le reçut avec plaisir pour son gendre. Dès le lendemain, les noces furent faites, ainsi que Riquet à la Houppe l'avoit prévu, et selon les ordres qu'il en avoit donnés longtemps aupara-vant.

MORALITÉ.

Ce que l'on voit dans cet écrit
Est moins un conte en l'air que la vérité même.
Tout est beau dans ce que l'on aime;
Tout ce qu'on aime a de l'esprit.

24

Charles Perrault, *Riquet à la houppe,* 1907; p. 24. (Ashmolean Museum, Oxford)

tions with Maurice Joyant of the Goupil Gallery in Paris, one of the major art dealers in Impressionism. Many of the unsold Eragny Press books were placed on deposit there. Roger Marx also suggested Lucien seek subscribers from the many bibliophile societies in Paris. With enough subscribers in France, Lucien would have a secure financial base from which to work. A group of at least forty subscribers in France would enable Lucien to avoid bargaining with the French dealers. Marx procured membership lists from several of the clubs including Le Livre contemporain. Subscription prospectuses were sent out to these various memberships. Within four months, Lucien had received twelve paid subscriptions.[111] The apathy of the French book collectors was not surprising to Lucien. To counter the French apathy, Marx promised Lucien that he would contact book collectors in Germany and Holland who were more enthusiastic.

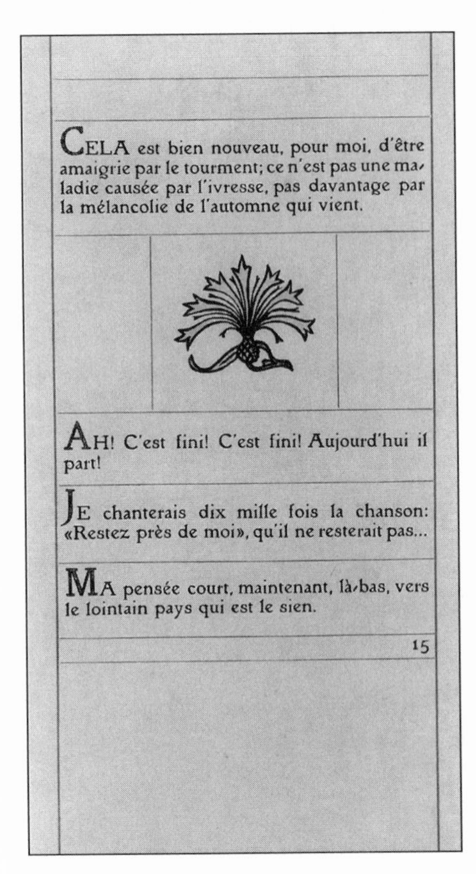
CELA est bien nouveau, pour moi, d'être amaigrie par le tourment; ce n'est pas une maladie causée par l'ivresse, pas davantage par la mélancolie de l'automne qui vient.

AH! C'est fini! C'est fini! Aujourd'hui il part!

JE chanterais dix mille fois la chanson: «Restez près de moi», qu'il ne resterait pas...

MA pensée court, maintenant, là-bas, vers le lointain pays qui est le sien.

15

Judith Gautier, *Album de poëmes tirés du livre de jade*, 1911; p. 15. (Ashmolean Museum, Oxford)

Of the 125 copies for sale, only about half the edition sold initially. From 1908 until 1911, when *Livre de jade* was completed, the Pissarros had not had a new book on the market. Thus, it may be assumed that much of their potential clientele in England and America had forgotten the Press. While they were able to attract some French customers, mainly from Les Cent bibliophiles and Le Livre contemporain, Lucien's notion of book design did not readily mesh with the French concept, which still advocated abundant white spaces on text pages. In fact, rarity of the edition was still more important than well-conceived design. In addition, at this point, around 1910–11, single prints were once again in vogue, making the sale of books more difficult.

Although the Pissarros were no longer actively printing for the English market, they did have large stocks of books left over. Over the next five years, several bookdealers and private buyers bought an occasional book, but the Eragny Press' major promoter came from a young man living in Kansas City, Missouri—Harry Alfred Fowler. A native Missourian born in 1889, Fowler was a young man enamored of the Arts and Crafts movement and an active collector of Kelmscott and Doves Press books. He was editor and publisher of an occasional magazine devoted to book-plates, bibliophilism, and art, entitled the *Ex Libran*. Fowler was put in touch with the Pissarros through J. M. Andrieni, who had written an article on the book-plates of the Eragny Press for the *Ex Libran*.[112] Fowler borrowed from the Pissarros electrotypes of the book-plates to illustrate Andrieni's article. From this initial contact, Fowler would remain in contact with the Pissarros over the next decade. As a collector, Fowler was interested in vellum copies; he placed an initial order for vellum copies of *A Brief Account of the Origin of the Eragny Press, Some Old French and English Ballads,* and *Songs by Ben Jonson*. He commissioned Lucien to design and print a book-plate which he would use only in his Eragny Press books. In November 1912, Fowler made a "pilgrimage" to Hammersmith. His visit to England and to the Pissarros inspired him to commission a book from the Eragny Press. He proposed that Lucien design and print twenty copies on vellum of William Cullen Bryant's poem "Thanatopsis." Fowler would pay all expenses. Having recently finished a book for a French bibliophile society, Lucien was in no rush to do it, but in due course, he commenced the design for

Fowler's book. Fowler, wanting to use as his copy text the first edition of the poem, delayed the project when he could not find a copy. In late July 1913, he believed that this might be for the best because he did not feel that he could afford the publication after all.

In January 1913, Fowler proposed to sell Eragny Press books in America, believing that if American collectors knew about the books they would want to purchase copies. He offered to work for a 20 percent commission on the copies he could sell, or for a 10 percent commission for all books sold in America by other dealers. He would not agree to take any specific number of copies, but rather would simply work to sell all that he could of them.[113] He planned to advertise the books in his new magazine, the *Biblio*, and hoped that his commission would cover the cost of advertising. Fowler did not want to enter into a business venture; he preferred to sell books for his pleasure and pastime. Lucien agreed to his plan and sent Fowler one hundred prospectuses. In fact, Fowler planned a strong advertising campaign. An advertisement would appear in the fifteen hundred copies of an issue of the *Biblio*; Fowler was preparing a small catalog of Eragny Press books in twenty-five hundred copies, and with the one hundred prospectuses a total of forty-one hundred notices would be sent to American book-lovers. On 1 April, Fowler sent Lucien his first statement of account: "No Sales."[114] Fowler had received several inquiries, however. April, May, and June passed and Fowler still had made no sales. In November, he finally sold one copy of *The Descent of Ishtar*. Fowler resolved

> . . . to continue patiently to endeavor to dispose of the copies. It is rather disgusting to think of the depraved taste of the average American book-buyer, is it not? But I think that it is due to lack of knowledge of the beauties of the books quite as much as to anything else.[115]

By April 1914, Fowler had sold two more books. Fowler continued to sell a book occasionally and he persisted in attempting the sale of their books until 1919 without much success.

Fowler was an enthusiastic supporter of the Pissarros. How effective his sales technique was is difficult to discern, but he was in contact with members of the Grolier Club and other book-collectors. It would seem that his sales attempts should have provided more results than they did, but the American market, like the British, was depressed as well as saturated with fine press productions. In any event, Fowler endeared himself to the Pissarros for all of his efforts, so that when they considered resuming the Press in 1920, after World War I, they thought of Fowler's "Thanatopsis" as the first book in their new series.

Commissions

Since his father's death, whenever Lucien grew perplexed and hesitant, he turned to his friend Roger Marx, a French civil servant and art critic. Marx had played a pivotal role in the official movement for the revitalization of the arts and crafts in the 1890s. Serving as Secretary to the Director of the Beaux-Arts from1883 to1888 and as Inspector General of Provincial Museums after 1889, he was well-placed to promote the decorative arts. Moreover, Marx was a prominent art critic and collector, and was highly regarded in the circles of artists and writers interested in the revitalization of the arts and crafts. He was called "the great apostle of a social art," like Morris in England.[116] It was natural, then, that Marx was able to arrange a commission for Lucien with one of the Parisian bibliophile clubs. Roger Marx introduced Lucien to Eugène Rodrigues, a lawyer and president of Les Cent bibliophiles. Les Cent bibliophiles had been founded by Alfred Piat in 1895; following his death in 1896, Eugène Rodrigues assumed the presidency of the society and continued to direct it until his own death in 1928. Rodrigues was a strong personality with a prophetic vision. Considered ahead of his time in his taste in books, Rodrigues preferred those which were well made from fine materials and which were well-designed. He had an abhorrence of reproductive engraving.[117] At last Lucien had found someone in France sympathetic to his ideals.

Marx proposed to Rodrigues that Lucien and Les Cent bibliophiles discuss a potential book project. Rodrigues met with Lucien in Paris on September 22,[118] where Lucien proposed to print an edition of Gerard de Nerval's *Histoire de la reine du matin* with twenty wood engravings, including illustrations, head and tail pieces, and ornamental initials, of which at least four would be in four colors. Lucien was not able to submit a more explicit plan for the book because as he worked on a project he refined his design. Rodrigues understood this completely. Lucien estimated a cost of 8,000 francs for the wood engravings and 2,000 francs for the actual printing. Lucien assured Rodrigues that while the book would be ornate, it would also be as typographic as possible. While Rodrigues was comfortable in giving Lucien so much control over the book, in the ensuing negotiation he did request more wood engravings.

Rodrigues announced Lucien's commission on 9 October 1907. He had recently reread de Nerval with great pleasure and was sure that this beautiful text would be appropriately interpreted by Lucien. Lucien's proposal of 10,000 francs was accepted with the stipulation that if Lucien were to introduce more illustrations into the text, the Bibliophiles would add a supplemental payment.[119] Paper, which was paid for by Les Cent bibliophiles, was especially commissioned from Perrigot-Masure with both the Eragny Press' and Les Cent bibliophiles' watermarks.[120]

Financial negotiations out of the way, Lucien began to experiment with the design. He began investigating printing with gold leaf and colors.[121] Because of the experimentation, work on the book went very slowly, three initial letters taking Lucien three months to produce. Because of this intense involvement with the book, all of Lucien's other projects came to a halt. The lack of income forced Lucien to ask Rodrigues for an advance of 1,000 to 1,500 francs. Lucien proposed and Rodrigues agreed that arrangements be made to pay him on a quarterly basis until the book was finished. This would allow him to continue to work on the book tranquilly and without interruption.[122] The book continued to evolve slowly; by mid-May, seven woodcuts were done. In late June 1908 the text was composed and the first

"The Explosion," wood engraving (NIF). Gerard de Nerval, *Histoire de la reine du matin et de Soliman prince des génies,* 1909. (Ashmolean Museum, Oxford)

proofs were sent to Paris for correction. In production for two years, the book was finished in October 1909 at a final cost of 4,493 francs 20 centimes. This amount was for materials and for the wages of the printer, but did not include any of the Pissarros' design work, engraving, or printing. Twenty months of intense work had gone into *Histoire de la reine.* Rather than the originally proposed twenty engravings, Lucien had included thirty-two engravings, of which twelve were in color. Much of the time had been spent in experimenting and perfecting printing with gold leaf. In trying to create a masterpiece, Lucien had literally short-changed himself. In adding twelve more engravings, Lucien had spent 60 percent more time. He thus believed that he should have a 60 percent supplement,[123] yet Les Cents bibliophiles only paid him a supplement of 25 percent. Lucien's underestimation of the cost of materials and labor confirms once again his poor business sense; it also demonstrates that art was far more important than money.

The book finished for Les Cents bibliophiles, Lucien entered into negotiations with Le Livre contemporain. Le Livre contemporain was founded by Pierre Dauze and Paul Gallimard in 1903 to encourage the "modern" style in book design. The society promoted original engraving and lithography, but was not against reproductive methods and techniques. An individual member could propose a book upon which the society would then discuss and decide. If a book were accepted for publication, two members of the society would be chosen to see the book through its production. The format, the method of production, the choice of type, etc. would all be decided by these two members, for whom the book would be representative of their personal taste. It was thus important for these members to present something to the society of which they could be proud.[124]

In late 1906, Lucien approached Pierre Dauze, then head of the Société des XX, about a study of Camille Pissarro which he wished to print. The text, to be written by Octave Mirbeau, would be accompanied by a portrait of Camille, designed and engraved by Lucien, as well as by several of Camille's drawings which Lucien would interpret into wood engravings.[125] Lucien submitted his plan for a book based on drawings by Camille Pissarro. The drawings for this book were those that had been prepared for a book on which Camille and Lucien were collaborating before Camille's death. It had not been finished and it was something that Lucien greatly wanted to do as a tribute to his father. The earlier negotiations with Dauze had fallen through and now in 1909, with Roger Marx acting as intermediary, the book was once again proposed to Dauze, now president of Le Livre contemporain.

The negotiations between Lucien and Le Livre contemporain were long and difficult. Because of the tradition of involvement in the preparation of a book for the society, it was important for Dauze to be immersed in the design of the book. Dauze, after having seen the book Lucien had created for Les Cent bibliophiles, wanted a book that was even more dazzling. It was important for his reputation in the club to ensure that this be so. Unfortunately, his ideas of typography and illustration did not mesh with Lucien's. Dauze neither appreciated Lucien's type, which he found to be too heavy, nor the spacing of the words, which made the pages too black.[126] These attributes were so essential to Lucien's design that he could not change his style that dramatically. Lucien had also carefully based the dimension of his page on the size of Camille's drawings. He wanted each page to be uniform. Dauze insisted on a more colorful book. Lucien had planned this book to be in chiaroscuro colors to suit the severe quality of Camille's drawings. The paper which Lucien planned to use Dauze found too thick. Dauze complained that the price was too high. Lucien explained that the high cost was due to the many trials needed for printing in color. In order to get the colors perfect and uniform, it was necessary to print almost double the amount.[127] Lucien had to insist that he be given free rein on the book. He assured Dauze that he could be certain that every effort would be made to make a successful book "as much for my personal satisfaction as for yours."[128]

Lucien began the book without a firm contract and without a text. The text for this work was to be specially commissioned and written to correlate with the agricultural subject matter of Camille's drawings. Jules Renard was approached by Dauze to write the text, but due to illness was not able to accept the commission. Émile Moselly, winner of the Goncourt prize in 1907, was chosen to replace Renard. He was given a restriction as to length and number of chapters. The text had to be tailored to fit the Eragny Press' small format, as well as to illustrate the twelve drawings of Camille Pissarro. A chapter written for each drawing could be no more than ten pages long. Because the text was treated as an after-thought,

Moselly was often forced to begin a chapter with a word which began with the initial letter that Lucien had already prepared.

The negotiations between Lucien and Le Livre contemporain took over thirteen months to complete. Because Dauze was obsessed with creating a work which would be more successful and at a better price than the one Lucien had created for Les Cent bibliophiles, Lucien found himself making adjustments to his proposal which Dauze would find acceptable. Dauze was not willing to allow Lucien to produce the book for a fixed price without a detailed explanation of the cost. It seems that he thought Lucien was trying to maneuver more money from his club than he had received from Les Cent bibliophiles. Lucien, however, felt that he had to charge more for this book because Dauze had insisted on fifty engravings (compared to the thirty-two for Les Cent bibliophiles). Lucien also needed compensation for his father's original drawings, which were to be given to the society upon the completion of the book. Lucien had to resort to pricing his woodblocks not by their artistic value but by their size, as was the trade convention. He asked for three francs per centimeter for each engraving. Dauze wanted his book to cost no more than the Les Cent bibliophiles' book, but he also wanted it to be enhanced with more engravings. Nothing Lucien proposed pleased him. Lucien had made all the concessions he could make in order to create the book which he had in mind. The bottom line was that Lucien was willing to reduce the price of the book if Dauze was willing to reduce the amount of work involved with making it. Dauze had wanted more color; Lucien rethought the book and found a means to obtain a satisfactory result by adding color to the initial letters, head and tail pieces. He consented to make his colored decorations for the same price as he had proposed for one color and he lowered the price of the ornaments by pricing the wood engravings by the centimeter. In telling Roger Marx of his plight, Lucien concluded that if a contractual agreement could not be reached, he would be forced to either go into debt to produce this book or he would be obliged to cut corners on the quality of the production.[129]

Lucien believed that he could produce this book for 15,000 francs. Because Lucien very much wanted to do this book, he finally accepted the terms of 15,000 francs with several conditions. The paper would be furnished by Le Livre contemporain. The book would have ten chapters printed in black, each with a head piece, an initial letter, and a tail piece printed in three colors, as well as the twelve drawings of Camille which would be printed in chiaroscuro. The text was to be no longer than 120 pages (twelve pages per chapter); if it were longer the price would be increased. All the drawings and woodblocks would become the property of Le Livre contemporain. The society had agreed to do the book in March 1910, but the contract was not signed until a year later, in March 1911.[130]

With the contract settled, many obstacles remained to be overcome. Moselly was slow in producing the text; moreover, he became critically ill in the summer of 1911, which delayed the text even more. Without a text, Lucien could not design the head and tail pieces, nor the initial letter for each chapter. The first chapter did not arrive from Moselly until September.

By late October, Lucien sent Dauze his first chapter specimen. Rather than carefully correcting any typographical errors that he might have noticed, Dauze made demands for an adjustment in Lucien's spacing. He found the page too solidly black.[131] Lucien reminded Dauze that as designer of the book, the color of the page would depend on his judgment alone. He resented Dauze for treating him like a commercial printer.[132] Moselly's text would continue to come irregularly to Lucien. The delay in receiving the text added to Lucien's expenses. Because the only work in the Press was the book for Le Livre contemporain, when there was no text his printer had nothing to do while waiting for more of the text, but he still had to be paid. All these delays added greatly to the book's expense. Fortunately, Le Livre contemporain was generous. They provided Lucien with an extra trimester payment which was not deducted from the final settlement payment. The book, entitled *La Charrue d'érable,* took the Pissarros and Thomas Taylor, their printer, over two years to complete. Dauze achieved his objective of making a finer book for his club than Lucien had produced for Les Cent bibliophiles. *La Charrue d'érable* is certainly Lucien's best work. His colors are subtle without being dull. He was able to capture in his initial letters and head and tail pieces the feeling of the French countryside which was portrayed in Camille's sketches and Moselly's text.

In 1914, Katherine Bradley, who wrote under the pseudonym Michael Field with her niece Edith Cooper, commissioned the last Eragny Press book. In 1906, the Michael Fields had approached the Pissarros about printing a little volume of poems on their dog, Whym Chow, who had recently died. The proposal fell through because of the expense. But now, with Edith Cooper dead and Katherine Bradley herself terminally ill, it had become a sacred duty to her that the little book be printed. She wanted twenty-five copies printed to give to her most intimate friends. Because she was anxious for the work to be finished before her death she hurried Esther, who was now responsible for the Press, along. *Whym Chow* was finished in April 1914. It was to be the last book printed at the Eragny Press.

Conclusions

Lucien certainly achieved a degree of success with the French bibliophiles—it was no easy task to receive commissions from two of the more prominent clubs—but his connections were neither broad enough nor necessarily relevant. The remaining associations which Lucien had in Paris were friends of his father and his own contemporaries. Both Félix Fénéon and Roger Marx did what they could to promote Lucien's work, upon which they must have looked favorably. While these men were both well-connected with collectors and bibliophiles, they had few actual connections with the book dealers and publishers who would have had the power to promote Lucien. Thus, when he had completed the works for these two bibliophile clubs, no more opportunities were available to Lucien in France.

Lucien's decision to live and work in England was a considerable factor in alienating him from his French contemporaries. It seems likely that if Lucien had returned to France his work would have had far more impor-

Title page. Émile Moselly, *La Charrue d'érable*, 1912/13. (Ashmolean Museum, Oxford)

tance, and he could quite possibly have been seen as a leader in the field of book design in France. Other designers and engravers, August Lepère, for example, became commercially successful in designing books for various publishers and book clubs.

Lucien's belief in the independent artist also cost him a great deal. Because he did virtually all the work himself, from designing to engraving his illustrations, his output was considerably limited. In France, it was not seen as a point of pride to do all the work oneself; there was still a deep chasm between designer and craftsman. A limited output prevented Lucien's designs from being well-represented in the marketplace.

If it is any consolation to Lucien and Esther, other artists' books in

France before the turn of the century did not have particularly vigorous sales. Toulouse-Lautrec's *Histoire naturelles* (1899), illustrated with his lithographs, took eighteen years to sell.[133] When Vollard finally took up publishing, after having been inspired by Lucien, his sales, early on in his publishing career, were discouraging. After World War I, the *livre d'artiste* would become exceedingly popular with collectors. Unfortunately, the Eragny Press did not resume printing after the war, when it might have found a more receptive clientele.

One of the major questions still to be answered concerns the lack of success in the sales of Eragny Press books for the Brook series. When Hacon & Ricketts was the publisher and distributor, the books of the Eragny Press were quickly bought. Charles Ricketts, with the help of Charles Holmes, undoubtedly was a man of much business acumen. Once Hacon & Ricketts was established, it began to prosper. At the peak of Vale Press' success, many of the woodcut engravings were destroyed by a fire at the Ballantyne Press. This provided Ricketts, who wanted to move onto other interests,[134] with an excuse to bring the Vale Press, as well as Hacon & Ricketts, to a close. Once the works in production were finished, the Press closed. This all happened concurrently with a declining economy, as well as with a waning interest in the products of the Arts and Crafts movement. Ricketts undoubtedly foresaw the decline. Before the economy was completely weakened, Ricketts closed the doors to Hacon & Ricketts and ended on a successful note.

During the time that Hacon & Ricketts were in business, a large clientele, both trade and private clients, was acquired. The business had evolved to a large enough size that Hacon & Ricketts had several employees working for them. In any case, Hacon & Ricketts were successful. When Lucien began to publish and distribute his own books, he had no network in place and no faithful clientele. These belonged to Ricketts. Ricketts, generous enough to provide the Pissarros with a list of his customers, both trade and private, and to recommend one of his employees to become secretary and business manager to the Eragny Press, left the Pissarros as well prepared and situated as he could. However, Ricketts could do very little about a faltering economy and a press which had little business acumen.

The Pissarros did not have any strategy for marketing their books. The books would speak for themselves. They may have naïvely believed that through prospectuses and calls paid to the London trade enough sales would result to enable them to make a profit. Hacon & Ricketts had bought Eragny Press books at half the retail price. By doing the marketing and distribution themselves, the Pissarros believed they would double their profit. Unfortunately, this was not the case. The Pissarros made some strategic errors. The choice of texts was not necessarily appropriate. In a market now more inclined to the text than to the physical appearance of the book, the Pissarros' choice of texts, such as their editions of Browning and Coleridge, which were available in cheap reprints, did not help their sales. Nor did the more obscure sixteenth-century music texts find a place in the market with a limited clientele to begin with. Music printing in two colors was a very time-consuming task. If they thought they could produce a profit from a book which required so much time and extra investments (music type, for example), then they were woefully unprepared for the market in which they undertook to sell their books. In addition, the texts they chose were not substantial enough. Books in such small formats could not possibly have been seen as a good value in a market which was seeking a good price. They were not conspicuously monumental and impressive. The books were too costly for the market, but not expensive enough for the time and labor which were put into them.

In retrospect, marketing miscalculations and errors are easy to see. The Pissarros were committed to producing useful works of art as well as they could make them and beyond economic considerations of reward. Even if they had been able to determine what motivated the market, the Pissarros would not have done anything any differently.

Notes

1. William S. Peterson, *A Bibliography of the Kelmscott Press* (1984), xl, and his *Kelmscott Press,* 102.
2. Franklin, *The Ashendene Press,* 27.
3. Annie Cobden-Sanderson, Hammersmith, to Esther L. Pissarro, The Brook, Hammersmith, 4 July 1905, Pissarro Collection, Ashmolean Museum. See also Marianne Tidcombe's *The Doves Press* (London: British Library and New Castle, Delaware: Oak Knoll Press, 2002) for a full discussion of the Doves Press.
4. Alan Crawford, *C. R. Ashbee: Architect, Designer, and Romantic Socialist* (New Haven and London: Yale University Press, 1985), 180.
5. Ricketts, A *Bibliography of the Books Issued by Hacon & Ricketts,* xvi.
6. Camille Pissarro, Paris, to Lucien Pissarro, Epping, England, Pissarro Collection, Ashmolean Museum. I am not able to locate the date of this letter.
7. Lucien Pissarro, Epping, to Camille Pissarro, Paris, 26 February 1896, Pissarro Collection, Ashmolean Museum.
8. Eragny Press Notebooks, [undated], Pissarro Collection, Ashmolean Museum.
9. Félix Fénéon, Paris, to Lucien Pissarro, London, [undated, 1895?], Pissarro Collection, Ashmolean Museum. I have not seen a copy of this advertisement.
10. Mr. F. Sears, Hotel Imperial, rue Christophe-Colombus, Paris; Mrs. A. B. Mason, 85 rue La Boétie, Paris; Mrs. George Tysan, 314 Dartsmouth Street, Boston, Massachusetts; Mme. Jackson, 16 rue des Bassins, Paris; Mrs. J. M. Sears, 12 Arlington Street, Boston, Massachusetts; Mr. Q. A. Shaw, Hotel Royal, Rome, Italy; Mr. H. L. Higginson, 191 Communwelth [Commonwealth] Avenue, Boston, Massachusetts; Mr. Martin Brimmer, 47 Beacon Street, Boston, Massachusetts; Mrs. Henry Whitman, 79 Mt. Vernon Street, Boston, Massachusetts; Mme. Perraud, 32 avenue Marceau, Paris; Mr. W. H. Hart, 105 rue Notre Dame des Champs, Paris.
11. Substantial sales of Lucien's early engravings in Holland as well as a sympathetic group of artists who supported his work corroborate Lucien's notion about his success in Holland.
12. Lucien Pissarro, Epping, to Camille Pissarro, Paris, 10 July 1896, Pissarro Collection, Ashmolean Museum.
13. Ibid., [after 21 November 1896].
14. Camille Pissarro, Rouen, to Lucien Pissarro, Epping, 6 November 1896, Pissarro Collection, Ashmolean Museum.
15. Surely John Lane had bought a part of the edition, but I have found no record of this for *The Book of Ruth and the Book of Esther.*
16. Quoted in Raymond Hesse, *Le livre d'art du XIXe siècle à nos jours* (Paris: La Renaissance du livre, [1927]), 64. Translation mine.
17. For a complete description of S. Bing, his background, and his establishment, Maison de l'art nouveau, see Gabriel Weisberg's *Art Nouveau Bing: Paris Style 1900* (New York: Abrams, 1986). Quoted in Weisburg, 46–47.
18. S. Bing, *Artistic America, Tiffany Glass, and Art Nouveau* (Cambridge, Mass.: MIT Press, 1970). Quoted in Weisburg, *Art Nouveau Bing,* 49.
19. Bing had first invited Charles Ricketts to design the catalog. The Vale type was considered very au courant by Bing. See Lucien Pissarro to Camille Pissarro, 14 March 1896, Pissarro Collection, Ashmolean Museum.
20. *Le Figaro,* 9 June 1896 (Tuesday).

21. Ibid.
22. *L'Art moderne,* 28 June 1896, 203–204.
23. See Una E. Johnson's *Ambroise Vollard, Editeur: Prints, Books, Bronzes* (New York: Museum of Modern Art, 1977).
24. Ambroise Vollard, *Recollections of a Picture Dealer,* trans. Violet M. MacDonald (Boston: Little, Brown, and Company, 1936), 170.
25. Lucien Pissarro, Epping, to Camille Pissarro, Paris, 3 September 1896, Pissarro Collection, Ashmolean Museum.
26. Camille Pissarro, Paris, to Lucien Pissarro, Epping, 3 September 1896, Pissarro Collection, Ashmolean Museum.
27. Vollard, who would soon become one of the most important publishers of *livres d'artiste,* would also find it difficult to sell his books.
28. Lucien Pissarro, Epping, to Julie Vellay Pissarro, Eragny, [1896], Pissarro Collection, Ashmolean Museum.
29. Lucien Pissarro, Epping, to Edmond Deman, Brussels, 15 August 1896, Pissarro Collection, Ashmolean Museum.
30. He would hear from Deman in mid-March 1897, inquiring about *Moralités légendaires.* Lucien responded that orders were now being handled by Mercure de France.
31. *La Revue blanche* made its debut in December 1889. Under the Natanson brothers, Alfred and Thadée, the review quickly began to establish itself as a major voice in the literary and artistic world. In 1893, *La Revue blanche* began to include an original print as the frontispiece to each issue, and in 1895 the review issued a portfolio of twelve prints. Because of this venture into publishing, Lucien had thought that they might be interested in undertaking the sale of his work.
32. See the letters of Emile Laforgue to Lucien Pissarro, Pissarro Collection, Ashmolean Museum. It appears that Emile Laforgue did not charge Lucien for the right to publish it. He was very pleased that his brother's work appeared in such a lovely setting.
33. Between March 1897 and September 1897, twenty-five copies were sold. Six copies were sold in 1898. In 1899, thirteen copies were sold. Twenty-one copies were sold in 1900, seventeen copies in 1901, and eighteen copies in 1902.
34. Charles Holmes, London, to Lucien Pissarro, Hammersmith, 12 September 1898, Pissarro Collection, Ashmolean Museum. Lucien wrote to Camille on 26 March 1897 that in seven days thirty copies were sold; by 12 April 1897 fifty copies had been sold by Hacon & Ricketts in fifteen days.
35. Ibid.
36. Lucien Pissarro, Bedford Park, to Camille Pissarro, Eragny, 21 April 1897, Pissarro Collection, Ashmolean Museum.
37. Ibid.
38. How the Pissarros made contact with Floury, I do not know, but it seems likely that he was a part of the large group sympathetic to the Impressionists.
39. Lucien Pissarro, Bedford Park, to H. Floury, Paris, 27 October 1897, Pissarro Collection, Ashmolean Museum.
40. Lucien Pissarro, Epping, to H. Floury, Paris, [late November 1897], Pissarro Collection, Ashmolean Museum.
41. Camille Pissarro, Paris, to Lucien Pissarro, Bedford Park, 1 April 1898, Pissarro Collection, Ashmolean Museum.
42. Lucien Pissarro, Bedford Park, to Camille Pissarro, Paris, 2 April 1898, Pissarro Collection, Ashmolean Museum.
43. In January 1898, Camille was looking for a copytext of *Les Contes* for Lucien. Camille Pissarro, Bedford Park, 28 January 1898, Pissarro Collection, Ashmolean Museum.
44. Lucien Pissarro, Bedford Park, to Camille Pissarro, Paris, 20 March 1898, Pissaarro Collection, Ashmolean Museum.
45. Camille Pissarro, Paris, to Lucien Pissarro, Bedford Park, 23 October 1898, Pissarro Collection, Ashmolean Museum.
46. Lucien Pissarro, Bedford, to Camille Pissarro, Paris, [1898], Pissarro Collection, Ashmolean Museum.
47. Charles Holmes, London, to Lucien Pissarro, Bedford Park, 7 June 1899, Pissarro Collection, Ashmolean Museum. Evidently, Hacon & Ricketts had certain customers to whom they supplied vellum copies when vellum copies were printed. Lucien would make a £1 clear profit from each vellum copy.
48. Ibid., 8 June 1899.
49. Ibid., 26 September 1899. Lucien received £65 for the 130 copies from Hacon & Ricketts.
50. Ibid., 12 Decemberr 1899.
51. Lucien Pissarro, Bedford Park, to Camille Pissarro, Paris, [before 21 April 1900], Pissarro Collection, Ashmolean Museum.
52. Ibid., 29 November 1900.
53. Lucien Pissarro, Epping, to Camille Pissarro, Paris, 28 April 1896, Pissarro Collection, Ashmolean Museum. Lucien writes: "Ricketts a deux livres charmants de prêts, mais il est boycotté de tous les côtés et il n'y a encore que 20 exemplaires de vendus!" Lucien is not clear why the trade is boycotting Ricketts. It is likely the trade did not appreciate the competition.
54. Charles Holmes, London, to Lucien Pissarro, Bedford Park, 5 and 7 March 1903, Pissarro Collection, Ashmolean Museum.

55. Lucien Pissarro, The Brook, Hammersmith, to John Lane, London, [September 1903], Pissarro Collection, Ashmolean Museum.
56. Lucien Pissarro, The Brook, Hammersmith, to John Lane, London, [undated, 1904?], Pissarro Collection, Ashmolean Museum.
57. Lucien Pissarro, Paris, to Esther Pissarro, The Brook, [1903], Pissarro Collection, Ashmolean Museum.
58. Lucien Pissarro, The Brook, Hammersmith, to Julie V. Pissarro, Eragny, 26 May 1904, Pissarro Collection, Ashmolean Museum.
59. Lucien Pissarro, The Brook, Hammersmith, to Albert Morelli, [London], 15 December 1904, Pissarro Collection, Ashmolean Museum.
60. Esther L. Pissarro, The Brook, Hammersmith, to Albert Morelli, [London], 27 December 1904, Pissarro Collection, Ashmolean Museum.
61. Esther L. Pissarro, The Brook, Hammersmith, to Albert Morelli, [London], [undated], Pissarro Collection, Ashmolean Museum.
62. Wilfrid Voynich was a dealer of incunables, but his wife, novelist Ethel Voynich—most remembered for *The Gadfly* (1897), a novel set in pre-1848 Italy which sold in vast quantities in translation in the Soviet Union—was a very good friend of Esther's.
63. List of Eragny Press books, unsold, December 1904:
Bibliography, 50 copies (pub. July 1903)
Ishtar, 84 copies (pub. December 1903)
Areopagitica, 64 copies (pub. December and April 1903)
Browning, 90 copies (pub. June 1904)
Christabel, 142 copies (pub. October 1904)
64. R. Keith Johnston, [London], to Lucien Pissarro, The Brook, Hammersmith, 29 November 1904, Pissarro Collection, Ashmolean Museum.
65. Lucien Pissarro, The Brook, Hammersmith, to Keith Johnston, [London], 5 December 1904, Pissarro Collection, Ashmolean Museum.
66. Esther L. Pissarro, The Brook, Hammersmith, to Keith Johnston, [London], 6 December 1904, Pissarro Collection, Ashmolean Museum.
67. Lucien Pissarro, Paris, to Esther L. Pissarro, The Brook, Hammersmith, [undated, 1903], Pissarro Collection, Ashmolean Museum.
68. Lucien Pissarro, Paris, to Esther L. Pissarro, The Brook, Hammersmith, 5 December 1903, Pissarro Collection, Ashmolean Museum.
69. Lucien Pissarro, Paris, to Esther Pissarro, The Brook, Hammersmith, 26 November 1903, Pissarro Collection, Ashmolean Museum.
70. Lucien Pissarro, Paris, to Esther Pissarro, The Brook, Hammersmith, [March 1904], Pissarro Collection, Ashmolean Museum.
71. Hacon & Ricketts, Account to the Eragny Press, 14 July 1903, Pissarro Collection, Ashmolean Museum.
72. Lucien Pissarro, Paris, to Esther Pissarro, The Brook, Hammersmith, [undated 1903], Pissarro Collection, Ashmolean Museum.
73. Raymond Hesse, *Histoire des sociétés de bibliophiles en France de 1820 à 1930* (Paris: L. Giraud-Badin, 1929), 49–51.
74. Lucien Pissarro, Paris, to Esther Pissarro, The Brook, Hammersmith, [19/20? March 1904], Pissarro Collection, Ashmolean Museum.
75. Lucien Pissarro, The Brook, Hammersmith, to Carteret, Paris, [June 1906], Pissarro Collection, Ashmolean Museum.
76. Located at 5 Henrietta Street, Covent Garden, London, W.C., with branches in New York, Paris, Berlin, etc.
77. Brown, Langham and Co. was located at 78 New Bond Street, London W.
78. Lucien Pissarro, The Brook, Hammersmith, to Perris and Cazenove, London, 6 May 1904, Pissarro Collection, Ashmolean Museum.
79. Ibid.
80. Esther L. Pissarro, The Brook, Hammersmith, to Brown, Langham, London, [undated, 1904], Pissarro Collection, Ashmolean Museum.
81. Esther L. Pissarro, The Brook, Hammersmith, to Brown, Langham, London, 25 June 1904, Pissarro Collection, Ashmolean Museum.
82. Ibid.
83. Frank Hollings, 7 Great Turnstile, Holborn, London.
84. Esther L. Pissarro, The Brook, Hammersmith, to Francis Edwards, London, 15 November 1904, Pissarro Collection, Ashmolean Museum.
85. Francis Edward, London, to the Eragny Press, The Brook, Hammersmith, 5 April 1905, Pissarro Collection, Ashmolean Museum.
86. E. L. Levetus, London, to Esther Pissarro, The Brook, Hammersmith, 5 April 1905, Pissarro Collection, Ashmolean Museum. Simpkin, Marshall and Co. was a retail and wholesale dealer as well as a publisher.
87. Esther Pissarro, The Brook, Hammersmith, to Simpkin Marshall and Co., London, 7 April 1905, Pissarro Collection, Ashmolean Museum.
88. Binyon wrote these poems for his wife, Cecilia.
89. L. Binyon, London, to Lucien Pissarro, The Brook, Hammersmith, 15 September [1904], Pissarro Collection, Ashmolean Museum.

90. Lucien Pissarro, The Brook, Hammersmith, to L. Binyon, London, 7 March 1905, Pissarro Collection, Ashmolean Museum.
91. Lucien Pissarro, The Brook, Hammersmith, to Julie V. Pissarro, Eragny, [June 1905], Pissarro Collection, Ashmolean Museum.
92. Scribner's Sons, New York, to J. M. Andreini, New York, 19 September 1905, Pissarro Collection, Ashmolean Museum.
93. Lucien Pissarro, The Brook, to Gardner C. Teall, New York, 10 October 1905, Pissarro Collection, Ashmolean Museum.
94. Gardner C. Teall, New York, to Lucien Pissarro, The Brook, Hammersmith, 24 October 1905, Pissarro Collection, Ashmolean Museum.
95. Ibid.
96. Ibid.
97. When *Songs by Ben Jonson* was finished, in addition to dedicating the work to Andrieni, the Pissarros also sent him a vellum copy. J. M. Andrieni, New York, to Esther and Lucien Pissarro, The Brook, Hammersmith, 30 April 1906, Pissarro Collection, Ashmolean Museum: "It is altogether too kind of you to send me a vellum copy. I do not feel justified in accepting it as a gift: the dedication is enough compliment and I beg you to let me pay for the copy. I should like to have it for my collection with Mr. and Mrs. Pissarro's autographs. You must bear with me when I tell you that I shall feel a great deal more comfortable that way—otherwise it will prevent me from being of use to you—as I wish to be—I wish to serve you for the pleasure I find in it, not for the hope of reward for my efforts in your behalf, such as they were, for I can see in it your very delicate appreciation thereof."
98. Esther L. Pissarro, The Brook, Hammersmith, to T. S. Moore, [London], 21 July 1906, Pissarro Collection, Ashmolean Museum. Esther blamed the lack of sales in America upon the April 1906 earthquake in San Francisco.
99. E. & L. Pissarro, The Brook, Hammersmith, to Messrs. G. P. Putnam and Sons, London, 22 May 1906, Pissarro Collection, Ashmolean Museum.
100. E. & L. Pissarro, The Brook, Hammersmith, to Messrs. Putnam's Sons, London, 31 October 1906, Pissarro Collection, Ashmolean Museum.
101. Esther L. Pissarro, The Brook, Hammersmith, to J. M. Andreini, New York, 11 December 1906, Pissarro Collection, Ashmolean Museum.
102. F.E.L. Watson, Lenox, Massachusetts, to E. & L. Pissarro, The Brook, Hammersmith, 15 January 1907, Pissarro Collection, Ashmolean Museum.
103. Lucien Pissarro, The Brook, Hammersmith, to F.E.L. Watson, New York, 10 February 1907, Pissarro Collection, Ashmolean Museum.
104. F.E.L. Watson, Lenox, Massachusetts, to E. & L. Pissarro, The Brook, Hammersmith, 2 December 1907, Pissarro Collection, Ashmolean Museum.
105. E. & L. Pissarro, The Brook, Hammersmith, to Macmillan and Co., London, 1 August 1906, Pissarro Collection, Ashmolean Museum.
106. Lucien Pissarro to Esther L. Pissarro, [undated], Pissarro Collection, Ashmolean Museum.
107. Lucien Pissarro, The Brook, Hammersmith, to F.E.L. Watson, Lenox, Massachusetts, 18 June 1907, Pissarro Collection, Ashmolean Museum. The Grolier Club of New York, founded in 1884, is the oldest and largest bibliophile society in the United States.
108. Grant Richards, London, to Lucien Pissarro, The Brook, Hammersmith, 16 July 1907, Pissarro Collection, Ashmolean Museum.
109. Ibid.
110. Lucien Pissarro, Eragny, to Esther Pissarro, The Brook, Hammersmith, 10 May [1910], Pissarro Collection, Ashmolean Museum.
11. Lucien Pissarro, The Brook, Hammersmith, to Roger Marx, Paris, 8 June 1911, Pissarro Collection, Ashmolean Museum. The subscribers were Pierre Revèrt (vellum), Louis Berthon (vellum), J. Doucet, Roger Braun, A. Mariani, L. Dubrugeaud, G. Morceau, F. Dreyfus, G. Tuonens, A. André, A. Blaiget, and H. Floury.
112. J. M. Andrieni's article, "Notes on Book-plates by Esther and Lucien Pissarro; and on Their Eragny Press," appeared in vol. 1, no. 3 (1912) of Fowler's *Ex Libran*. The Pissarros designed and printed bookplates mainly for family, personal friends and supportive collectors, like Andrieni and Fowler.
113. H. Alfred Fowler, Kansas City, Missouri, to Lucien Pissarro, The Brook, Hammersmith, 7 January 1913, Pissarro Collection, Ashmolean Museum.
114. Statement of Consigned Account, *Biblio,* H. Alfred Fowler, editor, 1 April 1913, Pissarro Collection, Ashmolean Museum.
115. H. Alfred Fowler, Kansas City, Missouri, to Lucien Pissarro, The Brook, Hammersmith, 15 November 1913, Pissarro Collection, Ashmolean Museum.
116. Anatole France, "Préface," in Roger Marx, *L'Art social* (Paris: Bibliothèque-Charpentier, 1913), viii.
117. Hesse, *Histoire des sociétés de bibliophiles en France*, 33–39.
118. Eugène Rodrigues, Paris, to Lucien Pissarro, The Brook, Hammersmith, 21 September 1907, Pissarro Collection, Ashmolean Museum.
119. Eugène Rodrigues, Paris, to Lucien Pissarro, The Brook, Hammersmith, 9 October 1907, Pissarro Collection, Ashmolean Museum.
120. Lucien Pissarro, The Brook, Hammersmith, to Perrigot-Masure, Paris, 12 February 1908, Pissarro Collection, Ashmolean Museum.

121. Lucien Pissarro, The Brook, Hammersmith, to Eugène Rodrigues, Paris, 27 February 1908, Pissarro Collection, Ashmolean Museum.
122. Ibid.
123. Ibid.
124. Ibid.
125. Lucien Pissarro, The Brook, Hammersmith, to Pierre Dauze, Paris, 19 December 1906, Pissarro Collection, Ashmolean Museum.
126. Lucien Pissarro, The Brook, Hammersmith, to Roger Marx, Paris, 19 February 1912, Pissarrro Collection, Ashmolean Museum.
127. Lucien Pissarro, The Brook, Hammersmith, to Pierre Dauze, Paris, 6 December 1909, Pissarro Collection, Ashmolean Museum.
128. Lucien Pissarro, The Brook, Hammersmith, to Pierre Dauze, Paris, 9 December 1909, Pissarro Collection, Ashmolean Museum. Translation mine: ". . . autant pour ma satisfaction personelle que pour la votre."
129. Lucien Pissarro, The Brook, Hammersmith, to Roger Marx, Paris, 6 January 1911, Pissarro Collection, Ashmolean Museum.
130. Esther L. Pissarro, The Brook, Hammersmith, to John Quinn, New York, 18 March 1911, Pissarro Collection, Ashmolean Museum.
131. Lucien Pissarro, The Brook, Hammersmith, to Pierre Dauze, Paris, 15 February 1912, Pissarro Collection, Ashmolean Museum.
132. Lucien Pissarro, The Brook, Hammersmith, to Roger Marx, Paris, 19 February 1912, Pissarro Collection, Ashmolean Museum.
133. W. J. Strachan, *The Artist and the Book in France: The Twentieth Century Livre d'Artiste* (London: Peter Owen, 1969), 35–36.
134. After the Vale Press closed, Ricketts turned to stage and costume design as well as journalism. He also painted occasionally in the style of Velasquez.

Chapter IV

Art and Design

Because of his decision to live and work outside of France, it is difficult to classify Lucien and to place his work as a book artist within a nationalistic context. He was an artist who had to remove himself from his French milieu in order to find his own distinctive style. In moving to London, Lucien withdrew from the French art scene in the early 1890s, an action that prevented him from promoting his ideas about book design in his native country. His removal from the art scene hindered him from establishing contacts and from directly influencing the artists in whose circle he would have moved. This withdrawal from France also cost him the recognition he deserved. While working in England, his major influence was still his French background; although he found some appreciation for his books in England, his designs were not as completely understood as if he had been English. He straddled the worlds of French art and English craft, creating a distinctive style which neither country could fully understand or identify as its own.

An Eragny Press book is a distinct blending of English Arts and Crafts style and French Impressionism. In arrangement and craftsmanship, an Eragny Press book meets the criteria established and followed by William Morris and his Kelmscott Press. In illustration and color, the books reveal Lucien Pissarro's Impressionist background. A delicate and charming design emanates from this amalgam of two national styles, appropriately so, since the proprietors, Lucien and Esther Pissarro, were French and English, respectively.

In comparison to the other private presses of the period, Eragny Press books are dismissed as inconsequential[1] because they lack the monumental size that is the hallmark of the deluxe book. Where the Kelmscott Press has its Chaucer, the Doves Press its Bible, the Ashendene Press its Dante, and the Essex House Press its Bible, the Eragny Press produced nothing at all in a folio size. The modest format of the Eragny Press creates a more intimate and personal book. The books, simple and charming, have no intention or presumption of presenting a masterpiece only through their size; rather they are monuments to color. The woodblock illustrations, created and produced by an artist with great sensitivity to color, assert a monumentality which size alone cannot rival. Unlike the production from the Kelmscott Press and other private presses which are permeated with a decorative minimalism or a cultivated Renaissance style, Eragny Press books are modern in their outlook, not looking back to an older, established tradition but rather seeking to be representative of one person's nature and vision.

Perhaps of all the revivalist private presses of the period, the Eragny Press alone created the true *livre d'artiste*. Eragny Press books have never been classified as *livres d'artiste* because they have been so readily categorized as products of the English private press movement. But the books really belong to this greater tradition. W. J. Strachan defines the *livre d'artiste* as

> a book containing illustrations carried out by the artist himself—a painter, sculptor, or original engraver (*peintre-graveur*)—who will have himself employed some autographic process for the execution of his designs. . . . In some cases the artist himself does the printing of the illustrations. . . . Each illustration in the *livre d'artiste* is as much an 'original' as each individual print, similarly produced, of a set of number prints such as one purchases in a gallery.[2]

An Eragny Press book meets the criteria set out by Strachan, who has traced the responsibility for the concept of the *livre d'artiste* to Ambroise Vollard, Parisian art dealer and publisher.[3] Vollard, in turn, credited Lucien Pissarro's first book, *The Queen of the Fishes,* with spurring him on in his attempt to publish.[4] Lucien's role in the development of the *livre d'artiste* has never been considered. His place within this tradition had been overshadowed by more prominent artists who popularized this art form. Yet, if his own output had been greater and his reputation more far-reaching, his books would have been seen as prototypes for this tradition.

Influences

Lucien's training in art began at an early age under the direction of his father. Not a naturally skilled artist, he came to his art more by temperament and perseverance. Molded by Impressionist theories after experimenting with and incorporating pointillism into his drawing and painting, his mature art was a refinement and redefinition of his earlier training. Lucien considered himself to be an artist of the School of Eragny. The School of Eragny, focusing on landscape and nature, was founded by Camille Pissarro, whose early followers included Paul Cézanne, Paul Gauguin, and Armand Guillaumin.

The underlying theory behind Camille Pissarro's concept of painting was the sensation—an expression of what is felt, an interplay between self and nature at the very moment of the experience. Color, light, and a simple design scheme are the key elements. An impressionist paints what he sees and what he sees happening without idealization but does not imitate or copy. He paints nature in his own style, expressing his own unique temperament. The only real forces are work, observation, and sensation. The style was not an academic one, but rather an original vision of nature. Lucien described the principles of the School of Eragny as he applied them to his wood-engraved designs as including a particular ornamentation which the Eragny countryside inspires, but which is, at the same time, a mixture of japonism and gothic, but also modern and impressionist. Lucien's entire body of work, both painting and wood engraving, lies on the simple premise of looking to nature and following one's own temperament.

When Lucien took up original wood engraving in the middle 1880s he was seeking a medium by which he could express his own character without competition with his father. Additionally, wood engraving had more commercial possibilities than painting (or so the Pissarros thought). Lucien's introverted personality seemed to suit the intimate medium of wood engraving. In his best engravings, Lucien was a successful miniaturist, for the size of the blocks limited his art to the miniature, the nonmonumental. Rather than piecing the woodblocks together to fit a large drawing, Lucien developed his technique to suit the natural size and grain of the wood. Moreover, by making his own engravings rather than permitting a professional engraver to interpret his drawings, nothing interfered with his personal vision.

When Lucien began as a wood engraver, under the direction of Auguste Lepère, his rustic style was outside the accepted tradition of wood engraving—his technique, preserving the drawn line in a simple and straightforward manner, was either too advanced or too crude for the public's taste. These innovations which Lucien made to wood engraving as an original art form have remained largely uncredited to him as a result of his move to England in 1890. His absence from France during the crucial years of 1891–95, when the woodcut finally was seen as an independent print medium, hindered his career considerably.[5]

His interest in creating books began long before he sought a vehicle for his engravings. As a teenager he made books for his younger brothers and sisters. Heavily influenced by the English picture books of Walter Crane, Randolph Caldecott, and Kate Greenaway, sent to the Pissarro family by Lucien's cousin Esther Isaacson, his initial attempts at designing books display a mixture of the English style with that of the French nursery books. These early designs, transcended and transformed once Lucien established the Eragny Press, embody all the charm and naïveté of Eragny Press books, but little attention was paid to the interaction between text and illustration. Lucien would not consider this aspect of book design until he came under the influence of Charles Ricketts.

Without doubt, the greatest influence on Lucien's art was his father, Camille. The complex relationship between Lucien and his father was a major influence, not so much upon the design of his books but on the character of the illustrations. In the early period of the Eragny Press, Lucien did not possess the necessary confidence his work required. Surpassed and diminished by his father's talent, Lucien found it difficult to find his own artistic voice. Lucien's preference of using Camille's drawings, rather than his own, as the basis for his engravings demonstrates his devotion to his father. As a great admirer of his father's work, Lucien was his paramount promoter. To produce engravings based on drawings by Camille Pissarro would have done more to enhance Camille's reputation

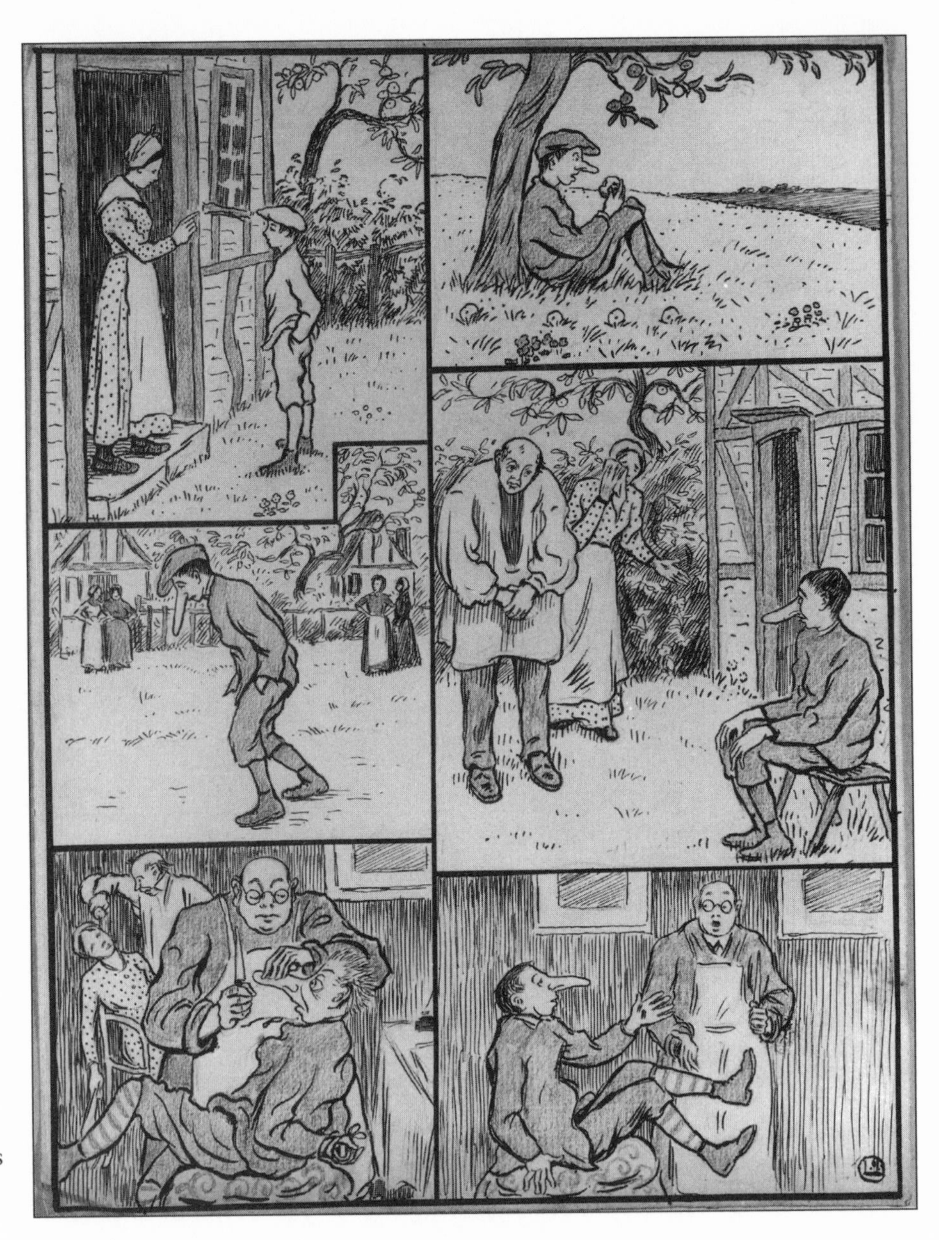

"Le Long nez," drawing for children's story, c. 1888. (Ashmolean Museum, Oxford)

than Lucien's, but it would have allowed the tentative younger artist to work in a medium without the responsibility for the art itself. But Camille tried to steer Lucien away from this course of collaboration. He preferred that Lucien develop his own style, which Camille perceived had a charm and quality all its own. They did collaborate finally on two works, *Les Travaux de champs* and *Daphnis et Chloe*. Neither book saw it to the production stages due to a variety of circumstances, mainly time constraints and financial considerations.[6]

In spite of Camille's generosity and encouragement of Lucien as an original artist, when Lucien yielded to the influence of Charles Ricketts Camille was not pleased. His meeting with Ricketts and Charles Shannon introduced Lucien to another artistic vision, one based on an historicism virtually unknown to Lucien at the time of his arrival in England. Ricketts looked to the old masters for his inspiration. Under Ricketts' Pre-Raphaelite influence, Camille believed that Lucien's work had become

Christian and sentimental, his figures elongated and unnatural looking,

> a sentimental element characteristically English and quite Christian, an element found in many of the Pre-Raphaelites . . . and elsewhere. . . . There are hundreds of ideas in your other engravings, which belong to you, anarchist and lover of nature, to the Lucien who reserves the great ideal for a better time when man, having achieved another mode of life, will understand the beautiful differently.[7]

Camille disliked the tendency in Ricketts toward idealization and allusion to the past, especially to ancient Greece and fifteenth-century Italian art. This tendency disturbed Lucien as well. Ricketts believed that it was "stupid to make things from nature,"[8] seeking instead convention and ornamentation. Lucien, adhering to his father's principles, was of the opinion that while it is necessary to be conventional, each artist must find his own convention. For the impressionist, convention was not what had come before—passed down through tradition—but was something that identified an artist's own style, the personal manner of visualization. Lucien's education was diametrically opposed to Ricketts' idealization of and borrowing from the masters. Convention, according to Camille, was to be found through sensation:

> Observe that it is a grave error to believe that all mediums of art are not closely tied to their time. Well, then, is this the path of Ricketts? No. It has been my view for a long time that it is not a question of pretty Italian elegance, but of using our eyes a bit and disregarding what is in style.[9]

These two divergent views about art would result in irreconcilable differences between Lucien and Ricketts. But in the meantime, Lucien fell under Ricketts' spell. Lucien's personality was too pliable and too easily influenced for him to have held firmly to his impressionist principles. In looking back over his life, Lucien regretted this artistic phase in his life.

Camille Pissarro and Ricketts differed in their views on another very important point. Camille saw in books the possibility of fine art, as valid in its own way as painting. Ricketts saw books as a branch of design. Under Ricketts' influence Lucien could not be persuaded that his engravings were art. Camille considered the illustrators of the past to be great artists.

> I do not doubt that Morris's books are as beautiful as Gothic art, but it must not be forgotten that the Gothic artists were inventors and that we have to perform, not better, which is impossible, but differently and following our own bent. The results will not be immediately evident. Yes, you are right, it is not necessary to be Gothic, but are you doing everything possible not to be? With this in view you would have to disregard friend Ricketts, who is, of course, a charming man, but who from the point of view of art seems to stray from the true direction, which is the return to nature.[10]

For Camille (and Lucien would understand this later as well), a book is great art when it communicates personal vision.

Camille, while disapproving of Lucien's new direction, continued to provide Lucien with critiques as well as words of encouragement and praise.

> Your style is inspired by nature . . . because you have a very personal side, very artistic, a time will come where this will be understood, one will have been astonished not to have seen it earlier . . .[11]

He praised the primitive and startling qualities of Lucien's engravings, while urging him to "evolve towards an art more of sensation, more free and which will conform to your nature."[12] Camille found those engravings that were heavily influenced by the Italian bias of Ricketts to be lifeless. But the engravings done before Ricketts' influence he found to have a personal savor, an intuition, a sincerity. These aspects of Lucien's true temperament were to Camille the height of art. Under Ricketts' influence, Lucien had deviated from the true path to take up, unquestioningly, Anglo-Italian art. Camille urged a return to nature.[13]

In determining how substantial Camille's influence was over Lucien, it is essential to recall that Lucien depended upon Camille for his financial backing. In displeasing Camille, he always ran the risk of losing his patronage, both financially and psychologically. While in retrospect, it seems unlikely that Camille would have withdrawn his financial support, since he was such an advocate of Lucien, it is conceivable that this may have been seen as a real threat to Lucien, who had no additional income except what he could earn from his art.

One significant concept which is seldom addressed when discussing printing as an artistic endeavor is the major expense involved with setting up a studio. The expense of painting—canvas, paints, and brushes—is very minimal by comparison. While Lucien began his press using commercial printers, he soon realized the necessity of printing the works himself in order to obtain quality craftsmanship. The presses and type necessary for Lucien to set up a printing studio were very cost-intensive items. Moreover, the paper to print even a small edition was a major outlay. Without Camille's financial support the Eragny Press would not have been possible. For Camille, art was more important than commercial and financial success. In continuing his patronage, he provided Lucien with the means to develop his style.

Lucien's high regard and respect for his father's genius made it difficult for him to develop his own artistic style. For most of his life, especially in his darker moments, Lucien saw himself as a second-rate imitator of his father.[14] In wood engraving, however, Lucien found his own unique style, still influenced by Camille, but very much a reflection of his own artistic voice and skill.

The meeting between Charles Ricketts and Lucien in November 1890 proved to be a momentous occasion. Their mutual interest in wood engraving resulted in a close association lasting over a decade. Under

Ricketts' cultivation and encouragement, Lucien grew from a wood engraver into a printer and book designer. Ricketts introduced Lucien to the Print Room at the British Museum, urging him to study old master drawings and engravings. He provided Lucien with an historical background in art that had been more or less circumvented in his education. The philosophical and theoretical differences between Ricketts and Lucien were not apparent at first. Initially their mutual interest in wood engraving overcame any perceptible differences. Ricketts was a natural aristocrat, an artist devoted to the life aesthetic. Surely his appreciation and cultivation of the most delicate and refined things intrigued Lucien, a man without artifice. Whereas Ricketts indulged himself in an atmosphere of luxurious artfulness, which the Vale Press and other artistic ventures demonstrate so aptly, Lucien turned to nature and to "sensation." Ricketts always toyed with the decadent and the artificial; Lucien, with nature and the expression of the sensation. Because Lucien was a gentle naïve, it is easy to see how he could have become fascinated with Ricketts.

An expert and highly skilled wood engraver, Ricketts introduced many of his engraving techniques and theories to Lucien. The most important technique Lucien learned from Ricketts was how to make a true engraving—learning to interpret with the tools. This was achieved by hollowing out the white areas to create the black line of the relief. With this new technique Lucien was able to render more life into his engravings. Under Ricketts' authority, Lucien's engravings not only became more mature but also more literary and more sentimental, especially in the figures' attitudes, expressions, and general physiognomies.

Ricketts introduced Lucien to the ornamental in art. Heavily influenced by the French writer Joris-Karl Huysmann, Ricketts defined the ornamental as the mystic in art, the naturalism of the unreal, the form defined by things of the spirit.[15] This definition could be applied to all the decorative arts. Ricketts believed the artist who best represented and embodied this mysticism was Rossetti. Lucien was attracted to these new ideas which were so alien to impressionism, but he did not find them completely sound. Under the influence of both Ricketts and Esther, Lucien's engravings became more literary and symbolic, acquiring what Camille called a sentimental tendency. By mid-1896 Lucien was slowly removing himself from Ricketts' artistic influence. Regretting his subordination to the force of Ricketts' authority, he realized the necessity for his return to nature with free sensations. Ricketts had borrowed too much from past masters, not following his own nature. Lucien realized the importance of achieving art through one's own experience rather than through imitation of another's experience.

But Lucien continued to defend both traditions to Camille. He praised the Pre-Raphaelites for creating the industrial arts movement; he did not believe that the two styles were irremediable enemies and believed that his task was to join them, or at least to create another style from the two.

While Lucien never deviated far from regarding his father as his true master and mentor, he easily and completely capitulated to Ricketts' charms. Under his father's influence he cultivated the concepts and attitudes to landscape and nature which would remain the backbone of his artistic expression all his life and which was the strong base to which he would return after his forays into both Neo-Impressionism (as a painter) and Pre-Raphaelitism (as an engraver). But it is to Charles Ricketts that Lucien's development as a typographer can be credited. Ricketts introduced Lucien to book design, especially the integration of type and illustration. Without this introduction, the Eragny Press would not have come into existence.

Ricketts, in a retrospective moment, credits the Eragny Press to his influence and a friendly loan of type.[16] The relationship between the two men is more complex and less one-sided than Ricketts suggests. Ricketts was a charismatic leader who capitalized upon Lucien to promote and further the goals of the Vale group. It was advantageous to have within the group someone who was connected to continental symbolist artists and who could further Ricketts' reputation abroad. In Lucien Ricketts found an associate who could articulately discuss many of the major art movements of their time and their relation to wood engraving.

The books which Lucien produced under Ricketts' influence are not as successful as those which capture his own style. In the correspondence between father and son, during this period so heavily influenced by Ricketts, Camille constantly harangued Lucien to follow his own nature, to look towards nature for his art. Time has proven Camille right. Sentimentalism invades Lucien's art under the Pre-Raphaelite influence. His work becomes too refined, too precious, too sweet—to the detriment of his unpolished, spontaneous Eragny Style. Ricketts, as a student and admirer of old master drawings and engravings, urged Lucien to look to them for his style, not to nature. There is no doubt that Ricketts was a much more skillful draughtsman than Lucien. He had a real genius for arrangement and artifice. In one of his more shrewd moments, Lucien wrote to his father that Ricketts had the qualities of an arranger and a high degree of comprehension of material, and that "he would be able to be a jeweler, a cabinet maker, or never mind what without difficulty."[17] In fact, the Vale books are artfully arranged, demonstrating artifice rather than personality. The books are carefully composed but lack a certain charm. In spite of Ricketts' influence, Lucien's books are rustically charming and display a personality that Vale books, by their artifice, do not.

These early years in London under Ricketts' guidance were important to Lucien. He established himself as an artist outside the sphere of his father's influence and in a different medium—engraving rather than painting. With their two divergent views—Ricketts heavily influenced by the Pre-Raphaelites and Lucien an impressionist—it is no wonder that the two eventually came to the parting of the ways. Ricketts was sophisticated, fond of artifice; Lucien, rustic and primitive.

Theories on the Aesthetic of the Book

Lucien summed up his aesthetic of the book with three simple criteria. He believed it necessary to have a beautiful type and good paper and, if the

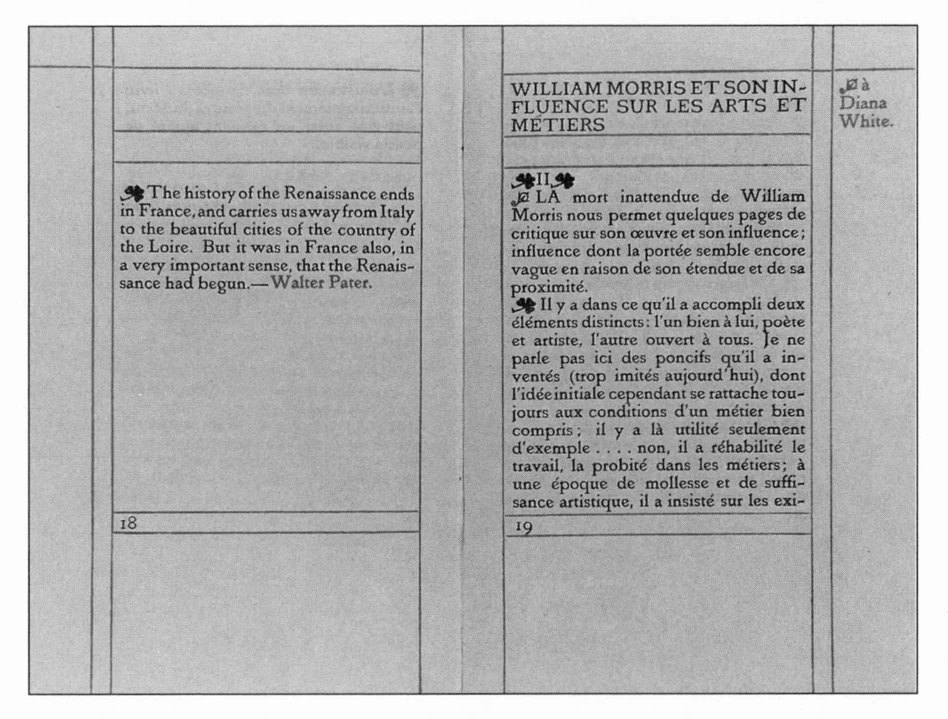

The history of the Renaissance ends in France, and carries us away from Italy to the beautiful cities of the country of the Loire. But it was in France also, in a very important sense, that the Renaissance had begun.—Walter Pater.

18

WILLIAM MORRIS ET SON INFLUENCE SUR LES ARTS ET MÉTIERS

II

LA mort inattendue de William Morris nous permet quelques pages de critique sur son œuvre et son influence; influence dont la portée semble encore vague en raison de son étendue et de sa proximité.

Il y a dans ce qu'il a accompli deux éléments distincts: l'un bien à lui, poète et artiste, l'autre ouvert à tous. Je ne parle pas ici des poncifs qu'il a inventés (trop imités aujourd'hui), dont l'idée initiale cependant se rattache toujours aux conditions d'un métier bien compris; il y a là utilité seulement d'exemple . . . . non, il a réhabilité le travail, la probité dans les métiers; à une époque de mollesse et de suffisance artistique, il a insisté sur les exi-

19

à Diana White.

Charles Ricketts and Lucien Pissarro, *De la typographie et de l'harmonie de la page imprimée: William Morris et son influence sur les arts et métiers,* 1898; pp. 18–19. (Ashmolean Museum, Oxford)

book were to be illustrated, that the illustrations and ornaments must harmonize with the complete page.[18] These principles would be followed throughout the work of the Eragny Press, but the most vital of these principles, for Lucien, was the harmony of the page. This idea was elaborated upon in a collaborative essay by Ricketts and Lucien.

Lucien and Ricketts met often to discuss not only wood engraving but the revitalization of the book. By 1896, these discussions took the form of a short essay, "De la typographie et de l'harmonie de la page imprimée," published by Hacon & Ricketts in 1898 along with another essay "William Morris et son influence sur les arts et métiers."[19] Written directly in French and aimed at continental markets, the essay was intended as a manifesto with which to promote in France, Belgium, and Holland their vision of the book. It is difficult to refute the long-held assumption which credits Ricketts for the theories outlined in this essay. The original manuscript, written in Lucien's hand,[20] implies, however, that a genuine collaboration existed between the two men. The generosity of Ricketts' participation within the collaboration should be noted since he had little to gain from the essay's publication. Ricketts' work was not particularly appreciated in France, nor did he have any interest in marketing his work on the Continent.

Their essay, "De la typographie . . . ," building upon theories put forth by William Morris, focuses on the relationship of the printed page to illustration. Attributing the "conscientious ideal" of a harmonious book to two or three manuscripts by William Morris and the renewal of interest in the intrinsic beauties of the book in England to Morris and Burne-Jones, Ricketts and Lucien also credited them with bringing forth a more profound knowledge of the resources of ornamentation and of the anatomy of letter forms. No matter how admirable an illustration may be in itself, they were critical of illustration which is added to a book without any relationship to it, without supporting the character or weight of the type.

The first printers, they believed, had the advantage of being heirs to a tradition of beautiful writing. Based on ancestral forms, a superior typography was created. But this period did not last long before it was corrupted, the letters losing their shape and strength at the hands of the engraver. By the nineteenth century, type had become "poor and bombastic." Ricketts and Lucien urged that only by seeking out the sources of letterforms, and by understanding the processes necessary to remake them, could one revitalize typography and give it an element of harmony, which they believed the current state of type lacked. They blamed the crisis upon the need to economize on space in order to save paper and thus to minimize the cost. In addition, both Ricketts and Lucien concluded that type, as well as wood engraving, taking into account the limitations and demands of the medium, ought to be designed with regard for the engraving process by which it was to be cut.

The art of page arrangement, the "mise-en-page," had also been lost over the centuries, taken over by the affectation of details. The danger that contemporary printers had fallen into was the temptation to create a book without any thought to the materials of book-making. The classic simplicity of page layout advocated by Ricketts and Lucien would, they claimed, appear to be archaic to the modern printer. They feared that printers were convinced that an attempt to return to a logical understanding of letter forms would also be a return to the archaic.

The contemporary illustrated book did not take into account the actual materials used to make a book, but allowed the illustration to dominate as something separate from the text. Illustrations which compete with the text weaken the purpose of the text by introducing discordant elements into the book as a whole. Illustration properly related to typographical forms is a note of decoration, the luminous point, integrated into the page. Illustration should accompany the book as gesture or décor, as an element of visual poetry. The text is enhanced by purely nonverbal means appropriate to the book.

Some of these ideas may have been borrowed from Maurice Denis, whose treatise on illustration written in 1890 recognized illustration as an evocation of a subject rather than as a story-telling device.[21] But, in Lucien and Ricketts' well-reasoned essay, this is the first time that the idea of harmony between text and illustration were combined.

Their interest in finding a means to understand drawing as it is applied to engraving material took Morris' theories one step beyond. They came to comprehend that drawings destined to be cut into the wood needed to be executed in a particular fashion which permitted the material to impart its own character, resulting in a wood engraving that was not merely a skillful reproduction of a drawing but was something unique in its own right. Thus it became important to both Ricketts and Lucien that the block be engraved by the artist, who alone, they believed, could bring out the distinctive qualities of the engraving.

In another essay written by Lucien entitled "Essai sur le livre compris comme objet d'art"[22] he offers a more detailed account of the origins, the deformations, and the dangers of superfluous ornamentation (*fioritures*) of type; on why wood engraving, especially original engraving, appears to be the most proper medium to harmonize with type; on the decadence of commercial printing and the dangers in abandoning the restrictions of materials; and on color engraving, which should not be based on water-colors or oil painting but should be conceived with the printing material in mind.

In order for ornaments and illustrations to be understood in an harmonic way, they must not be isolated from the text which they decorate. Wood engraving, especially original wood engraving, seems to be the medium most in sympathy with typographic characters. Each line of the drawing made by the engraving tool is the same sort of line as that for each letter made by the tool of the punch cutter. However, it is not sufficient for the illustration or ornament to be merely cut on the wood; the drawing must be conceived for the material to which it is destined. These major principles of book design and illustration were the ones which Lucien expressed and followed.

Lucien conceived of himself as both painter and engraver. The two mediums were not antipathetic. His drawings and paintings served as studies for his engravings. In his engravings, he believed that he refined his style.[23] He fought the notion that his engravings were decorations, believing instead that they were of an absolute realism.[24] Lucien began to see, surely under Ricketts' influence, his engravings in a context—not prints that would necessarily stand alone but prints that were appropriate to typography.[25] By printing his engravings in color he gave to them more of a painted quality than a decorative one but still produced an engraving which was appropriate to typography. Lucien had an amazing grasp of his medium, his tremendous technical skill developed after only a few years of experimentation with wood engraving. As a master of flat pattern, his style is refined and delicate. He tried to design his prints in terms of the material in which they were to be executed, and his ability to harmonize the weight of his type with the tonalities of his prints is remarkable.

Style

In 1911 Lucien, in a letter to Roger Marx, lamented that if he had a group of subscribers for his books it would permit him to produce a series of illustrated booklets (*plaquettes*) in the style of *The Queen of the Fishes,* his starting point, which he had been forced against his will to abandon in 1894.[26] This remark clarifies why an abrupt change in Lucien's style can be observed with the publication of his second book, *The Book of Ruth and the Book of Esther.* To remain in Ricketts' good graces, to have the use of the Vale type, and to have his works published by Hacon & Ricketts, Lucien had to conform to Ricketts' strictures on art and to his ideals.

The first book of the Eragny Press, *The Queen of the Fishes,* fully realized the School of Eragny style. Besides employing impressionist colors and gothic gold, the illustrations are rustically simple and natural without affectation. The figures are not stylized, but are drawn and cut on the wood based on Lucien's vision of the characters, not in imitation of someone else's style. The manuscript hand which Lucien employed for the text blends well with the illustrations. Lucien's first attempt at book design, while still not employing all the precepts of the harmonic book, was a dazzling success. The book, recalling Lucien's French background, utilizes little of the Arts and Crafts style. While he employs a border, the border is neither Kelmscott nor Vale, neither full of wine nor full of light, but of sinewy art nouveau style. It is not an elaborate intertwining border, but is composed of a gentle whiplash. *The Queen of the Fishes,* is an integrated whole; all the parts, both text and illustration, belong to each other.

But the burden of Ricketts' influence lay heavily upon Lucien to become more Pre-Raphaelite, to copy the ways of the old masters rather than to follow his own sensations. It must be noted, however, that this turn to the English Arts and Crafts style was not completely influenced by Ricketts, but also by Esther, who before her marriage to Lucien had been completely captivated by William Morris and his designs. Surely she

The Book of Ruth and the Book of Esther, 1896; pp. xvi–xvii. (Special Collections, Florida State University, Tallahassee)

Ruth resteth with the reapers.

shall have done eating & drinking. IV And it shall be, when he lieth down, that thou shalt mark the place where he shall lie, and thou shalt go in, and uncover his feet, and lay thee down; and he
xvi will

will tell thee what thou shalt do. V And she said unto her, All that thou sayest unto me I will do. VI And she went down unto the floor, and did according to all that her mother in law bade her. VII And when Boaz had eaten and drunk, and his heart was merry, he went to lie down at the end of the heap of corn: and she came softly, & uncovered his feet, and laid her down. VIII And it came to pass at midnight, that the man was afraid, and turned himself: and, behold, a woman lay at his feet. IX And he said, Who art thou? And she answered, I am Ruth thine handmaid; spread therefore thy skirt over thy handmaid; for thou art a near kinsman. X And he said, Blessed be thou of the LORD, my daughter: for
xvii thou

The Book of Ruth.

pressured Lucien to create a style more imitative of Morris. Those books, following the dictates of the Arts and Crafts movement, are exquisite examples of bookmaking, but they are not in Lucien's true style. The figures in the illustration became more stylized, more elongated in the Pre-Raphaelite style, and less rustic, simple, and natural. The borders became more intertwined and complicated, and the use of color subsided.

The Book of Ruth and the Book of Esther is more closely aligned with the Arts and Crafts style. The book, printed in black and red, is decorated with ornamental initials and shoulder notes. The illustrations, in black and white, are not surrounded by borders as a typical Arts and Crafts book would be, but are enclosed by two simple lines, one narrow, the other wide. While the illustrations still retain much of their Normandy flavor, the book itself is less in the Eragny temperament which *The Queen of the Fishes* embodies so well, in terms of quality of the engraving and its color, as well as the story line.

Ricketts, upon seeing *The Book of Ruth and the Book of Esther* for the first time, praised it very highly:

> It's funny you are not a decorator and the first cover of the book and the first ornamental initials that you made are completely successful.[27]

Lucien attributed his success to his naïve quality and to the School of Eragny which

> makes the things we make not seem connected to what is known and classical and has a very special aspect which pleases one and irritates another enormously. It is, by consequent [*sic*], original, of a style completely natural, and which, I am sure, although adapted from another art, preserves it.[28]

Surely, some of this change and gravitation to a style which met with Ricketts' approval must have been in some way a rebellion against his father. Lucien needed some time to try other styles before he could reconcile himself to his true style. His next books, *Moralités légendaires,* volumes one and two, in black and red, are heavier and darker than the previous two books. Employing a border more in keeping with the Vale style, the figures of Salomé and Ophelia are more Pre-Raphaelite women than French peasants drawn from nature. In spite of this, the two volumes are completely successful, but they are not necessarily what Lucien would have made if he had not been under Ricketts' influence.

Perrault's *Deux contes de ma mère l'oye,* printed in 1899, returns to a use of color, employing a greenish ink and gold, to create a more delicate woodcut illustration than in the previous books. However, the border which surrounds the woodcut, the same one used in the first volume of *Moralités légendaires,* while delicately styled, is not wholly appropriate to the wood engraving. This book is the first book that Hacon & Ricketts bought outright; and it is the last that Lucien produced with a color engraving, until the final book of the Vale series, *C'est d'Aucassin et de Nicolete.* Because color is the most important element of an Eragny Press

IVRESSE D'AMOUR. Li-Tai-Pé.

LE vent agite doucement, à l'entour du Pa-lais des Eaux, les fleurs embaumées des nénuphars.

SUR la plus haute terrasse de Kou-sou on peut apercevoir le roi de Lou, étendu noncha-lamment.

7

"Ivresse d'amour," wood engraving. Judith Gautier, *Album de poëmes tirés du livre de jade,* 1911; p. 7. (Ashmolean Museum, Oxford)

book, giving the most immediate sensation of life and being the area in which Lucien was most skilled as an artist, it is curious that color was neglected almost completely in the Vale series. The reason for this seems to be obvious. Printing in color is a time-consuming, labor-intensive task which makes for an expensive undertaking. As capital was always limited, it was important to produce a book quickly in order to make a prompt return on the investment. It is interesting to note that once Hacon & Ricketts was no longer the publisher of Eragny Press books, almost all the books for which Lucien designed the woodcuts have at least one color engraving. And, moreover, the Eragny Press was continually without financial resources during this period. In order to be a part of the Vale group, it was necessary for Lucien to compromise his art. While many of the later Vale series engravings are very much in keeping with Lucien's French temperament, they are still very different from what he set out to do with *The Queen of the Fishes*—which was to create an ensemble of the book and the sensation of art. The engravings from *The Queen of the Fishes* have a personal savor which distinguish them from those made under Ricketts' fifteenth-century-Italian influence.

In returning to the French markets, Lucien also returned to the style from which he had been diverted. With *Riquet à la houppe* (1907); *Histoire de la reine du matin et de Soliman prince des génies* (1909), produced for the Société des cent bibliophiles in Paris; the *Album de poëmes tirés du livre de jade* (1911), printed with the French market in mind; and *La Charrue d'érable* (1912/13), executed for Le Livre contemporain in Paris, Lucien returned to his Eragny style. Color, in these truly modern books, is their most prominent feature; the engravings are sensitive and delicate. They are experimental and innovative. None of the four employ black ink for the text, but use various shades of gray which harmonize with the impressionist colors used in the engravings. In addition there is a series of engravings used in the books. While the earlier books tend to have one major engraving and several ornamented initials, these books include specially designed head and tail pieces, historiated initials, and a variety of engravings at key points in the text, just as *The Queen of the Fishes* had so many years earlier. The five masterpieces of the Eragny Press, the books are monumental in their use of color and design. Lucien completely abandoned the Arts and Crafts style of Morris and Ricketts, producing an original vision of the book with perfect harmony and grace. Of all the books of the Press, these five are Lucien's *livres d'artiste* and the closest examples we have to true impressionist book art.

In creative vision, original style, and meticulous production skills, no other private press surpasses the art of an Eragny Press book. Combining the principles of Arts and Crafts book design and of impressionist sensation, Lucien Pissarro created the most original books of the private press movement and can be credited also with provoking an interest in France in the *livre d'artiste.* By being both the creative artist and the workman, Lucien combined his skills to create books which, because they are almost completely autographic, are the closest one comes to personal expression in book design. While many printers and designers of the period were adept in a variety of skills, none of the private press proprietors participated in all the processes of book production. Lucien saw a book from its inception through the actual printing, doing much of the work himself. Moreover, with Esther working by his side, to her own exacting, meticulous standards, Lucien had one of the best production teams available.

In his struggle for financial solvency, Lucien may have deviated from his true path toward original artistic vision, but his skill as an engraver and as an arranger are always evident in his work. Every Eragny Press book exhibits careful craftsmanship, an intrinsic element in the Arts and Crafts principles, as well as the Impressionist sensation. Most tellingly, one of Lucien's contemporaries described Eragny Press books as "lovely, delicate, sensitive to color, a breath rather than a statement, something that hinges one into the ethereal qualities of life and art."[29]

Notes

1. Colin Franklin has called the Press "a minor matter in the scheme of things."
2. Strachan, *The Artist and the Book in France*, 19.
3. Ibid., 21.
4. Vollard, *Recollections of a Picture Dealer*, 170.
5. For a discussion of Lucien's role in the revival of the woodcut as an original art form see Jacquelynn Baas, "Auguste Lepère and the Artistic Revivial of the Woodcut in France, 1875–1895" (Ph.D. diss., University of Michigan, 1982).
6. The drawings, which Camille had done for "Les Travaux des champs," were finally realized, however, in *La Charrue d'érable* (1912/13), commissioned by Le Livre contemporain. This commission provided Lucien with the means to complete the work as well as pay tribute to his late father.
7. Camille Pissarro to Lucien Pissarro, 8 July 1891, Pissarro Collection, Ashmolean Museum. Translated in Rewald, 226.
8. Lucien Pissarro to Camille Pissarro, [between 10 and 15 February 1891], Pissarro Collection, Ashmolean Museum.
9. Camille Pissarro to Lucien Pissarro, 19 August 1898, Pissarro Collection, Ashmolean Museum. Translated in Rewald, *The History of Impressionism*, 425–426.
10. Ibid. Translated in Rewald, *The History of Impressionism*, 425.
11. Camille Pissarro to Lucien Pissarro, 26 April 1892, Pissarro Collection, Ashmolean Museum. Translation mine.
12. Camille Pissarro to Lucien Pissarro, 27 January 1894, Pissarro Collection, Ashmolean Museum. Translation mine.
13. Camille Pissarro to Lucien Pissarro, 17 March 1903, Pissarro Collection, Ashmolean Museum.
14. Lucien Pissarro, Paris, to Esther L. Pissarro, The Brook, Hammersmith, [1910], Pissarro Collection, Ashmolean Museum.
15. Lucien Pissarro to Camille Pissarro, 23 May 1891, Pissarro Collection, Ashmolean Museum.
16. Charles Ricketts, London, to D. S. MacColl, [London], [1904], Ricketts Papers, MS. 58090, Letter 44, Department of Manuscripts, British Library, London.
17. Lucien Pissarro to Camille Pissarro, [after 2 December 1896], Pissarro Collection, Ashmolean Museum.
18. Lucien Pissarro to Camille Pissarro, 10 Apirl 1895, Pissarro Collection, Ashmolean Museum.
19. Charles Ricketts and Lucien Pissarro, *De la typographie et de l'harmonie de la page imprimée* (Paris: en vente chez Floury; London: Sold by Hacon & Ricketts, 1898). In their second essay, "William Morris et son influence sur les arts et métiers," they offered a few pages of criticism on Morris' work and his influence. Primarily they recognized Morris for having reestablished hard work and integrity in the crafts and for his creative influence which brought about the revival in decoration. An English translation by Richard K. Kellenberger can be found in the *Colby Library Quarterly* (ser. 3, no. 5): 69–75; (ser. 3, no. 12): 194–200.
20. The manuscripts are held in the Print Room, Ashmolean Museum.
21. M. Denis, *Théories, 1890–1910, du symbolisme et de Gauguin vers un nouvel ordre classique* (Paris: L. Rouart et J. Watelin, 1920), 1–13.
22. This essay remains unpublished; I do not know when or why Lucien wrote this essay or what plans he had for it.
23. Lucien Pissarro to Esther L. Pissarro, 15 March 1910, Pissarro Collection, Ashmolean Museum. "For

what is my purpose in painting landscape from nature? To learn in order to do my blocks away from nature and so bringing a sort of résumé or synthèse."

24. Lucien Pissarro to Camille Pissarro, 22 February 1894, Pissarro Collection, Ashmolean Museum.

25. Lucien Pissarro to Camille Pissarro, 5 May 1892, Pissarro Collection, Ashmolean Museum.

26. Lucien Pissarro, The Brook, Hammersmith, to Roger Marx, Paris, 6 January 1911, Pissarro Collection, Ashmolean Museum.

27. Lucien Pissarro to Camille Pissarro, [after 21 November 1896], Pissarro Collection, Ashmolean Museum. Translation mine.

28. Ibid.

29. W. L. Clause to Lucien Pissarro, 29 April 1941, Pissarro Collection, Ashmolean Museum.

Conclusion

Lucien Pissarro came to London in 1890 to investigate career prospects within the decorative arts movement. William Morris had become a symbol for the Pissarro family because of his role in raising the level of the applied arts and his vision of a new society in which art would be integrated with everyday life. The success of William Morris' firm, Morris & Co., led the Pissarros to believe that they could use their art to create useful products, more marketable than paintings. With this new awareness of craftsmanship that Lucien was to glean from his stay in England, the Pissarros planned to start their own atelier in France inspired by Morris and Co.

An introduction to Charles Ricketts and a significant relationship with Esther Bensusan changed the course of Lucien's career. Under Ricketts' influence, Lucien's early interest in book illustration was revived and he turned to book design as a vehicle for his wood engravings. Taking William Morris' successful Kelmscott Press as a model, Lucien established his own press in 1894. His early training with its emphasis on drawing, his initial work as a painter and chromolithographer, and his profound knowledge of the science of color converged, resulting in Lucien's Eragny Press books of quiet perfection.

While never achieving the fame and recognition of the Kelmscott or Vale Presses, the Eragny Press played a significant role in the history of fine printing. Just as Lucien served as a direct link in introducing Impressionism from France into England, he also served this same function in introducing Morris' principles of book design to the continent. His attempts to communicate Morris' design theories, as well as his own, to the continent, set forth in his essay *De la typographie et de l'harmonie de la page imprimée* are indicative of his goals to promote book design. Lucien's theories and books were highly regarded in France, Belgium, and Holland by his Symbolist and Impressionist friends, who helped to publicize the books through notices and reviews. Yet Lucien's reputation never reached beyond that limited audience, which severely restricted his breadth of influence. His natural timidness and modesty inhibited the promotion and publicizing of ideas not widely accepted by mainstream book collectors who should have constituted the bulk of Lucien's continental clientele. The idea of dark type solidly spaced and integrated with illustrations and ornaments on a page was foreign to French bibliophiles,

Initial N (Fern 300 [122]). *The Book of Ruth and the Book of Esther*, 1896. (Special Collections, Florida State University, Tallahassee)

who preferred the lighter, more refined Elsevier types with *hors-texte* illustration.

Lucien's decision, profoundly influenced by Esther, to live and work in England was, as Lucien understood in retrospect, a mistake. He felt out of place in England and had few close friends outside the Bensusan circle.[1] He never penetrated the Arts and Crafts circles and never, socially, reached the heart of the movement. If Lucien had returned to France after he developed his craft, it is highly likely he would have been more successful. Because Lucien's early work in England was promoted in France through an intermediary—his father—Lucien never created close contacts with those men on the Continent who could have promoted his work. Camille also discouraged his son from participating and associating with artists who did not, in his opinion, have the Pissarro integrity. Graphic art, as an affordable art for the masses, required some compromise, which the Pissarros were unwilling to accept. Lucien's books remained largely unknown on the Continent after twenty years in England. Lucien looked bitterly to the success of Auguste Lepère and his brother, Georges, who both began designing books at a much later time than he.[2] Commissions with two major French book clubs strengthened his reputation, but with the closing of the Press, these commissions did little to actually promote his work.

The Eragny Press' modest prosperity in association with Hacon & Ricketts was due to Ricketts' popularity and the effective marketing of the books by Charles Holmes, who was an experienced publisher when he agreed to manage Charles Ricketts' firm. The more pragmatic control which Ricketts and Holmes asserted over the design of the books—less color to keep costs down and a design more in keeping with stylistic trends of the period—made the books more attractive and less extravagant to the 1890s consumer. When Lucien's affiliation with Hacon & Ricketts ended, he began a gradual stylistic move back to his earlier work, *The Queen of the Fishes,* employing more color and undertaking more technically difficult work which ultimately resulted in his masterpiece, *La Charrue d'érable.* Any astute observer would have realized that the commercial success of the books was endangered by this renewed artistic integrity, but Lucien was uncompromising in his artistic vision.

> It is a good sign [to] have not sold more . . . you must take up a position: either you work as an artist, or look upon yourself as a tradesman . . . if you try to be one [a tradesman], you will lose your quality as an artist. Thus it is better . . . to continue . . . to follow your artistic feelings without thinking of sales. . . . Remember, in spite of the time it takes to arrive, that is the surest way. Sooner or later one finds one's place.[3] . . . Remember we don't work in order to earn our living, but because we cannot help it. If by chance you earn some money, all the better, but that is not the purpose.[4]

Lucien Pissarro, in his late seventies, wrote these words of advice to his nephew, John Bensusan-Butt, who at the time was aspiring to become an artist, Lucien's advice, passed on the counsel which his father had given him, but which he had not fully understood when he was the proprietor of the Eragny Press, struggling to make his living from his art. This unequivocal devotion to art as a personal vision eclipsed and diminished any plan for commercial and artistic success.

Esther Pissarro's role in the Press, once neglected, has been identified and defined. As Lucien's companion, Esther, as outspoken as Lucien was shy, supported him with perspicacious insights into his design and techniques and influenced him in his decision to adopt the Arts and Crafts style in his border designs. She was more than a helpmeet. After Lucien's major illness in 1897, she took on most of the presswork and eventually became printer to the Eragny Press. She acquired the necessary technical printing skills, though some were self-invented, and approached printing with a painstaking meticulousness. Because of Esther's unfailing craftsmanship, Eragny Press books are some of the finest printed of any private press of the period.

In considering this golden age of the private press, the triumvirate of the Kelmscott, Ashendene, and Doves presses is the one most likely to come to mind. Essentially these presses were run by men of wealth, who while practicing the Arts and Crafts ideals of fine design and workmanship had few pecuniary constraints. The Eragny Press and the Vale Press are removed and outside these traditional private presses. Both Lucien and Charles Ricketts, neither one wealthy, needed to earn a living from their presses. For them, it was a matter of financial necessity, not lofty ideals, to integrate art with everyday life.

In evaluating the Eragny Press, many critics have praised the books for their personal charm and delightfulness, but then have quickly dismissed them because they remain a "fairly minor matter in the whole movement"[5] or because they are "quite unlike anything to be found in the work of any other private press"[6] or because they are a "curious mixture"[7] of Impressionism and "art nouveau decoration."[8] This simplistic dismissal of the Eragny Press has had much to do with the standards of judgment of the private press books of this period. The books have been referred to as "minor" for three predominant reasons: format and size of text, output, and scale of operation. Printed in primarily an octavo format or smaller, and with short texts, Eragny Press books did not meet these critics' standard of monumentality for private press books of this era. The texts themselves were often of a foreign nature and certainly not a part of the English literary canon. In comparison to the books of the highly popular triumvirate of Kelmscott, Ashendene, and Doves, the Eragny Press books' smaller formats and shorter texts, as well as the Press' entire output—thirty-two books over a twenty-year period—are quite modest. And the scale of operation, with only Lucien, Esther, and a printer taking part in the work, was unassuming as well. These three criteria have been the basis on which the importance of the Eragny Press has been judged by the private press critics, though contemporary collectors are now seeing the Press' books for what they are—small gems.

Other standards of judgment are more germane to the Eragny Press than those which have been used in the past. Eragny Press books can best be appraised by three different criteria: workmanship; design and structural unity; and original artistic vision.

Lucien's careful guidance of the work through the Press, accompanied by Esther's high standards of perfection, resulted in superb craftsmanship. Lucien's willingness to be innovative within the medium, his experiments in printing with gold powder and leaf as well as music type, for example, is evidence of his commitment to his craft. The uncompromising use of materials—handmade paper fabricated to exacting standards, vellum carefully selected for its uniform qualities, and ink for its precise color—proclaims the integrity of the books. In addition, each book contains one or more autographic prints. Lucien's involvement in the work of the Press is a measure of the extent of his creative stake in the operation. The design of Eragny Press books is based on the principles and precepts of book design established by William Morris. But Lucien, as well as Charles Ricketts, took Morris' precepts one step further with his interest in original wood engraving. The Kelmscott Press and other private presses which included illustrations in their books saw wood engraving mainly as a convenient means to reproduce an illustration within the medium of letterpress printing. Lucien regarded engravings as original artistic expressions. Because he understood the limitations of his materials, translated his drawings onto wood, and engraved them himself, Lucien's books, essentially illustrations united with careful typographic design, form harmonious entities.

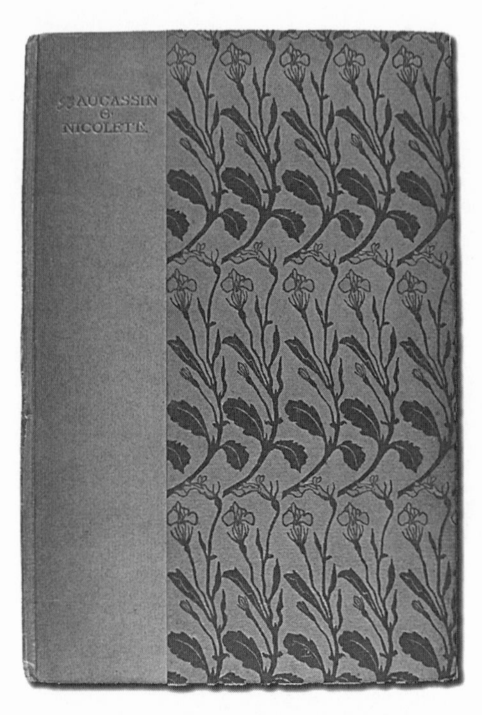

Binding. *C'est d'Aucassin et de Nicolete,* 1903. (Special Collections, Florida State University, Tallahassee)

His conscientious choice of appropriate binding design to complete his structure was an important innovation within the revivalist private press movement. Rather than placing his books within the confines of a temporary binding with the expectation that the collector would find appropriate covering, Lucien designed his own bindings. The charming and delicate paper covers, always colorfully printed, provide added decoration as well as incentive for looking further.

Lucien Pissarro approached book design as both a painter and an engraver, a rare combination within the private press tradition. Painting, during the Eragny Press period, became for him the dominant means of study, permitting him to maintain contact with nature and supplying him with a source for illustrations. His mastery of color synthesis gives his illustrations a luster reminiscent of medieval miniatures. Lucien's woodcut illustrations result from sensation, the feeling aroused by some immediate observation of the world in close relation to one's own feelings and nature.

Lyric impressionism paired with subtle gradations and varieties of color make Lucien's work unique and important. In the use of color, Pissarro had no equal in the private press movement. Essentially, his books are in the French tradition of *livres d'artiste*. This unique combination of French influences and English Arts and Crafts style reveal a supremely lyrical and elegant sense of design. No other revivalist private press comes close to the personal quality of an Eragny book.

It is perhaps ironic that the most personal of the private presses, the one with the most artistic integrity, should be founded on commercial considerations. It is unfortunate that Lucien did not possess boundless resources from which to invent and construct his books. The books, however, have a greater unity because of the control Lucien exercised, out of necessity, over their design and production.

At the expense of his stature and reputation, Lucien maintained a greater integrity of craftsmanship than any other revivalist private press. The impressiveness of design, the careful integration of woodcuts into the text, and the innovative use of color combined with personal vision, contribute to the significance of Eragny Press books. The shortage of capital, a major component obstructing Lucien's achievements, limited, not only the output, but the artistic vision as well. It is precisely because they are not like anything to be found within the work of the private presses that the books need to be acknowledged and appreciated. The Eragny Press so aptly demonstrates the pursuit of the Arts and Crafts ideal by a man who produced the best that he could, in spite of commercial considerations. The books of the Eragny Press are eloquent of the tender emotions which nature inspires. In their quiet perfection they provide a close and intimate view of the expression of feelings. In the Eragny Press, Lucien Pissarro found the proper medium for the articulation of his sensation and "the work which will count."[9]

Notes

1. Lucien Pissarro to Esther Pissarro, [1910], Pissarro Collection, Ashmolean Museum.
2. Ibid., 10 May [1910].
3. Quoted in John Bensusan-Butt, "Recollections of Lucien Pissarro in his Seventies," in *Lucien Pissarro, 1863–1944* (London: Anthony d'Offay, [1977]), 13.
4. Ibid., 26.
5. Franklin, *The Private Presses*, 93–94, 101–102.
6. Cave, *The Private Press*, 117.
7. John Lewis, *The Twentieth Century Book: Its Illustration and Design*, 2nd edition (New York: Van Nostrand Reinhold Company, 1984), 19.
8. Ibid.
9. Lucien Pissarro to Esther Pissarro, 28 July 1928, Pissarro Collection, Ashmolean Museum. On hearing that Esther had sold the printing press, Lucien wrote, "It is really the end of a period of our lives, and perhaps the one in which we did the work which will count. The true collaboration, the expression of our mutual love."

Part II

A Descriptive Bibliography of Eragny Press Books

INTRODUCTION

The Eragny Press produced thirty-two books over the course of twenty years, with no edition larger than 226 copies. The smallest edition was twenty-seven copies. Their average output was one and a half books a year. Their peak output was no greater than four books a year. In spite of the small edition sizes, the limited output, and the small formats, Eragny Press books were time-consuming to create and were produced almost entirely by the Pissarros, a couple working together to produce books completely outside the commercial industry—artists' books in every sense. The hallmarks of the Press were the color wood engravings, used mainly in the frontispieces of each book. Only five of the books had elaborate color, including gold, throughout and reflect the true nature of the Press. Nine were printed primarily in black and white—a means to increased output and better cash flow. The bibliography that follows describes the thirty-two books of the Press and includes ephemera only in relation to the books. For example, the Pissarros occasionally designed and printed bookplates for close friends and associates. They are not included here.

The illustrations and typographical decorations are referred to by their Fern numbers. In the late 1950s, Alan Fern edited the studio books of Lucien and Esther Pissarro, their "Catalogues de gravures sur bois," the record of wood engravings of the Press as well as engravings Lucien created before the establishment of the Eragny Press. Fern's catalog, though unpublished, remains the definitive guide to Lucien Pissarro's wood engravings, but it is not without flaws. Some of them are owing to lack of information about the engravings due to the period in which Fern worked; others are due to ideologies conflicting with the Pissarros' ideas concerning their books. The original studio book does not differentiate between pictorial engravings and typographical decorations (ornaments, borders, and floriated initials). Fern separated these into two different sections. He wrote, "These [the typographical elements] were often used several times and in different contexts, indicating that the artist regarded them as part of his typographical resources rather than as individual prints" (Fern, p. 100). This, however, was not the case. Orovida Pissarro noted that "it was a pity to divide the decorations from the illustrations often so carefully thought out and interrelated" (undated letter). In order to create a sense of wholeness as well as an artistic identity, the Pissarros used the typographical decorations more as a refrain or a counterpoint and fugue within the body of their work. The initials and borders create connections between the books and clearly show that there was a publishing program in place, despite the financial barriers to implementing it. The keywords here are unity, connection, and wholeness between the illustrative engravings and the ornamental. The Fern numbers and his rearrangement of the catalog do not reflect this. The studio book numbers are more reflective of how the Pissarros conceived of the flow of their work and follow the Fern number here in brackets. The Fern catalog also omits many of the engravings, primarily initials—but also some wood engravings, if the Pissarros neglected to place them in their studio book. Those items omitted from Fern are identified in the descriptive bibliography as (NIF).

There were seven different design series of initial letters used in Eragny Press books. The initials created for *Of Gardens* were used only in that book. Another set of initials, created for *The Little School*, and used in *Songs by Ben Jonson* and *Whym Chow*, are not included in Fern's catalog.

The Pissarros used quite unorthodox printing methods; the collational formulas reflect the ideal more than the reality. One can be safe in assuming that pages with complex wood engravings were printed separately from the more typographical pages. I have made note of this in the narrative portion of this section's bibliography when I was able to determine this through secondary sources—primarily the letters of Esther Pissarro to Thomas Leighton of Leighton, Son, and Hodge, the commercial bindery where all Eragny Press books were sent to be bound.

The Letters of Lucien to Camille Pissarro, 1883–1903, edited by Anne Thorold provides supporting documentation for this bibliography with copious illustrations of trial designs for the illustrative engravings, the floriated initials, and typography during the period where Lucien was polishing his skills under Camille's guidance. All letters and related items cited here may be found in the Pissarro Collection at the Ashmolean Museum, Oxford, unless otherwise indicated.

In the United States, the most complete collections of Eragny Press books are at the New York Public Library and the Sacramento Public Library. A handful of libraries have strong collections, but many hold only a few. The most complete collection in England is at the British Library. I was able to look at the collections of the Ashmolean, which holds the Pissarros' copies; The Bancroft Library of the University of California at Berkeley (Bancroft); The British Library (BL); Special Collections, The Florida State University, Tallahassee (FSU); The Huntington Library, San Marino, California (Huntington); the Library of Congress (LC); The New York Public Library (NYPL); the San Francisco Public Library (SFPL); and the William Andrews Clark, Jr., Library at the University of California, Los Angeles (UCLA).

EP1 • Margaret Rust. The Queen of the Fishes. 1895.

[in gold manuscript caps, hand-lettered and reproduced by means of process block] THE QVEEN OF THE FISHES. | AN ADAPTATION IN ENGLISH | OF A FAIRY TALE OF VALOIS. | [two orn: iris] BY MARGARET RVST [two orn: iris] | WITH ILLVSTRATIONS DESIG- | NED ON THE WOOD CVT AND | PRINTED BY LVCIEN PISSARRO. | SOLD BY JOHN LANE, AT THE | SIGN OF THE BODLEY HEAD. | IN VIGO STREET. LONDON. [orn: iris]

[1] [edition statement] [in green] [orn: iris] THE ISSUE IS STRICTLY | LIMITED TO ONE HUNDRED | AND FIFTY COPIES, OF WHICH, | ONE HUNDRED AND TWENTY | ARE FOR SALE, THIS IS: ... | NO ...... [in red manuscript hand] 104 [LP Mongram in red] [NYPL Copy]

SECOND ISSUE TITLE PAGE: [in gold manuscript caps, hand-lettered and reproduced by means of process block] THE QUEEN OF THE FISHES. | AN ADAPTATION IN ENGLISH | OF A FAIRY TALE OF VALOIS. | [double orn: iris] BY MARGARET RUST. [double orn: iris] | WITH ILLVSTRATIONS DESIG- | NED ON THE WOOD CUT AND | PRINTED BY LVCIEN PISSARRO. | PUBLISHED BY CH. RICKETTS | 31 BEAUFORT ST^{T} CHELSEA, | [orn: iris] LONDON. [orn: iris]

COLOPHON: [in black and orange type] "VALE PUBLICATIONS." [Pressmark I (Fern 93)] | THIS BOOK HAS BEEN PRIN- | TED IN 1894, BY LUCIEN | PISSARRO AT HIS | PRESS IN EPPING | [ESSEX.] [orn: iris] [in green ink] THE ISSUE IS STRICTLY LIMITED TO ONE HUNDRED | FIFTY COPIES, OF WHICH, | ONE HUNDRED AND TWENTY | ARE FOR SALE, THIS IS: ... | No .....

COLLATION: 8°: 12 double-folded Japanese-style leaves, pp. [1] 2–12 [13] 14 [15–16]

PAPER: Japanese vellum. Leaf: 195 x 127 mm.

TYPE: Hand-lettered and reproduced by means of process blocks

ILLUSTRATIONS, ORNAMENTS, AND INITIALS: [twelve wood-engraved illustrations: five color wood engravings with borders and seven in black and white; three ornaments in red; pressmark in black and white] p. [1]: "The Queen of the Fishes," four-block color engraving, 69 x 45 mm. (Fern 81 [SB 69]) within gold border, 57 x 77 mm. (Fern 277 [SB 83]). p. 2: "Child on Riverbank," 70 x 50 mm. (Fern 82 [SB 71]). p. 3: "Children Gathering Wood," 76 x 55 mm. (Fern 83 [SB 70]). p. 4: "Girl Reaching into Stream," four-block color engraving, 75 x 80 mm. (Fern 84 [SB 72]) within green border (Fern 277 [SB 83]). p. 5: "The

Wreathing" 89 x 32 mm. (Fern 85 [SB 74]). p. 6: "The Queen and her Attendants," 89 x 58 mm. (Fern 86 [SB 73]). p. 7: "On the River Bank," four-block color engraving, 83 x 78 mm. (Fern 87 [SB 75]) within green border, 83 x 78 mm. (Fern 277 [SB 83]). p. 8: "Bringing in Firewood," 78 x 51 mm. (Fern 88 [SB 75 ter]). p. 9: "Asleep by the Stream," 32 x 76 mm. (Fern 89 [SB 75 bis]). p. 10: "Fisherman," four-block color engraving, 67 x 79 mm. (Fern 90 [SB 77]) within green border (Fern 277 [SB 83]). p. 11: Ornament (Fern 278 [SB 84]) in red. p. 12: "Woodcutters," 58 x 78 mm. (Fern 91 [SB 76]) within green border (Fern 277 [SB 83]). p. 13: "In the Field," five-block color engraving (including gold), 116 x 78 mm. (Fern 92 [SB 78]). p. 14: Head-piece (Fern 279 [SB 85]) in red. p. 15: Cul-de-lampe (Fern 276 [SB 80]) in red. p. [16]: Pressmark, 71 x 51 mm. (Fern 93 [SB 79]). Shoulder notes in red.

CONTENTS: p. [i]: edition statement. p. [ii–vii]: blank. p. [viii]: title. pp. 1–15: text. p. [16]: colophon

BINDING: Soft apple green calfskin with gold stamped iris in upper right corner (published by Ch. Ricketts).

VARIANT BINDING: White vellum with gold stamped iris surrounded by leaves in upper right corner (sold by John Lane).

VARIANT BINDING: White vellum with gold stamped iris surrounded by leaves in upper right corner and lower right corner (trial copy, given to S. L. Bensusan).

PUBLICATION: 120 copies for sale (£1 or 30 frs.). Lucien had originally advertised the book at 25 frs; the price was increased with the rise in binding costs. Published in February 1895.

PROSPECTUS: [240 x 108 mm.] [large orn.] The Queen of the Fishes | [small type orn.] A STORY OF THE VALOIS | ADAPTED BY MARGARET RUST | BEING A PRINTED MANUSCRIPT | DECORATED WITH PICTURES | AND OTHER ORNAMENTS CUT | ON THE WOOD BY LUCIEN | PISSARRO, AND PRINTED BY | HIM IN DIVERS COLOURS AND | IN GOLD AT HIS PRESS IN | EPPING. (VALE PUBLICATIONS.) SOLD BY JOHN LANE, AT THE | SIGN OF THE BODLEY HEAD, IN VIGO STREET, LONDON. | [small orn.] Ready very shortly, 150 copies (120) | for sale, of which 50 have been sold in | France, Germany, Holland, Belgium, and | Italy, and 70 are for England and America, | crown 8vo., price £1 net. Each copy will be numbered and signed. | [small orn.] Printed on hand-made Japanese paper | and bound in vellum. | Subscribers are requested to use order | form on the other side. | [verso] [Order from].

VARIANT PROSPECTUS: [240 x 108 mm.] [column one] [large leaf orn] THE QUEEN OF THE FISHES. | Pressmark I | [orn] A STORY OF THE | VALOIS ADAPTED | BY MARGARET RUST | BEING A PRINTED | MANUSCRIPT DEC- | ORATED WITH PICTURES AND OTHER | ORNAMENTS CUT | ON THE WOOD BY | LUCIEN PISSARRO, | & PRINTED BY HIM | IN DIVERS COLOURs | & IN GOLD AT HIS | PRESS IN EPPING. | PUBLISHED BY C.H. | SHANNON. (VALE | PUBLICATIONS) 31 | BEAUFORT STREET | CHELSEA LONDON. | [column two] [in red] [orn.] Ready | very shortly | 150 copies | (120 for sale) | crown 8vo. | Price 1£ net | each copy | will be num- | bered & si- | gned. | [orn] Prin- | ted on hand- | made japa- | nese paper & | bound in | apple green calf. | [orn.] Subs- | cribers are | requested to | use order | form on the | other side. | [verso] [Order form].

THE QVEEN OF THE FISHES.
AN ADAPTATION IN ENGLISH
OF A FAIRY TALE OF VALOIS.
BY MARGARET RVST.
WITH ILLVSTRATIONS DESIGNED ON THE WOOD CVT AND
PRINTED BY LVCIEN PISSARRO
PVBLISHED BY CH.RICKETTS
31 BEAVFORT STT CHELSEA,
LONDON.

Title page. Margaret Rust, *The Queen of the Fishes,* 1895.

NOTES: Lucien began working on illustrations for the Eragny Press edition of *The Queen of the Fishes* in 1893. He used the English translation of Margaret Rust, a friend of Esther's. Earlier versions, in French and English, had been rejected by both French and English publishers. In the winter and spring of 1894, Lucien was engraving blocks and starting to acquire the necessary materials to produce the *The Queen of the Fishes.* He acquired his first press in late February. By late May, having finished writing the text, Lucien, impatient to begin printing his book, was waiting for Camille to send him a little money so he could begin production. In late December, he reported to Camille that he was producing his book little-by-little and on 8 February 1895 announced to Camille that the book was finished and would be sent to the binder the next day. The production cost 1,000 frs. and Lucien hoped to realize 2,500 frs. (£100) from the sale of the edition. Lucien and Ricketts had selected an apple-green calfskin for the binding. The colored calfskin was not expensive, only 2s6d per copy, but by the time *The Queen of the Fishes* was ready to be bound, the apple-green calfskin had become fashionable and the price had risen to 4s6d per copy. Lucien had already announced that his book would be bound in vellum, or for those willing to pay an additional four shillings, *The Queen of the Fishes* would be bound in the calfskin. Thirty subscribers had already bought copies bound in the calfskin and thus Lucien was obligated to have the books bound in the calfskin, at a loss of six pence per copy. By 8 March 1895, one hundred copies had been sold. Thirty copies were sold in Belgium and Holland; seventy copies were bought by John Lane, the English publisher who was planning to sell the books in the United States. Lane bought the copies outright, giving Lucien a quick profit of 1,000 frs. or five shillings per copy. Although Lucien realized his lack of business acumen, he still felt exploited by Lane. The profit was insufficient for the effort and time that had gone into the production. Lucien had hoped to make a larger profit to cover the expenses of his next book.

Lucien's business dealings with Lane were off to a shaky start. Eighty prospectuses had been sent to Lane, but Lane wanted five hundred copies. Printing five hundred prospectuses would cut considerably into profits. Shannon suggested that Lane be provided with 250 prospectuses and that Lane and Lucien share the expense. Lane had refused to pay Lucien for the books unless he obtained the prospectuses (C. H. Shannon to Lucien Pissarro, [undated, 1895?]).

The Queen of the Fishes was advertised in the 7 April 1895 issue of *L'Art moderne* with an illustration and in the May issue of *La Revue blanche* (edited by Félix Fénéon and Thadée Natanson), with an advertisement for *Ruth et Booz* (later to become *The Book of Ruth and the Book of Esther*).

Sixteen copies were sold in France; seventeen in Belgium; eleven in Holland; two in Germany; one in England; and two in the United States. Of the numbered copies, nos. 1–5 were sold to Deman in Brussels; 6–13 were sold by *Van Nu en Straks*; 14–15 Martinus Nijhoff; 17 to a buyer in Eragny; 18 Contet; 19 Toulouse-Lautrec (exchanged for a vellum copy); 20–25 Vincent van Gogh, Amsterdam; 26–27 Martinus Nijhoff, 28 T. S. Perry, Paris; 29 T. W. Gutbier; 20 and 31 Dietrich & Co., Brussels; 32 Madame L. Jackson, Paris; 33 Madame Arthur Tite, Ware; 34 Max Elskamp, Anvers; 35–36 Mrs. H. Whitman, Boston; 37 Dietrick; 38 T. S. Perry; 39–44 vellum *Revue blanche* (43 to Bing); 45 L. W. Gutbier; 47–48 Bing; 49 *Revue blanche*; 50 Gaillard; 51–120 John Lane (see *Letters of Lucien Pissarro to Camille Pissarro, 1883–1903*, pp. 427–428).

Of the thirty copies not for sale, copies were given to G. Geffroy, Camille Pissarro, Theo van Rysselberghe, Henri van de Velde, Georges Lecomte, Félix Fénéon, Charles Ricketts and Charles Shannon, H. Petitjean, Diana White, C. Destrée, Vincent van Gogh (Amsterdam bookdealer), May Morris, Margaret Rust (2 copies), H. Campbell, Georges Pissarro, Julie Pissarro, Sam Bensusan, Orovida Bensusan, Esther's mother (F. L. Bensusan), A. Hamon, E. G. Verity, Ida Henry, Alice Isaacson, and a "rich neighbor."

In February 1894, Lucien began negotiations for a separate French edition of *The Queen of the Fishes* with André Marty, a Paris publisher and print dealer. Although this did not work out, Lucien almost succeeded in negotiating a portfolio of the illustrations with Marty for the French market.

The wood engravings were created through an iterative process. Lucien would send proofs of an engraving to Camille who would provide critical feedback. Often, Camille would find Lucien's attempts unsuccessful, not capturing the characteristics of his figures—hands, for example, lacking the strength necessary for a woodcutter (for the engraving, "Les Bûcherons"). He appraised Lucien's choice of colors, finding the pistachio green border out of harmony with the colors of the flowers. But by the time Lucien was ready to go to press, Camille found the engravings to be beautiful, with delightful composition, and the colors clear. On seeing the book itself, Camille considered it to be truly charming and believed it would bring credit to Lucien. He thought the binding, however, to be too refined for the book.

Félix Fénéon found the book to have a joyful and disarming charm that delighted him and Durand-Ruel thought it a small marvel of good taste and faultless execution and hoped it would find the reception that it merited (Durand-Ruel to Lucien Pissarro, 27 April 1895).

On 20 March 1898, Camille wrote Lucien that his *Queen of the Fishes* had become a classic in Paris. This reignited Lucien's desire for a French edition of *The Queen of the Fishes* printed in Vale type. The project, however, would not come to fruition.

COPIES SEEN: Ashmolean (unnumbered copy). Bancroft (No. 144 Alice Isaacson | from her cousin | [LP Monogram]). BL (Sam Bensusan's copy; deposit copy). Huntington (No. 66 [LP monogram]). NYPL (No. 104 [LP monogram], John Shaw Billings Memorial Fund; John Lane ed.). SFPL (Provenance: Robert Grabhorn, No. 82 [LP monogram], from the collection of H. Nazeby Harrington).

EP2 • Bible. O.T. The Book of Ruth and the Book of Esther. 1896.

[in black and red] THE BOOK OF RUTH & | THE BOOK OF ESTHER. | WITH FIVE ILLUSTRA- | TIONS DESIGNED AND | CUT ON THE WOOD BY | LUCIEN PISSARRO, | [type orn: trefoil] PRINTED WITH HIS | OWN HAND & ISSUED | FROM HIS PRESS AT | EPPING (ESSEX).

COLOPHON: OF THIS EDITION ONLY | ONE HUNDRED & FIFTY | FIVE COPIES EXIST OF | WHICH ONE HUNDRED | & FIFTY ARE FOR SALE. | SOLD BY L. HACON AND | C.S. RICKETTS, AT THE | SIGN OF THE DIAL, FIF- | TY TWO WARWICK ST. | REGENT St. LONDON, W. | M.DCCC.XCVI.

COLLATION: 12°: π^4 a^4 b^4 c^8 d^4 e^8 g^7. 43 leaves, pp. [1 leaf] i–lxxxii [lxxxiii]

PAPER AND DIMENSIONS: Arnold's unbleached hand-made paper, with Vale watermark. Leaf: 172 x 95 mm.

TYPE: Vale

ILLUSTRATIONS, ORNAMENTS, AND INITIALS: [four black and white wood-engraved illustrations; fifteen initials in black and white] a1^{r}: Initial N (Fern 300 [SB 122]). a2^{r}: "Ruth, Orphar and Naomi," 76 x 65 mm. (Fern 99 [SB 97]). a4^{v}: Initial A (Fern 307 [SB 129]). a5^{v}: "Ruth Gleaning," 75 x 65 mm. (Fern 100 [SB 98]). b1^{r}: Initial T (Fern 308 [SB 130]). b1^{v}: "Reapers Resting," 76 x 65 mm. (Fern 101 [SB 99]). b3^{v}: Initial T (Fern 308 [SB 130]). b4^{v}: "The Elders," 78 x 65 mm. (Fern 102 [SB 100]). c3^{v}: Initial N (Fern 300 [SB 122]). c4^{v}: "Crowning of Esther," 75 x 65 mm. (Fern 103a [SB 101]). c6^{v}: Initial N. c7^{r}: Initial A (Fern 307 [SB 129]). d3^{r}: Initial A (Fern 307 [SB 129]). e1^{v}: Initial W (Fern 304

Boaz buyeth the inheritance.

I cannot redeem it.
VII Now this was the manner in former time in Israel concerning redeeming and concerning changing, for to confirm all things; a man plucked off his shoe,
xxii and

and gave it to his neighbour: and this was a testimony in Israel.
The Book of Ruth.
VIII Therefore the kinsman said unto Boaz, Buy it for thee. So he drew off his shoe.
IX And Boaz said unto the elders, and unto all the people, Ye are witnesses this day, that I have bought all that was Elimelech's, & all that was Chilion's & Mahlon's, of the hand of Naomi.
X Moreover Ruth the Moabitess, the wife of Mahlon, have I purchased to be my wife, to raise up the name of the dead upon his inheritance, that the name of the dead be not cut off from among his brethren, and from the gate of his place: ye are witnesses this day.
XI And all the people that were in the gate, and the elders, said, We are witnesses. The Lord make the woman that is come into
xxiii c thine

The Book of Ruth and the Book of Esther, 1896; pp. xxii–xxiii. (Special Collections, Florida State University, Tallahassee)

[SB 126]). e4^{r}: Initial N (Fern 300 [SB 122]). e6^{v}: Initial O (Fern 302 [SB 124]). f1^{r}: Initial S (Fern 299 [SB 121]). f3^{r}: Initial O (Fern 302 [SB 124]). g2^{r}: Initial N (Fern 300 [SB 122]). g6^{v}: Initial A (Fern 307 [SB 129]). Shoulder notes and catchwords in red.

CONTENTS: π1^{r}: Dedication: AFFECTIONATELY | DEDICATED TO | ESTHER & RUTH π1^{v}: title. a2^{r}: THE BOOK OF RUTH. | CHAPTER THE FIRST. a4^{v}: CHAPTER THE SECOND. b1^{r}: CHAPTER THE THIRD. b3^{v}: CHAPTER THE FOURTH. c3^{r}: THE BOOK OF ESTHER. c3^{v}: THE BOOK OF ESTHER. | CHAPTER THE FIRST. c7^{r}: CHAPTER THE SECOND. d3^{r}: CHAPTER THE THIRD. e1^{v}: CHAPTER THE FOURTH. e4^{r}: CHAPTER THE FIFTH. e6^{v}: CHAPTER THE SIXTH. f1^{r}: CHAPTER THE SEVENTH. f3^{r}: CHAPTER THE EIGHTH. g2^{r}: CHAPTER THE NINTH. g6^{v}: CHAPTER THE TENTH. g7^{r}: colophon.

ERRATA [slip]: Page ii line 7, read continued | for coninued. | Page lxxiv line 3, read provin- | ces for | ptovinces. | Page lxxv line 4, read hundred | for yundred.

BINDING: Quarter cream paper, gold stamped on upper left cover: [orn: flower] THE | BOOK OF | RUTH & | THE | BOOK OF | ESTHER. Michallet green paper boards with a repeat pattern of "snowdrop" (Fern 280 [SB 144]) printed in green ink. On spine gold stamped at top and bottom, flower ornament.

PUBLICATION: 150 copies for sale at 15s. Published in September 1896.

RELATED MATERIAL: Trial cover: green paper printed in green and white; Floriated initials, with note, "Built between 5 1/2 ems white to be used in 6 ems letters."; preliminary design for alphabet of floriated initials on graph paper; preliminary border design; proof sheet of p. xxii with verse numbers and ornaments in red.

PROSPECTUS: [1 leaf, 163 x 100 mm.)] [type orn: flower] VALE PUBLICATIONS | ISSUED FROM THE SIGN | OF THE DIAL BY HACON | AND RICKETTS, 52 WAR- | WICK STREET, REGENT | STREET, LONDON. W.

Now Ready: [woodcut initial T (NIF) 21 x 41 mm.] HE BOOK OF | RUTH AND THE | BOOK of ESTHER | [type orn: trefoil] Printed in the Vale | type, with initial let- | ters & five illustrations | designed & engraved | on the wood by Lu- | cien Pissarro. Printed | with his own hand, and his press | in Epping, in black and red | on Arnold's hand-made paper, with | the Vale water-mark. One hun- | dred & fifty copies print- ed, of | which one hundred & fifty are for | sale at fifteen shillings net. | [to the right] Order Form | over

[verso] ORDER FORM | TO Messrs. HACON AND | RICKETTS THE SIGN OF | THE DIAL 52 WARWICK | STREET REGENT ST. W. | Please send me .... cop... of | THE BOOK OF RUTH & | THE BOOK OF ESTHER, | for which I enclose cheque. | Value [one dotted line] | Name [one dotted line] | Address [two dotted lines] | Date [one dotted line] | NOTE.—Cheques should be | made out to the order of Messrs. | Hacon and Ricketts and crossed | "London and South Western | Bank" [type orn: rose]

NOTES: In the planning stages by late 1894, *The Book of Ruth*, originally entitled *Ruth et Booz*, was conceived as a small book illustrated by three black and white wood engravings. The text for *The Book of Ruth* was too short, however, and Lucien added another story, *The Book of Esther*, as well as one wood engraving. Due to time and finanacial constraints, Lucien did not plan for color; moreover, Esther could engrave black and white illustrations. In early March 1895, Lucien sent three drawings to Camille for *The Book of Ruth*, and by early April proofs for "Ruth Gleaning" and "Ruth and Naomi." Camille like their arrangement, but found the arms too long in "Ruth Gleaning." He found the figures to be indistinct in "Ruth and Naomi" and thought the background could be simpler. Although Lucien agreed with Camille's assessment, it was too late to remedy the problems.

By mid-September, Ricketts' type was not yet ready and the book was delayed, but by late November 1995 Lucien was busy setting the type. In early March, Lucien and Esther had spent two days printing more than 400 proofs of an ornament for the cover of *The Book of Ruth and the Book of Esther*. They had been waiting for paper to resume printing of the book (Lucien Pissarro to Julie Pissarro, 10 March 1896). The book was finally completed in September 1896. Lucien sent a copy to Camille in late September (Lucien Pissarro to Julie Pissarro, 27 September 1896).

Camille found the book to be sentimental. But Lucien, to the contrary, thought *The Book of Ruth and the Book of Esther* to be no more sentimental than *The Queen of the Fishes*. In fact, he found the book to be superior to *The Queen of the Fishes*, in the sense that it was better as a book, typographically speaking, with its ornamented letters and borders. He found there was no room for sentimentalism and could not see why Camille thought this.

In mid-December 1896, T. J. Cobden-Sanderson bought two copies of *The Book of Ruth and the Book of Esther.* Lucien saw this as an excellent sign (Lucien Pissarro to Camille Pissarro, before 13 December 1896).

The Book of Ruth and the Book of Esther was reviewed in *Nieuwe Rotterdamsche Courant*, 15 October 1896.

COPIES SEEN: Ashmolean, BL, Huntington (Provenance: Henry William Poor). FSU. NYPL (purchased from Goodspeed [21 Feb. 1952]). SFPL (Provenance: Robert Grabhorn with bookplate of Olive Percival).

EP3 • Jules Laforgue. Moralités légendaires. Volume I. 1897.

[type orn: leaf] JULES LAFORGUE. | [type orn: leaf] MORALITES LEGENDAIRES. [type orn: leaf] | [type orn: leaf] TOME PREMIER.

COLOPHON: LE FRONTISPICE, LES BORDURES | ET LES LETTRES ORNEES ONT | ETE DESSINES ET GRAVES SUR | BOIS PAR LUCIEN PISSARRO ET LE | LIVRE FUT ACHEVE LE QUATOR- | ZE JANVIER M.DCCC. XCVII. A EP- | PING, (ESSEX), ANGLETERRE. [type orn: leaf] | CETTE EDITION EST STRICTE- | MENT LIMITEE A DEUX CENT | VINGT EXEMPLAIRES, DONT | DEUX CENTS POUR LA | VENTE. | En vente chez Messrs. Hacon & Ricketts, at | the Sign of the Dial, 52, Warwick Street, | Regent Street, London, W. | & | A la Société du MERCVRE de FRANCE, | 15, rue de l'Echaudé-Saint-Germain, Paris.

COLLATION: Crown 8°: π^4 a^2 b^4–n^4. 58 leaves, pp. [i–vii] viii–cxi [cxii–cxvi]

PAPER AND DIMENSIONS: Arnold's unbleached hand-made paper with Vale watermark. Leaf: 210 x 130 mm.

TYPE: Vale

ILLUSTRATIONS, ORNAMENTS, AND INITIALS: [one black and white wood-engraved illustration with border; nine initials in black and white] $\pi 3^v$: "SALOMÉ," 130 x 86 mm. (Fern 105 [SB 102]) within border, 175 x 123 mm. (Fern 281 [SB 105]). π4^{r}: border, 175 x 399 mm. (Fern 281 [SB 106]), Initial I (Fern 298 [SB 120]). b1^{v}: Initial L (Fern 287 [SB 109]). c3^{v}: Initial S (Fern 292 [SB 114]). e2^{v}: Initial A (Fern 288 [SB 110]). e4^{v}: Initial O (Fern 291 [SB 113]). h1^{r}: Initial L (Fern 287 [SB 109]). i4^{v}: Initial O (Fern 291 [SB 113]). j4^{r}: Initial C (Fern 285 [SB 107]). l1^{r}: Initial E (Fern 286 [SB 108]). Catchwords.

CONTENTS: π1^{r}: Title. π1^{v}: blank. π2^{r}: Dedication: A TEODOR DE WYZEWA. π2^{v}: [type orn: leaf] La Reine de Saba à saint Antoine:—Ris | donc, bel ermite! Ris donc, je suis très gaie, tu | verras! Je pince de la lyre, je danse comme une | abeille et je sais une foule d'histories toutes à | ranconter plus divertissantes les unes que les | autres. [type orn: leaf] Gustave Flaubert. π3^{r}: blank. π3^{v}–e4^{r}: Salomé. e4^{v}–i4^{r}: Lohengrin, Fils de Parsifal. i4^{v}–n2^{r}: Perse et Andromede ou Le Plus Heureux des Trois. n2^{v}: Table [of Contents]. n3^{r}: colophon. n4: blank.

ERRATA: Errata. [slip]: Page xvii ligne 5, lire brocarts, au lieu de | brocards. | Page xviii ligne 12, lire kilométriquement, | au lieu de kilomètriquement. | Page xlvi ligne 21, lire Séléné, au lieu de | Sélène. Page lxi ligne 5, lire ressortissait au, au lieu | de ressortissait du. | Page lxvi ligne 8 & page lxvii ligne 5, lire | Tout est pas plus, au lieu de Tout | et pas plus.

BINDING: Quarter Michallet blue paper, gold stamped on upper left cover: [type: trefoil] JULES | LAFORGUE | MORALITES | LEGENDAI- | RES. [orn: trefoil]. Buff paper boards with a repeat pattern of "wood sorrel" (NIF) printed in green ink. On spine gold stamped: [orn: trefoil] Jules | Laforgue | Moralities | Légendai | res. [orn. trefoil] | Tome I.

PUBLICATION: 200 copies for sale at 16 shillings. The book was finished in early December 1896 and was bound by mid-March 1897.

RELATED MATERIAL: Two preliminary drawings for floriated initial I; preliminary binding paper printed on gray paper with wood sorrel in dark green ink and white ink with flowers; preliminary design for border.

NOTES: Upon receiving word from Félix Fénéon in late April 1896 that Dujardin had given permission for the publication of Laforgue, Lucien began printing the proofs for the first page, the frontispiece, borders, and ornamented letters. Lucien still had a small ornament to engrave. In late October, Lucien bought the paper for the Laforgue and finished printing it before mid-December 1896. By mid-April, fifty copies of the book had sold in England in fifteen days (Lucien Pissarro to Camille Pissarro, 12 April 1897).

Hacon & Ricketts paid Lucien's production expenses. The cost of the first volume, without counting for Lucien's time or the paper for the binding, came to £27 (or 675 frs.) or about four francs per copy. If all copies sold, the profit would be 1,725 frs.

When Camille saw the book, he found the book to be very beautiful, very successful. The first page with the engraving of Salomé, the typography, etc. was masterful and Camille hoped that others would find it very beautiful, but he thought that they might think it too English, Morris, Gothic. But for Camille, that was of little importance. He also found the binding to be charming, and in sum found it to be a beautiful book (Camille Pissarro to Lucien Pissarro, 19 March 1897).

T. S. Moore called the edition "exquisite" and found "the effect of the border page is magnificiently coloured; the Shamrock cover seems to be most fortunate, delicate and striking at the same time. Among the initials I have been divided between the O and the C, perhaps the former seems a little black otherwise I should prefer it . . ." (T. S. Moore to Lucien Pissarro, 18 March 1897).

One hundred copies to Mercure de France, 76 copies to Hacon & Ricketts, 5 deposit copies, Charles Holmes, the Vale Press, Camille and Julie Pissarro (2 copies), Félix Fénéon, Georges Lecomte, C. Destrée, Contet, Sam Bensusan, Charles Ricketts, L. Hacon, A. Vallette, Emile Laforgue, Wysema, T. S. Moore, John Gray, E. Dujardin, Emile Verhaeren, Diana White, A. Mcgregor, Th. Gaillard, P. Signac, H. Floury, Ruth Bensusan, Rudolph Pissarro, Ida Henry, F. & G. Chesterton.

In stock: 1 March 1904, 4 copies; 1 March 1905, 4 copies; 1 March 1906, 4 copies; 1 March 1907, 5 copies; 1 March 1908, 5 copies; 1 March 1909, 4 copies; 1 March 1910, 2 copies (Private ledger).

COPIES SEEN: Ashmolean (Inscribed: A mon Père témoignage d'affection—Lucien Pissarro). BL (deposited 4 June 1897). LC. NYPL (Bookplate: FROM THE BOOKS | OF CROSBY GAIGE). SFPL (Provenance: Robert Grabhorn with bookplate of Breslauer & Meyer, Buchhändler & Antiquare, Berlin, w.136 Leipzigerstr.).

EP4 • Jules Laforgue. Moralités légendaires. Volume II. 1898.

[type orn: leaf] JULES LAFORGUE. | [type orn: leaf] MORALITES LEGENDAIRES. [type orn: leaf] | [type orn: leaf] TOME SECOND.

COLOPHON: LE FRONTISPICE, LES BORDURES | ET DES LETTRES ORNEES ONT | ETE DESSINES PAR LUCIEN PIS- | SARRO ET GRAVES SUR BOIS PAR | ESTHER PISSARRO ET LE LIVRE | FUT ACHEVE D'IMPRIMER LE 24 | DECEMBRE M.DCCC.XCVIII. SUR | LEUR PRESSE A LONDRES. [double type orn: leaf] | CETTE EDITION EST STRICTE- | MENT LIMITEE A DEUX CENT | VINGT EXEMPLAIRES, DONT | DEUX CENTS POUR LA | VENTE. | En vente chez Messrs. Hacon & Ricketts, at | the Sign of the Dial, 52, Watwick [sic] Street, | Regent Street, London, W. | & | A la Société du MERCVRE de FRANCE, | 15, rue de l'Echaudé-Saint-Germain, Paris.

COLLATION: crown 8°: π^3 a^3 b^4–p^4 q^2. 64 leaves, pp. [i–v] vi–cxxvi [cxxvii–cxxviii]

PAPER AND DIMENSIONS: Arnold's unbleached hand-made paper with Vale watermark. Leaf: 212 x 130 mm.

TYPE: Vale

ILLUSTRATIONS, ORNAMENTS, AND INITIALS: [one black and white wood-engraved illustration; two borders; one initial in red; four initials in black and white; pressmark] $\pi2^v$: "Ophelia," 150 x 76 mm. (Fern 107 [SB 104]) within border (Fern 282 [SB 104]). $\pi3^r$: border (Fern 283 [SB 104 bis]). Initial D (Fern 289 [SB 107]) in red. $h1^v$: Initial J (Fern 290 [SB 112]). $i1^r$: Initial C (Fern 285 [SB 107]). $k2^v$: Initial L (Fern 287 [SB 107]). $l2^v$: Initial S (Fern 292 [SB 114]). $q2^v$: Pressmark II, 77 mm. diameter (Fern 111 [SB 152]). Catchwords.

CONTENTS: $\pi1^v$: blank. $\pi1^r$: title. $\pi2^r$: blank. $\pi2^v$–$h1^r$: Hamlet. $h1^v$–$l2^r$: Le Miracle des Roses. $l2^v$–$q1^r$: Pan et La Syrinx. $q1^v$: Table [of contents]. $q2^r$: colophon.

BINDING: Quarter Michallet blue paper, gold stamped on upper left cover: [orn: trefoil] JULES | LAFORGUE | MORALITES | LEGENDAI- | RES. [orn: trefoil]. Buff paper boards with a repeat pattern of "wood sorrel" (NIF) printed in green ink. On spine gold stamped: [orn: trefoil] Jules | Laforgue | Moralité | Légendai | res. [orn: trefoil] | Tome II.

PUBLICATION: 200 paper copies at 16 shillings. Although the colophon states a completion date of December 1898, the book was published in March 1899.

RELATED MATERIAL: Preliminary border sketch; border (Fern 282 [SB 104]) proof; preliminary drawing for border (Fern 283 [SB 104 bis]); preliminary drawing for border on graph paper; drawn border for (Fern 283 [SB 104 bis]) to size; magnified border (Fern 283 [SB 104 bis]); border (Fern 283 [SB 104 bis]) greatly reduced; initial D proof; drawn initials C, E, L, A.

PROSPECTUS: [type orn: leaf] THE VALE PUBLICATIONS [type orn: outline leaf] ISSUED FROM THE SIGN OF THE | DIAL BY HACON AND RICKETTS, | 52 WARWICK ST. REGENT ST W. | [Pressmark II]. | [in red] FEBRUARY 1., M.DCCC.XCIX.

[in red] [type orn: leaf] NOTICE [type orn: leaf] | [woodcut initial T (Fern 308 [SB 130])] he group in which it has | been customary to place | Laforgue no longer exists. | (Of Verlaine's Poëtes Mau- | dits, for example, not one| is now alive.) The repu- | tations concerned have nothing to regret in | the disuse of a classification invented for po- | lemical reasons, or merely idly for the sake of classification. | On the contrary, a com- |

Initial I (Fern 298 [SB120]). Used in: *Moralités légendaires*, vol. 1, 1897; *La Légende de St. Julien l'hospitalier*, 1900; *Autre poésies*, 1901; *Les Petits vieux*, 1901; *Some Poems by Robert Browning*, 1904. (Special Collections, Florida State University, Tallahassee)

mon cause of reaction does not make unity; | and it is in no way detrimental to an artist's | independence that he should be acquainted | with the aims of his friends in letters. Lafor- | gue's distinctive character as an artist is one | which has ever been most salutary to the lit- | erature of his country, specially prone as it is | to limit its range continually, refining more | and more upon tried methods. The freshen- | ing influence of his inquisitiveness & catho- | licity is very active in France at this moment [sic] | Beyond this diversity of appreciation, ren- | dering it complex, as an artistic standpoint | is bound to be, he was endowed with the | special gift of satire which marks the keenest | sympathies. If sympathy or conviction be | carried to its limit intellectual balance or bias | intervenes, producing a new manifestation, | graceful & amiable caricature, satire which | is an end in itself, a literary medium as it is | found in the Moralités Légendaires. | [to the right] John Gray

Page 2: [in red] Now ready: | [in black] LES MORALITES LEGENDAIRES | Vol. II, par Jules Laforgue [indent] Contents of Vol. I: Salomé, Lohengrin, | fils de Parsifal and Persé et Andromède. | [indent] Contents of Vol. II: Hamlet, ou les suites | de la prété filiale, Le Miracle des Roses and | Pan et la Syrinx. The frontispiece, double | border & initial letters, designed by Lucien | Pissarro and engraved on the wood by Es- | ther Pissarro. Printed in the Vale type, on hand-made paper, at their presses in London. | Two hundred & twenty copies printed for | England France & America; of which two | hundred are for sale at sixteen shillings net.

NOTES: Lucien began to design the floriated initials in April 1898. These were probably the capitals "J" and "D." The capitals "S" and "L" were reused from the first volume. Printing was underway by November 1898 and Lucien announced to Camille that the book was finished sometime before 27 December 1898 (Lucien Pissarro to Camille Pissarro, before 27 December 1898). However, in late January 1899, the Pissarros were proofreading and revising the pages of the book (Lucien Pissarro to Camille Pissarro, 27 January 1999). In mid-March, Lucien was anticipating the arrival of the books from the bindery (Lucien Pissarro to Camille Pissarro, before 16 March 1899). By late March, sixty copies had sold at Hacon & Ricketts in eight days (Lucien Pissarro to Camille Pissarro, 29 March 1899). Although Camille liked this second volume, he disapproved of the aesthetic in which the illustration "Ophelia" was conceived. He hoped that Lucien's next book would be more in keeping with the style of *The Queen of the Fishes* (Camille Pissarro to Lucien Pissarro, 18 and 28 December 1898).

Emile Verhaeren found the second volume to be exquisite—the impression, engravings, and ornamentation—a perfect combination (Emile Verhaeren to Lucien Pissarro, [undated 1898?]).

Paul Signac was flattered by the gift of Laforgue and noted the perfect harmony of the book (Paul Signac to Lucien Pissarro, 22 March 1899).

T. S. Moore wrote, "Thank you very much for your beautiful second volume. I shall enjoy reading it; as I have never seen these three of Laforgue's

Moralités they will have the charm of complete surprise as well as that of their satiric force and beauty" (T. S. Moore to Lucien Pissarro, 22 March 1899, University of London, Paleography Room, Letter 19/126).

Copies to: 70 Hacon and Ricketts (copies sent on 16 March 1899), 100 copies to Mercure de France (copies sent 17 March 1899), 5 deposit copies, Charles Ricketts, Camille Pissarro, Emile Verhaeren, A. Vallette, Félix Fénéon, Georges Lecomte, C. Destrée, T. S. Moore, Emile Laforgue, Th. Gaillard, P. Signac, A. Mcgregor, Diana White, Charles Holmes, L. Hacon, H. Floury, Ruth Bensusan, Rodolphe Pissarro, Ida Henry, F. & G. Chesterton, A. Teisser.

In stock: 1 March 1904, 16 copies; 1 March 1905, 16 copies; 1 March 1906, 16 copies; 1 March 1907, 16 copies; 1 March 1908, 17 copies, 1 March 1909, 16 copies; 1 March 1910, 14 copies; 1 March 1911, 12 copies (Private ledger).

COPIES SEEN: Ashmolean. BL (deposited 10 April 1899). LC. NYPL (FROM THE BOOKS | OF CROSBY GAIGE). SFPL (Provenance: Robert Grabhorn).

EP5 • Charles Perrault. Deux contes de ma mère l'oye: La Belle au bois dormant et Le Petit chaperon rouge. 1899.

[type orn: trefoil] LA BELLE AU BOIS DORMANT | & | [type orn: trefoil] LE PETIT CHAPERON ROUGE. | [type orn: bud] DEUX CONTES | DE MA MERE | LOYE [type orn: leaf] | [Geese Rondel within border] | PAR [type orn: leaf] | C. PER- RAULT | DE L'ACA- DEMIE | FRANÇAISE. | m.dccc.xcix. | [type orn: leaf]

COLOPHON: e4^r: Le frontispice, les bordures, les illustra- | tions, et les lettres ornées ont été dessinés | par Lucien Pissarro et gravés sur | bois par Esther & Lucien Pis- | sarro et le livre fut achevé | d'imprimer sur leurs | presses à Lon- | dres le 16 | Juillet | 1899. | [type orn: trefoil | [two type orns: trefoil] | [type orn: trefoil] | En vente chez Hacon & Ricketts, 52, | Warwick Street, Regent Street, London. | & | Chez Floury No. 1 Boulevard des Ca- | pucines, Paris. e4^v: Il a été tiré de cet ouvrage 224 exemplai- | res, dont 200 pour la vente. | [Pressmark II]

COLLATION: 8°: [a]^6 b^4 c^4 d^2 e^4. 20 leaves, pp. [1–6] 7–29 [30–32] 33–38 [39–40]

PAPER AND DIMENSIONS: Arnold's unbleached hand-made paper with Vale watermark. Leaf: 195 x 123 mm.

ILLUSTRATIONS, ORNAMENTS, AND INITIALS: [two wood-engraved illustrations in black and white; two wood-engraved illustrations in three colors; three borders and thirty-seven initials in black and white] [a]1^r: "Geese" within border [2 separate blocks], 89.5 mm. diameter

(Fern 113 [SB 154]). [a]2ᵛ: "La Belle au Bois Dormant," three-color wood engraving in black, green, and gold, 110 x 89 mm. (Fern 108 [SB 105]), within border (Fern 281 [SB 105-106]), Initial O (Fern 320 [SB 141]). [a]3ʳ: "La Belle au Bois Dormant" (Fern 109 [SB 106]) three-color wood engraving in black, green, and gold, 110 x 89 mm. within border (Fern 281 [SB 105-106]), Initial A (Fern 312 [SB 133]). [a]4ʳ: Initial I (NIF), Initial L (Fern 317 [SB 138]). [a]4ᵛ: Initial A (Fern 312 [SB 133]), Initial L (Fern 317 [SB 138]). [a]5ʳ: Initial C (Fern 313 [SB 134]). [a]5ᵛ: Initial C (Fern 313 [SB 134]), Initial L (Fern 317 [SB 138]), Initial A (Fern 312 [SB 133]). [a]6ʳ: Initial L (Fern 317 [SB 138]). [a]6ᵛ: Initial A (Fern 312 [SB 133]), Initial L (Fern 317 [SB 138]). b1ʳ: Initial E (Fern 314 [SB 135]). b1ᵛ: Initial A (Fern 312 [SB 133]). b2ʳ: Initial A (Fern 312 [SB 133]). b2ᵛ: Initial L (Fern 317 [SB 138]), Initial L (Fern 317 [SB 138]). b3ʳ: Initial I (Fern 316 [SB 137]). b3ᵛ: Initial A (Fern 312 [SB133]). b4ʳ: Initial C (Fern 313 [SB 134]). b4ᵛ: Initial I (Fern 316 [SB 137]), Initial L (Fern 317 [SB 138]). c1ʳ: Initial L (Fern 317 [SB 138]), Initial M (Fern 318 [SB 139]). c1ᵛ: Initial Q (Fern 320 [SB 141]). c2ʳ: Initial C (Fern 313 [SB 134]), Initial H (Fern 315 [SB 136]). c2ᵛ: Initial C (Fern 313 [SB 134]). c3ᵛ: Initial U (Fern 321 [SB 142]), Initial I (Fern 316 [SB 137]). d2ʳ: "Le Petit Chaperon Rouge," 113 x 93 mm. (Fern 98 [SB 96]). e1ʳ: Initial I (NIF), Initial L (Fern 317 [SB 138]), Initial U (Fern 321 [SB 142]). e1ᵛ: Initial L (Fern 317[SB 138]). e2ʳ: Initial L (Fern 317 [SB138]). e2ᵛ: Initial L (Fern 317 [SB 138]). e4ᵛ: Pressmark II, 76 mm. diameter (Fern 111 [SB 152]). Catchwords and shoulder notes.

CONTENTS: [a]1ʳ: title. [a]1ᵛ: Dedication: [type orn: bud] À Emile Verhaeren. [a]2ʳ: blank. [a]2ᵛ–c4ᵛ: La Belle au Bois. d1ʳ–e3ᵛ: Le Petit Chaperon Rouge. e4: colophon

BINDING: Quarter Michallet blue paper, gold stamped on upper left cover: [orn: trefoil] C. PERRAULT | DEUX CONTES | DE MA MÈRE | LOYE. [orn: trefoil]. Cream paper boards with repeat pattern of "lotus flower" (Fern 323 [145]) printed in blue. On spine gold stamped at top and bottom flower ornament.

PUBLICATION: 200 copies for sale, 130 copes sold by Hacon & Ricketts at 20 shillings, 70 copies sold by H. Floury, Paris. 4 copies on vellum (not for sale). Published in July 1899.

RELATED MATERIAL: Drawings for small initials [two pieces]; printed trial for cover block in blue (Fern 323 [145]); cover design in black; cover design in black with China ink correction.

NOTES: These tales of Perrault were originally planned to follow *The Book of Ruth and the Book of Esther,* and in contrast to the black and white of *Ruth,* the Perrault was to have a color engraving. Intervening, of course, were the two Laforgue volumes, as well as Lucien's illness. The illustrations, drawn before Lucien's illness, were engraved by Esther. Lucien had intended to publish two editions of *Deux contes,* one in French, the other English.

Copies to: 130 to Hacon & Ricketts, 70 to Mercure de France, 5 deposit, subscription copy. Gifts to Charles Holmes, Charles Ricketts, Emile Verhaeren, Camille Pissarro, Diana White, H. Floury, T. S. Moore, Georges Lecomte, Ruth Bensusan, Sam Bensusan, Orovida Bensusan, L. Hacon, A. Mcgregor.

COPIES SEEN: Ashmolean (vellum copy, bound in vellum with silk ties). Bancroft. BL (deposited 18 October 1899). NYPL. SFPL (Provenance: Robert Grabhorn).

EP6 • François Villon. Ballades. 1900.

[in black and orange] [caps] LES | [large caps] BALLADES | [caps] DE | MAISTRE FRANCOIS VILLON. | LONDON | HACON & RICKETTS | 17 CRAVEN STREET STRAND. | [type orn: trefoil] | [type orn: trefoil] | MCM [type orn: trefoil] | [type orn: trefoil]

COLOPHON: LE FRONTISPICE A ETE DES- | SINE ET GRAVE SUR BOIS PAR | LUCIEN PISSARRO. LA BOR- | DURE & LES LETTRES OR- | NEES ONT ETE DESSI- | NEES PAR L. PISSARRO | & GRAVEES PAR ES- | THER PISSARRO. | CETTE EDITION EST STRIC- | TEMENT LIMITEE A DEUX | CENT VINGT SIX EXEM- | PLAIRES, dont DEUX CENTS | POUR LA VENTE. | [two type orns: leaf] | [type orn: leaf]

COLLATION: 8°: $[a]^2$ b^4–l^4. 46 leaves, pp. [1–3] 4–88 [89–92]

PAPER AND DIMENSIONS: Arnold's unbleached hand-made paper with Vale watermark; four copies printed on old Japanese handmade paper. Leaf: 195 x 130 mm.

TYPE: Vale

ILLUSTRATIONS, ORNAMENTS, AND INITIALS: [Pressmark; wood-engraved illustration in black and white; border printed in black and red; one large initial in red; thirty-eight initials in red] [all initials printed in red] [a]1^r: Pressmark III, 76 mm. diameter (Fern 112 [SB 152]). [a]2^r: "Dames du temps jadis," 74 mm. diameter (Fern 119 [SB 157]); border in black and red, 205 x 130 mm. (Fern 326 [SB 157]); initial letter D in red surrounded by black and white foliage (Fern 289 [SB 111]). b1^r: Initial Q (Fern 293 [SB 115]). b2^r: Initial C (Fern 285 [SB 107]). b3^r: Initial O (Fern 291 [SB 113]). b4^r: Initial P (Fern 295 [SB 117]). c1^r: Initial D (Fern 301 [SB 123]). c2^v: Initial F (Fern 310 [SB 132]). c3^v: Initial P (Fern 295 [SB 117]). c4^v: Initial A (Fern 288 [SB

110]). d1^{v}: Initial E (Fern 286 [SB 108]). d2^{v}: Initial S (Fern 292 [SB 114]). d4^{r}: Initial Q (Fern 293 [SB 115]). d4^{v}: Initial S (Fern 299 [SB 121]). e2^{r}: Initial C (Fern 305 [SB 127]). e3^{r}: Initial A (Fern 307 [SB 129]). e4^{r}: Initial I (Fern 298 [SB 120]). f1^{r}: Initial A (Fern 307 [SB 129]). f2^{r}: Initial Q (Fern 293 [SB 115]). f4^{r}: Initial F (Fern 310 [SB 132]). g1^{r}: Initial F (Fern 310 [SB 132]). g2^{v}: Initial T (Fern 308 [SB 130]). g4^{r}: Initial Q (Fern 293 [SB 115]). h1^{r}: Initial L (Fern 287 [SB 109]). h2^{v}: Initial J (Fern 290 [SB 112]). h3^{v}: Initial T (Fern 308 [SB 130]). h4^{v}: Initial I (Fern 298 [SB 120]). i1^{v}: Initial J (Fern 290 [SB 112]). i2^{v}: Initial H (NIF). i4^{v}: Initial A (Fern 288 [SB 110]). j1^{v}: Initial C (Fern 285 [SB 107]). j2^{r}: Initial S (Fern 299 [SB 121]). j3^{v}: Initial S (Fern 303 [SB 125]). j4^{v}: Initial J (Fern 290 [SB 112]). k1^{r}: Initial C (Fern 285 [SB 107]). k2^{r}: Initial B (Fern 306 [SB 128]). k3^{v}: Initial C (Fern 285 [SB 107]). l1^{r}: Initial O (Fern 303 [SB 125]). l1^{v}: Initial R (Fern 296 [SB 118]).

CONTENTS: [a]1^{r}: Pressmark III. [a]1^{v}: title. [a]2^{r}: frontispiece. [a]2^{r}–l2^{v}: text. l3^{r}–l4^{r}: TABLES DES MATIERES. l4^{v}: colophon

BINDING: Quarter buff paper, gold stamped on upper left cover: [orn: trefoil] VILLON | BALLADES. White paper boards with repeat pattern of small five-petalled flowers (NIF) printed in pink. On spine gold stamped: [orn: trefoil] | VIL- | LON | [double orn: trefoil] | BAL- | LA- | DES. | [orn: trefoil]

PUBLICATION: 200 paper copies for sale at 30s. Published late July 1900.

RELATED MATERIAL: Prototype cover in black and white; [slip]: Of this edition of «LES BALLADES DE | FRANÇOIS VILLON» 222 copies have | been printed on Arnold's unbleached hand- | made paper and 4 copies on old Japanese | hand-made paper; of the latter, this is No. [in red] 2.

NOTES: In early September 1899, Lucien, telling Camille of his desire to publish a book by Villon, asked him to send Villon's work in one volume. He specified the edition of "Nouvelle collection Jannet," published in 1867, due to its careful editing (Villon, François. *Oeuvres complètes de François Villon. Nouvelle collection Jannet.* Paris: E. Picard, 1867). By this time, Lucien was sufficiently recovered from his stroke that he was able once again to engrave his own illustrations, leaving Esther to engrave the ornaments and borders.

By mid-February 1900, printing had begun on the Villon. The Pissarros hired a printer to help with printing in two colors. Not well-equipped to do color on a large scale, the Pissarros had problems with keeping paper damp, and given that they printed black one day, and red the next, the difference in a sheet of paper they found could be as much as two centimeters. Having the printer there allowed them to work more rapidly and alleviated the problem somewhat.

As late April 1900 approached, work on Villon progressed slowly. Lucien blamed it on having to pass each sheet of paper through the press twice. If he had two presses, a sheet could go from one press to another press immediately, thus ensuring perfect registration without needing to worry about paper expansion or contraction (Lucien Pissarro to Camille Pissarro, before 22 April 1900). Lucien hoped to finish Villon in early June.

In a draft letter (probably early June 1900) to Leighton, Lucien asked Leighton to make two sample bindings—one with a linen back with plain Michallet blue papers boards with a label placed on the left hand corner—modeled after Morris' books. The other sample was to be done up like a Ricketts' binding, in the same dark paper with the label on the left-hand corner.

Leighton received the proofs for the cover sheets of Villon on 7 June 1900 and returned a specimen copy to the Pissarros on 16 June. The charge for binding would be 64 shillings per 100 copies—rather more than it had been for *Deux contes.* Due to an inflationary period, prices had gone up nearly 25 percent, but because the Villon did not require too many materials, the increase was not as large as it could have been. On 17 July 1900, Leighton, unable to complete the binding of Villon, lacked twelve front cover papers. The Pissarros sent him proof sheets, more than likely that was all that remained. The four Japanese paper copies had to be rebound; they had been rushed and thus spoilt (Leighton to Lucien Pissarro, 20 July 1900). *Les Ballades de François Villon* was available in late July.

Ricketts bought 200 copies of the Villon, thus relieving Lucien of marketing his book. The purchase also provided Lucien with enough money so he could continue to produce additional books (Lucien Pissarro to Camille Pissarro, before 12 January 1900). Lucien, not pleased by the sales price Holmes decided upon, was convinced that the higher price of 30s rather than 21s would make little difference to buyers, especially given the escalating value of his books. The last public sale of *The Queen of the Fishes* had brought 220 frs. for it. Its published price was 25 frs. And *The Book of Ruth and the Book of Esther* had recently sold for 50 frs. Lucien's dilemma, of course, was that he sold his books too cheaply given how much time was involved in their making, and that buyers found them too expensive in comparison to machine-made books.

T. S. Moore found the Villon to be "delightful . . . looks cool and refreshing even in this terribly hot weather." He liked the color of the cover immensely: "[T]here you have a pull over every one else, you can make sure of really delightful tints." Moore continued, "The printing of so many pages both in red and black must have been a great labour. The very proper ladies in their garden of long ago are a very quaint comment on Villon who I suppose imagined them in the height of the then fashion, but they no doubt bring his sentiment nearer to us. I suppose it is Proserpina's Garden, and she, with her experience, has been over their wardrobe to much the same result as an old Quaker lady might" (T. S.

Moore to Lucien Pissarro, [undated]. University of London, Paleography Room, Letter 19/124).

Copies were given to Charles Holmes, Ernest Verity, Sam Bensusan, Ida Henry, Diana White (both paper and Japanese handmade paper), Cyril Kirby, T. S. Moore, Camille Pissarro (Japanese handmade paper), Alfred Pissarro (Japanese handmade paper), Emile Verhaeren, Georges Lecomte, Th. Gaillard.

COPIES SEEN: Ashmolean. BL (deposited 2 August 1900; another copy with Sybil Pye binding in gold tooled orange morocco, dated MCMXXVIII). NYPL (Bookplate: John Shaw Billings Memorial Fund; bound by the The Knickerbocker Press of G. P. Putnam's Sons in burgundy morocco with delicate gold tooling with original binding set in and with red marbled endpapers). SFPL (Provenance: Robert Grabhorn).

EP7 • Gustave Flaubert. La Légende de St. Julien l'hospitalier. 1900.

[orn: tudor rose] GUSTAVE FLAUBERT. | LA LÉGENDE DE SAINT | JULIEN L'HOSPITALIER.

COLOPHON: Le frontispice a été dessiné & | gravé sur bois par Lucien Pis- | sarro. La bordure et les lettres | ornées ont été dessinées par | Lucien Pissarro et gravées | sur bois par Esther | Pissarro. [orn: leaf] | MCM. | En vente chez Hacon & Ricketts | 17, Craven St., Strand, London. g6^r: Il a été tiré de cet ouvrage 226 ex. | dont 200 pour la vente. | [Pressmark III]

COLLATION: 16°: [a]^2 b^8–g^8. 52 leaves, pp. [1–3] 4–92 [93–104]

PAPER AND DIMENSIONS: Arnold's unbleached hand made paper with Vale watermark. Leaf: 144 x 98 mm.

TYPE: Vale

ILLUSTRATIONS, ORNAMENTS, AND INITIALS: [one wood-engraved illustration, one border; three initials, press mark in black and white] [a]1^v: "Deer in the Forest," 89 mm. diameter (Fern 118 [SB 159]). [a]2^r: border (Fern 325 [SB 160]); Initial L (Fern 322 [SB 143]). d3^r: Initial I (Fern 298 [SB 120]). f4^r: Initial I (Fern 298 [SB 120]). g6^r: Pressmark III, 76 mm. diameter (Fern 112 [SB 152]).

CONTENTS: [a]1^r: title. [a]1^v–g5^r: text. g5^v–g5^v: colophon. g6^v–g8^v blank

BINDING: Quarter buff cloth with Michallet blue boards with printed paper label on upper left cover: G. FLAUBERT | [double orns: leaf] | LA LÉGENDE | DE St. JULIEN | L'HOSPITA- | LIER.

LA
LÉGENDE DE ST.
JULIEN L'HOSPITALIER.

I

LE père et la mère de Julien habitaient un château, au milieu des bois, sur la pente d'une colline.

Les quatre tours aux angles avaient des toits pointus recouverts d'écailles de plomb, et la base des murs s'appuyait sur les quartiers de rocs, qui dévalaient abruptement jusqu'au fond des douves.

Les pavés de la cour étaient nets comme le dallage d'une é-

Opening pages. Gustave Flaubert, *La Légende de St. Julien l'hospitalier,* 1900. (Special Collections, Florida State University, Tallahassee)

PUBLICATION: 200 copies for sale at 15 shillings. Published in October 1900.

PROSPECTUS: [type orn: leaf] ISSUED BY HACON & RICK- | ETTS, THE VALE PRESS, 17 | CRAVEN ST., STRAND, LON- | DON | Now ready: | LA LEGENDE DE ST. JULIEN | L'HOSPITALIER. By Gustave Flau- | bert. With Frontispiece, border and | initial letter designed by Lucien Pissarro | and engraved on the wood by Esther & | Lucien Pissarro, and printed at their | press in London in the Vale Type, on | Arnold's unbleached hand-made paper. | Demy 16 mo. Two hundred and twenty- | six copies printed for England and | America, of which two hundred are for | sale, at fifteen shillings nett. | [to right] Order Form | over

[verso]: ORDER FORM | Please send to me .... cop........ of | LA LÉGENDE DE ST. JULIÉN L'HOSPITALIER, for which I en- | close cheque. | Value [one dotted line] | Name [one dotted line] | Address [3 dotted lines] | To [one dotted line] | [to right] Bookseller | [two dotted lines] | Hacon & Ricketts, 17 Craven St., W.C.

RELATED MATERIAL: Cover design of rabbits in dark green (Fern 110 [SB 151]), not used; earlier version of "Deer in the Forest," 89 mm. (Fern 117 [SB 158]); border drawing.

NOTES: The Pissarros began printing *St. Julien* either in late May or early June 1900. Hacon & Ricketts paid £106.6.1 on 13 November 1900 for the edition.

Copies were given to Georges Lecomte, Emile Verhaeren, T. S. Moore, Charles Holmes, Th. Gaillard, Diana White, Archibald Mcgregor, A. Teisser, Sam Bensusan, Camille Pissarro, Alfred Pissarro, Ida Henry, Cyril Kirby, Ernest Verity, B. Guinaudeau.

COPIES SEEN: Ashmolean. BL (deposited 18 October 1900; another copy with Sybil Pye binding in red morocco with gold tooling, dated 1901). FSU. NYPL (John Quinn copy, bought from Anderson Gallery, 7 April 1924; Bookplate John Shaw Billings Memorial Fund). SFPL (Provenance: Robert Grabhorn). William Andrews Clark Library, UCLA (Bookplate: William Andrews Clark Jr.)

EP8 • Gustave Flaubert. Un Coeur simple. 1901.

[within border])] GUSTAVE FLAUBERT. [type orn: tudor rose] UN CŒUR SIMPLE. | [Illus: Girl and Cow]

COLOPHON: Il a été tiré de cet ouvrage 226 ex. | dont 200 pour la vente. | [Pressmark III]. g8v Le frontispice a été dessiné & | gravé sur bois par Lucien Pis- | sarro. Les bordures et les lettres | orneés ont été dessinées par | Lucien Pissarro et gravées | sur bois par Esther | Pissarro. [tpe orn: leaf] | MCMI. | En vente chez Hacon & Ricketts | 17, Craven St., Strand, London.

Opening pages. Gustave Flaubert, *Un Coeur simple*, 1901. (Special Collections, Florida State University, Tallahassee)

COLLATION: 16°: π2 a^8–g^8. 58 leaves, pp. [1–3] 4–113 [114–116]

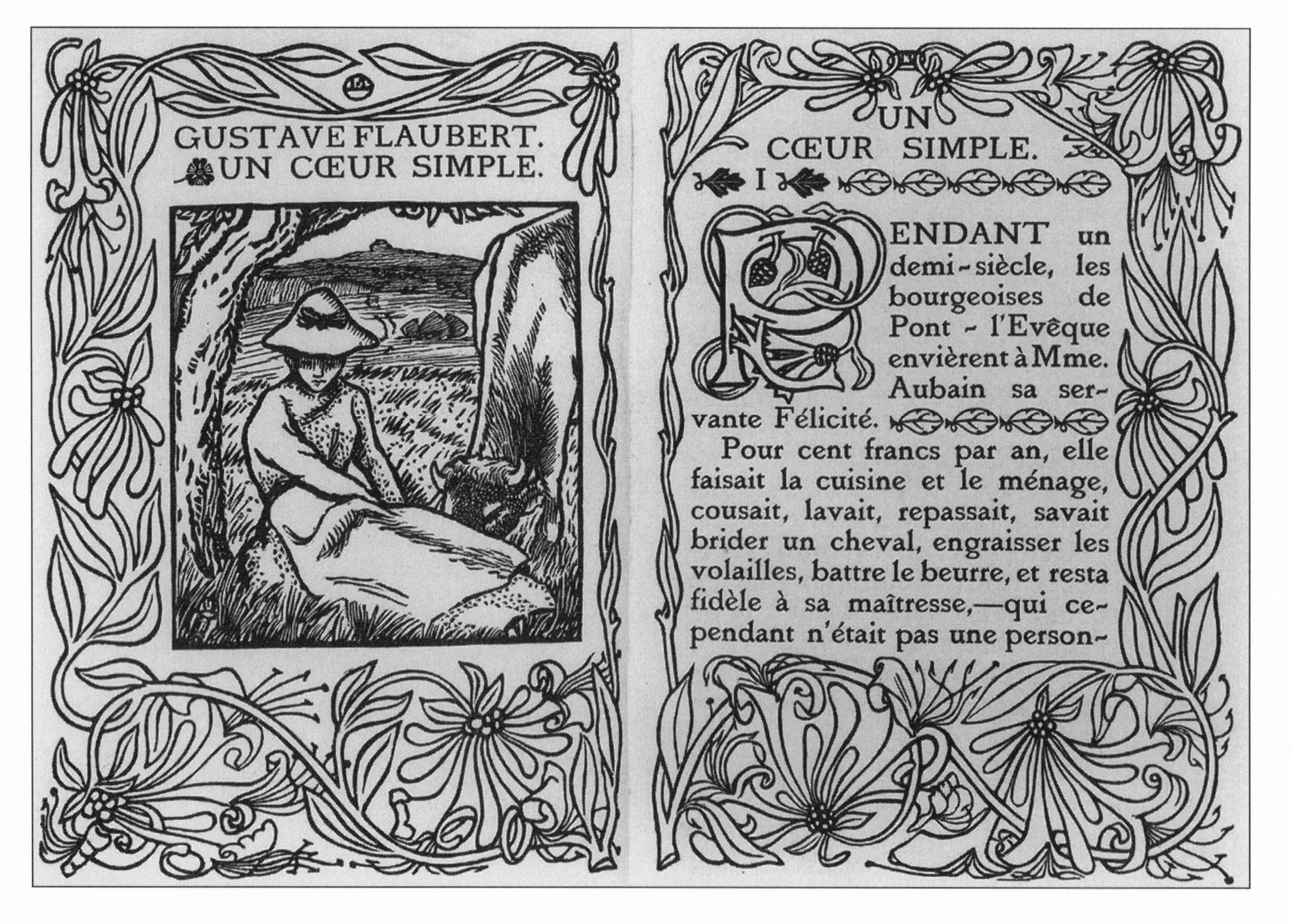

PAPER: Arnold's unbleached hand-made paper with Vale watermark. Leaf: 144 x 98 mm.

TYPE: Vale

ILLUSTRATIONS, ORNAMENTS, AND INITIALS: [one wood-engraved illustration, two borders; four initials, press mark in black and white] $\pi 1^{v}$: "Girl and Cow," 68 x 66 mm. (Fern 127 [SB 170]) within border, 130 x 94 mm. (Fern 327 [SB 170]). $\pi 2^{r}$: border, 128 x 91 mm. (Fern 325 [SB 160]); Initial P (Fern 295 [SB 117]). $a3^{r}$: Initial E (Fern 314 [SB 135]). $e6^{v}$: Initial I (Fern 316 [SB 137]). $g5^{r}$: Initial L (Fern 317 [SB 138]). $g8^{r}$: Pressmark III, 76 mm. diameter (Fern 112 [SB 152]).

CONTENTS: $\pi 1^{v}$: title. $\pi 2^{r}$–$g7^{v}$: text. g8: pressmark and colophon

BINDING: Quarter buff cloth with Michallett blue paper boards with printed paper label on upper left corner: GUSTAVE | FLAUBERT. | [double orn: leaf] | UN CŒUR | SIMPLE.

PUBLICATION: 200 copies for sale. Published in June 1901.

RELATED MATERIAL: Trial title page with a rondel encircling UN COEUR SIMPLE surrounded by foliage; Lucien Pissarro. Black crayon drawing, "Seated Girl," 1884.

NOTES: Lucien asked Camille to provide a drawing to illustrate *Un Coeur simple.* He suggested that Camille make a drawing from one of his painting of a small maid. He was having problems coming up with the design of the book. Camille declined Lucien's request and in mid-December 1900, Lucien sent him a proof of the illustration he was finishing for *Un Coeur simple.* The engraving was of a drawing Lucien had done before his illness. Camille found the engraving to be in the same genre as that of *The Queen of the Fishes* and suggested a few changes to the engraving. He thought the cow needed more definition and the girl's sleeve seemed too short.

Printing was underway by late April 1901. On Monday, 10 June 1901, 210 copies were sent to Hacon & Ricketts. The Pissarros received a check from Hacon & Ricketts for *Un Coeur simple* in the amount of £65.14.0 on 15 July 1901.

T. S. Moore found the book ". . . delightful, and the little shepherdess 'recueillie' prepares one for the tale with all its pathos and simplicity. The effect of the pale honeysuckle border over the double page is very delicate and suits the woodcut exactly. I do not know if I like the black leaf before the quotation marks it seems to jump on one too much. I dont [*sic*] remember to have seen it used so before these two little books of yours" (T. S. Moore to Lucien Pissarro, 10 July 1901, University of London, Paleography Room, Letter 19/132).

Copies were given to Charles Holmes, Georges Lecomte, Th.

Gaillard, C. Pissarro, A. Teissier, Emile Verhaeren, T. S. Moore, E. Verity, Diana White, A. Macgregor, Sam Bensusan, Alfred Pissarro, Burgler, and Ida Henry.

COPIES SEEN: Ashmolean. BL (deposited 24 June 1901; another copy with Sybil Pye binding in blue morocco with gold tooling, dated 1901). FSU. NYPL (John Shaw Billings Memorial Fund). SFPL (From the Library of R. H. St. J. Hornby Chantmarle, Dorset). William Andrews Clark Library, UCLA (Bookplate of William Andrews Clark).

EP9 • Gustave Flaubert. Hérodias. 1901.

GUSTAVE FLAUBERT. | [type orn: leaf] HÉRODIAS. [double type orn: leaf] | ["Herodias"within border]

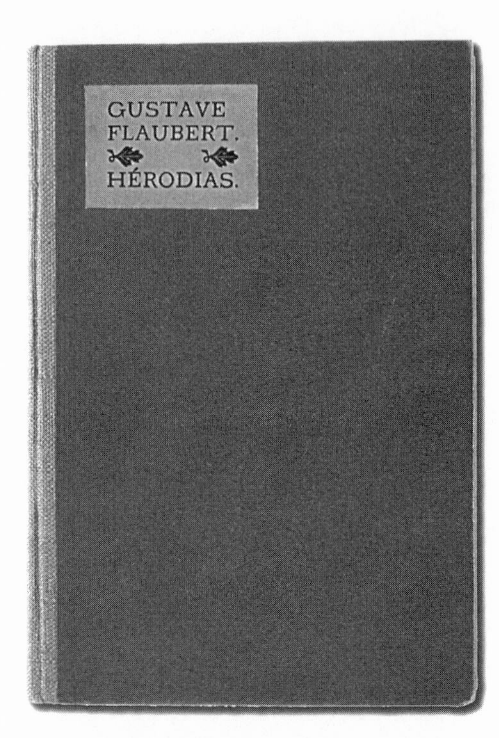

Binding. Gustave Flaubert. *Hérodias.* 1901. (Special Collections, Florida State University, Tallahassee)

COLOPHON: Le frontispice a été dessiné & | gravé sur bois par Lucien Pis- | sarro. Les bordures et les lettres | ornées ont été dessinées par | Lucien Pissarro et gravées | sur bois par Esther | Pissarro. [type orn: leaf] | MCMI. | En vente chez Hacon & Ricketts | 17, Craven St., Strand, London. $g3^v$ Il a été tiré de cet ouvrage 226 ex. | dont 200 pour la vente. | [Pressmark III (Fern 112 [SB 152])]

COLLATION; 16°: π^4 a^8–f^8 g^4. 56 leaves, pp. [1–3] 4–103 [104–108]

PAPER AND DIMENSIONS: Arnold's unbleached hand-made paper with Vale watermark. Leaf: 144 x 98 mm.

TYPE: Vale

ILLUSTRATIONS, ORNAMENTS, AND INITIALS: [one wood-engraved illustration, two borders, three initials, pressmark in black and white] $\pi 1^v$: "Hérodias" (Fern 130 [SB 175]) 67 x 65 mm. within border, 130 x 94 mm. (Fern 327 [SB 170]). $\pi 2^r$: border, 128 x 91 mm. (Fern 325 [SB 160), Initial L (Fern 322 [SB 143]). $b6^v$: Initial L (Fern 322 [SB 143]). $e1^v$: Initial L (Fern 322 [SB 143]). $g3^v$: Pressmark III, 76 mm. diameter (Fern 112 [SB 152]).

CONTENTS: $\pi 1^r$: blank. $\pi 3^v$: title. π^2-g^2: text. $g3^r$: colophon. $g3^v$: pressmark.

BINDING: Quarter buff cloth with Michallet blue paper boards with printed paper label on upper left front corner: GUSTAVE | FLAUBERT. | [double orn: leaf] HÉRODIAS.

PUBLICATION: 200 paper copies for sale. Published September 1901.
PROSPECTUS: [189 x 125 mm.] ISSUED BY HACON & RICKETTS | THE VALE PRESS, XVII CRAVEN | STREET, STRAND. | Now

ready: | [woodcut initial H (Fern 315 [SB 136]) ERODIAS by G. FLAUBERT. | With a frontispiece designed and | engraved on the wood by Lucien | Pissarro, & a double border designed by L. | Pissarro & engraved by Esther Pissarro. De- | my 16 mo. Two hundred & twenty copies | printed, by Lucien Pissarro at his Eragny | Press, on Arnold's hand-made paper with | the Vale water-mark, of which two hundred | copies are for sale at fifteen shillings net. | [to right] Order Form | over.

[verso]: [type orn: flower] NOTICE. To prevent disappointment, | orders should be sent, if possible, by return | of post. | Please send me .... cop... of | HERODIAS BY G. FLAUBERT, prin- | ted by Lucien Pissarro, for which I enclose | cheque. | Name [dotted line] | Address [three dotted lines] | To: [dotted line] | [dotted line] Bookseller, | [dotted line] | [dotted line] | Hacon & Ricketts, 17 Craven Street, W.C.

NOTES: Copies were given to Ida Henry, Camille Pissarro, Th. Gaillard, Diana White, A. Macgregor, A. Teisser, T. S. Moore, Charles Holmes, Emile Verhaeren, Sam Bensusan, Alfred Pissarro, Burgler, E. Verity, Georges Lecomte.

GUSTAVE FLAUBERT.
HÉRODIAS.

HÉRODIAS
I
LA citadelle de Machærous se dressait à l'orient de la mer Morte, sur un pic de basalte ayant la forme d'un cône. Quatre vallées profondes l'entouraient, deux vers les flancs, une en face, la quatrième au delà. Des maisons se tassaient contre sa base, dans le cercle d'un mur qui ondulait suivant les inégalités du terrain; &, par un chemin en zigzag tailladant le rocher, la ville se reliait à la forteresse, dont les murailles étaient hautes de

Opening pages. Gustave Flaubert, *Hérodias*, 1901. (Special Collections, Florida State University, Tallahassee)

COPIES SEEN: Ashmolean. Bancroft. BL (deposited 26 September 1901; another copy with Sybil Pye binding in green morocco with gold tooling, dated 1901). FSU. Huntington. NYPL (Bookplate John Shaw Billings Memorial Fund; purchased from Rota 15 Nov 1923). SFPL (Provenance: Robert Grabhorn). UCLA (Bookplate of William Andrews Clark).

EP10 • François Villon. Autres poésies. 1901.

[in black and red] AUTRES POESIES DE MAIS- | TRE FRANÇOIS VILLON & DE | SON ECOLE. | LONDON | HACON & RICKETTS

| 17 CRAVEN STREET STRAND. | [type orn: trefoil] | [type orn: trefoil] MCMI [type orn: trefoil] | [type orn: trefoil]

COLOPHON: LE FRONTISPICE A ETE DES- | SINE ET | GRAVE SUR BOIS PAR | LUCIEN PISSARRO. LA BOR- | DURE & LES LETTRES OR- | NEES ONT ETE DESSI- | NEES PAR L. PISSARRO | & GRAVEES PAR ES- | THER PISSARRO. | CETTE EDITION EST STRIC- | TEMENT LIMITEE A DEUX | CENT VINGT SIX EXEM- | PLAIRES, dont DEUX CENTS | POUR LA VENTE. | [double type orn: leaf] | [type orn: leaf]

COLLATION: Crown 8°: [a]^{2} b^{4}–h^{4}. 30 leaves, pp. [1] 2–55 [56–60]

PAPER AND DIMENSIONS: 222 copies printed on Arnold's unbleached hand-made paper with Vale watermark. Leaf: 194 x 125 mm. 4 copies printed on old Japanese hand-made paper. Leaf: 192 x 126 mm.

TYPE: Vale

ILLUSTRATIONS, ORNAMENTS, AND INITIALS: [one black and white wood-engraved illustration, two borders in green, one red initial, twenty-eight black and white initials] [a]1^{v}: Frontispiece: "Les Regrets de la Belle Hëaulmiere," 75 mm. in diameter (Fern 131 [SB 174 bis]) within border in green (Fern 328 [SB 155]). [a]2^{r}: border in green (Fern 326 [SB 157]). Initial A (Fern 307 [SB 129]) in red. b2^{v}: Initial M (Fern 297 [SB 119]). b3^{r}: Initial B (Fern 306 [SB 128]). b4^{r}: Initial A (Fern 307 [SB 129]). b4^{v}: Initial R (Fern 296 [SB 118]). c1^{r}: Initial J (NIF). c1^{v}: Initial J (NIF). c2^{v}: Initial O (Fern 291 [SB 113]). d1^{r}: Initial L (Fern 287 [SB 109]). d1^{v}: Initial A (Fern 307 [SB 129]). d2^{v}: Initial U (Fern 294 [SB 116]). d3^{r}: Initial S (Fern 292 [SB 114]). d4^{r}: Initial D (Fern 289 [SB 120]). e1^{r}: Initial P (Fern 295 [SB 117]). e1^{v}: Initial T (Fern 308 [SB 130]). e2^{r}: Initial A (Fern 307 [SB 129]). e2^{v}: Initial L (Fern 287 [SB 109]). e3^{v}: Initial Q (Fern 293 [SB 115]). e4^{v}: Initial H (NIF). f1r: Initial A (Fern 288 [SB 110]). f1^{v}: Initial E (Fern 286 [SB 108]). f2^{r}: Initial S (Fern 299 [SB 121]). f3^{r}: Initial C (Fern 305 [SB 127]). f3^{v}: Initial I (Fern 298 [SB 120]). f4^{v}: Initial D (Fern 301 [SB 123]). g1^{v}: Initial J (Fern 290 [SB 112]). g3^{r}: Initial P (Fern 295 [SB 117]). g4^{v}: Initial Q (Fern 293 [SB 115]). h1^{v}: Initial D (Fern 289 [SB 111]). h4^{v}: Pressmark III, 76 mm. (Fern 112 [SB 152]). Song refrains and shoulder notes in red.

CONTENTS: [a]1^{r}: title. [a]1^{v}: illustration. [a]2^{r}–c1^{v}: LES REGRETS DE LA BELLE HËAULMIERE. c2^{r}–h2^{v}: POÉSIES ATTRIBUÉES A VILLON. h3^{r}–h3^{v}: table [of contents]. h4^{r}: colophon. h4^{v}: pressmark.

BINDING: Quarter buff paper, gold stamped on upper left cover: [orn: trefoil] VILLON. | [orn: trefoil] AUTRES | POÉSIES. White paper boards with a repeat pattern of small five-petalled flowers (NIF) printed in pink. On spine gold stamped: [orn: trefoil] | VIL- | LON | [double orn: trefoil]

PUBLICATION: 200 copies for sale at 20 shillings. Published October 1901.

[on slip]: Of this edition of «AUTRES POE - | SIES DE FRANCOIS VILLON» 222 | copies have been printed on Arnold's un- | bleached hand-made paper and 4 copies on | old Japanese hand-made paper; of the later, | this is No. [in red] 1. [Also slip for No. 2]

PROSPECTUS: ISSUED BY HACON & RICKETTS | THE VALE PRESS, XVII CRAVEN | STREET, STRAND | Now ready: | [Initial A (Fern 312 [SB 133])] UTRES POESIES DE MAIS- | TRE FRANCOIS VILLON & DE SON ECOLE. With a fron- | tispiece, border & initial letters designed by | Lucien Pissarro, and engraved on the wood | by Lucien & Esther Pissarro. Crown octavo | Two hundred & twenty-six copies printed | by Lucien Pissarro at his Eragny Press, in | red & black throughout, on Arnold's hand- | made paper with the Vale water-mark; of | which two hundred copies are for sale at | twenty shillings net. | [type orn: flower] Note. The publication of LES SON- | NETS DE P. DE RONSARD, previous- | ly announced has been postponed till next year. | [to the right] Order Form over.

[verso]: [type orn: flower] NOTICE: To prevent disappointment, | orders should be sent, if possible, by return | of post. | Please send me .... cop... of AUTRES POESIES DE MAISTRE | FRANCOIS VILLON, printed by Lucien | Pissarro, for which I enclose cheque. | Name [dotted line] | Address [three dotted lines] | To [dotted line] | [dotted line] Bookseller, | [two dotted lines] | Hacon & Ricketts, 17 Craven Street, W.C.

NOTES: Camille found the proof of "Les Heaulmière" to be very beautiful, seeing a woman advanced in years, and weeping, her beauty gone. He suggested, however, that it might be better to dress the woman in costume and head-dress more contemporary to Villon's poem. It would be easy to change the engraving without changing the pose, which he found suitable to the subject matter. Although Lucien realized that his illustration was not in keeping with Heaulmière, his model was a Puritan Protestant one, a model that could hardly be suspected of serving to illustrate a courtesan.

Copies were given to Diana White, A. Macgregor, Ida Henry, Emile Verhaeren, T. S. Moore, Sam Bensusan, Burgler, E. Verity, Charles Holmes, Th. Gaillard, A. Teisser. The Japanese handmade paper copies were given to Diana White, Camille Pissarro, and Alfred Pissarro.

COPIES SEEN: Ashmolean (on old Japanese handmade paper; Inscribed: A mon père | bien affectueusement | Lucien Pissarro). Bancroft. BL (deposited 23 Oct 1901). NYPL (Bookplate of John Shaw Billings Memorial Fund, purchased at Anderson 2 May 1923, likely John Quinn's copy). SFPL.

EP11 • Emile Verhaeren. Les Petits vieux. 1901.

[type orn: leaf] Emile Verhaeren. | [type orn: leaf] LES PETITS VIEUX. [type orn: leaf] | LONDON | Hacon & Ricketts | 17 Craven Street, Strand. W. [p. 2] Il a été tiré de cet ouvrage 230 exemplaires dont 200 pour | la vente.

COLOPHON: [in black and peach] Le frontispice en coleur et les letters ornées ont été | dessinés par Lucien Pissarro et gravés sur bois par Lucien | et Esther Pissarro. | [type orn: leaf] MCMI. [type orn: leaf]

COLLATION: Fancy, 19 leaves

PAPER: Old Japanese paper on uncut pages, printed one side only. Leaf: 121 x 160 mm.

"Winter aconite" binding. Emile Verhaeren, *Les Petits vieux*, 1901. (Ashmolean Museum, Oxford)

TYPE: Vale

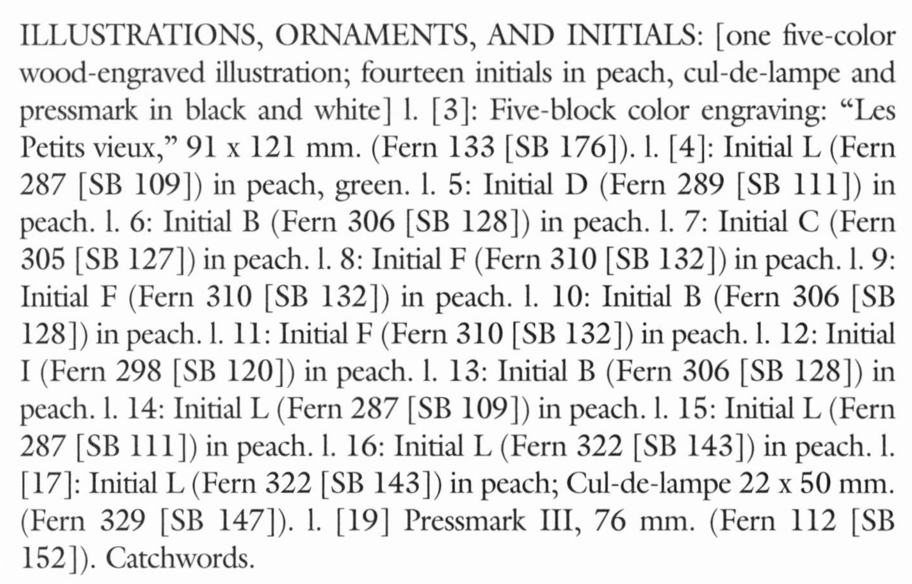

ILLUSTRATIONS, ORNAMENTS, AND INITIALS: [one five-color wood-engraved illustration; fourteen initials in peach, cul-de-lampe and pressmark in black and white] l. [3]: Five-block color engraving: "Les Petits vieux," 91 x 121 mm. (Fern 133 [SB 176]). l. [4]: Initial L (Fern 287 [SB 109]) in peach, green. l. 5: Initial D (Fern 289 [SB 111]) in peach. l. 6: Initial B (Fern 306 [SB 128]) in peach. l. 7: Initial C (Fern 305 [SB 127]) in peach. l. 8: Initial F (Fern 310 [SB 132]) in peach. l. 9: Initial F (Fern 310 [SB 132]) in peach. l. 10: Initial B (Fern 306 [SB 128]) in peach. l. 11: Initial F (Fern 310 [SB 132]) in peach. l. 12: Initial I (Fern 298 [SB 120]) in peach. l. 13: Initial B (Fern 306 [SB 128]) in peach. l. 14: Initial L (Fern 287 [SB 109]) in peach. l. 15: Initial L (Fern 287 [SB 111]) in peach. l. 16: Initial L (Fern 322 [SB 143]) in peach. l. [17]: Initial L (Fern 322 [SB 143]) in peach; Cul-de-lampe 22 x 50 mm. (Fern 329 [SB 147]). l. [19] Pressmark III, 76 mm. (Fern 112 [SB 152]). Catchwords.

CONTENTS: l. [1]: title. l. [2]: edition statement. l. [3]: illustration. l. 4–l. [17]: text. l. [18]: colophon. l. [19]: Pressmark II.

BINDING: Quarter gray paper with Michallet blue paper boards with a repeat pattern of "Winter aconite" (NIF) printed in two shades of green ink. On spine red gold stamped: EMILE VERHAEREN [leaf orn] LES PETITS VIEUX

PUBLICATION: 200 paper copies for sale at 20 shillings. Published December 1901.

PROSPECTUS: [1 leaf, 179 x 121 mm.] ISSUED BY HACON & RICKETTS | THE VALE PRESS, XVII CRAVEN | STREET, STRAND. | Now ready: [woodcut initial L (15 mm. x 17 mm.) (NIF)]

ES PETITS VIEUX [two type orns: leaf] | BY EMILE VERHAEREN. | With a frontispiece printed in | colours and initial letters designed by Lucien | Pissarro and engraved on the wood by Lu- | cien & Esther Pissarro, and a cover "Winter | aconite" printed in two colors. Two hun- | dred and thirty copies printed by Lucien | Pissarro at his Eragny Press, in red & black | throughout, on Japanese hand-made paper | of which two hundred copies for sale at | twenty shillings net. | [to the right] Order Form over.

[verso]: [type orn: bud] NOTICE.—To prevent disappointment, | orders should be sent, if possible, by return | of post. | Please send me .... cop.... of | LES PETITS VIEUX BY EMILE | VERHAEREN, printed by Lucien Pissar- | ro, for which I enclose cheque. | Name [dotted line] | Address [dotted lines] | [dotted line] | [dotted line] | To [dotted line] | [dotted line] Bookseller, | [dotted line] | [dotted line] | Hacon & Ricketts, 17 Craven Street, W.C.

Initial L (Fern 287 [SB 109]). Emile Verhaeren, *Les Petits vieux*, 1901.

NOTES: Copies to: Emile Verhaeren (four copies), Camille Pissarro, A. Teisser, Ida Henry, Louise Henry, A. Macgregor, Diana White, T. S. Moore, Charles Holmes, Burgler, E. Verity, Orovida Bensusan, Sam Bensusan, Georges Lecomte, Th. Gaillard, Laurence Binyon.

COPIES SEEN: Ashmolean. BL (deposited 1901). LC. NYPL (Bookplate of John Shaw Billings Memorial Fund). SFPL (Provenance: Robert Grabhorn with bookplate of William & Helena M. Hand).

EP12 • Sir Francis Bacon. Of Gardens. 1902.

[in black, red, and green] [type orn: leaf] OF GARDENS. [type orn: leaf] | AN ESSAY, BY FRANCIS | BACON. | [type orn: entwined leaves] | LONDON | HACON & RICKETTS | CRAVEN ST., STRAND. | [type orn: trefoil] | [type orn: trefoil] MCMII. [type orn: trefoil] | [type orn: trefoil]

COLOPHON: [in black and red] THE FRONTISPIECE has | BEEN DESIGNED & | ENGRAVED BY | [type orn: bud] LUCIEN PISSARRO. [type orn: bud] | [woodcut orn: two half-flowers] | THE DOUBLE BORDER | & INITIAL LETTERS | DESIGNED BY L. | PISSARRO & EN- | GRAVED BY | [type orn: bud] ESTHER PISSARRO. [type orn: bud] $e1^v$ [Pressmark III in green] $e2^r$ [type orn: leaf] THIS EDITION IS | STRICTLY LIMITED | TO 226 COPIES OF | WHICH 200 ARE | FOR SALE. | [cul-de-lampe]

COLLATION: 12°: b^4–d^4 e^2. 14 leaves, pp. [1–5] 6–23 [24–28]

PAPER AND DIMENSIONS: Arnold's unbleached hand-made paper with Vale watermark. Leaf: 173 x 95 mm.

TYPE: Vale

ILLUSTRATIONS, ORNAMENTS, AND INITIALS: [one black and white wood-engraved illustration, two borders in green, ten initials and one cul-de-lampe in red; pressmark in green] [b]2^r: "The Garden," 75 mm. diameter (Fern 137 [SB 153bis]). [b]2^v: border in green, 157 x 90 mm. (Fern 330 [SB 153]), Initial G (Fern 332 [SB 178]) in red. [b]3^r: border, 157 x 90 mm. (Fern 330 [SB 153]) in green. c1^r: Initial A (Fern 336 [SB 182]) in red. c2^r: Initial F (Fern 333 [SB 179]) in red. c4^r: Initial F (Fern 334 [SB 180]) in red. c4^v: Initial F (Fern 334 [SB 180) in red. d2^r: Initial F (Fern 334 [SB 180]) in red. d3^r: Initial F (Fern 334 [SB 180]) in red. d3^v: Initial F (Fern 334 [SB 181]) in red. d4^r : Initial F (Fern 333 [SB 179]) in red. d4^v: Initial S (Fern 335 [SB 181]) in red. [e]1^v: Pressmark III in green, 76 mm. diameter (Fern 112 [SB 152]). [e]2^r: Cul-de-lampe (Fern 276 (80]) [without THE END in red]. Catchwords.

CONTENTS: b1^r: blank. b1^v: title. b2^r: frontispiece. b2^v–d4^v: text. [e]1^r: colophon. [e]1^v: pressmark. [e]2^v: edition statement. [e]2^v: blank.

BINDING: Quarter cream paper, gold stamped on upper left cover: [orn: leaf] OF | GARDENS | BY | FRANCIS | BACON. [orn: leaf]. Michallet blue paper boards with a repeat pattern of "rose" (Fern 284 [SB 150]) printed in red and green ink.

PUBLICATION: 200 paper copies for sale at 16 shillings. Published April 1902.

RELATED MATERIAL: Trial border; trial paper covers; drawings for initials.

PROSPECTUS: [1 leaf, 182 x 125 mm.] Includes Initial O (Fern 302 [SB 124]).

NOTES: Leighton sent a sample copy to Esther on 7 April 1902. By 17 April the edition was bound and ready to ship.

Copies given to Camille Pissarro, A. Macgregor, Diana White, Mrs. Clotilde Wollersen, Ida Henry, T. S. Moore, Laurence Binyon, Jacob Bensusan, Ruth Bensusan, Burgler, E. Verity, Charles Holmes, Georges Lecomte.

COPIES SEEN: Ashmolean. Bancroft. BL (deposited 12 May 1902). FSU (Inscribed: To Ethel & Lucien | from Esther & | Lucien Pissarro. | July 16th 1902.). NYPL. SFPL (Provenance: Robert Grabhorn).

"Rose" binding. Francis Bacon, *Of Gardens,* 1902. (Special Collections, Florida State University, Tallahassee)

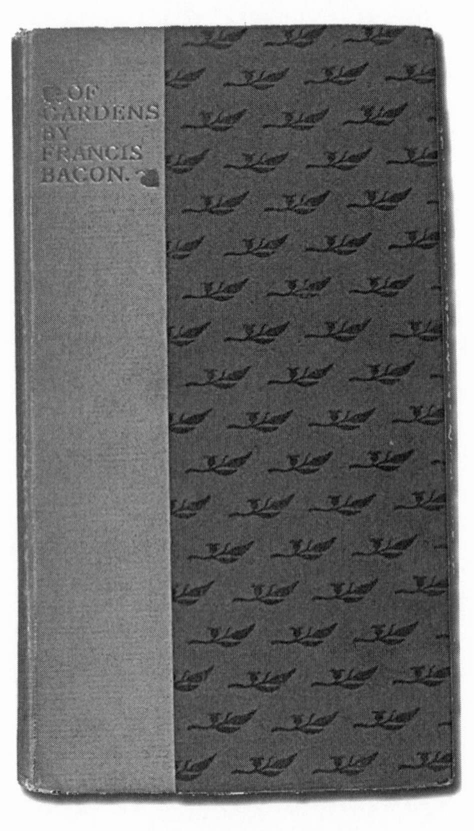

EP13 • Pierre de Ronsard. Choix de sonnets. 1902.

[in black and red] [within border ["Girl Picking Flowers"] [orn, 14 x 93 mm.] [Initial C] HOIX DE [orn] | SONNETS DE | P. DE RONSARD.

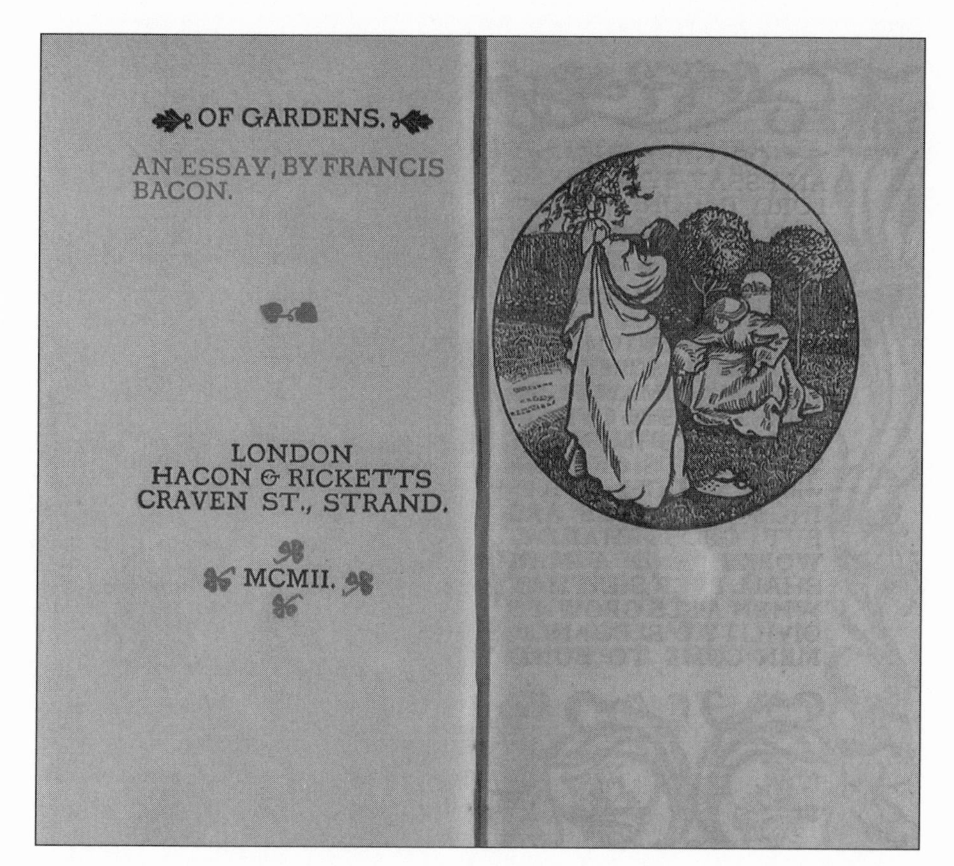
OF GARDENS.
AN ESSAY, BY FRANCIS BACON.
LONDON
HACON & RICKETTS
CRAVEN ST., STRAND.
MCMII.

Title page and frontispiece. Francis Bacon, *Of Gardens,* 1902. (Special Collections, Florida State University, Tallahassee)

COLOPHON: Le frontispice a été dessiné et gravé sur bois | par Lucien Pissarro. La bordure et les lettres | ornées ont été dessinées par L. Pissarro et | gravées sur bois par Esther Pissarro, | et le livre fut achevé d'impri- | mer en Juillet 1902 sur leurs | presses, The Brook, | Hammersmith, | London, | W. | [type orn: leaf] | [type orn: entwined leaf] | [type orn: leaf] | En vente chez Hacon & Ricketts, 17, Craven | Street Strand. l4^{r}: Il a été tire de cet ouvrage 226 exemplaires, | dont 200 pour la vente. | [Pressmark III within border]

COLLATION: 8°: [a]^{2} b^{4}–j^{4} [k]^{4} l^{4}. 46 leaves, pp. [1–4] 5–79 [80–92]

PAPER AND DIMENSIONS: Arches. Leaf: 213 x 141 mm.

TYPE: Vale

ILLUSTRATIONS, ORNAMENTS, AND INITIALS: [one black and white wood-engraved illustration; three black and white borders; one red initial, seventy-six initials and one pressmark in black and white] [a]1^{v}: "Girl Picking Flowers," 114 x 92 mm. (Fern 135 [SB 177]) within border (Fern 331 [SB 177 bis]). [a]2^{r}: border (Fern 331 [SB 177 bis]), Initial Q (Fern 357 [SB 203]) in red. b1^{r}: Initial N (Fern 354 [SB 200]). b1^{v}: Initial E (Fern 344 [SB 190]). b2^{r}: Initial B (Fern 340 [SB 186]). b2^{v}: Initial L (Fern 352 [SB 198]). b3^{r}: Initial J (Fern 347 [SB 196]). b3^{v}: Initial U (Fern 361 [SB 207]). b4^{r}: Initial A (Fern 341 [SB 187]). b4^{v}: Initial J (Fern 347 [SB 196]). c1^{r}: Initial S (Fern 359 [SB 205]). c1^{v}:

Initial Q (Fern 357 [SB 203]). c2^{r}: Initial O (Fern 355 [SB 201]). c2^{v}: Initial A (Fern 341 [SB 187]). c3^{r}: Initial P (Fern 356 [SB 202]). c3^{v}: Initial C (Fern 342 [SB 188]). c4^{r}: Initial S (Fern 359 [SB 205]). c4^{v}: Initial Q (Fern 357 [SB 203]). d1^{r}: Initial A (Fern 341 [SB 187]). d1^{v}: Initial A (Fern 341 [SB 187]). d2^{r}: Initial D (Fern 343 [SB 189]). d2^{v}: Initial Q (Fern 357 [SB 203]). d3r: Initial V (Fern 362 [SB 208]). d3^{v}: Initial P (Fern 356 [SB 202]). d4^{r}: Initial D (Fern 343 [SB 189]). d4^{v}: Initial Q (Fern 357 [SB 203]). e1^{r}: Initial M (Fern 353 [SB 199]). e1^{v}: Initial M (Fern 353 [SB 199]). e2^{r}: Initial L (Fern 351 [SB 197]). e2^{r}: Initial L (Fern 351 [SB 197]). e2^{v}: Initial D (Fern 343 [SB 189]). e3r: Initial A (Fern 341 [SB 197]). e3^{v}: Initial M (Fern 353 [SB 199]). e4^{r}: Initial M (Fern 353 [SB 199]). e4^{v}: Initial J (Fern 342 [SB 188]). f1^{r}: Initial M (Fern 353 [SB 199]). f1^{v}: Initial A (Fern 341 [SB 187]). f2^{r}: Initial C (Fern 341 [SB 187]). f2^{v}: Initial V (Fern 362 [SB 208]). f3^{r}: Initial H (Fern 350 [SB 193]). f3^{v}: Initial J (Fern 346 [SB 195]). f4^{r}: Initial J (Fern 347 [SB 196]). f4^{v}: Initial A (Fern 341 [SB 187]). g1^{r}: Initial P (Fern 356 [SB 202]). g1^{v}: Initial L (Fern 351 [SB 197]). g2^{r}: Initial C (Fern 342 [SB 188]). g2^{v}: Initial T (Fern 360 [SB 206]). g3^{r}: Initial L (Fern 352 [SB 198]). f3^{v}: Initial V (Fern 362 [SB 208]). f4^{r}: Initial V (Fern 362 [SB 208]). g4^{v}: Initial C (Fern 342 [SB 188]). h1^{r}: Initial C (Fern 342 [SB 188]). h1^{v}: Initial A (Fern 341 [SB 187]). h2^{r}: Initial O (Fern 355 [SB 201]). h2^{v}: Initial J (Fern 346 [SB 195]). h3^{r}: Initial V (Fern 362 [SB 208]). h3^{v}: Initial Q (Fern 357 [SB 203]). h4^{r}: Initial C (Fern 342 [SB 188]). h4^{v}: Initial Q (Fern 357 [SB 203]). i1^{r}: Initial I (Fern 345 [SB 194]). i1^{v}: Initial A (Fern 341 [SB 187]). i2^{r}: Initial D (Fern 343 [SB 189]). i2^{v}: Initial Q (Fern 357 [SB 203]). i3^{r}: Initial B (Fern 340 [SB 186]). i3^{v}: Initial J (Fern 347 [SB 196]). i4^{r}: Initial J (Fern 346 [SB 195]). i4^{v}: Initial J (Fern 347 [SB 196]). j1^{r}: Initial J (Fern 346 [SB 195]). j1^{v}: Initial M (Fern 353 [SB 199]). j2^{r}: Initial B (Fern 340 [SB 186]). j2^{v}: Initial J (Fern 347 [SB 196]). j3^{r}: Initial O (Fern 355 [SB 201]). j3^{v}: Initial L (Fern 351 [SB 197]). j4^{r}: Initial J (Fern 347 [SB 196]). j4^{v}: Initial R (Fern 358 [SB 204]). [k]1r: Initial J (Fern 346 [SB 195]). [k]1^{v}: Initial J (Fern 347 [SB 196]). [k]2^{r}: Initial R (Fern 358 [SB 204]). l4^{r}: Pressmark III, 76 mm. diameter (Fern 112 [SB 152]) within border, (variant of Fern 328 [SB 155] but flowers are white outlined in black).

CONTENTS: [a]1^{r}: blank. [a]1^{v}: frontispiece. [a]2^{r}–[k]2^{r}: text. [k]2^{v}: blank. [k]3^{r}–l2^{r}: Table des Matieres. l2^{v}: blank. 13^{r}: colophon. 13^{v}: blank. l4^{r}: colophon, pressmark. l4^{v}: blank.

BINDING: Quarter buff paper, pale gold stamped on upper left cover: RONSARD. | [type orn: entwined leaves] | CHOIX DE | SONNETS. Michallet blue paper boards with a repeat pattern of "May blossom" (Fern 339 [SB 216]) printed in buff and green ink.

PUBLICATION: 200 paper copies for sale at 30 shillings. Published September 1902.

HOIX DE SONNETS DE P. DE RONSARD

CHOIX DE SONNETS DE P. DE RONSARD

AMOURS DE CASSANDRE.

I.

QUI VOUDRA VOIR COMME AMOUR ME SURMONTE, COMME IL M'ASSAUT, COMME il se FAIT VAINQUEUR, COMME IL RENFLAME ET RENGLACE MON CŒUR, COMME IL REÇOIT UN HONNEUR DE MA HONTE:

QUI VOUDRA VOIR UNE JEUNESSE PRONTE A SUIVRE EN VAIN L'OBJET DE DE SON MALHEUR, ME VIENNE LIRE, IL VOIRRA MA DOULEUR, DONT MA DEESSE ET MON DIEU NE FONT CONTE.

IL COGNOISTRA QU'AMOUR EST SANS RAISON, Un DOUX ABUS, une BELLE PRISON, UN VAIN ESPOIR QUI DE VENT NOUS VIENT PAISTRE:

Frontispiece and title page. *Choix de sonnets de P. de Ronsard*, 1902. (Ashmolean Museum, Oxford)

PROSPECTUS: ISSUED BY HACON & RICKETTS | THE VALE PRESS, XVII CRAVEN | STREET, STRAND. | Now ready: | [woodcut initial C (Fern 305)] HOIX DE SONNETS DE | P. DE RONSARD. [two type orns: leaf] | With a Frontispiece designed | and engraved on the wood by | Lucien Pissarro, a border and | a new set of initials de- | signed by Lucien Pissarro, and a may | blossom cover, printed in two colors. Small | quarto. Two hundred and twenty-six copies | printed by E. & L. Pissarro at their Eragny | Press, on "Arches" hand-made paper with | their own water-mark, of which two hun- | dred copies are for sale at thirty shillings net. | [to the right] Order Form over.

[verso]: [type orn: bud] NOTICE.—To prevent disappointment, | orders should be sent, if possible, by return | of post. | Please send me .... cop.... of | CHOIX DE SONNETS DE P. DE | RONSARD, printed by E. & L. Pissarro, | for which I enclose cheque. | Name [dotted line] | Address [dotted lines] |[dotted line] | [dotted line] | To [dotted line] | [dotted line] Bookseller, | [dotted line] | [dotted line] | Hacon & Ricketts, 17 Craven Street, W.C. [350 prospectuses were printed]

RELATED MATERIAL: Design for title page of large drawn letters CHOIX DE SONNETS de P. De Ronsard, "to be reduced to exactly

15/16 of an inch"; Trial title page with border (almost identical to final border); drawing for large S.

NOTES: Esther and T. Taylor began composing *Choix de sonnets* on Saturday, 17 May 1902. The book was finished in mid-September. It is the first book printed on paper made especially for the Eragny Press. Lucien found this first lot of paper to be a bit too white (Lucien Pissarro to Camille Pissarro, before 24 September 1902).

On Monday, 25 August 1902, Esther sent all but the frontispiece and 7 sheets of signature I to Leighton. In late August 1902, the binding was underway, but not without difficulties. Esther thought Leighton was too slow in returning the sample copy and the price for binding the edition too high. He reminded her that during the week the lettering for the binding had been engraved and the book completely bound. The Ronsard, too, was a larger book, and as Leighton mentioned, "3/4 of an inch each way, is a considerable difference in the cost of binding" (Leighton to Esther Pissarro, 28 August 1902). The binding was ready for delivery on 17 September 1902.

Camille thought that Lucien had surpassed himself this time—"It's all simply superb," he wrote, the binding in a charming and subdued tone, the engraving large and well-suited to the ornaments and the letters and all together in good taste and without affectation (Camille Pissarro to Lucien Pissarro, 20 October 1902).

Copies given to Diana White, Mrs. Wollersen, York Powell, C. Kirby, Charles Holmes, A. Teisser, Emile Verhaeren, Camille Pissarro, Th. Gaillard, Georges Lecomte.

COPIES SEEN: Ashmolean (Inscribed: A mon cher père Lucien Pissarro). Bancroft. BL (deposited 6 October 1902). NYPL (Bookplate of John Shaw Billings Memorial Fund, purchased at the Anderson Gallery, 7 April 1924, probably John Quinn copy). SFPL.

EP14 • Charles Perrault. Historie de peau d'ane. 1902.

[in black and red][type orn: trefoil] CHARLES PERRAULT. | HISTOIRE DE PEAU D'ANE. | [Illustration ("Geese")] | [type orn: bud] | (CONTE DE MA MÈRE LOYE) | MCMII.

COLOPHON: [type orn: bud] Les trois illustrations ont été dessinées | et gravées sur bois par T. Sturge Moore. | Le frontispice, les bordures et les lettres | ornées ont été dessinés par Lucien | Pissarro et gravés sur bois par L. et | E. Pissarro. Le livre fut achevé | d'imprimer en Septembre 1902 | par L. et E. Pissarro sur leurs | presses, "The Brook," | Hammersmith, W. | [triple type orn: leaf] | [double type orn: leaf] | [type orn: leaf] | En vente chez Hacon & Ricketts, 17, | Craven Street, Strand. c4^{v}: Il a été tire de cet ouvrage 230 exem- | plaires dont 200 pour la vente. | [Pressmark III]

COLLATION: 8°: [a]^4 [b]^4 1 l. c^4 1 l. d^4 e^4. 22 leaves, 1–16 17–24 25–38 [39-40]

PAPER AND DIMENSIONS: Arches. Leaf: 205 x 126 mm.

TYPE: Vale

ORNAMENTS, ILLUSTRATIONS, AND INITIALS: [four black and white wood-engraved illustrations, three borders, 21 initials, and press-mark in black and white] [a]2^v: "Geese," 73 mm. diameter (Fern [SB 113 [SB 154]) within border (NIF). [a]4^v: Illustration by T. S. Moore, 93 x 90 mm. Caption: "Jamais on n'avait rien vu de si beau et | de si artistement ouvré. (Page 18.)"; Initial I (Fern 316 [SB 137]); and [b]1^r double-page border, 190 x 244 mm. (Fern 281 [SB 105–6]). [b]1^r Initial L (Fern 317 [SB 138]). [b]1^v: Initial O (Fern 319 [SB 140]). [b]2^v: Initial

"La joie de se trouver si belle lui donna evie de s'y baigner, ce que'elle exécuta," wood engraving by T. S. Moore. Charles Perrault, *Historie de peau d'ane,* 1902. (Ashmolean Museum, Oxford)

L (Fern 317 [SB 138]). [b]3[r]: Initial E (Fern 314 [SB 135]). [b]3[v]: Initial L (Fern 317 [SB 138]). [b]4[r]: Initial L (Fern 317 [SB 138]), [b]4[v]: Initial L (Fern 317 [SB 138]). [inserted leaf][v]: Illustration by T. S. Moore, 85 x 73 mm. Caption: "Elle soupirait de n'avoir pour témoin | de sa beauté qui ses moutons et ses din- | donc. (Page 23.) c3[r]: Initial L (Fern 317 [SB 138]), Initial P (NIF). c3[v]: Initial U (Fern 321 [SB 142]). c4[v]: Initial U (Fern 321 [SB 142]). [inserted leaf][r]: Illustration by T. S. Moore, 85 x 74 mm. Caption: "La joie de se trouver si belle lui donna | envie de s'y baigner, ce qu'elle exécuta. | (Page 23.). d1[r]: Initial I (Fern 316 [SB 137]), Initial L (Fern 317 [SB 138]). d2[v]: Initial Q (Fern 320 [SB 141]). d3[v]: Initial L (Fern 317 [SB 138]), Initial I (Fern 316 [SB 137]). d4[v]: Initial L (Fern 317 [SB 138]). e1[r]: Initial A (Fern 312 [SB 133]), Initial L (Fern 317 [SB 138]). e3[v]: Initial L (Fern 317 [SB 138]). e4[v]: Pressmark III, 76 mm. diameter (Fern 112 [SB 152]). Catchwords.

CONTENTS: [a]1[r]: half-title. [a]1[v]: blank. [a]2[r]: blank. [a]2[v]: title. [a]3[r]: Flaubert quote. [a]3[v]: blank. [a]4[r]: blank. [a]4[v]–e3[v]: text. e[4]: colophon.

BINDING: Quarter Michallet blue paper, gold stamped on upper left cover: [type orn: trefoil] C. PERRAULT. | PEAU D'ANE. [type orne: trefoil]. Cream paper boards with a repeat pattern of "lotus flower" (Fern 323 [SB 145]) printed in blue. On spine gold stamped at top and bottom flower ornament.

PUBLICATION: 200 copies for sale at 21 shillings. Published in late November 1902.

PROSPECTUS: [190 x 122 mm.] ISSUED BY HACON & RICKETTS | THE VALE PRESS, XVII CRAVEN | STREET, STRAND. | Now ready | [woodcut initial H, 41 x 42 mm. (NIF)] ISTOIRE DE PEAU | D'ANE PAR CH. | PERRAULT. [two type ons: trefoil] | With a frontispiece | designed and engraved | on the wood by Lucien | Pissarro, a border and | initial letters designed | by L. Pissarro and engraved on the wood by | Esther Pissarro, and three illustrations de- | signed and engraved on the wood by T. S. | Moore. Crown 8vo. Two hundred and thirty | copies printed by E. & L. Pissarro at their | Eragny Press, on 'Arches' handmade paper | with their own watermark, of which two | hundred copies are for sale at twenty-one | shillings nett. | Order Form over.

[verso]: [type orn: bud] NOTICE. (To prevent disappointment, orders should be sent, if possible, by return of post. | Please send me .... cop.... of HISTOIRE DE EAU D'ANE PAR | CH. PERRAULT, printed by E. & L. Pis- | arro, for which I enclose cheque. | Name [dotted line] | Address [three dotted lines] | To [dotted line] | [dotted line] Bookseller, | [two dotted lines] | Hacon & Ricketts, 17 Craven Street, W.C.

NOTES: *Peau d'ane* may have been planned by autumn 1901, if not earlier. Laurence Binyon found the copy text for the Pissarros in the British Museum (Des Periers. Jean Bonaventure. *Nouvelles récréations et joyeux devis de B. des Periers, suivis du Cymbalum mundi, réimprimés par les soins de D. Jouaust. Avec une notice, des notes et un glossaire par Louis Lacour.* Paris, 1874.) The story of Peau d'ane is in vol. 2 (Laurence Binyon, 12 October 1901).

T. S. Moore, who contributed the wood engravings for the book, wrote to Lucien in a letter dated 5 February 1902, "I am affraid [*sic*] I have done nothing yet towards Peau d'Ane but hope to soon, but I am wholly fallen away from art lately." Printing was underway on 30 August 1902. On 12 November 1902, Lucien wrote to Camille that the book was finished. Camille (letter to Lucien, 21 November 1902) found the book very well done and truly ornamental. Camille also noted the number of engravings—three—commenting that one engraving is not enough for a volume.

Leighton was preparing a sample copy of the Perrault in early October and had in hand the two little flower blocks for the spine of the book. He promised Esther he would keep the cost of the binding as low as possible. The quoted price to bind the edition was 72 shillings per 100 copies. The quote included side lettering, or one lettering anywhere. Esther found the price too high. Leighton assured her that it was the same price as he charged Hacon & Ricketts.

Leighton was having difficulties with the size of the sample binding. He had understood that the book was to be the same size as *Deux contes de ma mère l'oye.* In order to do that, Leighton would have to remove half an inch from the height. And if this were so, from where? And if wasn't to be trimmed, the printed sides for the binding were too short. Perhaps, he wondered, Esther wanted the book trimmed to fit the printed sides. If this were indeed the case, the book would be considerably larger than *Deux contes* (Leighton to Esther Pissarro, 7 October 1902).

A fire occurred at a house adjoining Leighton's bindery and the cover papers to *Peau d'ane* were spoiled by the smoke. Leighton asked Esther to send him an invoice for the cost of paper and reprinting the cover papers and he would try to obtain the money from his insurance company (Leighton to Esther Pissarro, 23 October 1902). A few days later he found that only 140 pairs of cover paper had been spoiled and he still found the cover paper to be a little short, adding that "nothing must be said to the insurance people about this however but please put it right when reprinting" (Leighton to Esther Pissarro, 27 October 1902). Leighton advised Esther to insure their books when they were at the binder. (Leighton to Esther Pisssarro, 29 October 1902).

In addition to the fire, the engravings were placed in incorrect order. The plates had been printed side-by-side and Leighton had to place those four pages around signature c. Leighton wondered how they could have reversed the order of the engravings without putting them upside down, unless the order had been reversed in printing. Esther wanted the engravings to face the text rather than backing the text (Leighton to Esther Pissarro, 14 and 21 November 1902).

Copies to: Diana White, Mrs. Wollersen, A. Teissier, Camille Pissarro, Cyril Kirby, Ernest Verity, Charles Holmes.

COPIES SEEN: Ashmolean. BL (deposited 5 December 1902). NYPL (Bookplate of John Quinn; Bookplate of John Shaw Billings Memorial Fund, bought at the Anderson Gallery auction, 11 Feb. 1924 for $7.50). SFPL (Provenance: Robert Grabhorn with bookplate of William Randolph Keltie Young). UCLA.

ABREGÉ DE L'ART POETIQUE FRAN-
ÇOIS PAR PIERRE DE RONSARD.
A ALPHONSE DELBENE, ABBÉ DE
HAUTE-COMBE EN SAVOIE.
PISSARRO
E·ET·L.
LONDON.
ERAGNY PRESS
MDCCC
CCIII.
LONDON
HACON & RICKETTS,
17 CRAVEN STREET, STRAND.

Title page. Pierre de Ronsard, *Abrégé de l'art poétique françois,* 1902. (Ashmolean Museum, Oxford)

EP15 • Pierre de Ronsard. Abrégé de l'art poétique françois. 1902.

[within a border of five pieces] ABREGÉ DE L'ART POETIQUE FRAN- | ÇOIS PAR PIERRE DE RONSARD. [double type orn: leaf] | [line of border] | A ALPHONSE DELBENE, ABBÉ DE | HAUTE-COMBE EN SAVOIE. [double type orn: leaf] | [type orn: bud] [Pressmark III within border] | M | D| C | C | C | C | I | I | I. | LONDON | HACON & RICKETTS, | 17 CRAVEN STREET, STRAND.

COLOPHON: Les ornaments et les lettres ornées ont été | dessinés par Lucien Pissarro et gravés | par Esther Pissarro, et le livre fut | achevé d'imprimer en Jan- | vier MCMIII. sur leurs presses, The Brook, | Hammersmith, | London, | W. | [type orn: leaf] | [type orn: entwined leaf] | [type orn: leaves] | Il a été tiré de cet ouvrage 226 exemplaires | dont 200 pour la vente.

COLLATION: 8°: $[a]^{2}$ b^{4} c^{4} [c^{3} tipped in] d^{4}–f^{2}

PAPER: Arches. Leaf: 213 x 142 mm.

TYPE: Vale and Greek

ILLUSTRATIONS, ORNAMENTS, AND INITIALS: [two borders, eighteen ornaments, twelve initials, one pressmark in black and white] [a]1^{v}: Border (NIF); Pressmark III, 76 mm. diameter (Fern 112 [SB 152]). [a]2^{v}: Initial C (Fern 342 [SB 188]); Border (NIF). b4^{r}: Cul-de-lampe (Fern 329 [SB 147]). b4^{v}: Vignette (Fern 278 [84]); Initial P (Fern 356 [SB 262]). c1^{r}: Cul-de-lampe (Fern 276 [80]) [without THE END]). c1^{v}: Ornament (Fern 279 [85]); Initial T (Fern 360 [SB 206]). c2^{r}: Cul-de-lampe (Fern 329 [SB 147]). c2^{v}: Vignette (NIF); Initial E (Fern 344). c3^{r}: Cul-de-lampe (NIF). c3^{v}: Vignette (NIF); Initial T (Fern 360 [SB 206]). d1^{r}: Vignette (NIF); Initial L (Fern 351 [SB 197]). d1^{v}: Vignette (NIF); Initial T (Fern 360 [SB 206]). d2^{r}: Tail-piece (NIF). d2^{v}: Vignette (Fern 278 [84]); Initial L (Fern 352 [SB 198]). e1^{r}: Vignette (NIF); Initial L (Fern 351 [SB 197]). e2^{v}: Vignette (Fern 279 [85]); Initial L (Fern 352 [SB 198]). e3^{r}: Cul-de-lampe (NIF). e3^{v}: Vignette (NIF); Initial L (Fern 352 [SB 198]). e4^{v}: Vignette (NIF); Initial T (Fern 360 [SB 206]). f4^{r}: Cul-de-lampe (Fern 329 [SB 147]).

CONTENTS: [a]1^{r}: blank. [a]1^{v}: title. [a]2^{r}–f4^{r}: text. f4^{v}: colophon

BINDING: Quarter buff paper, gold stamped on upper cover: RONSARD. | [double type orn: leaf] | ABREGÉ DE | L'ART POE- | TIQUE. Michallet blue paper boards with a repeat pattern of "May blossom" (Fern 339 [SB 216]) printed in buff and green.

PUBLICATION: 200 copies for sale at 15 shillings. Published March 1903.

RELATED MATERIAL: Drawings for initials L, L, P, D, and ornament.

PROSPECTUS: ISSUED BY HACON & RICKETTS | THE VALE PRESS, XVII CRAVEN | STREET, STRAND. | Now ready: | [woodcut initial A (Fern 307 [SB129])] BREGÉ DE L'ART | POETIQUE FRAN- | ÇOIS par PIERRE DE RONSARD [two type orns: leaf] | With decorations & initial | letters designed by Lucien | Pissarro & engraved on the wood by Esther | Pissarro, and a may blossom cover, printed | in two colors. Small quarto. Two hun- | dred and twenty six copies printed by E. | & L. Pissarro at their Eragny Press, on | "Arches" hand-made paper with their own water-mark, of which two hundred copies | are for sale at fifteen shillings nett. | Order Form over.

[verso]: [type orn: bud] NOTICE.—To prevent disappointment, | orders should be sent, if possible, by return | of post. | Please send me .... cop... of | ABREGÉ DE L'ART POETIQUE FRANÇOIS VILLON PAR P. DE RONSARD, | printed by E. & L. Pissarro, for which I | enclose cheque. | Name [dotted line] | Address [dotted lines] | [dotted line] | [dotted line] | To [dotted line] | [dotted line] Bookseller, | [dotted line] | [dotted line] | Hacon & Ricketts, 17 Craven Street, W.C.

NOTES: Printing began 10 January 1903 and ended 10 February 1903. The Pissarros were frantically trying to finish printing *Abrégé*. Lucien sent a completed copy to Camille on 16 March 1903. Camille found the book to be very successful, but was impatient to see Lucien's new type, the Brook, in one of his books.

Two trial copies were printed on old Ingres paper, one pale pink, the other pea green.

In stock: 1 March 1904, 26 copies; 1 March 1905, 26 copies; 1 March 1906, 26 copies; 1 March 1907, 27 copies; 1 March 1908, 27 copies; 1 March 1909, 27 copies; 1 March 1910, 27 copies; 1 March 1911, 27 copies (Private ledger).

Copies given to E. Verity, Camille Pissarro, C. Kirby, Emile Verhaeren, A. Teissier, Charles Holmes, Th. Gaillard, Mrs. Wollersen, Diana White.

COPIES SEEN: Ashmolean. BL. LC. NYPL (Bookplate of John Shaw Billing Memorial Fund; purchased from Anderson Gallery on 7 April 1924, probably John Quinn's copy). SFPL (Provenance: Robert Grabhorn acquired in Salisbury by Albert Sperisen, June 1944, bookplate of C. R. and J. E. Ashbee with letter from Lucien Pissarro to Mr. Ashbee).

Pierre de Ronsard, *Abrégé de l'art poétique françois*, 1902; p. 18. (Ashmolean Museum, Oxford)

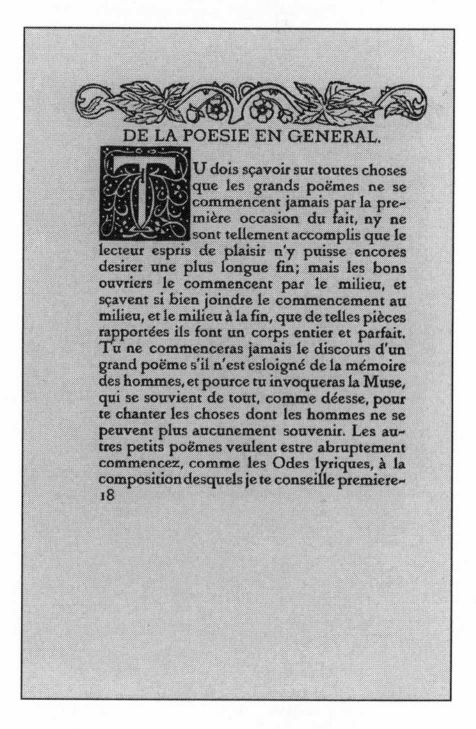

DE LA POESIE EN GENERAL.

TU dois sçavoir sur toutes choses que les grands poëmes ne se commencent jamais par la première occasion du fait, ny ne sont tellement accomplis que le lecteur espris de plaisir n'y puisse encores desirer une plus longue fin; mais les bons ouvriers le commencent par le milieu, et sçavent si bien joindre le commencement au milieu, et le milieu à la fin, que de telles pièces rapportées ils font un corps entier et parfait. Tu ne commenceras jamais le discours d'un grand poëme s'il n'est esloigné de la mémoire des hommes, et pource tu invoqueras la Muse, qui se souvient de tout, comme déesse, pour te chanter les choses dont les hommes ne se peuvent plus aucunement souvenir. Les autres petits poëmes veulent estre abruptement commencez, comme les Odes lyriques, à la composition desquels je te conseille premiere-

18

UCLA (Bookplate "From the library of | C. H. St. J. Hornby | Chantmarie, Dorest" and bookplate "Lex William Andrews Clark, Jr.").

EP16 • C'est d'Aucassin et de Nicolete. 1903.

[type orn: leaf] C'EST D'AUCASSIN ET DE | NICOLETE.

COLOPHON: THIS EDITION OF AUCASSIN & | NICOLETE HAS BEEN PRINTED | FROM THE EDITION PUBLISHED | BY MESSRS. MACMILLAN & CO. IN | MDCCCXCVII. AND BEEN SEEN | THROUGH THE PRESS AND RE- | VISED BY THE EDITOR, FRANCIS | WILLIAM BOURDILLON, M.A. | The Frontispiece has been designed and en- | graved by Lucien Pissarro. This is the | last book printed in the Vale Type | by Esther and Lucien Pissarro | at the Eragny Press, The | Brook, Hammersmith, and completed | May, 1903. i1^v: This edition is strictly limited to 230 copies, | of which 200 are for sale. | [Pressmark III within border]

COLLATION: 8°: $[a]^2$ b^2 c^4–h^4 i^2. 30 leaves, pp. [i–ii] [1–2]–55 [56–58]. [a]1 and [a]2 are tipped in and separate leaves; d1 tipped in.

PAPER AND DIMENSIONS: Arches. Leaf: 215 x 145 mm.

TYPE: Vale, Music

ILLUSTRATIONS, ORNAMENTS, AND INITIALS: [one five-color wood-engraved illustration, two borders, three ornaments, and pressmark in black and white, one initial in red] [a]2^r: "Nicolete," five-color wood-engraved illustration, 101 x 97 mm. (Fern 141 [SB 219bis]); woodcut orn: Tudor rose (NIF); [in red] "ET DE LE FOILLE AUTRESI, | UNE BELLE LOGE EN FIST"; woodcut orn: Tudor rose, surrounded by a repeated wood-engraved ornament (sixteen) border (NIF). b1^r: [in large caps] C'EST D'AUCAS- | SIN ET DE NICO- | LETE; woodcut ornament (NIF); Initial Q (NIF) in red. i1^r: Cul-de-lampe (Fern 329 [SB 147]). i2^v: Pressmark III, 76 mm. diameter (Fern 112 [SB 152]) within border (NIF).

CONTENTS: [a]1^v: title. [a]2^r: frontispiece. [a]2^v: blank. b1^r–i1^r: text. i1^v: blank. i2^r: colophon. i2^v: pressmark.

BINDING: Quarter cream paper, gold stamped on upper left cover: [orn: trefoil] AUCASSIN | & | NICOLETE. Buff paper boards with a repeat pattern of "verbena" (Fern 368 [SB 148]) printed in blue and green ink. On spine gold stamped at top and bottom flower ornament.

PUBLICATION: 200 copies for sale at 30 shillings. Published June 1903.

RELATED MATERIAL: Drawing for initial Q; trial paper cover for binding in black and white.

PROSPECTUS: [1 leaf, 210 x 147 mm.]

NOTES: Francis William Bourdillon (1852–1921), English poet and scholarly editor of poems and chronicles from the Old French, was the editor of *Aucassin and Nicolette: A Love Story*, translated into modern English and published by Kegan Paul and Co. in 1887. The Pissarros were considering using his translation as their copytext. Bourdillon had a long-held dream of Aucassin and Nicolette in an edition after the old French, but knew this was hardly what the Pissarros had in mind. Bourdillon asked the Pissarros for £10 for the use of his text. He explained that he had had no return on his translation—"only much trouble and a good deal of expense." Bourdillon was also concerned that another printing might hurt the sale of the 1887 publication, but he also knew he would regret not having the pleasure of seeing the text in the Vale type (F. W. Bourdillon to Lucien Pissarro, 18 February 1903). Lucien counter-offered a payment of £5 and two copies of the book with an acknowledgement of the 1887 edition. The offer was accepted.

Bourdillon modified the text for the Pissarros, making it more readable, eliminating brackets and other scholarly apparatus, and suggesting alternative readings to make the text read intelligently. He made these revisions on the Eragny Press proofs (F. W. Bourdillon to Lucien Pissarro, 29 February 1903). He also advised them on how to print the music. Printing began on Wednesday, 11 February 1903.

T. S. Moore liked "the cover enormously the colour sets off the design and makes it much more pleasing than I had remembered. The wood-cut also gains by appearing in its right place, and the book as a whole appears to me one of the most charming you have made" (T. S. Moore to Lucien Pissarro, 18 June 1903).

Copies to: Charles Holmes, E. Verity, T. S. Moore, York Powell, Camille Pissarro, Diana White, Mrs. Wollersen, C. Kirby, Robert Steele, A. Teissier, Emile Verhaeren, F. W. Bourdillon (2 copies).

In stock: 1 March 1904, 4 copies; 1 March 1905, 3 copies; 1 March 1906, 3 copies; 1 March 1907, 4 copies; 1 March 1908, 4 copies; 1 March 1909, 4 copies; 1 March 1910, 4 copies; 1 March 1911, 4 copies (Private ledger).

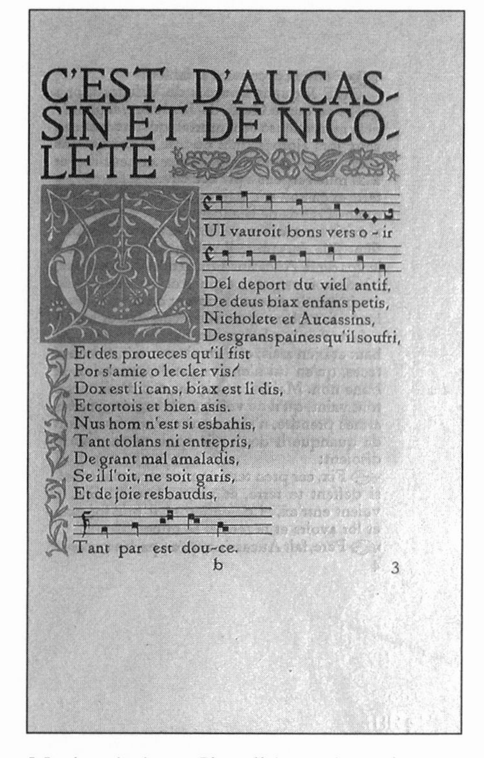
C'EST D'AUCASSIN ET DE NICOLETE

QUI vauroit bons vers o - ir
Del deport du viel antif,
De deus biax enfans petis,
Nicholete et Aucassins,
Des grans paines qu'il soufri,
Et des proueces qu'il fist
Por s'amie o le cler vis?
Dox est li cans, biax est li dis,
Et cortois et bien asis.
Nus hom n'est si esbahis,
Tant dolans ni entrepris,
De grant mal amaladis,
Se il l'oit, ne soit garis,
Et de joie resbaudis,
Tant par est dou-ce.

b 3

Music printing. *C'est d'Aucassin et de Nicolete*, 1903. (Special Collections, Florida State University, Tallahassee)

COPIES SEEN: Ashmolean. BL (deposited 2 July 1903; another copy: Ex Libris Campbell Dodgson). FSU. LC. NYPL. SFPL.

EP17 • T. S. Moore. A Brief Account of the Origin of the Eragny Press. 1903.

[type orn: entwined leaves] A BRIEF ACCOUNT OF THE | ORIGIN OF THE ERAGNY PRESS & A | NOTE ON THE RELATION OF

THE | PRINTED BOOK AS A WORK OF ART | TO LIFE BY T. STURGE MOORE. | A BIBLIOGRAPHICAL LIST OF THE | ERAGNY BOOKS PRINTED IN THE | VALE TYPE BY ESTHER & LUCIEN | PISSARRO ON THEIR PRESS AT EP- | PING, BEDFORD PARK, AND THE | BROOK, CHISWICK, IN THE ORDER | IN WHICH THEY WERE ISSUED.

COLOPHON: [type orn: trefoil] THIS IS THE FIRST BOOK PRIN- | TED IN THE «BROOK TYPE» BY | ESTHER & LUCIEN PISSARRO | AT THE ERGANY PRESS, | THE BROOK, HAMMER- | SMITH. FINISHED | IN JUNE 1903 | [four type orn: leaf] | [type orn: trefoil] SOLD AT THE ERAGNY PRESS. g4ᵛ: [type orn: entwined leaves] This edition is strictly limited to 235 pa- | per and 6 vellum copies, of which 200 paper | and 3 vellum copies are for sale. | [Pressmark III]

COLLATION: Small demy 8°: [a]^4 b^4–g^4. 28 leaves, pp. [1 l.] [1–3] 4–24 [25] 26 [27] 28 [29] 30 [31] 32 [33–34] 35–36 [37] 38 [39] 40 [41] 42 [43] 44 [45] 46 [47] 48 [49] 50 [51] 52 [53-55]

PAPER AND DIMENSIONS: Arches. Leaf: 205 x 132 mm.

ILLUSTRATIONS, ORNAMENTS, AND INITIALS: [fourteen wood-engraved illustrations and pressmark in black and white] d1ʳ: Pressmark I, 68 x 50 mm. (Fern 93 [79]). d2ʳ: "Ruth Gleaning," 75 x 65 mm. (Fern 100 [98]). d3ʳ: "Salome," 132 x 87 mm. (Fern 105 [102]). d4ʳ: "Ophelia," 151 x 77 mm. (Fern 107[104]). e1ʳ: Pressmark II (Inter Fructus Folia), 76 mm. diameter (Fern 111 [152]). e2ᵛ–e3ʳ: "La Belle au bois," 109 x 89 mm. (Fern 108–109 [105-106]). e4ʳ: "Geese" with border, 88 mm. diameter (Fern 113 [154]). f1ʳ: "Deer in the Forest," 88 mm. diameter (Fern 118 [159]). f2ʳ: "Dames du temps jadis," 73 mm. diameter (Fern 119 [157]). f3ʳ: "Girl and Cow," 68 x 66 mm. (Fern 127 [170]). f4ʳ: "Hérodias," 67 x 66 mm. (Fern 130 [175]). g1ʳ: "Les Regrets de la belle Hëaulmiere," 73 mm. diameter (Fern 131 [174 bis]). g2ʳ: "The Garden," 74 mm. diameter (Fern 137 [153bis]). g3ʳ: "Girl Picking Flowers," 115 x 94 mm. (Fern 135 [177]). g4ᵛ: Pressmark III, 76 mm. diameter (Fern 112 [152]). Catchwords.

CONTENTS: [a]1ᵛ: [type orn: entwined leaves] DEDICATED TO CH. RICKETTS. [a]2ʳ: PREFACE. [a]2ᵛ: blank. [a]3ʳ: [type orn: entwined leaves] A BRIEF ACCOUNT OF THE | ORIGIN OF THE ERAGY PRESS. [a]4ʳ: [type orn: entwined leaves] NOTE ON THE RELATION OF | THE PRINTED BOOK AS A WORK OF | ART TO LIFE. b4ᵛ: A BIBLIOGRAPHICAL LIST OF THE ERAGNY PRESS BOOKS. c4ᵛ: blank. d1ʳ–g3ʳ: Illustrations with verso pages blank. g4ʳ: colophon. g4ᵛ: pressmark.

BINDING: Quarter buff paper, gold stamped on upper left cover: T. S. MOORE. | [orn: entwined leaves] ABOUT | ERAGNY | BOOKS. |

[orn: entwined leaves]. White paper boards with a repeat pattern of "daisy" (Fern 369 [SB 149]) printed in green and pink.

PUBLICATION: 200 paper copies for sale at 25 shillings and 3 vellum copies for sale at 5 guineas. Published in July 1903.

RELATED MATERIAL: Preliminary cover paper printed in black and white; trial cover paper printed in green only.

PROSPECTUS: [211 x 97 mm.] [Pressmark III] | (No. 1) [type orn: trefoil] NOW READY: | A BRIEF ACCOUNT OF THE ERAGNY PRESS | & A NOTE ON THE | RELATION OF THE | PRINTED BOOK TO | LIFE. By T. STURGE | MOORE. A BIBLIO- | GRAPHICAL LIST of | the ERAGNY PRESS | BOOKS PRINTED IN | THE VALE TYPE | BY ESTHER & LU- | CIEN PISSARRO ON | THEIR PRESS AT | EPPING, BEDFORD | PARK & CHISWICK

Page 2: [type orn: trefoil] The Book is Illustrated with fifteen wood- | cuts reprinted from | various blocks that | have appeared in the | books, & A cover prin- | ted in two colours. | Small demy 8vo. Print- | ed on «Arches» Hand- | made paper with E. & L. | P. Monogram as water | mark. | [type orn: trefoil] The book has been | printed in the «Brook» | fount (PICA), designed | by Lucien Pissarro and | cut by E.P. Prince. This | fount will be used for | future Eragny Press | books. | [type orn: trefoil] Two hundred & thir- | ty-Five Paper and Six Vellum copies have been | printed, of which two hundred copies | are for sale at Twenty | five shillings nett. & Three Vellum copies at Five Guineas nett.

Page 3: ORDER FORM | To the Secretary of the Eragny Press, The Brook, Hammersmith. | All cheques to be made pay- | able to Lucien Pissarro & ****** London and South Western Bank, Chiswick Branch.

Page 4: [Blank]

NOTES: Printing was finished on Saturday, 11 July 1903.

Esther thought the cost of binding *A Brief Account* was too high due to the unnecessary interleaving. Leighton explained to her that interleaving was necessary to prevent off-set with solid engravings and the cost of interleaving a book was considerable. The high cost came not from the interleaving paper itself, but from cutting all the leaves of each book in order to place the interleaves within the pages. As Leighton had had standing instructions from Hacon & Ricketts to interleave pages with solid engravings, he assumed this was the Pissarros' practice as well. Because Esther had not requested interleaving, Leighton lowered the cost of the binding.

Charles Ricketts commented to Michael Field, ". . . have you seen T. S. Moore's preface to a catalogue of Eragny Books it contains some charming follies about books large lip-smacks in fact and large quotations from my french pamphlet, I will lend it to you on your return, as it costs £1" (Charles Ricketts to Michael Field, [15 July 1903]. British Library ADD 58088, no. 20).

Copies were given to: 5 deposit copies, 4 copies to the Press, Robert Steele, Mrs. Ethel Voynich, Pollard, Charles Holmes, Emile Verhaeren, Camille Pissarro, A. Teissier, Diana White, Mrs. C. Wollersen, C. Kirby, E. Verity, T. S. Moore (6 copies, 1 vellum), C. Ricketts (paper and vellum), A. Macgregor, Sam Bensusan, Orovida Bensusan, E. P. Prince, Albert Morelli, Burgler, Ida Henry, C. Destrée, Gabriel Mourey, Jacob Bensusan, Orovida Bensusan, Alfred Pissarro.

Seventy-five copies were sold to the London trade, including 52 to Lane; 32 copies to the Country Trade; 8 copies were sold in Germany and Holland; and 24 copies to the Pissarros' private customers.

In stock: 1 March 1904, 55 copies; 1 March 1905, 49 copies; 1 March 1906, 45 copies; 1 March 1907, 33 copies; 1 March 1908, 35 copies; 1 March 1909, 30 copies; 1 March 1910, 27 copies; 1 March 1911, 25 copies (Private ledger).

COPIES SEEN: Ashmolean (inscribed: J.S.L. Bensusan from | Esther and | Lucien Pissarro [in both the Pissarros' hands]). Bancroft. BL (deposited 30 July 1903). LC (2 copies; one with bookplate: Frederic & Bertha | Goudy | [monogram] | Collection | Library of Congress. Handwritten note on g4^{r}: Mr. & Mrs. Goudy visited the Pizzarros [*sic*] at their home in 1925). NYPL (Bookplate of John Quinn; Bookplate of John Shaw Billings Memorial Fund, purchased from Anderson Gallery, 14 January 1924). SFPL (Provenance: Robert Grabhorn; Ex libris Oscar Aurelius Morgner).

EP18 • John Milton. Areopagitica. 1903.

[in black and red] [in large caps.] AREOPAGITICA. | [in caps.] A SPEECH OF MR. JOHN MILTON FOR THE LIBERTY OF | UNLICENS'D PRINTING, TO THE PARLAMENT OF ENGLAND. [type orn: leaf] | [double type orn: leaf] | [four lines of Greek] | [five lines of English translation]

COLOPHON: [in black and red] [type orn: trefoil] IN THIS REPRINT OF THE AREOPAGITICA THE TEXT | AND SPELLING OF THE FIRST EDITION (1644) HAVE BEEN | FOLLOWED CLOSELY, BUT ITALICS ARE NOT USED & | THE QUOTATION FROM EURIPIDES ON THE TITLE PAGE HAS BEEN EMENDED. [type orn: trefoil] | THE BORDER AND INITIAL LETTERS HAVE BEEN DESIGNED BY | LUCIEN PISSARRO & ENGRAVED ON THE | WOOD BY ESTHER PISSARRO. THE | BOOK HAS BEEN PRINTED BY | THEM AT THEIR ERAGNY | PRESS, THE BROOK, HAMMERSMITH, W. [type orn: trefoil] FIN- | ISHED IN OCTO- | BER, 1903. | [triple type orn: leaf] | [double type orn: leaf] | [type orn: leaf] | SOLD BY THE ERAGNY PRESS, LONDON, | AND JOHN LANE, NEW YORK. i4^{v}: [type orn: trefoil] THIS EDITION IS STRICTLY LIMITED TO TWO HUNDRED | AND TWENTY-SIX

PAPER AND TEN VELLUM COPIES OF | WHICH TWO HUNDRED PAPER & EIGHT VELLUM COPIES | ARE FOR SALE.

COLLATION: 4°: [a]^{2} b^{2}–h^{2} i^{4}. 20 leaves, pp. [1–3] 4–37 [38–40]

PAPER AND DIMENSIONS: Arches. Leaf: 266 x 200 mm.

TYPE: Brook and Selwyn Image's Greek type

ILLUSTRATIONS, ORNAMENTS, AND INITIALS: [one large initial in red; one border, thirty initials, and one pressmark in black and white] [a]2^{r}: Initial T in red (Fern 370 [SB 220]); "Clematis" border (Fern 371 [SB 320]). b1^{r}: Initial I (Fern 316 [SB 137]). b1^{v}: Initial I (Fern 316 [SB 137]). b2^{r}: Initial I (Fern 316 [SB 137]). b2^{v}: Initial B (NIF). c1^{r}: Initial S (NIF). c1^{v}: Initial S (NIF). c2^{r}: Initial B (NIF); Initial N (NIF). c1^{v}: Initial S (NIF). c2^{r}: Initial B (NIF); Initial N (NIF). e2^{r}: Initial A (Fern 312 [SB 133]). e2^{v}: Initial I (Fern 316 [SB 137]). f1^{v}: Initial A (Fern 312 [SB 133]). f2^{r}: Initial A (Fern 312 [SB 133]). f2^{v}: Initial A (Fern 312 [SB 133]). g1^{v}: Initial W (NIF); Initial A (Fern 312 [SB 133]). g2^{r}: Initial N (NIF); Initial F (NIF). g2^{v}: Initial T (NIF); Initial T (NIF); Initial T (NIF). h1^{r}: Initial L (Fern 317 [SB 138]). h2^{r}: Initial F (NIF). h2^{v}: Initial W (NIF). i1^{r}: Initial W (NIF); Initial A (Fern 312 [SB 133]). i2^{v}: Initial T (NIF). i3^{r}: Initial A (Fern 312 [SB 133]). i4^{v}: Pressmark III, 76 mm. diameter (Fern 112 [SB 152]).

CONTENTS: [a]1^{r}: blank. [a]1^{v}: title. [a]2^{r}–i3^{r}: text. i3^{v}: blank. i4^{r}: colophon. i4^{v}: pressmark

BINDING: Quarter cream paper, Michallet blue paper boards with title printed in green ink: AREOPAGITICA. | BY JOHN MILTON. with an inset of "carnation and flames" wood engraving (NIF, variant of Fern 372 [SB 221]) printed on Michallet blue paper in three colors (green, red, and yellow) placed in the upper right corner.

PUBLICATION: 38 copies for sale at 31 shillings 6 pence; 10 vellum copies for sale at 7 guineas. Published March 1904.

RELATED MATERIAL: Preliminary drawings for large initial T, two designs on graph paper; preliminary design for border (rejected); drawing of carnation.

PROSPECTUS: [Pressmark III] | (No. 2) [type orn: trefoil] NOW READY: | AREOPAGITICA. A | SPEECH FOR THE | LIBERTY OF UN LI- | CENC'D PRINTING BY JOHN MILTON. | [type orn: leaf] WITH A CLEMATIS BORDER AND | INITIAL LETTERS | DESIGNED BY LU- | CIEN & | ENGRAVED on THE | WOOD BY ESTHER | PISSARRO, & WITH | A CARNATION CO- | VER PRINTED IN TWO COLOURS. [type orn: leaf] | SMALL DEMY 4to.

Page 2: [type orn: leaf] TWO HUNDRED & TWEN- | TY SIX COPIES PRINTED IN | THE BROOK TYPE ON AR- | CHES HAND-MADE PAPER | BY E. AND L. PISSARRO, OF WHICH TWO HUNDRED are FOR SALE IN ENGLAND & | AMERICA AT THIRTY-ONE | SHILLINGS AND SIX PENCE NETT. | [type orn: leaf] TEN VELLUM COPIES | HAVE BEEN PRINTED AND | OF THE EIGHT COPIES FOR | SALE, TWO STILL REMAIN | TO BE SOLD AT SEVEN | GUINEAS NETT.

Page 3: [Order form]

PROSPECTUS II: [type orn: trefoil] THE ERAGNY PRESS, THE | BROOK, HAMMERSMITH, W. (No. 2a) | [type orn: trefoil] SPECIAL NOTICE | [Initial I (Fern 298)] t is with much | pleasure that E. | & L. Pissarro are | able to announce | that the collated | sheets of forty | copies and the | sample copy of | MILTON'S AREOPAGITICA | (small demy 4to) have been saved | from the fire which occurred at the | binders (Messrs. Leighton, Son & | Hodge), in November, 1903. When | sending their notice, E. & L. Pis- | sarro had every reason to believe the | whole edition had been destroyed. [type orn: trefoil] of these copies, 38 are now for | sale in England & America, & they | have a distinctive binding of blue | Michallet paper, with a label (a car- | nation & flames printed in 3 colours) on the right hand top corner. [type orn: trefoil] The reprinted edition will be | ready early in April; but as feared | the block used for the border page | was only strong enough to print | 160 copies, of these, 136 are for | sale in England and America.

Page 2: [type orn: trefoil] This reprinted edition will be | bound as originally intended with | a carnation cover printed in two colours, but the colophon will be | necessarily changed. [type orn: trefoil] The price per copy of both issues will be thirty-one shillings | and six pence net. [type orn: trefoil] As the number of the first prin- | ted edition is exceedingly small, the | first refusal will be given to those | subscribers who ordered copies | from the original prospectus issued | last November, but then orders | must be received before March the | 24th. Should the demand for these | copies be greater than the number | for sale, orders will be executed | consecutively. | [type orn: trefoil] IN THE PRESS | [type orn: trefoil] «ROBERT BROWNING»: A | selection of poems and lyrics, with | a frontispiece designed & engraved | by Lucien Pissarro and printed in | five colours. Crown 8vo. Probable | price: Twenty-five shillings net.

Page 3: [Order Form] | [in red, at bottom of page] A copy of the book can be seen at | Mr. E. J. van Wisselingh's Gallery, 14 Brook Street, London, W.

NOTES: Printing began on Monday, 24 August 1903. Sheets were sent to Leighton on 9 November 1903. On 24 November the Pissarros heard of the fire at Leighton, Son and Hodge.

The initials, B, F, N, S, T, and W in the same design as Fern 312–321 [SB 133–142]) were added for *Areopagitica*.

COPIES SEEN: Ashmolean. SFPL (Provenance: Robert Grabhorn, vellum copy bound by Sangorski & Sutcliffe, London; with added slip: A few of the sheets [including the Colophon] | printed for this vellum copy of «Milton's Areo- | pagitica» were accidentally destroyed, & were | reprinted when second edition was produced). UCLA (Bookplates: Ex libris Joseph Manuel Andreini, designed and printed by the Eragny Press with a wood engraving of a girl attending sheep with initials J·M·A [Fern 172 (SB 245bis)]; and with bookplate of William Andrews Clark, Jr.).

EP18a • John Milton. Areopagitica. 1904 (reprint).

[in black and red] [in large caps.] AREOPAGITICA. | [in caps.] A SPEECH OF MR. JOHN MILTON FOR THE LIBERTY OF | UNLICENC'D PRINTING, TO THE PARLAMENT OF ENGLAND. | [type orn: leaf] | double type orn: [leaf] | [leaf orn: leaf] | [four lines of Greek] | [five lines of English translation]

COLOPHON: [in black and red] [type orn: trefoil] IN THIS REPRINT OF THE AREOPAGITICA THE TEXT | AND SPELLING OF THE FIRST EDITION (1644) HAVE BEEN | FOLLOWED CLOSELY, BUT ITALICS ARE NOT USED AND | THE QUOTATION FROM EURIPIDES ON THE TITLE PAGE | HAS BEEN EMENDED. [type orn: trefoil] THE BORDER & INITIAL LETTERS | HAVE BEEN DESIGNED BY LUCIEN PISSARRO & ENGRAVED | ON THE WOOD BY ESTHER PISSARRO. THE FIRST PAPER | ISSUE PRINTED BY THEM AT THEIR ERAGNY PRESS, | THE BROOK, HAMMERSMITH, FINISHED IN OCTO- | BER, 1903, WAS PARTLY DESTROYED BY FIRE, | AT THE BINDERS, ONLY THE SAMPLE | COPY AND 40 UNBOUND COPIES BEING | SAVED, OF WHICH THE LATTER | ARE FOR SALE. THE SECOND | ISSUE, CONSISTING OF 160 | COPIES, OF WHICH 134 | ARE FOR SALE, WAS | FINISHED IN | MARCH, 1904. | [double type orns: leaf] | [type orn: leaf] | SOLD BY THE ERAGNY PRESS, LONDON, | AND | JOHN LANE, NEW YORK

COLLATION: 4°: [a]^2 b^2–h^2 i^4. 20 leaves, pp. [1–3] 4–37 [38–40]

PAPER AND DIMENSIONS: Arches. Leaf: 266 x 200 mm.

TYPE: Brook

ILLUSTRATIONS, ORNAMENTS, AND INITIALS: [one large red initial, one border, 30 initials and pressmark in black and white] [a]2^r: Initial T in red (Fern 370 [SB 220]); "Clematis" border (Fern 371 [SB 320]). b1^r: Initial I (Fern 316 [SB 137]). b1^v: Initial I (Fern 316 [SB 137]). b2^r: Initial I (Fern 316 [SB 137]). b2^v: Initial B (NIF). c1^r: Initial S (NIF). c1^v: Initial S (NIF). c2^r: Initial B (NIF); Initial N (NIF). c1^v:

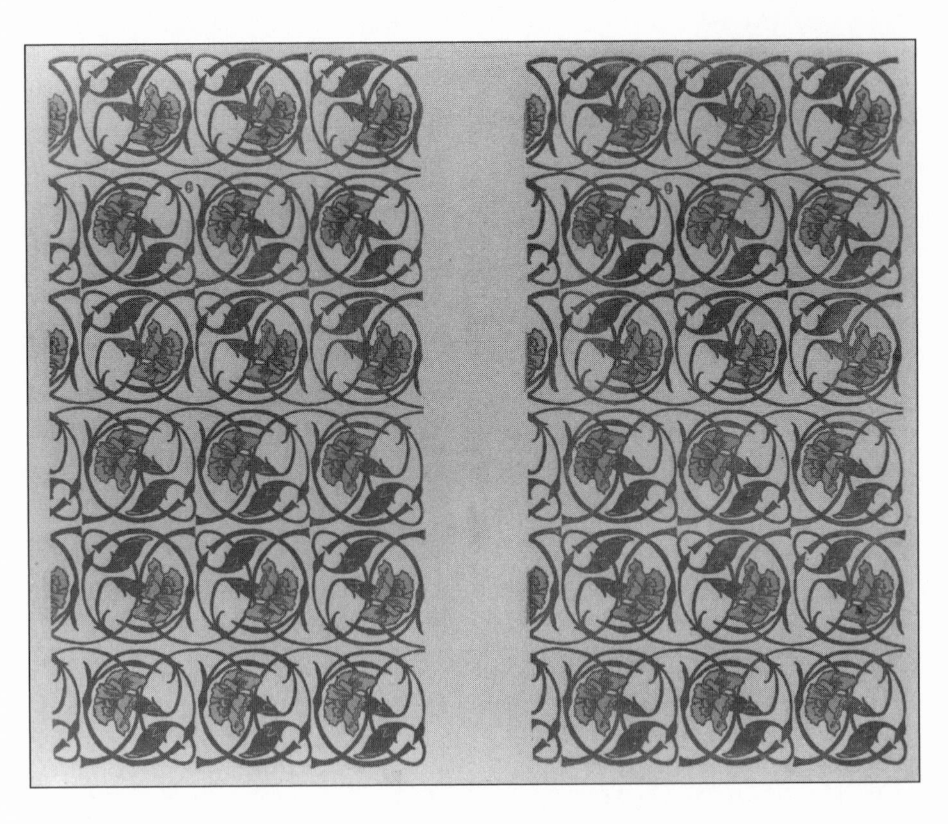

"Carnation" binding paper. John Milton, *Areopagitica,* 1904 (reprint). (Ashmolean Museum, Oxford)

Initial S (NIF). c2^{r}: Initial B (NIF); Initial N (NIF). e2^{r}: Initial A (Fern 312 [SB 133]). e2^{v}: Initial I (Fern 316 [SB 137]). f1^{v}: Initial A (Fern 312 [SB 133]). f2^{r}: Initial A (Fern 312 [SB 133]). f2^{v}: Initial A (Fern 312 [SB 133]). g1^{v}: Initial W (NIF); Initial A (Fern 312 [SB 133]). g2^{r}: Initial N (NIF); Initial F (NIF). g2^{v}: Initial T (NIF); Initial T (NIF); Initial T (NIF). h1^{r}: Initial L (Fern 317 [SB 138]). h2^{r}: Initial F (NIF). h2^{v}: Initial W (NIF). i1^{r}: Initial W (NIF); Initial A (Fern 312 [SB 133]). i2^{v}: Initial T (NIF). i3^{r}: Initial A (Fern 312 [SB 133]). i4^{v}: Pressmark III, 76 mm. diameter (Fern 112 [SB 152]).

CONTENTS: [a]1^{r}: blank. [a]1^{v}: title. [a]2^{r}–i3^{r}: text. i3^{v}: blank. i4^{r}: colophon. i4^{v}: pressmark

BINDING: Quarter Michallet blue paper, pale gold stamped on upper corner: AEROPAGITICA. | [orn: trefoil] A SPEECH BY | JOHN MILTON. Buff paper boards with a repeat pattern of "carnation" (NIF) printed in pink and green.

PUBLICATION: 134 copies for sale at 31 shillings 6 pence. Published March 1904.

NOTES: A fire at the bindery of J. J. Leighton, Son, and Hodge in late November 1903 destroyed all but forty paper and ten vellum copies of *Areopagitica*. Lucien, in Paris, after the death of his father, did not wish to reprint *Areopagitica,* preferring that the edition "lapse into rarity." He suggested to Esther that she have bound the copies that had already been sold and any copies that were not sold be sent to Lane. He cautioned that it would be very expensive to redo the composition for an edition of 100 and even more burdensome because they probably would not sell. Lucien also warned Esther of their precarious financial state and reminded her that they no longer had the necessary capital, given the loss of his pension from Camille, to wait for an edition to sell. But by 3 December 1903, Esther had already announced the reprinting. Only ten copies had been sold and with the fifty copies Lane was entitled to, only sixty copies were necessary to meet their obligations.

By late January 1904, Esther was carefully going through the copies and sheets that were salvaged. In early March, she asked Leighton to look through the copies and provide an estimate for how long it would take to get the books cleaned and resewn. During this period, Esther must have been resetting the type and printing for she asked Leighton in a letter dated 2 March 1904 if he could have both the fire edition and the reprint edition ready by 21 March.

Meanwhile, in Paris, Lucien was looking for paper for the cover at chez Contet, an art materials supplier, finding only similar paper to what they had used earlier, but nothing exact. He noted that it was difficult to make the exact same shade twice of the blue Ingres paper. Lucien suggested that they bind the fire copies in light blue and print the label in a darker blue. Lucien bought the paper on 14 March.

On 17 March, Esther sent to Leighton by parcel post twenty-one sheets of blue Michallet paper for fire copy covers, six sheets of yellow paper for the backs, a pattern card, and a label to make the sample case. Esther wanted the covers stamped with a square stamp and the label placed within the square inset. Esther received thirty-nine bound copies 26 March 1904. Esther sent the reprinted edition, except for the frontispiece, to Leighton on 28 March, but discovered, to her great disappointment, that a spelling error on the frontispiece page necessitated its reprinting. Esther promised the new sheets by Thursday, 31 March, and wanted Leighton to return the bound copies by 16 or 18 April. In addition to Esther's own delays, by 19 April, Esther was scolding Leighton for not having enough paper to complete the binding of the edition. Forty copies remained to be bound. By 26 April, Esther had 159 copies in hand. She returned eight copies to be rebound—three because the backs were dirty and five because the endpapers were badly stuck on the sides. Except for these copies, she was extremely pleased with the binding. She found the stamping to be beautifully done.

The Pissarros sent copies of *Areopagitica* to T. S. Moore, who found it to be "magnificient" (T. S. Moore to Esther Pissarro, 28 April 1904) and to Selwyn Image as a thank-you gift for the use of his Greek type. He found the book to be beautiful: "I assure you I value both the gift and the giving amazingly . . ." (Selwyn Image to the Pissarros, 6 May 1904).

In stock: December 1904, 64 copies; 1 March 1905, 59 copies, 1 vellum; 1 March 1906, 55 copies, 1 vellum; 1 March 1907, 40 copies, 1 vellum; 1 March 1908, 45 copies; 1 March 1909, 37 copies; 1 March 1910, 34 copies; 1 March 1911, 33 copies (Private ledger).

COPIES SEEN: Ashmolean. BL (deposited 27 April 1904). LC (Goudy Collection). NYPL (Bookplate of John Shaw Billings Memorial Collection, purchased 9 November 1923). SFPL (Ex Libris Joseph Manuel Andrieni and Eragny Press bookplate of JMA [Fern 172 (SB 245bis)]).

EP19 • Diana White. The Descent of Ishtar. 1903.

[in black and red] THE DESCENT OF ISHTAR. | BY DIANA WHITE. | [double type orn: leaf] | [type orn: leaf]

COLOPHON: [in black and red] [type orn: leaf] THE FRONTISPIECE HAS | BEEN DESIGNED BY DIANA | WHITE & ENGRAVED ON | THE WOOD BY ESTHER | PISSARRO. [type orn: leaf] THE DOUBLE | BORDER AND INITIAL LET- | TERS WERE DESIGNED BY | LUCIEN PISSARRO AND EN- | GRAVED BY ESTHER PIS- | SARRO. [type orn: leaf] THE BOOK HAS | BEEN PRINTED by THEM | AT THEIR ERAGNY | PRESS, THE BROOK, | HAMMERSMITH. | [type orn: leaf] FINISHED IN | DECEMBER, | 1903. | [type orn: leaf] | [type orn: leaf] SOLD BY THE ERAGNY | PRESS, LONDON, | AND | JOHN LANE, NEW YORK. f2^v: THIS EDITION IS STRICTLY | LIMITED TO 226 COPIES, OF | WHICH 200 ARE FOR SALE. | [Pressmark III]

Frontispiece. Diana White, *The Descent of Ishtar*, 1903. (Ashmolean Museum, Oxford)

COLLATION: Small demy 12°: a^2 [b]^2 c^4 d^2 e^4 f^2. 16 leaves, pp. [1–3] 4–30 [31–32]

PAPER AND DIMENSIONS: Arches. Leaf: 190 x 100 mm.

TYPE: Brook

ILLUSTRATIONS, ORNAMENTS, AND INITIALS: [one black and white wood-engraved illustration; two borders and one ornament in green; five initials in red; pressmark in black and white] [b]3^v: "O That Ishtar Might Hear Me," wood engraving by Diana White, 92 x 62 mm. within border, 157 x 90 mm. (Fern 330 [SB 153]) in green. b4^r: border, 157 x 90 mm. (Fern 330 [SB 153]) in green; Initial A (Fern 307 [SB 129]) in red. c1^v: Initial N (Fern 300 [SB 122]) in red. d2^r: Initial N (NIF) in red. e1^r: Initial N (NIF) in red. e3^v: Initial W (Fern 304 [SB 126]) in red. f1^v: Cul-de-lampe (Fern 329 [SB 147]) in green. f2^v: Pressmark III, 76 mm. diameter (Fern 112 [SB 152]).

CONTENTS: [a]1^r: title. [a]1^v: Dedication: To C.F.W. [a]^2: Preface by D[iana]. W[hite]. [b]1^r: blank. [b]1^v–f1^v: text. f^2: colophon.

BINDING: Quarter Michallet blue paper with printed paper label: [in red] [type orn: leaf] THE DE- | SCENT OF | ISHTAR. | BY DIANA |

WHITE. Green paper boards with a repeat pattern of "daisy" (designed by Diana White) printed in green ink.

PUBLICATION: 200 paper copies for sale at 12 shillings 6 pence; 8 vellum copies for sale at 3 guineas. Published in January 1904.

RELATED MATERIAL: Sample binding; original woodblock design to be reduced to 2 3/4 inches.

NOTES: *Ishtar*, a collaboration between the Pissarros and Diana White, was underway by November 1903. Lucien had been called to Paris on the 10th of November to attend to his father, who had taken ill. Camille Pissarro died on the 12th of November and Lucien remained in Paris until March 1904. Thus, Esther was left to carry out the production with the assistance of Diana White.

A new initial N was created for *Ishtar* (NIF), adding to the same series of initials used in *The Book of Ruth and the Book of Esther*. The border was first used in *Of Gardens*.

Writing from Paris on 26 November 1903, Lucien asked Esther to print only 150 copies of *Ishtar*, even though the colophon would indicate 200 copies. Lucien rationalized it as a small, not very serious, lie; better than announcing 200 copies and then printing 250. The smaller edition, he believed, would give early buyers an advantage. Lucien urged Esther to not employ too rigid an honesty here, because their way of life depended upon it. With Camille's death, they could no longer depend on him for future funds, and moreover, Camille's paintings were not selling at the prices that had been expected after his death. Repeatedly in his letters to Esther, Lucien asks about the edition size. Given her silence on the topic, Lucien assumed that she stubbornly printed 200 copies, which would leave them with more stock than they could sell. He suggested to Esther that in business, stubbornness is a greater cause of failure than weakness. Esther must have argued that because of their arrangement with Lane to print 200 copies, it would be dishonest to do otherwise, but Lucien countered that the arrangement was only there to keep them from printing an even greater number. Two hundred and twenty copies were sent to the bindery.

Lucien found Diana White's engraving for *Ishtar* to be too English. The figures, elongated and highly stylized, were not in keeping with the Eragny style.

Esther sent a sample copy to the bindery on Monday, 14 December 1903, telling Leighton the sheets would be ready on Thursday. Leighton had promised to deliver the books on Christmas Eve. The frontispiece had yet to be printed, but would be delivered to the bindery on the 21st. On the 17th, signatures c-d and e-f, the cover papers, the endpapers, and the labels were sent. The color of the cover sheets varied because they had to be printed at night. Esther blamed the short winter days for this, finding it impossible to keep on time as more than half the work done by artificial light had to be discarded.

Esther had intended that for the cover paper three perfect daisy groups be shown on alternate rows, but Leighton's binders tried to maintain the proportion of the blue paper rather than the printed papers and thus altered the intended proportions of the printed sides. Esther found the printed labels as attached to the covers to be messy. Leighton countered that he had not been given enough time (Leighton to Esther Pissarro, 28 December 1903). Although the book was published in January 1904, Esther's battles with the bindery continued. In late January 1904, Esther complained to Leighton that of twenty-nine copies, there was not a straight label and not one that had perfect sides. Leighton suggested that if Esther printed the labels more accurately to the edge of the paper, the labels would not be so difficult to cut and if she provided more time, the bindery could deal with the work satisfactorily (Leighton to Esther Pissarro, 3 February 1904). By the end of February the sides met her standards but the printed labels were still sloppily attached and not in the correct position. Esther wanted the labels to be placed in the middle.

A notice announcing *Ishtar* appeared in the *New York Times,* 13 February 1904.

Paul Durand-Ruel, the agent for Camille Pissarro's paintings and the owner of an important gallery in Paris, received a copy of *Ishtar* from Lucien in January, calling the book a typographic jewel and a piece of good luck for all bibliophiles. But he, too, complained of the glued label on the cover, though finding it of little importance, seeing that the contents was so exquisite (Durand-Ruel to Lucien Pissarro, 25 January 1904).

Two hundred twenty-two copies were produced due to a counting error in one of the gatherings.

By December 1904, 84 copies of *Ishtar* remained unsold. Copies could be seen at E. J. Van Wisselingh, 14 Brook Street, London, W., and at Mr. Tregaskis, The Caxton Head, Holborn.

In stock: 1 March 1904, 89 copies; 1 March 1905, 82 copies; 1 March 1906, 64 copies; 1 March 1907, 51 copies; 1 March 1908, 66 copies; 1 March 1909, 58 copies; 1 March 1910, 55 copies; 1 March 1911, 50 copies (Private ledger).

COPIES SEEN: Ashmolean. BL (deposited 13 February 1904). LC. NYPL. SFPL (Provenance: Robert Grabhorn; inscribed: To Mr. Roger Milès from Lucien Pissarro).

EP20 • Robert Browning. Some Poems. 1904.

SOME POEMS BY ROBERT BROWNING.

COLOPHON: [in black and <u>red</u>] [type orn: trefoil] THE FRONTISPIECE HAS BEEN DE - | SIGNED AND ENGRAVED ON THE | WOOD BY LUCIEN PISSARRO. THE | INITIAL LETTERS WERE DESIGNED BY LUCIEN PISSARRO AND EN- | GRAVED BY

ESTHER PISSARRO. | THE BOOK HAS BEEN PRINTED | BY THEM AT THEIR ERA- | GNY PRESS, THE BROOK, | HAMMERSMITH, & | FINISHED IN | JUNE, 1904. | [triple type orn: leaf] | [double type orn: leaf] | [type orn: leaf] | [type orn: trefoil] SOLD BY THE ERAGNY | PRESS, LONDON, | AND | JOHN LANE, NEW YORK. $i4^r$: This edition is strictly limited to 215 paper | and 11 vellum copies, of which 200 paper and | 9 vellum copies are for sale. | [Pressmark III]

COLLATION: small demy 8°: $[a]^3$: b^4–i^4. 35 leaves, pp. [1–4] 5–64 [65–70]

PAPER AND DIMENSIONS: Arches. Leaf: 208 x 133 mm.

TYPE: Brook

ILLUSTRATIONS, ORNAMENTS, AND INITIALS: [one five-color wood-engraved illustration; one border in peach, ten initials in red, one pressmark] $[a]2^r$: Five-block color engraving: "Women and Roses," 128 x 99 mm. (Fern 122 [SB 167]) surrounded by a border of roses and leaves, 145 x 110 mm. (NIF) in peach. $[a]3^r$: Initial W (NIF) in red. $b2^r$: Initial O (Fern 291 [SB 113]) in red. $b4^r$: Initial H (NIF) in red. $d1^r$: Initial M (Fern 297 [SB 119]) in red. $e2^r$: Initial I (Fern 298 [SB 120]) in red. $e3^r$: Initial T (Fern 308 [SB 125]) in red. $f1^v$: Initial L (Fern 287 [SB 109]) in red. $f4^v$: Initial V (NIF) in red. $g3^r$: Initial G (NIF) in red. $h3^v$: Initial H (NIF) in red. $i4^r$: Pressmark III, 76 mm. diameter (Fern 112 [SB 152]).

CONTENTS: $[a]1^r$ blank. $[a]1^v$: title. $[a]2^r$: frontispiece. $[a]2^v$: blank. $[a]3^r$ – $i1^v$:text. $i2^r$: blank. $i2^v$: contents. $i3^r$: colophon. $i3^v$: blank. $i4^r$: pressmark. $i4^v$: blank

BINDING: Quarter Michallet blue paper, medium gold stamped on upper left corner: [orn: trefoil] SOME POEMS | BY ROBERT | BROWNING. Cream paper boards with a repeat pattern of "wild rose" (NIF) printed in peach and green.

PUBLICATION: 200 paper copies for sale at 30 shillings and 9 vellum copies for sale at £7. Published June 1904.

PROSPECTUS: [207 x 100 mm., 4 pages]

RELATED MATERIAL: Three sample binding cases.

NOTES: In March 1904, Lucien and Esther were getting ready to begin the Browning. Robert Steele selected the poems. By early May, they were working on the Browning and Esther thought she was ready to send sheets to the bindery on 14 June and asked for the bound volumes to be

"Wild rose" binding. *Some Poems by Robert Browning,* 1904. (Special Collections, Florida State University, Tallahassee)

Title page and frontispiece. *Some Poems by Robert Browning,* 1904. (Special Collections, Florida State University, Tallahassee)

returned by 29 June. As usual, problems ensued. On 14 June, she sent Leighton the sheets for 215 books, including paper for the endpapers. However, the colophon and pressmark as well as the pp. 19–20 insertion were not quite ready, as they had to be removed and corrected pages inserted. Esther ordered tissue to be placed at the frontispiece, page 5, and the pressmark page. On 16 June, the frontispiece and last sheet were sent to Leighton. The frontispiece was not straight and given that, Leighton thought it impossible to deliver the books by the date Esther required. Leighton thought that each frontispiece would need to be cut individually, both time-consuming and costly, or the binders could simply take their chances with the frontispieces (Leighton to Esther Pissarro, 16 June 1904). The correspondence between Leighton and Esther indicate that there were two cancels which were hooked into one another. Leighton promised to keep the turnovers as small as possible, though larger turnovers were not a problem "since it is a sign of genuine honest work" (Leighton to Esther Pissarro, 17 June 1904). The paper Esther selected for the back of the Browning, according to Leighton, was unsuitable because it split easily in the joints of the binding (Leighton to Esther Pissarro, 28 June 1904).

A letter from Albert Morelli, the Pissarros' business manager, dated 10 May [1904], indicates that there were two prospectuses. The earlier prospectus showed the price at 25 shillings or perhaps 20 shillings (according to Morrelli's recollections); the later at 30 shillings. Morelli anticipated poor sales of the Browning due to the high price. Lane, for the American edition, also had difficulties with the price. He did not think that the five-color wood-engraved frontispiece nor red initials throughout the book warranted the price; but by 1 June 1904, Lane had ordered 50 copies (Morelli to Esther Pissarro, 10 May and 1 June 1904). By December 1904, 90 copies of Browning remained unsold.

In stock: March 1, 1905, 85 copies, 1 vellum; 1 March 1906, 81 copies, 1 vellum; 1 March 1907, 70 copies; 1 March 1908, 79 copies; 1 March 1909, 78 copies; 1 March 1910, 76 copies; 1 March 1911, 75 copies (Private ledger).

COPIES SEEN: Ashmolean. BL (deposited 4 July 1904). FSU. NYPL (unopened copy). SFPL (Provenance: Robert Grabhorn; inscribed: à Madame la Comtesse Leutrum | wishing her many happy returns | of March 31st 1929 | from | Lucien Pissarro | & Esther Pissarro; with plate of W. Heffer & Sons, Ltd. Booksellers, New & Second-hand, Cambridge England).

EP21 • Samuel Taylor Coleridge. Christabel, Kubla Khan, Fancy in Nubibus, and Song from Zapolya. 1904.

[type orn: trefoil] CHRISTABEL, [type orn: trefoil] KUBLA KHAN, | [type orn: trefoil] FANCY IN NUBIBUS, AND [type orn: trefoil] SONG | FROM ZAPOLYA. | BY SAMUEL TAYLOR COLERIDGE.

COLOPHON: [in black and red] [type orn: trefoil] THE FRONTISPIECE HAS BEEN DE- | SIGNED & ENGRAVED on THE WOOD | BY L. PISSARRO; THE BORDER AND | INITIAL LETTERS WERE DESIGNED | BY L. PISSARRO & ENGRAVED BY E. | PISSARRO. [type orn: trefoil] THE BOOK has BEEN | PRINTED BY THEM AT THEIR | ERGANY PRESS, THE | BROOK, HAMMER- | SMITH, & FIN- | ISHED IN | OCTO- | BER, | 1904. | [type orn: leaf] | SOLD BY THE ERAGNY | PRESS, LONDON, | AND | JOHN LANE, NEW YORK. g2^v: [type orn: trefoil] This edition is strictly limited to 226 paper | and 10 vellum copies, of which 200 paper and | 8 vellum copies are for sale. | [Pressmark III]

COLLATION: small demy 8°: [a]^1 [b]^4 c^4–f^4 g^2. 23 leaves, pp. [i–ii] [1–2] 3–4 [5–7] 8–41 [42–44]

PAPER AND DIMENSIONS: Arches. Leaf: 210 x 135 mm.

TYPE: Brook

ILLUSTRATIONS, ORNAMENTS, AND INITIALS: [one chiaroscuro wood-engraved illustration in green; large initial in orange and green; three initials and pressmark in black and white] [b]1^v: “Christabel,” 96 mm. diameter, chiaroscuro wood engraving in green (Fern 153 [SB 224]). [b]5^v: Initial T (NIF) in orange and green; border of Virginia creeper, 180 x 110 mm. (Fern 373 [SB 184]). f3^r: Initial I (Fern 298 [SB 120]). f4^v: Initial O (NIF). g1^r: Initial A (Fern 288 [SB 110]). g2^v:

Pressmark III, 76 mm. diameter (Fern 112 [SB 152]).

CONTENTS: [a]1r: blank. [a]1v: frontispiece. [b]1r: Title. [b]1v: blank. [b]2: Preface to Christabel [in red]. [b]3: blank. [b]4r–e4v: Christabel. Part the First. f1r: Kubla Khan. f1v–f2v: Preface [in red]. f3r–f4r: Kubla Khan. f4v: Fancy in Nubibus or the Poets in the Clouds. g1r: Song from Zapolya (Act ii, Scene i). g1v: blank. g2r: colophon. g2v: Pressmark III.

BINDING: Quarter gray paper, gold-stamped on upper left corner: [type orn: trefoil] CHRISTABEL, | KUBLA KHAN, | FANCY IN NUBI- | BUS, & A SONG, | BY SAMUEL T. COLERIDGE. Green paper boards with a repeat pattern of "violets" (NIF) printed in mauve and dark green.

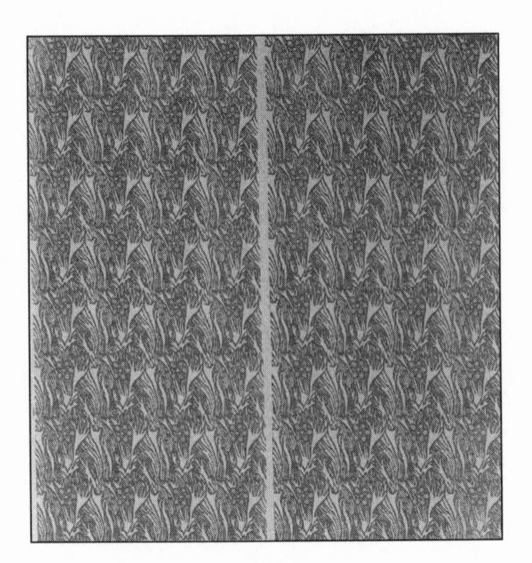

"Violet" binding paper. Samuel Taylor Coleridge, *Christabel, Kubla Khan, Fancy in Nubibus, and Song from Zapolya,* 1904. (Ashmolean Museum, Oxford)

PUBLICATION: 200 copies for sale at 1 guinea and 8 vellum for sale at 5 guineas. Published in October 1904.

NOTES: The poems for this volume were selected by Diana White. The Pissarros, in looking at various marketing schemes, looked at several options. One option was to not have a frontispiece in color with a lower price. When production began they had not decided in what direction to go. Lucien asked Esther to count the leaves in such a way that the frontispiece could be added or not. The chiaroscuro print may have been a compromise—still a colored print but one requiring fewer blocks.

For most of the production of this work, Lucien was away from the Brook.

John Lane ordered 26 copies for the American market. An announcement appeared in the *New York Times,* 10 December 1904. One hundred forty two copies of Christabel remained unsold as of December 1904.

In stock: 1 March 1905, 135 copies, 2 vellum; 1 March 1906, 102 copies, 2 vellum; 1 March 1907, 86 copies; 1 March 1908, 91 copies; 1 March 1909, 87 copies; 1 March 1910, 86 copies; 1 March 1911, 84 copies (Private ledger).

COPIES SEEN: Ashmolean. BL (deposited 20 October 1904). LC (Goudy Collection; unopened copy). NYPL (Bookplate of John Shaw Billings Memorial Fund, purchased 19 June 1928). SFPL (Provenance: Robert Grabhorn; signed by Lucien Pissarro).

EP22 • Some Old French and English Ballads. 1905.

[in black and large red caps] [type orn: trefoil] SOME OLD FRENCH AND ENGLISH | BALLADS [woodcut orn: flowers] | EDITED BY ROBERT STEELE.

COLOPHON: [in black and red] [woodcut orn: flowers] THIS EDITION OF OLD FRENCH | AND ENGLISH BALLADS HAS BEEN | EDITED by ROBERT STEELE. [woodcut orn: flowers] THE

| FRONTISPIECE HAS BEEN DESIGNED | AND ENGRAVED ON THE WOOD BY | L. PISSARRO. [woodcut orn: flowers] THE MUSIC TYPE | HAS BEEN DESIGNED SPECIALLY | FOR THIS WORK FROM XVIth. | CENTURY MODELS. [woodcut orn: flowers] THE | BOOK HAS BEEN PRINTED | BY E. & L. PISSARRO AT | THEIR ERAGNY PRESS, | The BROOK, HAMMER- | SMITH, & FINISHED | IN FEBRUARY, | MCCCCMV. [*sic*] | [quadruple type orn: leaf] | [triple type orn: leaf] | [double type orn: leaf] | [type orn: leaf] | [type orn: leaf] SOLD BY THE ERAGNY | PRESS, LONDON, | AND JOHN LANE, NEW YORK. p2^{v}: [type orn: trefoil] This edition is strictly limited to 200 paper | and 10 vellum copies. | [Pressmark III]

COLLATION: small demy 8°: [a]^{2} [b]^{2} c^{2}–p^{2}. 32 leaves, pp. [1 l.] 1–60 [61–62]

PAPER AND DIMENSIONS: Arches. Leaf: 208 x 135 mm.

TYPE: Brook, Music

ILLUSTRATIONS, ORNAMENTS, AND INITIALS: [one five-color wood-engraved illustration; twenty initials in red; pressmark in black and white] b2^{v}: Five-block color wood engraving: "Les Princeses au pommier doux," 91 mm. diameter (Fern 154 [SB 225]); Initial D (Fern 343 [SB 189]) in red. c2^{v}: Initial L (Fern 351 [SB 197]) in red. d1^{v}: Initial P (Fern 356 [SB 202]) in red. d2^{v}: Initial I (Fern 345 [SB 194]) in red. e2^{r}: Initial L (Fern 351 [SB 197]) in red. f2^{r}: Initial H (Fern 350 [SB 193]) in red. g1^{r}: Initial L (Fern 351 [SB 197]) in red. h1^{r}: Initial M (Fern 353 [SB 199]) in red. i1^{r}: Initial I (Fern 345 [SB 194]) in red. j1^{r}: Initial Q (Fern 357 [SB 203]) in red. j2^{r}: Initial P (Fern 356 [SB 202]) in red. k1^{r}: Initial T (Fern 360 [SB 206]) in red. k2^{r}: Initial O (Fern 355 [SB 201]) in red. l1^{r}: Initial A (Fern 341 [SB 187]) in red. l2^{v}: Initial T (Fern 360 [SB 206]) in red. n1^{r}: Initial I (Fern 345 [SB 194]) in red. n2^{v}: Initial E (Fern 344 [SB 190]) in red. o1^{v}: Initial C (Fern 365 [SB 213]) in red. o2^{v}: Initial W (NIF) in red. p1^{r}: Initial G (Fern 349 [SB 192]) in red. p2^{v}: Pressmark III, 76 mm. diameter (Fern 112 [SB 152]). Music staves printed in black, notes in red; refrains printed in red.

CONTENTS: [a]1^{r}: title. [a]1^{v}: All rights reserved. [a]^{2}–[b]1^{r}: Preface. [b]1^{v}: Contents. [b]2^{r}: blank. [b]2^{v}: Frontispiece. [b]2^{v}–p1^{v}: text. p2^{r}: colophon. p2^{v}: pressmark.

BINDING: Quarter Michallet blue paper, gold-stamped on upper left corner: [orn: trefoil] SOME OLD | FRENCH & | ENGLISH | BALLADS. Buff paper boards with a repeat pattern of "winter jasmine" (NIF) printed in two shades of green ink.

PUBLICATION: 175 paper copies for sale at 35 shillings and 8 vellum copies at 7 guineas. Published March 1905.

PROSPECTUS: [1 leaf, 206 x 96 mm., with order form on verso, initial S (Fern 303 [SB 125]) in red] No. 6.

RELATED MATERIAL: Woodblock print before reduction of "winter jasmine"; watercolor sketch for title page (not used); rondel with title in middle and with green border (not used); border sketch (not used).

NOTES: *Some Old French and English Ballads* was the Pissarros' second venture into music printing, the first being *C'est d'Aucassin et de Nicolete.* The Pissarros had music type cut, designed from sixteenth-century models, specially for this volume and planned to use it in future books. Shanks and Son, the type foundry, advised the Pissarros on 7 October 1904 that the casting of the music type was taking longer than had been anticipated. The type was not supplied much before mid-October. In addition to the delivery delay of the music type, music printing was more time consuming than the Pissarros had thought and the book, originally planned for a January publication date, was pushed back to March 1905.

Robert Steele was paid £5 for his role as editor and given a vellum copy and several paper copies.

Sheets and endpapers were sent to the bindery on 27 February 1905. Only 200 frontispieces were printed and Esther asked Leighton to ensure that none of them were spoiled. She was unable to include the printed papers for the covers as they had run out of paper and had to wire Paris for additional paper to be sent at the first post. The sample book was completed by 3 March and Esther found it agreeable. Tissue inserts were needed for the title, the preface, the preface contents, pages 59 and 60, and the pressmark; seven sheets in all. Esther found that the book opened better than usual. Fifty copies were ready on 8 March, with the remaining 150 copies to come two days later. Either due to a miscount or perhaps a mishap, a rejected signature n was used in one of the books. The vellum copies had not yet been collated and sewn, but would be bound in limp vellum with silk ties, sewn with silk threads, and as usual placed in white boxes.

Twenty-six copies were sent on 9 March to John Lane. On 27 March, Esther inquired of Lane when they would require their second delivery of copies—according to their contract, Lane was to buy 50 copies.

Notices appeared in the *Athenaeum,* 27 May 1905; the *Illustrated London News,* 15 April 1905; and *Figaro* (Paris), 1 April 1905.

In stock: 1 March 1906, 70 copies, 1 vellum; 1 March 1907, 51 paper, 2 vellum; 1 March 1908, 54 copies, 1 vellum; 1 March 1909, 37 copies, 1 vellum; 1 March 1910, 36 copies, 1 vellum; 1 March 1911, 27 copies, 1 vellum (Private ledger).

COPIES SEEN: Ashmolean. Bancroft. BL (deposited 14 March 1905). Huntington. NYPL (Bookplate of John Shaw Billings Memorial Fund). SFPL (Provenance: Robert Grabhorn).

EP23 • Laurence Binyon. Dream-Come-True. 1905.

[type orn: trefoil] DREAM-COME-TRUE. | POEMS BY LAURENCE BINYON.

COLOPHON: [type orn: trefoil] IN THIS, THE ONLY EDITION | OF «DREAM-COME-TRUE», THE | FRONTISPIECE HAS BEEN DE- | SIGNED & CUT ON THE WOOD | BY LAURENCE BINYON, AND | THE DECORATIONS WERE DE- | SIGNED BY LUCIEN PISSARRO | & ENGRAVED BY ESTHER | PISSARRO. THE BOOK HAS | BEEN PRINTED by THEM | AT THEIR «ERAGNY | PRESS», THE BROOK, | HAMMERSMITH, | & FINISHED | IN APRIL, 1905. | [type orn: trefoil] SOLD BY THE ERAGNY | PRESS, LONDON, | AND | JOHN LANE, NEW YORK. $f2^r$: [type orn: trefoil] This edition is strictly limited to 175 | paper and 10 vellum copies, of which | 150 paper and 8 vellum copies are for | sale | [Pressmark III]

COLLATION: Small demy 12°: a^2 $[b]^2$ c2 d^4–e^4 f^2. 16 leaves, pp. [1–7] 8–28 [29–32]

PAPER AND DIMENSIONS: Arches. Leaf: 180 x 105 mm.

TYPE: Brook

ILLUSTRATIONS, ORNAMENTS, AND INITIALS: [one black-and-white wood-engraved illustration, two borders and one ornament in green, one initial in red, fifteen initials and pressmark in black and white] $a2^r$: Eragny Press monogram in green (NIF). $[b]1^v$: woodcut illustration by Laurence Binyon, 59 x 63 mm. surrounded by border (Fern 330 [SB 153]) in green; Initial W (NIF) in red. $[b]2^r$: border (Fern 330 [SB 153]) in green. $[b]2^v$: Initial C (Fern 313 [SB 134]). $c1^v$: Initial U (Fern 321 [SB 142]). $c2^r$: Initial L (Fern 317 [SB 138]). $c2^v$: Initial O (Fern 319 [SB 140]). $d1^r$: Initial W (NIF). $d1^v$: Initial B (NIF). $d2^r$: Initial N (NIF). $d2^v$: Initial V (NIF). $d3^r$: Initial W (NIF). $d3^v$: Initial O (Fern 319). $d4^v$: Initial W (NIF). $e1^v$: Initial O (Fern 319 [SB 140]). $e2^v$: Initial W (NIF). $e3^v$: Initial B (NIF). $e4^v$: Initial S (NIF). $f2^r$: Pressmark III, 76 mm. diameter (Fern 112 [SB 152]).

CONTENTS: $a1^r$: title. $a1^v$: blank. $a2^r$: monogram. $a2^v$: contents. $b1^r$: blank. $b1^v$–$e4^v$: text. $f1^r$: colophon. $f1^v$: blank. $f2^r$: pressmark. $f2^v$: blank

BINDING: Quarter Michallet blue paper with printed paper label on upper left cover: [type orn: trefoil] DREAM- | COME- | TRUE. | BY | L. BINYON. Cream paper boards with a repeat pattern of "daisy" (NIF) printed in pink and green ink.

PUBLICATION: 150 paper copies for sale at 12 shillings 6 pence and 8 vellum copies at 3 guineas. Published in May 1905.

Laurence Binyon, *Dream-Come-True,* 1905; frontispiece. (Ashmolean Museum, Oxford)

RELATED MATERIAL: Photograph for cover design before reduction; binding sample with light turquoise quarter board.

PROSPECTUS: [215 x 94 mm.] Prospectus 7 | Dream-Come-True, Poems by Laurence Binyon. | NOTICE: Mr. Pissarro has long desired the opportunity | which at last presents itself, of publishing some work | by a living English poet, since he has before this | had the good fortune to publish a poem by the | eminent Belgian, Emile Verhaeren

Lovers of well built books not only desire beautiful | reprints of classics, but will, he feels convinced, | be glad to acquire the adequately embodied work of | a poet, whose reputation as a choice and rare | artist in words, has gradually risen so high, | as that of Mr. Binyon now stands. Mr. Binyon | has assured him moreover that these poems will not | again be grouped alone or under their | present titles. Therefore in «DREAM-COME-TRUE» they | must always possess a quite unique significance | in their creator's eyes as, doubtless, in those of his | admirers. Proper to their present issue besides, | is the woodcut frontispiece designed and engraved | by the author; for it will not again be used | in any book.

NOTES: The first in what the Pissarros called their Modern Series, *Dream-Come-True* was proposed by Laurence Binyon. Binyon, an expert on Japanese and Chinese art as well as a lyric poet, worked in the Department of Prints and Drawings at the British Museum. He wrote to the Pissarros, in September 1904: "I was going through some recent poems of mine the other day, & the idea came into my head of printing a tiny book of about 12 love poems & I wondered if there would be any chance of your caring to print them. I dare say your programme is full for sometime, perhaps they are not in your line: if so, please say so quite frankly. It would of course be a great honour & pleasure to appear in your beautiful type."

Binyon sent his manuscript to the Pissarros in late January 1905; by early March 1905, Lucien provided Binyon with an estimate for the book—£44.14.0, of which 20 percent of the cost was for Lucien's work on the book. Lucien believed the book would produce £45 from selling the advance orders (73 copies). If the full edition sold, there would be an additional £50 to split between them.

Binyon designed and cut the wood engraving for this little book. Binyon's design was revised by Selwyn Image. In an earlier letter Binyon noted, "I have tried to think of a woodcut, & if I had the gift of drawing & designing I would do one. If I had plenty of time I could elaborate something, but I have no time, & it wouldn't be good enough to go with your beautiful type."

By late March 1905, the poems were in proofs. Binyon added one more poem, recently written, to round out the book. Binyon's wood engraving was not yet finished. Binyon sent his completed block on 6 April and sheets were sent to Leighton on 18 April for binding. Leighton had difficulties in matching the blue Michallet paper. Esther was not happy with the binding, but as Leighton pointed out to her she had not allowed sufficient time for binding, and in the case of *Dream-Come-True* she broke one of the major rules of book production—she was too much in a hurry to take the time to look at the sample to ensure that it had been done to her specifications (Leighton to Esther Pissarro, 4 May 1905).

Although Diana White's *Ishtar* was not conceived as part of the Modern Series, it became a de facto part of the series, when *Dream-Come-True* was printed in the same format and bound with the same printed papers. Two new initial letters were added to the series (Fern 312–322), V and another O.

One of Binyon's poems, "Ricordi," was printed in the *Academy* before *Dream-Come-True* appeared. Binyon suggested that prospectuses be sent to the *Times*, the *Athenaeum*, the *Saturday Review*, *Outlook*, *Chronicle*, *Daily News*, *Telegraph*, and the *Speaker*, asking each to put in a paragraph in their literary news. Notices appeared in the *Academy*, 13 May 1905 and 15 April 1905; the *Athenaeum*, 22 September 1905; and the *New York Times*, 24 June 1905.

By 9 May, 89 paper copies and 6 vellum copies had been sold. By 19 September 1905 only 5 copies remained and by 29 November the book was out-of-print.

In stock: 1 March 1906, 1 copy, 3 vellum; 1 March 1907, 1 vellum; 1 March 1908, 1 vellum; 1 March 1909, 1 vellum; 1 March 1910, 1 vellum; 1 March 1911, 1 vellum.

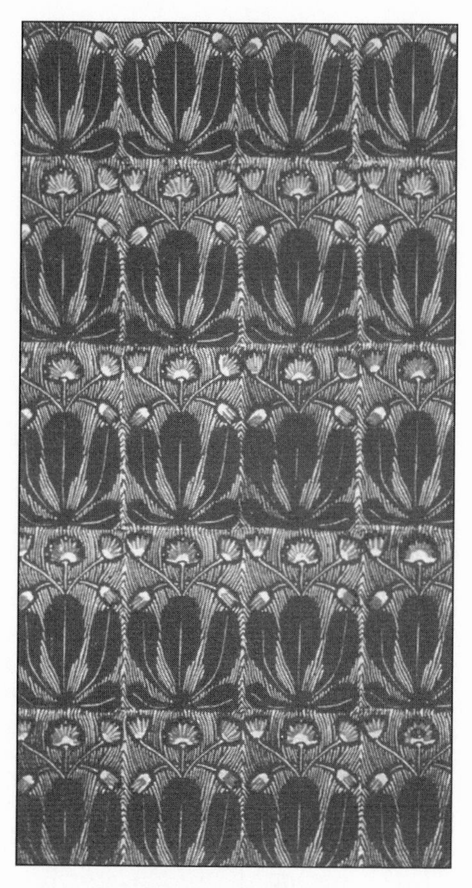

"Daisy" binding paper. Laurence Binyon, *Dream-Come-True*, 1905. (Ashmolean Museum, Oxford)

COPIES SEEN: Ashmolean. Bancroft (John Quinn copy, inscribed by Lawrence Binyon: To my friend | John Quinn | Lawrence Binyon | Dec. 1921). BL (deposited 8 May 1906; another copy bound in dark blue morocco with heavy gold tooling with gilt edge on top. Bound by Bagculey, Newcastle-Under-Lyme, 1905; another copy placed at the Adult Class Department, Malet Place, London, W.C. 1. "This book was given by the executors of the late Dr. Albert Mansbridge, C.H. Founder of the National Central Library"). LC (Bookplate of William Macgregor). NYPL. SFPL (Provenance: Robert Grabhorn with bookplate of William and Helena M. Hand). UCLA (Bookplate of William Andrews Clark).

EP24 • T. S. Moore. The Little School. 1905.

[type orn: entwined leaves] THE LITTLE SCHOOL, | A POSY OF RHYMES, | BY T. STURGE | MOORE. | [wood engraving of cherubs by T. Sturge Moore, 45 x 33 mm.]

COLOPHON: [type orn: trefoil] THANKS ARE DUE TO THE | EDITORS OF THE «DIAL» AND | THE «ACADEMY» FOR PER- | MISSION TO REPRINT SOME | FEW OF THE POEMS IN THIS, | THE FIRST EDITION OF «THE | LITTLE SCHOOL» WHICH will REMAIN UNIQUE in THE NUM- | BER AND ARRANGEMENT OF | ITS CONTENTS, ITS FOUR |

WOODCUTS by THE AUTHOR | & ALL FEATURES COMMON | TO «ERAGNY PRESS» BOOKS. | [type orn: trefoil] PRINTED BY LUCIEN & | ESTHER PISSARRO AT | THE BROOK, HAM- | MERSMITH, & | FINISHED IN JULY, 1905. | SOLD BY THE ERAGNY | PRESS, LONDON, | AND | JOHN LANE, NEW YORK. h2^{v}: [type orn: trefoil] This edition is strictly limited to | 175 paper and 10 vellum copies, of | which 150 paper and 8 vellum copies | are for sale. | [Pressmark III]

COLLATION: Small demy 12°: a^2 b^4 c^2 d^4 e^2 f^4 g^2 h^4. 24 leaves, pp. [1–7] 8–45 [46–48]

PAPER AND DIMENSIONS: Arches. Leaf: 180 x 105 mm.

TYPE: Brook

ILLUSTRATIONS, ORNAMENTS, AND INITIALS: [three wood-engraved illustrations, one cul-de-lampe, twenty-four initials, and one pressmark in black and white; monogram in green] a1^{r}: wood engraving of cherubs by T. S. Moore, 45 x 33 mm. b1^{r}: Eragny Press monogram in green (NIF). b2^{v}: wood engraving of mother and child by T. S. Moore, 36 x 75 mm.; Initial H (NIF). b3^{v}: Initial L (NIF). b4^{r}: Initial A (NIF). b4^{v}: Initial S (NIF). c1^{r}: Initial K (NIF). c2^{r}: wood engraving, “Frolicking Wind,” by T. S. Moore, 36 x 75 mm.; Initial T (NIF). d1^{r}: Initial T (NIF). d1^{v}: Initial B (NIF). d2^{r}: Initial S (NIF). d2^{v}: Initial T (NIF). d3^{r}: Initial H (NIF). d4^{r}: Initial L (NIF). e1^{r}: Initial T (NIF). e2^{r}: Initial L (NIF). e2^{v}: Initial S (NIF). f1^{r}: Initial O (NIF). f1^{v}: Initial L (NIF). f2^{v}: Initial T (NIF). f3^{r}: Initial L (NIF). f4^{r}: Initial O (NIF). f4^{v}: Initial W (NIF). g1^{v}: Initial T (NIF). g2^{r}: Initial I (NIF). h1^{r}: W. h2^{r}: Cul-de-lampe by T. S. Moore, 36 x 29 mm. h2^{r}: Initial T. h4^{v}: Pressmark III, 76 mm. diameter (Fern 112 [SB 152]).

CONTENTS: a1^{r}: title. a1^{v}: blank. a2^{r}: dedication: [type orn: trefoil] TO SYBIL PYE, [type orn: trefoil] | THE MISTRESS | OF THE LITTLE SCHOOL, | WHO WISHED THESE POEMS | MADE FOR, AND BROUGHT |THEM HOME TO CHIL- | DREN, THIS BOOK | IS GRATEFULLY | DEDICATED | BY T. S.M. | [triple type orn: leaf] | [double type orn: leaf] | [type orn: leaf]. a2^{v}: blank. b1^{r}: Eragny Press monogram. b1^{v}: contents. b2^{r}: blank. b2^{v}–h3^{r}: text. h3^{v}: blank. h4: colophon

BINDING: Quarter gray boards, gold-stamped on upper left corner: [orn: trefoil] THE | LITTLE | SCHOOL. | BY T. | STURGE | MOORE. Cream paper boards with a repeat pattern of “daffodil” (NIF) printed in green and yellow ink.

PUBLICATION: 150 paper copies for sale at 18 shillings and 8 vellum copies at 4 guineas. Published in July 1905.

Title page, wood engraving by T. S. Moore. T. S. Moore, *The Little School*, 1905. (Ashmolean Museum, Oxford)

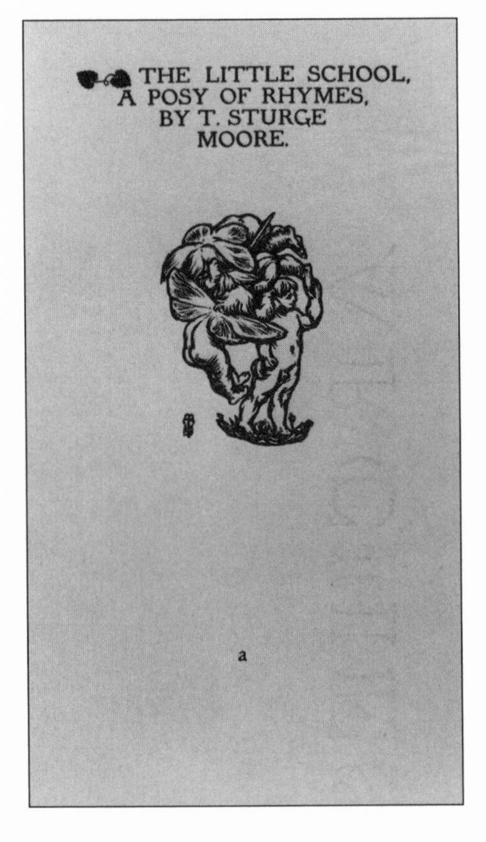

RELATED MATERIALS: Drawings for initials P, A, L, L, I, S, W, T, H, K, O, B to be reduced by half; photograph with letters reduced by half; second copy, H cutout; design for cover; drawings with Chinese ink for initials F, M, E, Y, D, N, C, R, J, V, G, J, U, O.

PROSPECTUS: [208 x 97 mm., 4 pages] No. 8 The Little School | NOTICE: In continuation of a series, begun with | Mr. Binyon's «Dream-Come-True» and planned to include choice work, unpublished before, by living | writers, Mr. Pissarro is glad to announce the issue of a | collection of short poems for children by | T. Sturge Moore.

The «Little School» is a happy marriage | of the two arts, which Mr. Moore has pursued | since the early days of the «Dial» and for which | he has won distinguished recognition as a poet | and as an original wood-engraver whose work is destined | to be prized among the finest of its kind.

The book will never be reprinted in its present form.

p. [3] IX. Hands

p. [4] Order form

NOTES: Following quickly behind Binyon's *Dream-Come-True,* T. S. Moore's *The Little School* was no. 2 (and the last) in the Pissarro's Modern Series. As in Diana White's *Ishtar* and Binyon's *Dream-Come-True,* the author also contributed the woodcuts—in this case, four. The book was in production by May 1905 and was handled primarily by Esther; Lucien was in Finchingfield, England, painting. Esther was anxious for the books to be delivered from the bindery by 3 July 1905 due to the schedule of the publishing season. But that delivery date was not to be. Esther wrote Leighton on 4 July, "We are most disappointed that you should again not send the book to time. . . . It is most annoying—I take every possible care & give you everything to time & yet you would never keep to date." And two days later, "I am more annoyed than I can tell you. The books, altho' three days late from absolutely no fault of mine and altho the 2nd sample was perfectly satisfactory have come and among them I cannot find one that is as I want them to be." Esther continued, "You evidently cannot manage these small orders which require careful work & I suppose we shall have to make other arrangements. If you look at my sample cover card—the one I sent in giving the order & if you will refer to my past letter you will understand why I am quite in despair of your ever doing the work properly" (Esther Pissarro to Leighton, 6 July 1905). Leighton, upset by Esther's complaint, could not imagine how the work went wrong (Leighton to Esther Pissarro, 7 July 1905).

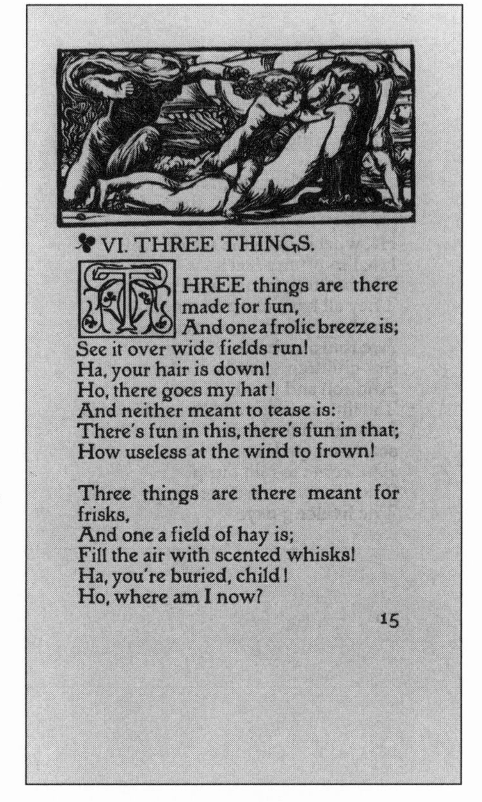

VI. THREE THINGS.

THREE things are there made for fun,
And one a frolic breeze is;
See it over wide fields run!
Ha, your hair is down!
Ho, there goes my hat!
And neither meant to tease is:
There's fun in this, there's fun in that;
How useless at the wind to frown!

Three things are there meant for frisks,
And one a field of hay is;
Fill the air with scented whisks!
Ha, you're buried, child!
Ho, where am I now?

15

"Frolicking Wind," wood engraving by T. S. Moore. T. S. Moore, *The Little School,* 1905. (Ashmolean Museum, Oxford)

In 1901, T. S. Moore had written to Sybil Pye, "I would like to write poems giving a spontaneous & childish expression of joy in the aesthetic and edifying elements of all necessary everyday actions, like eating, sleeping, washing, dressing, walking, talking, etc. . . ." (T. S. Moore to Sybil Pye, 28 December 1901. University of London, Paleography Room, 21/2).

Notices appeared in *Art Journal,* April 1906, and *Burlington Magazine,* October 1905.

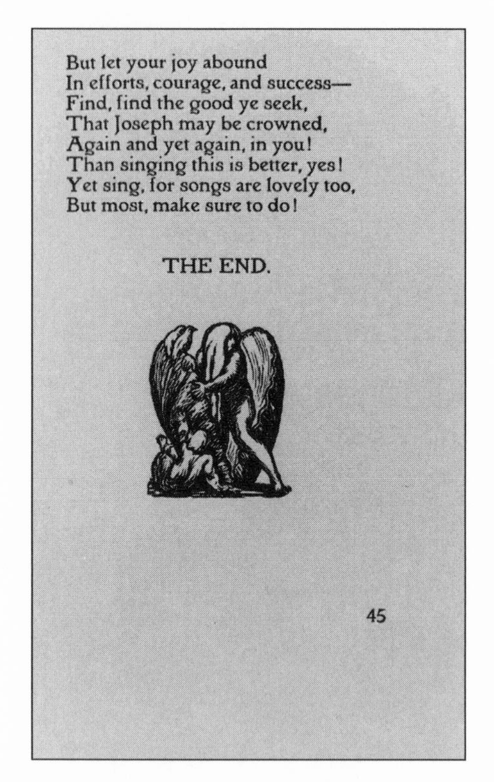
But let your joy abound
In efforts, courage, and success—
Find, find the good ye seek,
That Joseph may be crowned,
Again and yet again, in you!
Than singing this is better, yes!
Yet sing, for songs are lovely too,
But most, make sure to do!

THE END.

45

Cul-de-lampe, wood engraving by T. S. Moore. T. S. Moore, *The Little School*, 1905. (Ashmolean Museum, Oxford)

In stock: 1 March 1906, 27 copies, 3 vellum; 1 March 1907, 9 copies, 2 vellum; 1 March 1908, 21 copies, 2 vellum; 1 March 1909, 16 copies, 2 vellum; 1 March 1910, 15 copies, 2 vellum; 1 March 1911, 13 copies, 2 vellum (Private ledger).

COPIES SEEN: Ashmolean. BL (two copies, one from The Henry Davis Collection with a green morocco binding by Sybil Pye, dated 1906). LC (Inscribed: To Mr. Roger Marx from Lucien Pissarro). NYPL (Bookplate of John Shaw Billings Memorial Fund). SFPL (Provenance: Robert Grabhorn).

EP25 • John Keats. La Belle dame sans merci. 1905.

[in black and red] [within a frame of fleuron type ornaments and within single rules] LA BELLE DAME SANS MERCI. | [rule] | BY JOHN KEATS. | [rule] | New Year ["Vue d'Eragny"] mcxxxxvi | [rule] | The Eragny Press, The Brook, Hammersmith

COLOPHON: [in black and red] [vertical rule] [type orn: trefoil] PRINTED AND SOLD BY E. & L. | PISSARRO THE ERAGNY PRESS, | THE BROOK, HAMMERSMITH, LONDON, W. d4^{r}: [vertical rule] [type orn: trefoil] This edition is strictly limited to two | hundred paper and ten vellum copies.

COLLATION: 32°: $[a]^{4}$ b^{4}–d^{4}. 16 leaves, pp. [i–iii] iv–xxviii [xxvix–xxxii]

PAPER AND DIMENSIONS: Arches. Leaf: 73 x 106 mm.

TYPE: Brook

ILLUSTRATION AND ORNAMENTS: [one wood-engraved illustration in black and white; two initials in red] [a]1^{v}: "Vue d'Eragny," 23 mm. diameter (Fern 68 [SB 45]). [a]2^{r}: Initial A (Fern 307 [SB 129]) in red. c1^{r}: Initial O (Fern 302 [SB 124]) in red.

CONTENTS: [a]1^{r}: half-title: [in black and red] [type orn: trefoil] LA BELLE DAME SANS MERCI. | BY JOHN KEATS. [a]1^{v}: title. [a]2^{r}–d3^{r}: text. d3^{v}–d4^{r}: colophon. d4^{v}: blank.

ERRATA: Erratum. | Page 2, for mcxxxxvi., read mdccccvi [in BL copy]

BINDING: Quarter Michallet blue paper with printed paper label: [type orn: trefoil] LA | BELLE | DAME | SANS | MERCI. | BY | JOHN KEATS. Cream paper boards with a repeat pattern of "roses" (Fern 284 [SB 150]) printed in green and yellow ink.

PUBLICATION: 200 paper copies for sale at 5 shillings and 10 vellum copies at 1 guinea. Published in December 1905.

RELATED MATERIAL: Two sample case bindings.

PROSPECTUS: [208 x 94 mm., 1 leaf with order form on verso] No. 9. [Initial L (Fern 287 [SB 109])]

NOTES: The smallest book of the Eragny Press, the book was published on 7 December 1905 as a New Year's booklet. Because it was impossible for the Pissarros to finish the *Songs by Ben Jonson* in time for the Christmas season, they decided to do this little book so they would have something to offer their clients.

On 11 December 1905, Campbell Dodgson placed an order for *La Belle dame sans merci*. Presumably the Pissarros shipped the book to him that day, for in a letter dated 13 December, Dodgson noted that the book is dated 1146 rather than 1906. They started reprinting the title page that very same day, but stopped when they discovered that many of their customers wished to keep the books with the error. The Pissarros did not want one part of the edition with the fault and the other without, so they did not proceed with the reprinting. Instead, they printed an errata slip.

The binding process, as usual, was full of animosity. Leighton had difficulties in getting the sides correct. On the front side, the center rose was in about the right position, but those roses to the right were too high and those to the left too low, yet the side was cut through the center of the calyx of the rose. Leighton wondered if the paper had not stretched in printing. When the books arrived, Esther did not think the backs of the book were bound in the paper she had provided, but she did find on the whole that the bindings looked nice and were less stiff in the opening—but, nearly every page had offset (Esther Pissarro to Leighton, 7 December 1905). Leighton reminded Esther in a note dated 8 December, that set off is due to haste. When 100 copies arrived on 18 December, they were sent without the usual protective covers. Esther asked Leighton to send her the paper, appropriately cut, so they could send out the books. Set off was still a problem and several of the books were not clean. "Altogether we are not at all satisfied," wrote Esther to Leighton (18 December 1905). Esther must have questioned the charge for binding *La Belle dame sans merci*. In a letter dated 6 February 1906, Leighton explained to her that "little books of this kind which require such very exact work, are really more costly than larger books, upon which any slight variation is not so discernable."

Notices for *La Belle dame sans merci* appeared in the *New York Times* on 27 January 1906 and *Burlington Magazine*, February 1906.

The Pissarros sent copies of their New Year's book to Diana White, Laurence Binyon, T. S. Moore, Charles Holmes, Claude Monet, J. D. Symon, Barclay Squire, Robert Steele, Charles Ricketts, Georges Lecomte, Félix Fénéon, Emile Verhaeren, and to other friends and relatives. In all, they presented forty copies, in addition to those given for copyright deposit.

In stock: 1 March 1906, 63 copies; 1 March 1907, 44 copies; 1 March

1908, 56 copies; 1 March 1909, 42 copies; 1 March 1910, 41 copies; 1 March 1911, 36 copies (Private ledger).

COPIES SEEN: Ashmolean. BL (deposited 29 December 1906). NYPL (Inscribed, "To S. L. Bensusan from Esther & [Lucien did not write his name in]). SFPL (2 copies; one paper, the other, vellum. Provenance: Robert Grabhorn with bookplate of William and Helena M. Hand).

EP26 • Ben Jonson. Songs by Ben Jonson. 1906.

[in black and red] [vertical rule] [type orn: trefoil] SONGS BY BEN JONSON. [woodcut orn] | [rule]] | [type orn: trefoil] A SELECTION FROM THE PLAYS, | [rule] | MASQUES, AND POEMS, WITH THE | [rule] | EARLIEST KNOWN SETTINGS OF | [rule] | CERTAIN NUMBERS. | [rule] | [illustration: "Minstrel,"] | [type orn: trefoil] THE ERAGNY PRESS, THE BROOK, | [rule] | HAMMERSMITH, LONDON, W. | [rule]

COLOPHON: [in black and red] [type orn: trefoil] THE COLOURED FRONTISPIECE | HAS BEEN DESIGNED & ENGRAVED | ON THE WOOD BY L. PISSARRO. THE | BORDER & INITIAL LETTERS WERE | DESIGNED BY L. PISSARRO AND EN- | GRAVED BY E. PISSARRO. THE BOOK | HAS BEEN PRINTED BY E. AND L. | PISSARRO AT THEIR ERAGNY PRESS | AND FINISHED IN APRIL, 1906. | This edition is strictly limited to one hundred | & seventy-five paper | and ten vellum copies. [double type orn: leaf] | [Pressmark III] | [type orn: trefoil] SOLD BY THE ERAGNY PRESS, | THE BROOK, HAMMERSMITH, LON- | DON, W.

COLLATION: Small demy 8°: $[a]^2$ $[b]^2$ c^2–p^2. 32 leaves, pp. [2] [1–5] 6–59 [60–62]

PAPER AND DIMENSIONS: Arches with Eragny Press monogram. Leaf: 208 x 130 mm.

TYPE: Brook, Music

ILLUSTRATIONS, ORNAMENTS, AND INITIALS: [one four-color wood-engraved illustration, forty-six initials in red, one border and press-mark in black and white] $[a]2^r$: "Minstrel," four-color wood-engraved illustration, 80 mm. diameter (Fern 155 [SB 226]). $[b]2^r$: border (NIF); Initial A (NIF) in red; Initial S (Fern 292 [SB 114]) in red. $b2^v$: Initials O, T (NIF) in red. $c1^r$: Initials O, N (NIF) in red. $c1^v$: Initials I, L (NIF) in red. $c2^r$: Initials W, T (NIF) in red. $c2^v$: Initials B, F (NIF) in red. $d1^r$: Initial C (NIF) in red. $e2^r$: Initial S (NIF) in red. $f1^r$: Initials I, T (NIF) in red. $g1^r$: Initial K (NIF) in red. $g1^v$: Initials F, D (NIF) in red. $h2^r$: Initial S (NIF) in red. $h2^v$: Initial F (NIF) in red. $i1^r$: Initial C (NIF) in red. i1^v: Initial O (NIF) in red. i2^r: Initials M, H (NIF) in red. j1^r: Initials C, I (NIF) in red. j2^v: Initial I (NIF) in red. k2^r: Initial Y (NIF) in red. l2^r: Initial S (NIF) in red. m1^r: Initial H (NIF) in red. m2^v: Initial O (NIF) in red. n1^r: Initials O, G (NIF) in red. n1^v: Initials S, B (NIF) in red. n2^r: Initials I, T, T (NIF) in red. n2^v: Initials S, T (NIF) in red. o1^r: Initial O (NIF) in red. o1^v: Initial P (NIF) in red. o2^r: Initial C (NIF) in red. o2^v: Initial C (NIF) in red. p1^r: Initial R (NIF) in red. p2^v: pressmark, 76 mm. diameter (Fern 112 [SB 152]). Side notes and music staves in red.

CONTENTS: [a]1^r: dedication: [type orn: trefoil] DEDICATED TO J. M. ANDREINI. [a]1^v: blank. [a]2^r: title. [a]2^v: blank. [b]1^r: preface.

Title page. *Songs by Ben Jonson*, 1906. (Ashmolean Museum, Oxford)

[b]1^{v}: blank. [b]2^{r}–p1^{r}: text. p1^{v}–p2^{r}: contents. p2^{r}: errata. p2^{v}: colophon and pressmark

BINDING: Quarter Michallet blue paper, light gold-stamped on upper left corner: [type orn: trefoil] SONGS BY | BEN JONSON. Cream paper boards with a repeat pattern of "speedwell" (NIF) printed in green and blue ink.

PUBLICATION: 150 paper copies for sale at 40 shillings and 8 vellum copies at 7 guineas. Published in April 1906.

PROSPECTUS: [207 x 94 mm., 1 leaf with order form on verso] No. 10 [Initial S in red (Fern 299 [SB 121])]

NOTES: In June 1905, the Pissarros were debating whether to produce a Ben Jonson or a Baudelaire book. Baudelaire was rejected because it would be too long. They consulted Laurence Binyon at the British Museum; he introduced them to William Barclay Squire, who saw the music of the nine songs through the Press. The Pissarros needed considerable help in fully understanding the music. Squire provided that help and offered countless suggestions. T. S. Moore helped the Pissarros to select, along with Diana White, the Ben Jonson poems.

Early on, Lucien saw the book as having a small format, printed in red and black throughout, and he planned to use the honeysuckle border originally used in the Flaubert books for the frontispiece. He began experimenting with design for the book during his stay in Finchingfield in June 1905. Lucien had a difficult time of coming up with an illustration—the only thing he could come up with, helped by Diana White, was the god Pan playing the flute, but in order to do an illustration with Pan, it would be necessary to go to the British Museum to study the legs of Pan.

That summer while Lucien was off painting, Esther was working on the engravings for the frontispiece and the cover design. The book was designed to be the companion volume to *Some Old French and English Ballads.* They had planned to price it as they did *Ballads,* but *Songs by Ben Jonson* was so much work, "so long & so difficult," that they had to raise the price. It took three months to print the Ben Jonson.

The book was at the bindery by early April 1906. On 18 April, Leighton asked Esther to approve the sample binding and requested an additional twenty-five sheets of signature p and eight sheets of the dedication page in order to complete the binding. Esther may have been trying to cut costs when she asked Leighton to omit the interleaving paper, but given the trouble with set off in *La Belle dame sans merci,* Leighton was not willing to take any chances with complaints—but he got them anyway. The back was too pinched; the book did not open easily; signature k was not in place; the pages set off; the cover was badly stamped; and the cover paper needed to be forwarded by 1/16 inch. The Pissarros ran out of the paper needed to finish binding the book.

The Pissarros considered the Ben Jonson, up to 1906, to be their best book, but it sold badly. In writing to T. S. Moore on 21 July 1906, Esther explains, "The Ben Jonson which is really our best book has sold deplorably. Our American prospectuses arrived two days after the San Francisco disaster with the result we have sold in all three copies in America. For the rest we have sold about 35 copies and six vellums. The book cost £112 to produce allowing nothing for our work & it has yielded about £89—We have given up our printer as we felt we must not increase our debt to his master so you see things are very nasty. If Lucien had not sold a few things outside the books we should be in an even more terrible position. He is to have an exhibition in Germany in the autumn of his works so he paints in the morning & we print in the afternoon. We feel he ought to show his things more & more as the books seem so hopeless." Given their dire straits, Lucien asked Claude Monet for a loan (Lucien Pissarro to Claude Monet, 27 September 1906). Monet obliged.

The book was dedicated to J. M. Andrieni, a New York lawyer and book collector, who had been very helpful to the Pissarros in their American ventures. Andrieni received a vellum copy of the work and replied to the Pissarros, "It is certainly very complimentary to dedicate B. Jonson's to me and I trust you will have all the success with it which I wish you. It is a handsome book and I hope American collectors will appreciate it. I know the Times Editor will give you a full notice" (J. M. Andrieni, 30 April 1906).

Emery Walker said of *Songs by Ben Jonson*: ". . . a beautiful specimen of your press, and I am very proud to possess it. . . . I think it is the prettiest specimen of modern music typography I have seen" (Emery Walker to Esther Pissarro, 10 January 1910).

Notices appeared in the *Illustrated London News*, 5 May 1906; the *Athenaeum*, 19 May 1906; and *Burlington Magazine*, June 1906.

In stock: 1 March 1907, 72 copies, 1 vellum; 1 March 1908, 75 copies, 1 vellum; 1 March 1909, 59 copies, 1 vellum; 1 March 1910, 57 copies, 1 vellum; 1 March 1911, 53 copies, 1 vellum (Private ledger).

COPIES SEEN: Ashmolean. BL [lacks spine]. Bancroft. NYPL (Bookplate of John Shaw Billings Memorial Fund). SFPL.

EP27 • Christina Rossetti. Verses. 1906.

[type orn: trefoil] VERSES BY CHRISTINA G. ROSSETTI. | [type orn: trefoil] REPRINTED FROM G. POLIDORI'S | EDITION OF 1847. EDITED BY J. D. SYMON. | [Pressmark III] | THIS REPRINT IS MADE BY ARRANGE- | MENT WITH MESSRS. MACMILLAN & | CO., LTD., AND SOLD AT THE ERAGNY | PRESS, THE BROOK, HAMMERSMITH, | LONDON, W.

COLOPHON: [type orn: trefoil] THIS REPRINT OF CHRISTINA G. | ROSSETTI'S EARLIEST VERSES FOL- | LOWS THE TEXT OF G. POLIDORI'S | EDITION OF 1847, & HAS BEEN EDITED |

AND SEEN THROUGH THE PRESS BY | J. D. SYMON. [type orn: trefoil] THE DECORATIONS | HAVE BEEN DESIGNED BY LUCIEN | PISSARRO AND ENGRAVED ON THE | WOOD BY ESTHER & LUCIEN PISSAR- | RO, BY WHOM THE BOOK, FINISHED | IN OCTOBER 1906, HAS BEEN PRIN- | TED AT THEIR ERAGNY PRESS. | [type orn: trefoil] This edition is strictly limited to 175 paper | and 10 vellum copies.

COLLATION: small demy 8°: [a]^{1} b^{6} c^{4}–j^{4} k^{2}. 41 leaves, pp. [i–ii] i ii–v [vi] [1–2] 3–75 [76]

PAPER AND DIMENSIONS: Arches. Leaf: 212 x 128 mm.

TYPE: Brook

ILLUSTRATIONS, ORNAMENTS, AND INITIALS: [one historiated initial and one ornament in red; forty-two initials and pressmark in black and white] [a]1^{r}: Pressmark III, 76 mm. diameter (Fern 112 [SB 152]). b1^{r}: Initial O (Fern 319 [SB 140]). b3^{r}: Ornament, 66 x 73 mm. (Fern 376 [SB 295]) in red. b4^{r}: Historiated initial O, "Woman Kneeling Picking Flowers," 60 x 62 mm. (Fern 167 [SB 241]). c3^{v}: Initial I (Fern 316 [SB 137]). d1^{r}: Initial I (Fern 316 [SB 137]). d2^{r}: Initial H (Fern 315 [SB 136]). d3^{r}: Initials T, S (NIF). d4^{v}: Initial Y (NIF). e2^{r}: Initial L (Fern 317 [SB 138]), Initial F (NIF). e2^{v}: Initial I (Fern 316 [SB 137]). e3^{r}: Initial A (NIF). e3^{v}: Initial W (NIF). e4^{r}: Initial W (NIF). e4v: Initial T (NIF). f1^{r}: Initial W (NIF). f2r: Initial O (Fern 319); Initial L (Fern 317 [SB 138]). f3^{r}: Initial W (NIF). f3^{v}: Initial I (Fern 316 [SB 137]). g1^{v}: Initial O (Fern 319 [SB 140]). g2^{r}: Initial S (NIF); C (Fern 313). g2^{v}: Initial O (Fern 319 [SB 140]). g3^{v}: Initial L (Fern 317 [SB 138]). g4^{r}: Initial C (Fern 313 [SB 134]). g4^{v}: Initial G (NIF). h1^{r}: Initial W (NIF). h1^{v}: Initial A (NIF). h2^{v}: Initial W (NIF). h3^{v}: Initial L (Fern 317). i1^{r}: Initial I (Fern 316 [SB 137]); T (NIF). i2^{r}: Initial N (NIF). i2^{v}: Initial O (Fern 319 [SB 140]). i3^{r}: Initial L (Fern 317 [SB 138]). i3^{v}: Initial T (NIF); R (NIF). i4^{v}: Initial O (Fern 319 [SB 140]). j2^{r}: Initial S (NIF). j3^{r}: Initial T (NIF). j4^{r}: Initial A (NIF); H (Fern 315 [SB 136]). k1^{r}: Initial N (NIF).

CONTENTS: [a]1^{r}: title. [a]1^{v}: blank. b1^{r}–b2^{r}: Preface by J. D. Symon. b2^{v}: blank. b3^{r}: second title. b3^{v}: A FEW WORDS TO THE READER by G. Polidori. b4^{r}–k2^{r}: text. k2^{v}: colophon.

ERRATA: [type orn: trefoil] ERRATA. | PAGE 21, line 12: for «band», read «bands» | Page 40, line 8: for «his», read «His»

BINDING: Quarter Michallet blue paper, gold-stamped on upper left corner: [orn: entwined leaves] VERSES. | CHRISTINA | G. ROSSETTI. Buff paper boards with a repeat pattern of "saxifrage" (NIF) printed in green and yellow ink.

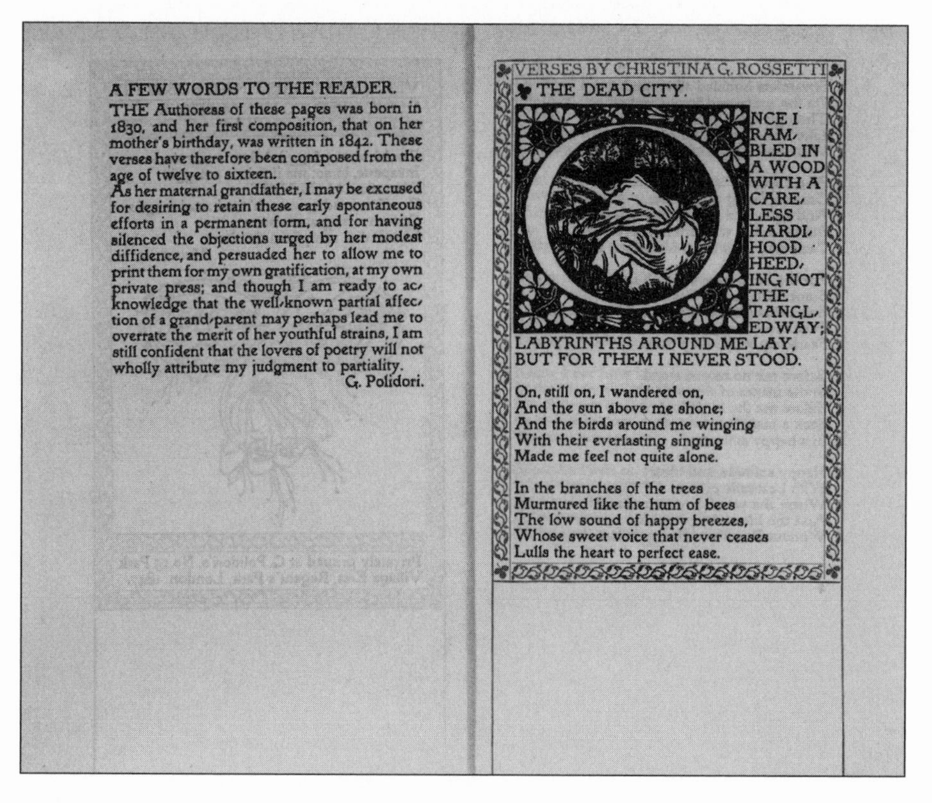

A FEW WORDS TO THE READER.

THE Authoress of these pages was born in 1830, and her first composition, that on her mother's birthday, was written in 1842. These verses have therefore been composed from the age of twelve to sixteen.

As her maternal grandfather, I may be excused for desiring to retain these early spontaneous efforts in a permanent form, and for having silenced the objections urged by her modest diffidence, and persuaded her to allow me to print them for my own gratification, at my own private press; and though I am ready to acknowledge that the well-known partial affection of a grand-parent may perhaps lead me to overrate the merit of her youthful strains, I am still confident that the lovers of poetry will not wholly attribute my judgment to partiality.

G. Polidori.

VERSES BY CHRISTINA G. ROSSETTI

THE DEAD CITY.

ONCE I RAMBLED IN A WOOD WITH A CARELESS HARDIHOOD HEEDING NOT THE TANGLED WAY; LABYRINTHS AROUND ME LAY, BUT FOR THEM I NEVER STOOD.

On, still on, I wandered on,
And the sun above me shone;
And the birds around me winging
With their everlasting singing
Made me feel not quite alone.

In the branches of the trees
Murmured like the hum of bees
The low sound of happy breezes,
Whose sweet voice that never ceases
Lulls the heart to perfect ease.

Opening pages. *Verses by Christina G. Rossetti*, 1906. (Ashmolean Museum, Oxford)

PUBLICATION: 150 copies for sale at 1 guinea and 8 vellum at 5 guineas. Published November 1906.

RELATED MATERIAL: Drawing for title-page ornament with initial O (not used); ink drawing of binding design with instructions "increase to 3 inches"; enlarged binding design (photo) in brown and white; leather piece with gold stamping with two different designs. One, an initial O; the other an O with a "Japanese" scene.

NOTES: Troubles continued with Leighton, Son, and Hodge. The second sample copy of the binding was returned to Esther on 2 November 1906. The stamping was still neither firm nor clear enough; the endpapers were unequal, but the size of the boards was finally right. Esther did not wish the book to be any more expensive than usual (given the cost they incurred to procure copyright permission). Leighton replied on 3 November that he was proceeding with the binding and every possible care would be taken. "I must point out, however, that it is quite impossible to lower the left-hand endpaper without raising the right hand one. It is not a practical plan to make the squares larger without cutting more off the book. You are aware, of course, that leather binders in binding single copies of books do that, I do not therefore say that what you want cannot be done. It would be enormously costly, however, and would not be quite in character, I think, with a binding issued from the Press. That is, however, the last process, if you wish the endpaper cut out like a leather bound book please let me know." On 10 November, Esther sent three sheets of paper for the endpapers, having not supplied enough in the beginning, and the ones she sent were far from fresh—having run out of their paper supply. Leighton needed additional copies of signatures f and g—for which Esther could only send one and two respectively. And she sent the insertions for signature d. By this time, the bound books were to Esther's liking. But when she received the 12 final copies on 28 November she complained that she had to clean off finger marks.

J. D. Symon, who wrote the preface, received 5 copies of *Verses*. He found the book to be charming. He wrote to the Pissarros (11 Nov. 1906), ". . . I feel the honour of inclusion in your series more than I deserve, untried literary person as I am, whose laziness had let all those years slip away with never a justification of my craft. Your faith is as great as it is flattering."

Notices appeared in the *Evening News* (London), November 1906, and the *Illustrated London News*, 1 December 1906.

In stock: 1 March 1907, 90 copies, 3 vellum; 1 March 1908, 88 copies, 3 vellum; 1 March 1909, 81 copies, 3 vellum; 1 March 1910, 78 copies, 3 vellum; 79 Rossetti, 2 vellum (Private ledger).

COPIES SEEN: Ashmolean. BL (deposited 17 November 1906). Bancroft. Huntington. NYPL (Bookplate of John Shaw Billings Memorial Fund). SFPL (Provenance: Robert Grabhorn).

EP28 • Charles Perrault. Riquet à la houppe. 1907.

[in black and red] [type orn: trefoil] RIQUET À LA HOUPPE. | [on right top shoulder] (Deux | Versions | d'un Con- | te de ma Mère Loye.) | "Geese," | M.DCCCC.VII.

COLOPHON: [in black and red] [type orn: trefoil] IN THIS EDITION of RIQUET | À LA HOUPPE THE FIRST | VERSION IS by Ch. PERRAULT | AND THE SECOND, TAKEN | FROM a MANUSCRIPT in THE | MAZARINE LIBRARY, PARIS, | IS BY AN UNKOWN AU- | THOR OF THE XVIIth CEN- | TURY. | [type orn: trefoil] The two illustrations were de- | signed and engraved on the wood by | Lucien Pissarro. The ornaments and | initial letters were designed by L. | Pissarro & engraved by E. Pissarro. | The book has been printed by them | at their Eragny Press, The Brook, | Hammersmith, & finished in April, | 1907. h3^{v}: [type orn: trefoil] This edition is strictly limited to | 80 copies on paper and 8 on vellum. | Of the paper copies, 75 are printed | in red & black throughout & 5 in gray | and orange. | [type orn: trefoil] Sold by the Eragny Press. | h4^{r}: [Pressmark III]

COLLATION: small demy 16°: $[a]^{1}$ b^{4}–d^{4} $[e]^{1}$ f^{4}–h^{4}. 26 leaves, pp. [1–3] 4–25 [26–27] 28–48 [49–52]

PAPER AND DIMENSIONS: Arches. Leaf: 133 x 107 mm.

TYPE: Brook

ILLUSTRATIONS, ORNAMENTS, AND INITIALS: [two four-color engraved historiated initials; forty-three initials in red; two cul-de-lampes and pressmark in black and white] [all initial letters are in red] [a]1^{r}: "Geese," 78 mm. (Fern 113 [SB 154]). b1^{r}: four-block color historiated intial IL, "Riquet à la houppe. I.," 98 x 68 mm. (Fern 169 [SB 242]). b1^{v}: Initial T (NIF) in red. b2^{r}: Initial A (NIF). b3^{r}: Initial A (Fern 312 [SB 133]). b3^{v}: Initial Q (Fern 320 [SB 141]). b4^{r}: Initial U (NIF). b4^{v}: Initial C (NIF). c1^{v}: Initial L (Fern 317 [SB 138]). c2^{r}: Initial Q (NIF). c2^{v}: Initial L (Fern 317 [SB 138]). c3^{r}: Initial E (NIF). c4^{r}: Initial L (Fern 317 [SB 138]). c4v: Initial E (Fern 314 [SB 135]). d1^{v}: Initial S (NIF). d2^{v}: Initial L (Fern 317 [SB 138]). d3^{r}: Initial Q (Fern 320 [SB 141]). d3^{v}: Cul-de-lampe (NIF). [e]1^{r}: four-block color historiated initial U, "Riquet à la houppe. II.," 97 x 78 mm. (Fern 170 [SB 243]). f1^{r}: Initial U (Fern 321 [SB 142]). f1v: Initial M (Fern 318 [SB 139]); A (Fern 312 [SB 133]). f2^{r}: Initial V (NIF); A (Fern 312 [SB 133]). f2^{v}: Initial U (Fern 321 [SB 142]); P (NIF). f3^{r}: Initial L (Fern 317 [SB 138]); E (Fern 314 [SB 135]). f3^{v}: Initial C (NIF); S (NIF). f4^{r}: Initial U (NIF); Q (Fern 320 [SB 141]). f4^{v}: Initial I (Fern 316 [SB 137]). g1^{r}: Initial R (NIF). g1^{v}: Initial L (Fern 317 [SB 138]). g2^{r}: Initial E (Fern 314 [SB 135]). g2^{v}: Initial R (NIF); L (Fern 317 [SB 138]). g3^{r}: Initial I (Fern 313 [SB 134]). g3^{v}: Initial L (Fern 317 [SB 138]). g4^{r}: Initial I (Fern 313 [SB 134]). h1^{r}: Initial L (Fern 317 [SB 138]); M (Fern 318 [SB 139]). h1^{v}: Initial L (Fern 317 [SB 138]); L (Fern 317 [SB 138]]). h2^{r}: Initial U (Fern 321 [SB 142]). h2^{v}: Cul-de-lampe (NIF). h4^{r}: Pressmark III, 76 mm. diameter (Fern 112 [SB 154]). Red rules.

CONTENTS: [a]1^{r}: title. [a]1^{v}: blank. b1^{r}–d3^{v}: Riquet à la houppe. I. d4^{r}–h3^{r}: Riquet à la houppe. II. h3^{v}: blank. II. h3^{v}–h3^{v}: colophon. h4^{r}: pressmark.

BINDING: Quarter vellum with printed paper label inset on upper left corner with woodcut ornament (NIF) printed in black, pink and green: [within rule] RIQUET À | [rule] [orn] la HOUPPE. Michallet blue paper boards.

PUBLICATION: 75 paper copies for sale at 25 shillings and 8 vellum copies at 4 guineas. Published in May 1907.

RELATED MATERIAL: Drawing for a cul-de-lampe of two bachelor buttons (not used).

PROSPECTUS: [210 x 101 mm., 1 leaf with red initial R (SB 296)] No. 12. Riquet à la houppe | Notice: The first of these two versions is by Charles Perrault; | the second is from a XVIIth Century manuscript | in the Mazarine Library in Paris. It is by an | unknown writer, who at the same time as Perrault, | had the idea of collecting French folk tales. His | version is very different from Perrault's celebrated | tale, and is nearer the legend of the gnome | Ruebezahl as Musaeus gathered it from the | peasants of the Hartz mountains.

With two original woodcuts designed and engraved by L. Pissarro, | in which large decorative initials frame small illustrations. | These are printed in four colours.

NOTES: The Pissarros considered using tinted vellum for the binding; the choice was between a pale buff or white. They finally settled on the white vellum (Esther Pissarro to Leighton, 5 May 1907 and 10 May 1907). The binding process was no easier for this edition than any of the others. Leighton's binders had written on four of the copies' endpapers "shabby copy," thereby rendering them "useless." Esther sent more paper for the new endsheets and requested that they reuse the cases again because there were no more labels. Esther complained about the sewing; she thought it unnecessary to use double thread for so small a book, and the needle was leaving large holes which let glue through (Esther Pissarro to Leighton, 7 June 1907). On 10 June 1907, Esther sent the eight vellum copies to Leighton to be bound. She asked that they be sewn with silk, as usual (Esther Pissarro to Leighton, 10 June 1907).

Riquet à la houppe was published on 20 May (Esther Pissarro to Mr. Watson, 6 May 1907).

With the publication of a French text, the first since 1903 and the first French text printed in the Brook type, Lucien once again sought out a French distributor. He wrote to Alfred Vallette, director of the Mercure de France (Lucien Pissarro to Alfred Vallette, 4 June 1907). Vallette had assisted Lucien with *The Queen of the Fishes* and *Moralités legendaries.* The Mercure de France was the only French publisher that Lucien believed understood his work. He was eager to cultivate a French clientele once again, partly because the English market for Eragny Press books had become so dismal.

Reviewed in the *Athenaeum*, 20 July 1907.

Roger Marx called the small book "delicious" (Roger Marx to Lucien Pissarro, 4 August 1907).

In stock: 1 March 1908, 10 copies, 2 vellum; 1 March 1909, 3 copies, 2 vellum; 1 March 1910, 1 copy, 2 vellum; 1 March 1911, 1 copy, 1 vellum (Private ledger).

COPIES SEEN: Ashmolean. Bancroft. BL (deposited 12 June 1907). LC (Bookplate of Louise M. Glazier; unopened). NYPL (Bookplate of John Shaw Billings Memorial Fund). SFPL.

EP29 • Gerard de Nerval. Histoire de la reine du matin et de Soliman prince des génies. 1909.

[in black and gray-green] GERARD DE NERVAL. | [woodcut orn (NIF)] [large caps. in gold outlined in gray-green]: HISTOIRE [woodcut orn (NIF)] | DE LA REINE DU | MATIN & DE SOLI- | MAN

PRINCE DES | [woodcut orn (NIF)] GÉNIES [woodcut orn (NIF)] | [small caps.]: LES CENT BIBLIOPHILES | [vignette, 55 x 94 mm. (Fern 195 [SB 279])] | THE ERAGNY PRESS, «THE BROOK», | [type orn: two flowers] | HAMMERSMITH, LONDON, W. [type orn: two flowers] | M. D. CCCC. IX

COLOPHON: [in black and gray-green] [type orn: trefoil] CETTE LÉGENDE EXTRAITE DU | «VOYAGE EN ORIENT», A ÉTÉ IMPRI- | MÉE POUR LA SOCIÉTÉ DES CENT BI- | BLIOPHILES. [type orn: trefoil] LES ILLUSTRATIONS | DESSINÉES PAR LUCIEN PISSARRO & | GRAVÉES SUR BOIS PAR ESTHER & | LUCIEN PISSARRO. [type orn: trefoil] LE PAPIER SPÉCIALEMENT FABRIQUÉ PAR LES PA- | PETERIES D'ARCHES AVEC DES CHIF- | FONS PUR FIL. | [Pressmark III] | [type orn: trefoil] LE LIVRE COMMENCÉ EN DÉCEM- | BRE 1907 FUT TERMINÉ EN AOÛT | 1909 SUR LES | PRESSES D'ÉRAGNY PAR | LUCIEN & ESTHER PISSARRO AVEC | L'AIDE DE T. TAYLOR.

COLLATION: 8°: $[a]^2$: π^1 $[b]^1$ c^2–z^2 $2a^2$–$2n^2$. 80 leaves, pp. [1–5] 12–159 [160]

PAPER: Arches with Les Cent Bibliophiles and Eragny Press watermarks. Leaf: 222 x 140 mm.

TYPE: Brook

ILLUSTRATIONS, ORNAMENTS, AND INITIALS: [thirty-two wood engravings: twelve historiated initials printed in four colors (primarily in greens, blues, yellows, oranges) and gold; thirteen illustrations printed in green-gray ink; six ornaments printed in green-gray ink and gold (where indicated); and one opening-page illustration within border in four colors] $\pi 1^r$: five-color engraved border and illustration, 184 x 107 mm. (Fern 174 [SB 256]); Historiated initial P, 30 x 19 mm. (NIF). $c4^v$: Cul-de-lampe, 32 x 64 mm. (NIF). $d1^r$: Historiated initial P, 49 x 32 mm. (Fern 175 [SB 247]). $e1^r$: "The Procession," 67 x 74 mm. (Fern 176 [SB 258]). $f2^v$: "The King and His Favorite," 64 x 72 mm. (Fern 177 [SB 257]). $h1^v$: Historiated initial N, 46 x 49 mm. (Fern 178 [SB 248]). $i2^r$: "The King Before His Subjects," 67 x 74 mm. (Fern 181 [SB 263 bis]). $m1^v$: Historiated initial C, 45 x 45 mm. (Fern 182 [SB 259]). $o2^v$: "At the Fountain," 66 x 73 mm. (Fern 183 [SB 264]). $p1^r$: Cul-de-lampe, 18 x 61 mm. (Fern 196 [SB 267]). $p1^v$: Historiated initial A, 46 x 47 mm. (Fern 184 [SB 251]). $r1^v$: Historiated initial T, 74 x 79 mm. (NIF). $r2^r$: "The Explosion," 74 x 81 mm. (NIF). $s2^r$: "The Fire," 71 x 79 mm. (Fern 197 [SB 268]). $u1^r$: Cul-de-lampe, 42 x 61 mm. (Fern 186 [SB 265]). $u1^v$: Historiated initial I, 47 x 42 mm. (Fern 187 [SB 255]). $v2^r$: "The Blessing," 65 x 71 mm. (Fern 198 [SB 277]). $x2^v$: Historiated initial C, 44 x 44 mm. (Fern 188 [SB 249]). $y1^r$: "Women by the Stream," 80 x 72 mm. (Fern 199 [SB 270]). $y2^v$: "Balkis au Lavis," 67 x 72 mm.

(Fern 200 [SB 269]). z2^{v}: "Woman in Thought," 63 x 69 mm. (Fern 156 [SB 227]). 2b2^{v}: "Messenger and Women," 75 x 79 mm. (Fern 201 [SB 271]). 2c1^{v}: Historiated initial S, 47 x 46 mm. (Fern 189 [SB 253]). 2c2^{v}: "The Old Priest," 68 x 72 mm. (Fern 202 [SB 272]). 2e2^{v}: Cul-de-lampe, 20 x 91 mm. (Fern 374 [SB 280]). 2f1^{r}: Historiated initial A, 47 x 50 mm. (Fern 203 [SB 273]). 2g2^{r}: "The Audience," 75 x 75 mm. (Fern 204 [SB 278]). 2h1^{r}: Cul-de-lampe, 49 x 96 mm. (Fern 205 [SB 274 bis]). 2h1^{v}: Historiated initial L, 48 x 46 mm. (Fern 190 [SB 245]). 2j2^{r}: "Le Narcotique," 67 x 71 mm. (Fern 206 [SB 275]). 2k1^{v}: Historiated initial T, 47 x 49 mm. (Fern 207 [SB 274]). 2m2^{v}: Headpiece in gray-green ink and gold, 38 x 89 mm. (Fern 208 [SB 276]). 2n2^{v}: Pressmark III, 76 mm. diameter (Fern 112 [152]).

CONTENTS: [a]1^{r}: half title: [type orn: trefoil] HISTOIRE DE LA REINE DU MATIN | ET DE SOLIMAN BEN-DAOUD. [a]1^{v}: Tirage à 130 exemplaires numérotés. No. [followed by number and name]. [a]2^{r}: blank. [a]2^{v}: title. π1^{r}: frontispiece. π1^{r}–c2^{v}: I. ADONIRAM. d1^{r}–h1^{v}: II. BALKIS. h1^{v}–l2^{v}: III. LE TEMPLE. m1^{r}–p1^{r}: IV. MELLO. p1^{v}–r1^{r}: V. LA MER D'AIRAIN. r1^{v}–u1^{r}: VI. L'APPARITION. u1^{v}–x2^{r}: VII. LE MONDE SOUTERRAIN. x2^{v}–2c1^{r}: VIII. LA LAVOIR DE SILOE. 2c1^{v}–2e2^{v}: LES TROIS COMPAGNONS. 2f1^{r}–2h1^{r}: X. L'ENTREVUE. 2h1^{v}–2k1^{r}: XI. LE SOUPER DU ROI. 2k1^{v}–2n2^{r}: XII. MAKENACH. 2n2^{v}: colophon.

BINDING: Soft green morocco, outer and inner covers gold stamped with repeat pattern of "carnation." Spine gold stamped: [from bottom to top] [orn: trefoil] GERARD DE NERVAL [orn: trefoil] HISTOIRE DE LA REINE DU MATIN ET DE SOLIMAN.

PUBLICATION: 130 copies printed for the French book club, La Société des Cent Bibliophiles.

RELATED MATERIAL: Drawings on post card for initials B, F, N (not used); drawing, young boy playing string instrument; watercolor drawing of initial P with bird; mounted cul-de-lampe.

NOTES: Although Camille had met Eugène Rodrigues in late 1897 and had hoped that he would commission a book from Lucien, nothing came of that meeting. Introduced to Eugène Rodrigues by Roger Marx, Lucien began negotiations with Rodrigues, president of La Société des cents bibliophiles, on 22 September 1907. Successful negotiations ended on 9 October 1907. Rodrigues wanted a large-format edition with color wood engravings. But an Eragny Press book could not be in a large format due to the difficulties with registration in printing two or three colors. Lucien suggested a format similar to the *Songs by Ben Jonson* and sent a copy to Rodrigues for his approval. Paper was also an issue. Lucien, when last in Paris, went to Perrigot-Masure. Lucien considered the paper that he had specially made there to be optimal for printing in color, but

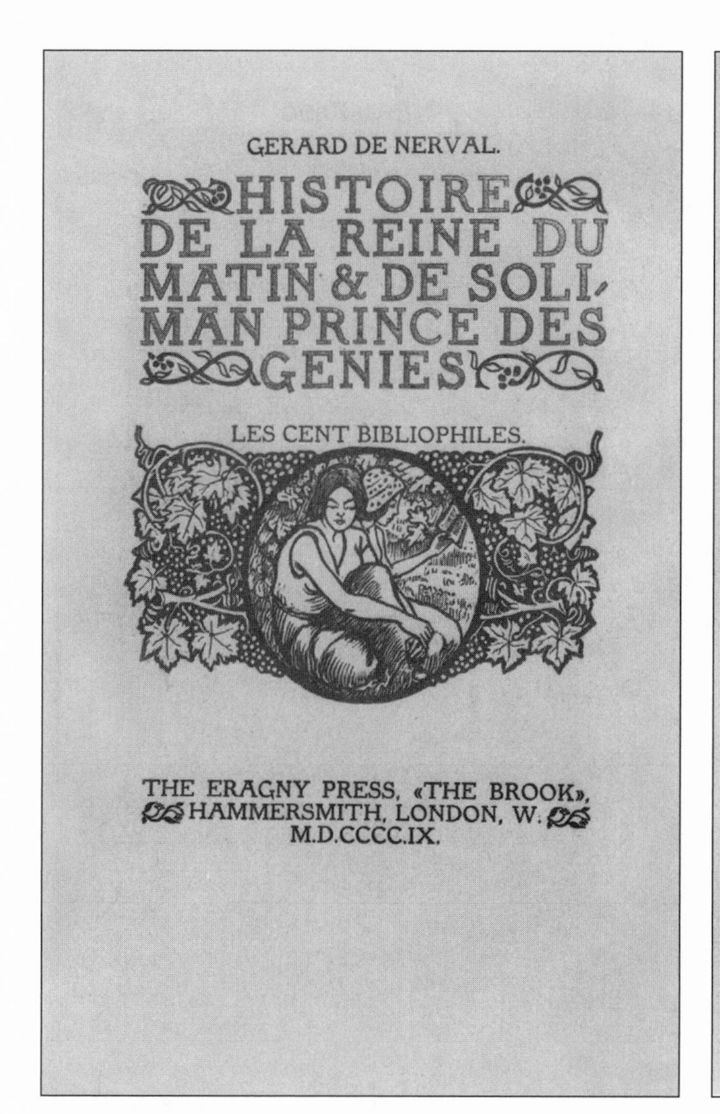

Title pages. Gerard de Nerval, *Histoire de la reine du matin et de Soliman prince des génies,* 1909. (Ashmolean Museum, Oxford)

the Société wished to have a more opaque paper, like the Japanese vellum used in *The Queen of the Fishes.* Lucien explained to Rodrigues that Japanese vellum works very well for engravings but not for typography. Lucien noted that the book of de Nerval would be a highly ornamented book and as typographic as possible, remaining strictly within the limits of the art (Lucien Pissarro to Eugène Rodrigues, 25 November 1907 and 4 December 1907).

Lucien ordered the paper on the 7 February 1908 from Perrigot-Masure. He insisted on the following specifications:

1. the quality, marks, weight, etc. must conform to the sample
2. the pulp should be very clean
3. paper to be made in half sheets of 275 x 435 mm.
4. must contain only two watermarks, that of Eragny and that of the Cents bibliophiles and they must be placed exactly as indicated (Lucien Pissarro to Perrigot-Masure, 7 February 1908)
5. twelve reams would be required (Lucien Pissarro to Perrigot-Masure, 12 February 1908)

In late February 1908, Lucien sent Rodrigues proofs of his first engravings. He had decided to make the initial letters in color because he considered color engravings to be preferable in a small format. For sometime, Lucien had been looking for a means to continue to print color with gold, a considerably difficult technique to do at the Press. He hoped to have, for the first time, initial letters printed in both gold and color (Lucien Pissarro to Eugène Rodrigues, 27 February 1908).

On 27 June 1908, Lucien sent Rodrigues the first proofs of the text for proofreading. By mid-October, Lucien had finished signatures f and g, having previously sent signatures c, d, e, and h. Signatures f and g were done after h so that two color formes could be done together for purely technical reasons. Lucien apologized for the slow progress, noting that the printing in gold was giving them enormous trouble (Lucien Pissarro to Eugène Rodrigues, 11 October 1908).

By mid-February 1909 Lucien apologized again to Rodrigues for the lack of progress. The three months of autumn and the winter months made color printing difficult due to the short days and artificial light. Lucien hoped to have the book finished by either June or July (Lucien Pissarro to Eugène Rodrigues, 15 February 1909).

During the last week in February, discussions concerning the binding were underway. Lucien initially proposed a portfolio tied with ribbons on which the title page would be printed in a combination of colors and, leaving himself some leeway, perhaps in some other arrangement. Lucien also suggested that the books be boxed. He noted there was time enough to make this decision (Lucien Pissarro to Eugène Rodrigues, 21 February 1909). A week later, Lucien proposed to do the binding in calfskin imprinted with an overall design—this would be a less expensive option than the earlier proposal (Lucien Pissarro to Eugène Rodrigues, 3 March 1909). On 16 April, Lucien sent two sample bindings to Rodrigues. The sample marked A would cost 5.60 frs. and that marked B would cost 2.50 frs. Either one would be boxed in a white carton. Lucien also reported to Rodrigues that he had not been able to decide on a definite design for the binding ornament so that it was difficult to know what the cost would be for stamping the leather—it would depend on the size of the block and the intricacies of the engraving, but in any case, it would still be a small part of the cost of the binding (Lucien Pissarro to Eugène Rodrigues, 16 April 1909). Rodrigues preferred the cheaper calfskin and thought that lining them with board would not make the binding limp enough. Esther inquired of Leighton whether the binding could be lined with leather and what would be the cost. Color had not yet been decided. Esther asked Leighton to send her color samples of the leather (Esther Pissarro to Leighton, 26 April 1909). The cost for this style was 4.35 frs. (Lucien Pissarro to Eugène Rodrigues, 6 May 1909). By 13 May, Lucien had in hand a sample binding based on Rodrigues' suggestion. Lucien proposed a sand color for the binding (Lucien Pissarro to Eugène Rodrigues, 13 May 1909).

Realizing that the book could not be finished by the end of June, Lucien wrote to Rodrigues to ask for an additional eight weeks. Although the days were longer, the warm weather of late spring made working with the paper more difficult. Lucien was devasted thinking that Rodrigues might not understand all the delays (Lucien Pissarro to Eugène Rodrigues, 25 May 1909). Lucien had ordered the calfskin and as soon as it arrived he sent a sample to Rodrigues for him to see the sand color. The color wasn't exactly the shade that Lucien had hoped for, but the manufacturer said that the divergence in the color was caused by the differences in calfskin which takes dye differently (Lucien Pissarro to Eugène Rodgrigues, early June 1909). He hoped that Rodrigues' members would think the book would be worth the wait.

Initial N. Gerard de Nerval, *Histoire de la reine du matin et de Soliman prince des génies,* 1909.

The Pissarros logged their printing time. For those signatures printed in color, six printings were necessary. An experiment with the frontispiece required 11 days; to actually print it required another 22 days. Signature d in 7 colors required 14.5 days; signature h in 6 colors, 9.5 days; signature m in 6 colors, 17.5 days; signature p in 6 colors, 11.5 days; signature r in 7 colors, 11.5 days; signature u in 7 colors, 13 days; signature x in 6 colors 12 days; signature 2c in 7 colors, 10.5 days, signature 2f in 6 colors, 7 days; signature 2h in 7 colors, 9.5 days; signature 2k in 6 colors, 5.5 days for a total of 155 days. Those sheets printed in black and gray required two printings. Signatures c and e in 2 colors, 7 days; signatures f and g in 3 colors, 5.5 days; k and l in black only, 3.5 days; i and j in 2 colors, 4.5 days, n and o in 3 colors, 8 days; q and s in 2 colors, 6 days; t and v in 2 colors, 5.5 days; w and y in 3 colors, 5.5 days; z–2a in 2 colors, 4 days; 2b–2d in 2 colors, 5.5 days; 2e–2g in 2 colors, 5.5 days; 2i–2k in 2 colors, 7 days; 2j–2m in 3 colors (gold), 10 days; 2n in 2 colors, 6.5 days— for a total of 84 days.

On 15 August, Lucien sent the final sheets of the book to Rodrigues. Bound copies would be ready in three weeks, but the books were not sent to Paris until 22 October 1909. At that point, Lucien made an accounting of the production expenses (not including the cost of the ornament for the binding and the cost of the binding itself). The expenses came to 4,493.20 francs. This figure did not include the labor costs of the Pissarros, who worked for twenty months on the book. In justifying the expenses, and asking for an additional supplement, Lucien noted that he did everything he could to make the book a success. Thirty-two engravings, of which twelve were printed in four colors and in 23-carat gold leaf, presented countless difficulties. The book as originally planned was to have at least twenty engravings, four of which were to be in color. At Rodrigues' suggestion, Lucien added twelve more engravings, eight of which were in color and all the color engravings. Gold too added considerably to the printing time. Thus, he believed, he was justified in asking for a supplement. Lucien included a list of expenses classified by category (Lucien Pissarro to Rodrigues, 22 October 1909).

Although La Société des cents bibliophiles did supplement the original agreement by 2,500 frs., they were resistant to doing so. As Lucien noted, the question of the supplement had nothing to do with the artistic aspects of the book, only commercial considerations—that it would cost more to print a poor design in five colors than it would a masterpiece in one color. Lucien argued that he could have made a book equally ornate and less expensive to produce, but he did not restrict himself by cost. He made the book without thinking of the time and the difficulties caused by printing in color and gold. He had hoped the supplement would be more in keeping with the percent of additional work—at least 30 percent rather than 25 percent of the original agreement. Lucien wished to vindicate himself to Rodrigues. Lucien noted that he would like to ignore the monetary aspect, in that what concerned him was his work; he assured Rodrigues that it pained him to have to bring up matters which could spoil even a part of his pleasure over the book (Lucien Pissarro to Eugène Rodrigues, 13 November 1909).

As part of the contract, Lucien sent the woodblocks to the Société. (Fern indicates that the blocks were destroyed. I have not confirmed whether the blocks are with the Société.)

Lucien asked Rodrigues if he might deposit a copy of de Nerval in the British Museum and Rodrigues consented (Lucien Pissarro to Eugène Rodrigues, 27 June 1908). (I have not been able to locate a copy in the British Library.)

COPIES SEEN: Ashmolean. Bancroft (Ex-libris Harry Alfred Fowler, No. 43 M. Rémy Garnier, bound by "C. McL-1912"). NYPL (No. 94 Auguste Tricaud).

EP30 • Judith Gautier. Album de poëmes tirés du livre de jade. 1911.

[within vertical and horizontal red rules] [in red and gray] [rule] [type orn: trefoil] JUDITH GAUTIER | DE L'ACADÉMIE GONCOURT. | [rule] | [rule] | [large caps in gold outlined in gray] ALBUM DE POEMES | [rule] | TIRES DU LIVRE DE | [rule] | [rule] | JADE | [rule] | [rule] | [ideogram] |[ideogram] | [rule] | THE ERAGNY PRESS, THE BROOK, | HAMMERSMITH, LONDON, W. | M.D.CCCC.XI. | [rule] | 1 | [rule]

COLOPHON: [gold initial outlined in gray] I [in gray] N THIS, THE 14th BOOK PRINTED IN | THE BROOK TYPE, THE COLORED | ILLUSTRATIONS & ORNAMENTS | HAVE BEEN DESIGNED BY LUCIEN | PISSARRO & ENGRAVED ON THE | WOOD BY LUCIEN AND ESTHER | PISSARRO. | [red rule] | [gold initial] T [in gray] HE BOOK HAS BEEN PRINTED | BY E. AND L. PISSARRO AT THEIR | ERAGNY PRESS, WITH THE HELP | OF T. TAYLOR, AND FINISHED IN | SEPTEMBER, 1911. | [red rule] | [gold initial] S [in gray] OLD BY THE ERAGNY PRESS, | THE BROOK, HAMMERSMITH, | LONDON, W. | [red rule] | [in red] This edition is strictly limited to 125 copies | for sale and 5 copies for the Museums. | Nos. 1 to 10 are on Roman vellum and the | remainder on Japanese vellum. | [p. 27] Pressmark III.

COLLATION: 8°: 27 folded pages printed on 1 side only

PAPER: Japanese vellum. Leaf: 196 x 120 mm.

TYPE: Brook

ILLUSTRATIONS, ORNAMENTS, AND INITIALS: [seven five-block color wood-engraved illustrations; one three-block color cul-de-lampe; one initial, nine ornaments and cul-de-lampes and pressmark in dark gray] [all pages within horizontal and vertical red rules] p. 3: Initial T, 49 x 51 mm. (Fern 220 [SB 294]) p. 7: Five-block color illustration, "Ivresse d'amour," 72 mm. diameter (Fern 214 [SB 288]). p. 8: Cul-de-lampe (NIF). p. 9: Five-block color illustration, "Chant des oiseaux le soir," 66 mm. diameter (Fern 221 [SB 293]). p. 10: Cul-de-lampe (NIF). p. 11: Five-block color illustration, "L'Empereur," 70 mm. diameter (Fern 222 [SB 292]). p. 13: Five-block color illustration, "Mes yeux fixes," 66 mm. diameter (Fern 215 [SB 285]). p. 14: Bachelor button ornament (NIF). p. 15: Bachelor button ornament (variation) (NIF). p. 16: Bachelor button cul-de-lampe (Fern 377 [SB 296]). p. 17: Five-block color print, "Froidure printanière," 67 mm. diameter (Fern 216 [SB 286]). p. 18: Ornament (Fern 379 [SB 297]). p. 19: Ornament (Fern 378 [SB 297]). p. 20: Cul-de-lampe (NIF). p. 21: Five-block color print, "Dans le palais," 65 mm. diameter (Fern 217 [SB 285bis]). p. 22: Cul-de-lampe (Fern 376 [SB 295]). p. 23: Five-block color illustration, "Le Lotus rouge," 69 mm. diameter (Fern 218 [SB 287]). p. 24: Lotus ornament (Fern 381 [SB 300]). p. 25: Cul-de-lampe (3 woodblocks), 56 mm. diameter (Fern 223 [SB 304]). p. 27: Pressmark III, 76 mm. diameter (Fern 112 [152). Shoulder notes in red.

CONTENTS: p. 1: Title. p. 2: subscriber's name. pp. 3–6: Preface by Diana White. pp. 7–25: text. p. 26: colophon. p. 27: pressmark.

BINDING: Full soft cream kid, green kid spine, bound in the Japanese manner; upper cover with title and ornament gold-stamped: JUDITH | GAUTIER. | [orn: fan] ALBUM DE | POEMES TIRES DU | LIVRE DE | JADE.

Binding. Judith Gautier, *Album de poëmes tirés du livre de jade*, 1911. (Ashmolean Museum, Oxford)

PUBLICATION: 130 copies printed. 125 copies on Japanese vellum for sale at £4. Five copies [unnumbered] for the museums.

RELATED MATERIAL: Drawing on graph paper for ornament on p. 20; tracing of drawing; Chinese characters used on title page.

PROSPECTUS: [in French, 1 leaf, 199 x 128 mm., on Japanese vellum, notes that vellum edition is out-of-print]; [in English, 1 leaf, 199 x 132 mm., on paper, with order form on verso, printed in red and gray].

NOTES: Roger Marx introduced Lucien to Judith Gautier, who agreed to allow Lucien to print her poems. In the negotiations, Lucien assured Miss Gautier the edition would be very limited and suggested a price of somewhere between 50 and 100 francs, depending on the number of copies printed as well as the number of illustrations. She would receive 5 copies. Miss Gautier generously gave Lucien some previously unpublisheed work, which he refused. This was an experimental work and if it did not succeed he did not want her previously unpublished work to be in something that might be badly done. However, if this were a success, he would be charmed to print some of her unpublished poems at a later time.

Work commenced on *Livre de jade* on Monday, 8 May 1911, with the preparation of the press; printing was finished on Monday, 9 October 1911.

Judith Gautier found the book to be well composed and of a remarkable perfection (Judith Gautier to Lucien Pissarro, 6 December 1911).

Campbell Dodgson on receiving the book wrote that it was exquisitely finished and the woodcuts looked beautiful on vellum (Campbell Dodgson to the Pissarros, 14 November 1911).

For T. S. Moore, the book was "in every sense exquisite." He thought the pictures among Lucien's best and the "burnished gold the red lines the many colours, necessitate looking back 4 centuries before one could find any rival to it" (T. S. Moore to the Pissarros, 3 December 1911).

Initial T (Fern 220 [SB 294]). Judith Gautier, *Album de poëmes tirés du livre de jade,* 1911.

L. W. Hodson wrote, "I have just received from Mr. Quaritch your Poemes tirés du Livre de Jade which I think in many ways the most beautiful little book of recent times. Seldom has the sympathetic 'study of appearances' so perfectly allied itself to the literature it clothes" (L. W. Hodson to the Pissarros, 21 January 1913).

In an undated letter to the Pissarros, Christine Angus Sickert, wife of Walter Sickert, wrote: "Your enchanting little book has just arrived and as Walter has gone to his usual evening resort—I am writing to thank you so very much for it. It is indeed all that its title conveys of charm and beauty made tangible and everything about it so delightful in design & colour. I have already spent a very pleasant half hour with it and hope to make a more thorough acquaintance with it this evening. I don't think we have ever been as pleased with our names as they appear in your beautiful lettering in that particularly delicate tone of gray or is it green?"

The Pissarros gave copies to Judith Gautier (4 paper copies and 1 vellum copy), Pierre Dauze, Roger Marx (1 paper copy and 1 vellum copy), Diana White, Samuel L. Bensusan, Robert Steele, T. S. Moore, Emile Verhaeren, Thomas Taylor, and Ida Henry.

COPIES SEEN: Ashmolean. BL (deposited 4 December 1911, No. 14). NYPL (No. 116. Bound with dark green kid with gold kid spine with gold-stamped carnation rondel; bookplate of John Shaw Billings Memorial Fund, purchased from Anderson Gallery, 7 April 1924, probably John Quinn's copy). SFPL (Provenance: Robert Grabhorn, on japanese vellum, No. 117).

EP31 • Émile Moselly. La Charrue d'érable. 1912/13.

[within border] ÉMILE MOSELLY. | [in large caps] LA CHARRUE D'ÉRABLE | [orn: apple] | [in caps] PARIS | LE | LIVRE CONTEMPORAIN. | M.CM.XII.

COLOPHON: [type orn: trefoil] L'ILLUSTRATION HORS TEXTE DE | CE LIVRE A ÉTÉ SPÉCIALEMENT DES- | SINÉE PAR CAMILLE PISSARRO POUR | TRE GRAVÉE PAR SON FILS LUCIEN | PISSARRO LEQUEL, CHARGÉ D'ORNER | LE TEXTE & DÉSIREUX D'Y MAINTENIR | L'UNITÉ DE DÉCORATION, Y A, DANS CE | BUT, ADAPTÉ LE PLUS SOUVENT POS- | SIBLE DES CROQUIS DE SON PÈRE. | [type orn: trefoil] TOUTES LES GRAVURES SUR | BOIS ONT ÉTÉ EXÉCUTÉES PAR | LUCIEN ET ESTHER PISSARRO. | [type orn: trefoil] PAR LEURS SOINS, ET A- | VEC L'AIDE DE T. TAYLOR, | L'OUVRAGE ENTIÈRE- | MENT TIRÉ SUR LES | PRESSES D'ÉRA- | GNY À ÉTÉ | ACHEVÉ | D'IMPRI- | MER | EN | DÉCEMBRE, M.CM.XII. w2^v: [Pressmark III] | [type orn: trefoil] The Eragny Press, The Brook, Hammersmith, | London.

COLLATION: 8°: [a]^2 [b]^2 c^2 π^1 d^2 e^2 f^3 g^2 h^3 i^2 j^3 k^2 l^3 m^2 n^3 o^2 p^3 q^2 r^3 s^2 t^3 u^2 v^3 w^2. 54 leaves, pp. [1–6] 7–105 [106–108]

PAPER AND DIMENSIONS: Arches with Le Livre Contemporain and Eragny Press watermarks. Leaf: 210 x 148.

TYPE: Brook

ILLUSTRATIONS, ORNAMENTS, AND INITIALS: [twelve wood-engraved illustrations, ten historiated initials, ten cul-de-lampes, one border; unless otherwise noted all wood engravings were printed from three color blocks in shades of peach, green, dark green, and blue] p. 3: Title-page border, 185 x 120 mm. (Fern 225 [SB 337]). p. 5: "Landscape," 33 x 92 mm. (Fern 209 [SB 281bis]). p. 7: "Peasant Women Gossiping," 62 x 90 mm. (Fern 227 [SB 310]); Historiated initial A for "La Baratte," 42 x 46 mm. (Fern 226 [SB 30]). p. 18: Cul-de-lampe for "La Baratte," 45 x 63 mm. (Fern 228 [SB 311]). p. 19: "Threshers," 64 x 91 mm. (Fern 229 [SB 314]); Historiated initial L for "Messidor," 42 x 47 mm. (Fern 230 [SB 315]). p. 26: Cul-de-lampe for "Messidor," 79 x 53 mm. (Fern 231 [SB 317]). p. 27: "Les Semailles," 64 x 91 mm. (Fern 232 [SB 312]); Initial P for "La Semailles," 42 x 47 mm. (Fern 233 [SB 313]). p. 38: Cul-de-lampe for "Lavandière nocturne," 56 x 46 mm. (Fern 234 [SB 321]). p. 39: "Lavandière nocturne," 63 x 92 mm. (Fern 235 [SB 318]); Initial H for "Lavandière nocturne," 41 x 47 mm. (Fern 236 [SB 320]). p. 46: Cul-de-lampe for "Sous les pommes," 61 x 54 mm. (Fern 248 [SB 328]). p. 47: "Harvester resting," 65 x 92 mm. (Fern 219 [SB 291]); Initial L for "Herbes coupées," 41 x 47 mm. (Fern 238 [SB 316]). p. 58: Cul-de-lampe for "Herbes coupées. p. 59: "Labour," 64 x 91 mm. (Fern 240 [SB 325]); Initial T for "Labour," 41 x 47 mm. (Fern 210 [SB 281 ter). p. 66: Cul-de-lampe for "Labour" 25 x 62 mm. (Fern 241 [SB 326]). p. 67: "Les Marchés," 66 x 92 mm. (Fern 242 [SB 308]); Initial L for "Bétail à vendre," 40 x 47 mm. (Fern 243 [SB 324]). p. 78: Cul-de-lampe for "Bétail à vendre," 75 x 54 mm. (Fern 245 [SB 326]). p. 79: "La Moissons," 64 x 92 mm. (Fern 224 [SB 306]); Initial O for "La Moisson," 43 x 47 mm. (Fern 246 [SB 327]). p. 86: Cul-de-lampe for "La Moisson," 44 x 48 mm. (Fern 247 [SB 335]). p. 87: "Sous les pommiers," 66 x 91 mm. (Fern 244 [SB 322]); Initial L for "Sous les pommiers," 40 x 47 mm. (Fern 248 [SB 328]). p. 98: Cul-de-lampe for "Sous les pommiers," 69 x 45 mm. (Fern 249 [329]). p. 99: "La Noce Normande," 62 x 90 mm. (Fern 250 [SB 331]); Initial C for "La Noce normande," 41 x 47 mm. (Fern 251 [SB 330]). p. [106]: Cul-de-lampe for "Fin," 52 x 51 mm. (Fern 252 [SB 332]). p. [108]: Pressmark III, 76 mm. diameter (Fern 112 [152]).

CONTENTS: p. [1]: half-title: LA CHARRUE D'ÉRABLE. p. [2]: Tiré à 116 exemplaires. p. [3]: title. p. 4: blank. pp. [5–6]: Table des matières. pp. 7–18: La Baratte. pp. 19–26: Messidor. pp. 27–38: Les Semailles. pp. 39–46: Lavandière nocturne. pp. 47–58: Herbes coupées. p. 59–66: Labour. pp. 67–78: Bétail à vendre. pp. 79–87: La Moisson. pp. 87–98: Sous les pommiers. pp. 87–99: La Noce normande. p. [107]: colophon. p. [108]: pressmark.

BINDING: Full soft-green leather, gold-stamped on upper right cover: E. MOSELLY. | LA CHARRUE | D'ÉRABLE | [orn: three apples] | LE LIVRE | CONTEMPORAIN. Inside cover gold-stamped in repeat pattern of "apple" and Livre contemporain monogram.

PUBLICATION: 116 copies printed for Le Livre contemporain.

RELATED MATERIAL: Drawing of title-page; drawing of monogram; drawings for initials J, P, D, C, A, L with apple motif background (not used); ornament, circle entwined with apples (not used); ornamented frame (not used).

NOTES: Lucien procured a copy to present to the British Museum (Campbell Dodgson to Lucien Pissarro, 22 March 1913). (I was not able to locate a copy at the British Library.)

Leighton did a dummy binding for a vellum and calf binding in late September 1912.

COPIES SEEN: Ashmolean. NYPL (No. 116 Mme. Vve C. Pissarro, inscribed: "To Diana from Esther & Lucien June 1919"). SFPL (Provenance: Robert Grabhorn, No. X).

EP32 • Michael Field. Whym Chow, Flame of Love. 1914.

[in black and red] [in large caps] WHYM CHOW | FLAME OF LOVE | [in caps] BY MICHAEL FIELD. | «Leave the fire ashes, what survives is gold.» | PRIVATELY PRINTED AT | THE ERAGNY PRESS, THE BROOK, | HAMMERSMITH, LONDON, W. | M.CM.XIV.

COLOPHON: THESE POEMS WERE WRITTEN IN | 1906 AND WERE PRINTED IN THE | EARLY SPRING OF 1914. | [Pressmark III]

COLLATION: 8°: [a]^4 b^4–g^4 h^2. 30 leaves, pp. [1–9] 10–58 [59–60]

ILLUSTRATIONS, ORNAMENTS, AND INITIALS: [twenty-nine initials in red] [none of the initials are in Fern's catalog] b1^r: large Initial I. b1^v: Initial O. b2^v: Initial C. b3^v: Initial O. b4^r: Initial I. b4^v: Initial W. c1^v: Initial I. c2^r: Initial J. c3^v: Initial M. c4^v: Initial O. d1^v: Initial T. d2^r: Initial W. d2^v: Initial C. d3^r: Initial T. d3^v: Initial O. d4^v: Initial T. e1^r: Initial A. e2^r: Initial W. e2^v: Initial O. e3^v: Initial D. e4^r: Initial M. f1^v: Initial S. f3^v: Initial T. f4^r: Initial L. g1^v: Initial I. g3^r: Initial W. g4^r: Initial W. h1^r: Initial O. h2^v: Initial A.

CONTENTS: [a]1^r: half-title: WHYM CHOW, FLAME OF LOVE. [a]1^v: [in red] Born October 29th, 1897, | Died January 28th, 1906. [a]2^r: Of 27 copies, No. 27. [a]2^v: blank. [a]3^r: title. [a]3^v: blank. [a]4^r: Contents. [a]4^v: blank. b1^r–h1^v: text. h2^r: blank. h2^v: colophon.

BINDING: Full red suede, printed label inset in right upper corner: WHYM | CHOW: FLAME | OF | LOVE. | [orn: fan leaf]

PUBLICATION: Privately printed for the poet Katherine Bradley in an edition of 27 copies. The book was finished in late April 1914.

RELATED MATERIAL: Drawing and design in red for initial I.

NOTES: Katherine Bradley and Edith Cooper (who together used the pseudonym Michael Field), wrote to Lucien, in early February 1906, of the death of their chow dog. They asked him to print half a dozen copies of a remembrance card for Whym in the "beautiful" Brook type. The card was to have the quotation "Heave the fire-ashes" in black and on the inside in red, "what ye bind on earth." They asked Lucien to send a rough proof with a statement of the cost; they wanted the order executed at once; and they wanted the matter to be kept entirely private. "As our Whym was most beautiful, we should like everything consecrated to his memory to be beautiful, and your fine type would comfort us." By 9 February Michael Field had received two different proofs. They liked the arrangement and selected a smooth vellum card stock on which they planned to place a photograph of Whym on the inside leaf. Whether

Lucien charged for the remembrance card or not is unknown, but either in addition to the fee or in lieu of, Michael Field gave him a vellum copy of *The Tragic Mercy,* the finest they considered of their earlier work.

In an undated letter, Michael Field enclosed a copy of the remembrance card, "We are sending to you & your husband, who were such understanding comforters to us in our loss of our Beloved Whym Chow one of our cards with his portrait, that you may know the face of this divine creature you joined with us to mourn. Please show it to no one—it is a secret between our households & seals a very warm sense of friendship."

REMEMBRANCE CARD: [78 x 103 mm.] p. 1: [in black caps] WHYM CHOW | FLAME OF LOVE | [in black type] Born October 29th, 1897 | Died January 28th, 1906 | [in red] «Leave the fire ashes, what survives is | gold.» [p. 2] [in red] that which ye bind on earth shall be | bound in heaven [p. 3] [portrait of Whym Chow]

Edith Cooper had died in 1913. Katherine Bradley, the surviving Michael Field, ask the Pissarros to print a book of poems devoted to Whym Chow. On 8 February 1914, Esther Pissarro, in her first solo printing job, sent an estimate to Katherine Bradley for *Whym Chow* with a title page in black and red. The quoted price was 50 guineas. By mid-March, Miss Bradley had proofs in hand and had decided that not only should the titlepage be in red and black, but the initial capitals should be also in red throughout. Esther suggested to Miss Bradley that this would almost double the cost, adding, "we will not ask you more than a quarter of the original price for the extra work and if we can it shall be less" (letter of Esther Pissarro to Katherine Bradley, 19 March 1914). The charge was, in the end, 60 guineas.

Work began on *Whym Chow* on Monday, 23 February 1914, and was finished on Thursday, 30 April 1914.

On 26 April 1914, Esther wrote to Leighton telling him that they had chosen the all-red cover. There would be no gold or other stamping. She asked Leighton to use different binding board so that it would not stain the paper (this is a problem in almost all the Eragny books). She was ready to send sheets for the sample copy, noting that a quarter sheet should be put around the first sheet so that the back of the table of contents would not be seen when looking at the first poem.

COPIES SEEN: Ashmolean. BL (deposited 8 October 1921 [not a copyright deposit]: Presented to the British Museum Library by Emily Fortex and Mary Sturgeon. 15.7.21. [Inscribed by the donors]: The occasion of the poems was a spiritual crisis in the poets' lives, arising out of their grief for the death of their much loved dog—Whym Chow. [in pencil] only twenty-seven copies printed. This is no. 25).

Bibliography

Manuscript Sources

Oxford:

Pissarro Collection. Department of Western Art, Print Room. Ashmolean Museum.

London:

Charles Ricketts and Charles Shannon Papers. Add. 58085–58118. Department of Manuscripts. British Library.

Thomas Sturge Moore Papers. Paleography Room. University of London.

The Hague:

Van Royen Papers. Rijksmuseum Meermanno–Westreenianum / Museum van het Boek.

Printed Sources

All for Art: The Ricketts and Shannon Collection. Exhibition selected and catalogue edited by Joseph Darracott. Fitzwilliam Museum, Cambridge, 9 October–3 December 1979. Cambridge: Cambridge University Press, 1979.

Andreini, J. M. "Notes on Book-plates by Esther and Lucien Pissarro; and on Their Eragny Press." *Ex Libran* 1, no. 3 (1912): 39–43.

L'Art ancien S.A. *A Collection of Books Designed by Charles Ricketts.* Zurich: L'Art ancien S.A., 1972.

The Artist and the Book, 1860–1960, in Western Europe and the United States. Boston: Museum of Fine Arts, Boston, and Harvard College Library, Department of Printing and Graphic Arts, 1961.

Arts Council of Great Britain. *Exhibition of Designs and Wood-engravings for the Eragny Press, 1894–1914.* London: Arts Council, [1950].

———. *Lucien Pissarro, 1863–1944: A Centenary Exhibition of Paintings, Watercolours, Drawings, and Graphic Work.* [London]: Arts Council, 1963.

Baas, Jacquelynn. "August Lepère and the Artistic Revival of the Woodcut in France, 1875–1895." Ph.D. diss., University of Michigan, 1982.

——— and Richard S. Field. *The Artistic Revival of the Woodcut in France, 1850–1900.* Exhibition catalogue. Ann Arbor: The University of Michigan Museum of Art, 1984.

Bailly-Herzberg, Janine. "Essai de reconstitution grâce à une correspondance inédite du peintre Pissarro du magasin que le fameux marchand Samuel Bing ouvrit en 1895 à Paris pour lancer l'Art Nouveau." *Connaissance des arts* 283 (September 1975): 72–81.

——— and Aline Dardel. "Les illustrations françaises de Lucien Pissarro." *Nouvelles de l'estampe* 54 (November–December 1980): 8–16.

Balston, Thomas. *The Cambridge University Press Collection of Private Press Types: Kelmscott, Ashendene, Eragny, Cranach.* [Cambridge]: Printed by the University Printer for His Friends, Christmas 1951.

Beckwith, Alice H.R.H. "Eragny Press." In *British Literary Publishing Houses, 1881–1965,* edited by Jonathan Rose and Patricia Anderson. Detroit and London: Bruccoli, Clark, Layman, 1991.

———. "Fairy Tales and French Impressionism: Medieval Content in Eragny Press Books." In *The Year's Work in Medievalism V,* edited by Leslie Workman, Kathleen Verduin, and Ulrich Muller. Goppingen, Austria: Kummerle Verlag, 1996.

———. "Pre-Raphaelites, French Impressionists, and John Ruskin, Intersection at the Eragny Press." In *Pre-Raphaelite Art in Its European Context,* edited by Susan Casteras and Alicia Faxon. London and Toronto: Associated University Presses, 1995.

Bensusan-Butt, John. *The Eragny Press, 1894–1914: Short-title List with Notes.* [s.l.: s.n.], 1974.

———. *Recollections of Lucien Pissarro in His Seventies.* Wiltshire: Compton Press, 1977.

Brettell, Richard, and Christopher Lloyd. *Catalogue of Drawings by Camille Pissarro in the Ashmolean Museum, Oxford.* Oxford: Oxford University Press at the Clarendon Press, 1980.

Bowers, Fredson. *Principles of Bibliographical Description.* Winchester: St. Paul's Bibliographies, 1986.

Calloway, Stephen. *Charles Ricketts: Subtle and Fantastic Decorator.* Foreword by Kenneth Clark. London: Thames and Hudson, 1979.

Cate, Phillip Dennis, editor. *The Graphic Arts and French Society, 1871–1914.* New Brunswick and London: Rutgers University Press, 1988.

Cave, Roderick. *The Private Press.* 2nd edition. New York and London: R. R. Bowker Company, 1983.

Chambers, David. *Lucien Pissarro, Notes on a Selection of Wood-Blocks Held at the Ashmolean Museum, Oxford.* Oxford: Ashmolean Museum, 1980.

Clément-Janin. "Peintres-graveurs contemporains: Lucien Pissarro." *Gazette des beaux-arts* (1919): 337–351.

Cobden-Sanderson, T. J. *The Arts and Crafts Movement.* Hammersmith: Hammersmith Publishing Society, 1905.

———. *Four Lectures.* Edited, with an introductory essay on Cobden-Sanderson's life and ideals with details of his American pupils and his lecture in the United States in 1907, by John Dreyfus. San Francisco: Book Club of California, 1974.

Cooper, Douglas. *The Courtauld Collection: A Catalogue and Introduction.* With a memoir of Samuel Courtauld by Anthony Blunt. London: University of London, Athlone Press, 1954.

Crawford, Alan. *C. R. Ashbee: Architect, Designer, and Romantic Socialist.* New Haven and London: Yale University Press, 1985.

Darracott, Joseph. *The World of Charles Ricketts.* New York and Toronto: Methuen, Inc., 1980.

Delaney, J.G.P. *Charles Ricketts: A Biography.* Oxford: Clarendon Press, 1990.

Denis, Maurice. *Théories, 1890–1910, du symbolisme et de Gauguin vers un nouvel ordre classique.* 4th edition. Paris: L. Rouart et J. Watelin, 1920.

Diers, Michael. "Von der Arbeit und dem besonderen Vergnügen am schönen Buch: Lucien Pissarro als Buchkünstler." *Imprimatur* 11 (1984): 137–155.

Fern, Alan Maxwell. "The Wood-Engravings of Lucien Pissarro with a Catalogue Raisonné." Ph.D. diss., University of Chicago, 1960.

FitzGerald, Fiona. "The Prints of Lucien Pissarro from 1886 to 1896." M.A. thesis, University of East Anglia, 1981.

Franklin, Colin. *The Ashendene Press.* Dallas: Bridwell Library, Southern Methodist University, 1986.

———. *The Private Presses.* London: Studio Vista, 1970.

Gaskell, Geoffrey Ashall. *Glaister's Glossary of the Book.* Berkeley and Los Angeles: University of California Press, 1979.

Gould, Brian. "'The Brook' Chiswick: The Home of the Eragny Press." *Private Library* (1971): 140–147.

Halperin, Joan Ungersma. *Félix Fénéon: Aesthete and Anarchist in Fin-de-Siècle Paris.* Foreword by Germaine Brée. New Haven and London: Yale University Press, 1988.

Hesse, Raymond. *Histoire des sociétés de bibliophiles en France de 1820 à 1930.* Preface d'Henry Beraldi. Paris: L. Giraud-Badin, 1929.

———. *Le Livre d'art du XIXe siècle à nos jours.* Paris: La Renaissance du livre, [1927].

Hogben, Carol, and Rowen Watson, eds. *From Manet to Hockney: Modern Artists' Illustrated Books.* Introduction by Carol Hogben. London: Victoria and Albert Museum, 1985.

Holme, Charles. *The Art of the Book: A Review of Some Recent European and American Work in Typography, Page Decoration, and Binding.* London, Paris, New York: The Studio Ltd., 1914.

Holmes, Charles. *Self and Partners (Mostly Self): Being the Reminiscences of C. J. Holmes.* New York: Macmillan Co., 1936.

Image, Selwyn. *Selwyn Image Letters.* Edited by A. H. Mackmurdo. [London]: G. Richards, 1932.

Johnson, Una E. *Ambroise Vollard, Editeur: Prints, Books, Bronzes.* New York: Museum of Modern Art, 1977.

Kellenberger, Richard K. "Typography and the Harmony of the Printed Page." Trans. from the French of Charles Ricketts. *Colby Library Quarterly* 3, no. 12 (November 1953): 194–200.

———. "William Morris and His Influence on the Arts and Crafts." Trans. from the French of Charles Ricketts. *Colby Library Quarterly* 3, no. 13 (February 1954): 69–75.

Lewis, John. *The Twentieth Century Book: Its Illustration and Design.* 2nd ed. New York: Van Nostrand Reinhold Company, 1984.

Lucien Pissarro, 1863–1944. 2 November to 3 December 1977. Exhibition catalogue. London: Anthony d'Offay, 1977.

Manson, J. B. "Notes on Some Wood-Engravings of Lucien Pissarro." *Imprint* (April 17, 1913): 240–247.

Marx, Roger. *L'Art social.* Préface par Anatole France. Paris: Bibliothèque-Charpentier, 1913.

Meadmore, W. S. *Lucien Pissarro: Un Coeur Simple.* Introduction by John Rewald. London: Constable and Company Ltd., 1962.

Morris, William. *The Collected Works of William Morris.* With introductions by his daughter May Morris. Vol. 22, "The Art of the People," 28–50. London, New York: Longmans, Green and Company, 1910–1915.

———. *The Ideal Book: Essays and Lectures on the Arts of the Book.* Edited by William S. Peterson. Berkeley and Los Angeles: University of California Press, 1982.

Naylor, Gillian. *The Arts and Crafts Movement: A Study of Its Sources, Ideals, and Influence on Design Theory.* Cambridge, Mass.: Harvard University Press, 1971.

Parry, Linda. *William Morris Textiles.* London: Weidenfeld and Nicolson, 1983.

Perkins, Geoffrey. *The Gentle Art: A Collection of Books and Wood Engravings by Lucien Pissarro.* Zurich: L'Art ancien S.A., 1974.

Peterson, William S. *A Bibliography of the Kelmscott Press.* Oxford: Clarendon Press, 1984.

———. *The Kelmscott Press: A History of William Morris's Typographical Adventure.* Berkeley: University of California Press, 1991.

Pissarro, Camille. *Camille Pissarro, Letters to His Lucien.* Edited by John Rewald with the assistance of Lucien Pissarro. Reprint of the 3rd, rev. and enlarged edition of 1972 (1st edition: 1944). Santa Barbara and Salt Lake City: Peregrine Smith, 1981.

———. *Correspondance de Camille Pissarro.* Tome 1: 1865–1885. Edited by Janine Bailly-Herzberg. Paris: Presses Universitaires de France, 1980.

———. *Correspondance de Camille Pissarro.* Tome 2: 1886–1890. Edited by Janine Bailly-Herzberg. Paris: Éditions du Valhermeil, 1986.

———. *Correspondance de Camille Pissarro.* Tome 3: 1891–1894. Edited by Janine Bailly-Herzberg. Paris: Éditions du Valhermeil, 1988.

———. *Correspondance de Camille Pissarro.* Tome 4: 1895–1898. Edited by Janine Bailly-Herzberg. Paris: Éditions du Valhermeil, 1989.

———. *Correspondance de Camille Pissarro.* Tome 5: 1899–1903. Edited by Janine Bailly-Herzberg. Paris: Éditions du Valhermeil, 1991.

Pissarro, Lucien. *Notes on the Eragny Press, and a Letter to J. B. Manson.* Edited with a supplement by Alan Fern. Cambridge: Privately printed, 1957.

———. *The Letters of Lucien to Camille Pissarro, 1883–1903.* Edited by Anne Thorold. Cambridge: Cambridge University Press, 1993.

Pratt, Barbara. *Lucien Pissarro in Epping.* Loughton, Essex: Barbara Pratt Publications, 1982.

Ranson, Will. *Private Presses and Their Books.* New York: R. R. Bowker Company, 1929.

Rewald, John. *The History of Impressionism*. 4th, rev. ed. New York: Museum of Modern Art, 1973.

———. "Lucien Pissarro: Letters from London, 1883–1891." *Burlington Magazine* 91 (1949): 188–192.

———. *Post-Impressionism: From Van Gogh to Gauguin*. 3rd ed., rev. New York: The Museum of Modern Art, 1978.

Ricketts, Charles. *A Bibliography of the Books Issued by Hacon and Ricketts.* London: Sold by Charles Ricketts; New York: John Lane, 1904.

———. *Charles Ricketts, R.A.; Sixty-five Illustrations Introduced by T. Sturge Moore*. London: Cassell, [1933].

———. *A Defence of the Revival of Printing*. London: Hacon and Ricketts, 1899.

———. *Letters from Charles Ricketts to "Michael Field," 1903–1913.* Edited by J. G. Paul Delaney. Edinburgh: Tragara Press, 1981.

———. *Self-Portrait.* Taken from the letters and journals of Charles Ricketts. Collected and compiled by T. Sturge Moore. Edited by Cecil Lewis. London: P. Davies, [1939].

———. *Some Letters from Charles Ricketts and Charles Shannon to "Michael Field" (1894–1902)*. Edited by J. G. Paul Delaney. Edinburgh: Tragara Press, 1979.

Robb, Brian. "The New Wood-Engravings of Lucien Pissarro." *Signature*, new ser. 6 (1948): 36–47.

Rothenstein, William. *Men and Memories, 1872–1938.* Edited by Mary Lago. Columbia: University of Missouri Press, 1978.

Salaman, Malcolm C. *British Book Illustration Yesterday and Today, with Commentary.* Edited by Geoffrey Holmes. London: The Studio, 1923.

Söderberg, Rolf. *French Book Illustration, 1880–1905.* Translated by Roger Tanner. Stockholm: Almqvist and Wiksell, 1977.

Stansky, Peter. *Redesigning the World: William Morris, the 1880s, and the Arts and Crafts.* Princeton: Princeton University Press, 1985.

Strachan, W. J. *The Artist and the Book in France: The Twentieth Century Livre d'Artiste.* London: Peter Owen, 1969.

Sturge Moore, Thomas. *A Brief Account of the Origins of the Eragny Press.* Hammersmith: The Eragny Press, 1903.

Symons, A.J.A. "An Unacknowledged Movement in Fine Printing." *Fleuron* 7 (1930): 83–119.

Thorold, Anne. *Camille Pissarro and His Family: The Pissarro Collection in the Ashmolean Museum.* Oxford: The Museum, 1993.

———. *A Catalogue of the Oil Paintings of Lucien Pissarro.* With a Preface by Christopher Lloyd and an Introduction by John Bensusan-Butt. London: Athelney Books, 1983.

———. *Lucien Pissarro: His Influence on English Art, 1890–1914.* Canterbury: Canterbury City Council Museums, 1896.

———. "The Pissarro Collection in the Ashmolean Museum, Oxford." *Burlington Magazine* 120 (October 1978): 642–645.

Tidcombe, Marianne. *The Doves Press.* London: British Library and New Castle, Delaware: Oak Knoll Press, 2002.

Urbanelli, Lora. *The Book Art of Lucien Pissarro, with a Bibliographical List of the Books of the Eragny Press, 1894–1914.* Wakefield, Rhode Island: Moyer Bell, 1997.

———. *The Wood Engravings of Lucien Pissarro and a Bibliographical List of Eragny Books.* Cambridge: Silent Books; Oxford: Ashmolean Museum, 1994.

Vollard, Ambroise. *Recollections of a Picture Dealer.* Translated by Violet N. MacDonald and now first published in any language; with thirty-two plates in collotype. Boston: Little, Brown and Company, 1936.

Weisberg, Gabriel. *Art Nouveau Bing: Paris Style 1900.* New York: Abrams; Washington, D.C.: Smithsonian Institution Traveling Exhibit Service, 1986.

Whiteley, Jon. "Lucien Pissarro, Roger Marx, and the *Gazette des Beaux-Arts.*" *Gazette des beaux-arts* 140 (2002): 243–248.

Willrich, Erich. "Lucien Pissarro als Buchkünstler." *Zeitschrift für Bildende Kunst* 42 (1907), 32–35.

Index

Illustrations are indicated in italic numerals and are listed after the text references. Eragny Press books are listed by title in SMALL CAPITALS.